MW01504977

A BROVELLI BROTHERS' MYSTERY

THE CASE OF THE '61 CHEVY IMPALA

TOM MESCHERY

CAVEL
PRESS

KENMORE, WA

CAMEL PRESS

A Camel Press book published by Epicenter Press

Epicenter Press
6524 NE 181st St.
Suite 2
Kenmore, WA 98028

For more information go to:
www.Camelpress.com
www.Coffeetownpress.com
www.Epicenterpress.com

Author's website: http://mescherysmusings.blogspot.com

This is a work of fiction. Names, characters, places, brands, media, and incidents are the product of the author's imagination or are used fictitiously.

Design by Rudy Ramos

The Case of the '61 Chevy Impala
2022 © Tom Meschery

ISBN: 9781942078685 (trade paper)
ISBN: 9781942078692 (ebook)

Printed in the United States of America

To Jon Jackson, for being a pal, for supporting my writing, and for invaluable suggestions. And for writing some of the best detective fiction there is on the planet.

And
To Melanie Marchant Meschery, my wife, my friend and line-editor extraordinaire.

Acknowledgments

I am grateful to my friends, Saint Mary's College classmates, Don and Ron Dirito who were the inspiration for the Brovelli Boys and for the long afternoon they spent providing me with information about the used car business, and regaling me with their humorous stories of life selling used cars.

Jennifer McCord, thank you for liking my novel and embracing the antics of my twins, the Brovelli Boys. I am grateful for your careful editing and many thoughtful suggestions.

Jon Jackson, your commentary on all things to do with literature have been pure pleasure and invaluably instructive. Thank you for your early suggestion to change the point of view of my novel. It made a huge difference. And thank you for those marvelous hard-boiled detective novels you have written that made me want to write mysteries.

I cannot thank my wife Melanie Marchant Meschery enough for the many times she read this manuscript, (five by my last count) patiently correcting mechanical errors and suggesting changes. The Brovelli Boys would not have come to life without her.

CHAPTER 1
CRIME SCENE

There is no trap so deadly as the trap you set for yourself.
from <u>Farewell My Lovely</u> by Raymond Chandler

I was staring into the trunk of a 1961 Chevrolet Impala. "The fucking trunk shouldn't have a dead body in it," I said to my twin brother, Vincent. "It didn't have a dead body in it when Sweets drove it off the lot." Stay calm I told myself.

My twin looked at me, like *duh*.

"It's a fucking dead woman," I said, my voice rising a couple of decibels. "You see that hole in her head?"

"No."

"Right there." I pointed. Her dark hair almost obscured it. Small. No blood, but definitely a hole. I could have stuck a pencil in it. I felt my stomach turn. Was I alarmed? You bet your ass I was. Vincent and I were standing in front of the office of Brovelli Brother's Used Cars, the business we'd owned for the last three years since our pop, Big Sal Brovelli, retired and handed the keys over to us. I'm Vincent's other half, Victor Brovelli. Occasionally, people shorten our names to Vince and Vic. Vincent doesn't seem to mind, but I do. Vic reminds me of victim, while Victor is all about winning. But if someone calls me Vic, I don't get too upset. Most of my friends know better.

"I don't think she's been dead for long," Vincent said. "I don't smell anything."

"*Smell, smell*, are you shitting me? Smell, who cares," I said, "Do you recognize her?"

"Not without seeing her face," he said. "And don't ask me to turn her over."

1

"Fine, you coward." The body was tucked into the fetal position, mini skirt revealing long brown legs. No stockings, no shoes, crimson toenails. I reached down.

"No, no, don't do that."

I jumped back, smacking my head against the open trunk lid. "Sonavabitch, sonavabitch."

"Stop yelling," Vincent said. "You want Sylvia to hear you." Sylvia Vitale was our accountant and our cousin on our mother's side of the family.

"She's in the office balancing her checkbook." I touched the back of my head. "I'm bleeding."

"It's a scratch," Vincent said. "You touch the body, and your fingerprints will be all over her. Get some gloves or something."

I was examining my hands for parts of my brain, thinking I'd like to brain my twin. I grabbed the buffer rag laying on the hood of the '64 Ford Galaxy I'd been polishing when Vincent drove in. A little voice inside my head was saying, *don't do it, don't do it*. But I've been known not to follow my own advice. I placed the rag on the dead woman's shoulder and with two hands shifted her so I could get a good look at her face. One arm flopped over. A Mickey Mouse watch encircled her slim wrist.

We both said her name at the same time, "Winona."

"I forgot her last name," I said.

"Davis," Vincent said.

Beautiful Winona Davis was a temp we'd hired when Sylvia, our accountant, took a week off to visit her father in San Diego for his birthday celebration. Winona was Sweets' girlfriend. We'd sold this cherry midnight blue '61 Impala to Sweets Monroe three months ago.

Her forehead was exposed but I couldn't see an exit hole. Which meant what? The bullet was still in there? In a waxy kind of way, beautiful Winona remained beautiful.

Vincent said. "Call the cops."

"Yeah," I said and started in the direction of the office. Half way there, I turned back. "You know, they'll arrest Sweets, and Pop will go absolutely ape-shit."

"It's a murder, Victor. You gotta call the cops."

I was almost to the office steps. Something occurred to me. I turned back toward my twin.

"The cops will turn our car lot into a crime scene and close it down for

God knows how long." Lately, sales at the Brovelli Brothers Used Cars had been for crap. All right, worse than crap. We were teetering on the edge of having our worst year. A couple of months of bad sales, and we could disappear into the abyss of failed used car dealerships, which would not only do us in, but put a serious dent in our father and mother's retirement.

"Hold on, hold on," I said. "Let's think about this."

"What's to think about? Be logical, Victor. This is about Sweets not about us."

Sweets Monroe was one of our repeat customers, albeit an unconventional one. His car-buying routine goes like this: Sweets shows up, marches his skinny butt up and down the rows of cars, with his hands clasped behind his back, checking out the stock, strutting like one of those Sergeant Majors in British war movies inspecting the troops. He test drives a couple of cars he likes, selects one, gives us tax and drives away. License is his responsibility. We carry the paper, knowing we'll never see another payment and don't expect to. The banks would never touch such a deal, which works sort of like a loaner. Around the fourth month without a dime from Sweets, we go looking to repo our car. Usually we find it right away, like Vincent did this morning. Sweets has never tried to avoid us. He accepts the inevitable, and there are no hard feelings. Like I said, he is a repeat customer. He would manage for a while driving around on his beat-up motorcycle, then he'd come in, pick out another car, and the game would start all over again. Crazy, huh?

You might ask why the Brovelli Brothers would put up with this. Because this was the verbal agreement Sweets and Pop had come to eight years ago, after Sweets saved Pop's business from the Amigos, the local gangbangers who were determined to drive Brovelli Motors from its East 14th Street location. According to Pop, Sweets saved our mom from becoming a widow. It is Pop's belief that the Brovelli family is beholden to Sweets, big time. I can't argue with that.

We inherited Pop and Sweets' weird handshake-agreement, unhappily, but with the solemn promise we'd honor it. Being from the "old country," Pop's belief in honor, onore, boarders on fanaticism. Since we knew eventually we were going to get the car back from Sweets, we went along with the program. Sweets was a fixture in this neighborhood, a burglar, a womanizer, and a bad dresser. But with all Sweet's faults, he possesses a goofy surfer disposition and a ready smile. It was rumored that Sweets, after a particularly successful burglary, would bring baskets of food and an envelope of cash to local single moms in need of which there were plenty in Oakland. The basket always contained hard candy for the kids – sweets from Sweets, so to speak. The cynical inhabitants of the neighborhood claimed that Sweets only gave to single moms who were good looking. Sweets claims that's a lie. Considering Sweets' Robin Hood rep and the fact that he only hits rich neighborhoods, most folks around here gave the burglar a pass. As far as our cars were concerned, Sweets never abused the vehicles. The cars we repo'd from him were as sharp inside and out as the day he drove them off the lot. Until today - blood being damn hard to clean up.

"You gonna call the cops or am I?" Vincent asked.

I began pacing.

"For Christ's sake, Victor, the woman's been shot. We've been selling cars to a frigging murderer."

"Sweets Monroe may be a burglar," I said, "but you know as well as I do that he could never kill anyone. Somebody stuck his girlfriend in the trunk so the cops would blame him."

"What does it matter? If we don't call the cops, they'll arrest us as accessories. With our asses stuck in jail, we'll lose business. We can't afford to lose business right now. Start making sense, will you.'

"Let me think," I said. "Close the trunk. Customers heading this way."

Vincent slammed it down. I waved him in the direction of a young Asian couple. He looked at me like I was crazy thinking of a sale at a time like this, but he smiled one of his perfect smiles, slipped on the blue Brooks Brother's blazer he was holding, buttoned it, and walked toward them with his hand outstretched. *Mr. Slick*.

Women have often told me that Vincent is a handsome hunk and his smile is irresistible. We're identical twins, but I've never heard women compliment me on my looks. We're both one inch short of six feet with black curly hair, hazel eyes, dimples, and swarthy southern Italian complexions, except mine is marred by a scar on my cheek that starts just below the center of my left eye and curves like a cradle around my cheek bone to the middle of my left ear, the result of a line drive that tagged me as I was stealing second. But who's complaining. The scar gives me a certain edgy look, you know, the kind some women can't resist.

I resumed pacing. My bro was right. If the cops arrested us as accessories to murder, Pop couldn't handle the lot by himself, not at his age with a bad ticker, and not in the sketchy financial condition it was in. A murder investigation could drag on for a long time and our bottom line would drop closer to the bottom of the Grand Canyon, a direction it had been heading for the last six months that Vincent claimed was due to the craziness in the county. As he put it, The Shameless Sixties. I don't find anything shameless going on, but Vincent is a bit of a prude. I won't go into how deep our debt is. Let's just leave it that our line of credit at banks is stretched like a fat woman's Pantyhose. Thank God for Morris Bank and Trust that still believed in us. That could disappear too if our neighborhood customers began avoiding us with the heat hanging around. Distrust of cops in Oakland was endemic, particularly, recently, with the Vietnam War in full swing, President Johnson announcing he won't seek a second term, and the Black Panthers making all sorts of scary noises. Not to mention that the cops would definitely impound the Impala. I looked at the Impala and wanted to cry. It was a four-door ebony sedan with white double S trim. Of the 490,000 plus existing Impalas, only 453 came with the double S trim, which starts like spear points just back of the headlights and widens as they extend down the side of the body coming to rest at the taillights.

I looked out onto East 14th Street, home to our family dealership since Pop started the business in 1950. The city of Oakland's East 14th Street began at First Avenue in downtown and extended south to the city limits of San Leandro, although the street name remained the same until it turned into Mission Boulevard in the city of Hayward. There were plenty of used car lots like ours on East 14th and some new car dealership, although you'd find most of the most prosperous new car dealership I liked to refer to as the "Big Dogs" on Broadway in downtown, Oakland. Altogether there were over 900 separate properties that did business along East 14th. Name a business and you'd find it somewhere along the length of our street.

The noise of morning rush hour traffic was starting to ebb. It was March, gray and chilly in the Bay Area. Considering there was a dead body in the trunk of our car, I welcomed the cool weather. In the distance I could hear the whoosh and roar of airplanes taking off and landing at the Oakland Airport, so many planes since World Airways started transporting troops to Vietnam. At regular intervals came the whine of the big rigs speeding along Nimitz Freeway that runs from the Bay Bridge south to San Jose the length of the San

Francisco Bay and parallel to East 14th Street. The distant wail of an ambulance, a pissed-off motorist blasting his horn, nearby, a car pealing rubber, a waste disposal truck backfiring. *City rock-and-roll, my kind of rhythm.*

It was time for a plan.

My first thought was to get the Impala off the lot and pretend we never saw it. Let Sweets fend for himself. As I went over this in my head, I imagined our Pop tending his vegetable garden, his wide body, encased in blue overalls, bending over his Early Girls and Heirlooms. What would he think of this idea? He wouldn't like it. To leave Sweets hanging would be dishonorable. To not call the cops, however, would be illegal. Pop versus cops – there was only one possible choice.

Vincent returned to tell me the couple said they'd be back tomorrow. He knew better. Once a customer walks away, I reminded him. Odds are they're gone for good. They'll be back, Vincent insisted. I had a lot more on my mind than starting an argument.

"We can't do it," I said.

"Can't do what?" Vincent asked.

"We can't call the cops."

"Okay, I get it. That's easily taken care of. I drive the car back where I found it. You pick me up, and we cut Sweets lose."

"You're missing the point."

"Which is what? This isn't about Pop's deal with Sweets, is it?"

"It's about honor, Vincent. Sweets saved Pop's business, our business now. Pop would want us to help Sweets." To be honest, I wasn't thinking only of Pop and honor, but about that beautiful Impala being impounded and beat to shit by bunch of the city's finest searching for evidence. It is no secret that when it comes to cars, I'm an incurable romantic.

"Well, we're not our pop," Vincent said. "At least I'm not.

"We've got no choice, Vincent. "A portion of Pop and Mom's retirement comes from sales."

"I know that. I know. But, come on, all that old country honor stuff doesn't cut it in today's world."

I smacked Vincent in the chest, knocking him back. He kept his balance and came at me, fists balled and stopped, nose to nose. Neither of us spoke, staring each other down.

I broke the silence. "Look, Vincent, if it hadn't been for Sweets, we wouldn't have a father. We're talking moral responsibility here."

"There's nothing moral about Sweets."

Vincent is far less tolerant of Sweets than I am, and his take on Sweets' charitable contributions, agrees with those who believe Sweet's benevolence has more to do with trying to seduce single moms.

"Look at it another way, Vincent," I said. "There's no way if this gets out it's going to help sales. Hey, like, do you want to buy a car from the Brovelli's? Might find a stiff in the trunk. Stuff like that."

"I don't know, Victor, I don't know."

"*Stai zitto*," I said. "Just give me Sweet's telephone number."

"Don't tell me to shut up," he said, this time, smacking me hard on the chest. I tripped and fell on my ass. I bounced back on my feet already swinging. He stood there, glaring at me, his chin jutting out, like okay, go ahead, I dare you. I don't know about other twins, but it seems to me that half of our lives have been spent toe to toe staring into each other's angry eyes like mirrors. I rarely back down to Vincent, but we were wasting time. My right-hand-cross stopped inches from his jaw.

"This is stupid," I said. "I'm sorry, all right?"

Vincent shrugged, and his shoulders sagged.

"Yeah," he said.

"Look, this is not the big deal you're making it out to be. We give Sweets a chance to get out of this *casino*, by giving him a heads-up."

"It's more than a screw-up," Vincent said.

When I'm tense, I find myself speaking Italian, not a characteristic shared by my twin, who accuses me of sounding like fake Italian mobsters in the movies. In Italy if one is really stressed, the term casino is often prefaced by *fottuta casino*, meaning fucking mess.

Vincent said, "If Sweets gets involved, it will be a frigging mess all right. If we don't call the cops this is going to come back and bite us on the ass; you know that, don't you?"

Probably, Vincent was right. I held out my hands, palms up. I said. "We've worked hard."

He let out a long sigh, reached into his inside jacket pocket and withdrew a little leather-bound book. He shook his head and handed it to me. "Under S, for murderer," he said. "This is on you Vittorio."

We walked to the office where I dialed. On the fourth ring, I heard a sleepy voice, "Yo, you gotta be kidding me."

Mouthing the word, *personal,* I waved Sylvia out of the office. She shrugged her shoulders, like what the hell, shook a Pall Mall out of her pack, and left without commenting on my rudeness. I waited until she was out the door and on the car lot, before answering Sweets. "Have you checked on the whereabouts of your girlfriend lately?"

"Which Brovelli is this? I can't tell your voices apart. I'm not taking kindly to being waked up. You know I work nights, and what do you mean, my girlfriend? I'm presently a man without a main squeeze."

"Yeah, well, main squeeze or past squeeze, you're not going to like the condition she's in." I told him about Vincent repo'ing the Impala and that we found Winona in the trunk with a bullet in the back of her pretty head. Sweets let out a sound like he was being strangled.

I said. "I'm sorry, Sweets, really, but our butts are on the line here. We need to talk right away."

"Winona," he said again. "You're screwing with me? You sure?"

"Tall, great body. Brown skin about your color. Slanty eyes. Always wears a Mickey Mouse watch."

"I'm on my way."

"No, no, not here. I'll meet you at your place."

"Bad idea," Sweets said. "Meet me at Lenny's near the airport."

"On Hegenberger Road. Okay, I'm leaving right now." I hung up the phone. For a moment I stared at my desktop calendar. It was the 29th of March. In two days it would be April. I had a feeling I would never forget this day. I left the office and headed for the Impala almost knocking Sylvia down. She gave me the finger as I peeled rubber.

CHAPTER 2
SWEETS

The Other Dude Did It

Ten minutes later I was parked in front of Lenny's Breakfast Grill listening to KNBR FM. The Beatles were singing "Hey Jude" about not letting him down. Music usually helped me relax. Not today. It was Friday. I decided from now on I'd hate Fridays.

Through my rear-view mirror, I saw a motorcycle pull in, and Sweets get off. Sweets is about my height but a lot skinnier than me. His skin's the color of cocoa and his hair is bottle-blonde, a portion of which stands up on the crown of his head like the top feathers of a cockatoo. His eyes are deep set and green. It's hard to gauge Sweets' age. He says he's thirty, but he's a lot like an impressionist painting; understandable from a distance, but up close it gets fuzzy, so I'd put Sweets' age somewhere in the forties. He wears lots of jewelry, except when he's breaking into houses. His clothes are always a size too small and an eclectic mix of colors and styles, none of which I've ever seen worn by another human being, as if they'd been designed by someone from a different galaxy. He talks like a surfer and walks like a hipster. His impish smile saves him from looking like a lunatic. Sweets grew up in Louisiana and claims his great ancestor was the pirate Jean Lafitte. His nickname refers to the enormous amount of candy he consumes. Some people occasionally call him bird-man, but not to his face because it's rumored Sweets carries a razor blade somewhere on his eccentric being.

I stepped out of the Impala. He waved a lollipop in the direction of his motorcycle.

"Had to dig out the old standby since you guys stole my wheels," he said, pointing to a beat-to-shit Harley Road King. There were killer bikers like the Hells Angels and Satans who would not look kindly on someone who mistreated a Harley this way. To them, it would be like beating your pet dog. Or should I say hog? Since Sweets' new address would soon be San Quentin's death row, why would he care?

"Get over here," I said. I opened the trunk of the car halfway. "Is this Winona?" He bent down and looked inside. I was hoping that maybe I was wrong.

"Muthafukaaaa," he said, dragging the word out so each syllable resonated, the last vowel sounding like a long-anguished sigh, like he was strangling.

I took his reaction to mean yes. I closed the trunk, and we walked into the restaurant. I ordered two cups of coffee. Sweets ordered the Double Pancake breakfast special with scrambled eggs, bacon on the side.

"You're kidding," I said.

"When I'm nervous, I eat," he explained.

"What are we going to do about this?" I asked. "We need to think fast. There's no fucking way this is getting back to us. Since Winona is your girlfriend and this is your car, you're the prime suspect."

"It's not my car. You repo'ed it."

"It was in your possession when the body entered the trunk, Sweets. We didn't repo it until this morning."

"Dude, I didn't kill Winona," he said, his voice rising to a squawk.

A couple of guys sitting at the counter looked over. "Keep it down, Sweets. I know you didn't kill anyone. I'm just saying that's what the cops will think. Look, I'm way out on a limb just being here and not reporting the body immediately. *Capisci?*"

"For which I'm grateful, Victor, truly."

"Vincent is all for calling the cops."

"Give me a minute for my brain to kick in."

There might have been plates clattering and customers talking and doors opening and closing, and waitresses calling out orders, but I wouldn't have heard anything; the silence from the other side of the booth was deafening. Finally, Sweets said, "If the cops pin this on me, I'm going to jail big time. You know they'll make the connection, and the cops are always dragging my ass in every time there's a tweeny weenie burglary."

"You got any ideas? Vincent and I are willing to help, but only so far."

"You guys want refills?" the waitress asked as she put Sweets' breakfast in front of him. She had no lips and no chin and enough hair for two women. The way she was looking at us, I was afraid she'd heard Sweets and was being nosy.

I waved her away. Sweets called her back and ordered a side of strawberry waffles with extra whipped cream. Sweets' metabolism probably burns up most of the food he swallows before it hits his stomach. In keeping with his personality, his eyes were twitching, and his fingers drumming, and his knees beneath the table jiggling. He looked as if at any moment, he'd fly away.

"All right, this is what we do," he said. "We find a more dignified resting place for Winona's body than the trunk of the car. After we do that, you detail the Impala, and I go find an alibi."

"I hope you're not talking about some midnight burial, cuz that's not happening."

"No, we remove her from the Impala and place her where she'll be found and given a decent burial."

"What's with the we?"

"You and me, Victor. I can't do this without you. I can't carry Winona all by myself. Winona is a big girl. She outweighs me. Besides, I hurt my arm recently on a job."

Probably climbing in a window I thought. "It's daylight," I said.

"We wait until night."

"Where the hell can we leave Winona?"

Sweets stuffed his mouth and chewed. "Got it," he said with his mouth full. "Satans."

"Aw, geez."

The Satans were the badest motorcycle club in the United States, worse than the Hells Angels and the Mongols combined. Their clubhouse was on East 14th about a dozen or so blocks from our lot. "You gotta be kidding," I said.

"I'm not joking," Sweets said. "I'll break into their club house. I've been inside. There's a comfy looking couch in their conference room. We'll put a blanket over her, put a pillow under her head, kind of tuck her in, you know, be real respectful."

"Aw, geez," I said again. "You're nuts. That honcho of theirs, you know, Sunny something. He's been coming by the lot hitting on Sylvia. He brought her a bunch of roses one time. She chased him off, but he keeps coming back. He looks mean. He acts mean, and I'm sure he doesn't like me. I don't want anything to do with those freaks."

"This will take the pressure off me."

"How so?"

"We put the heat on the Satans. Look, as far as I know Winona ran away from home when she was thirteen. She used to ho. . ."

"What, what?"

"Ho, whore, Jesus, Victor. But she got out of the game and started temp working. Cleaning up her act. There's no family. She used to have a roommate, but lives alone now. The cops will have to check out the Satans first before they start looking around for other suspects. Yours truly, for instance."

For a moment I couldn't breathe. When the air decided to return to my lungs, I leaned across the table and swatted him across the forehead. "You are one crazy Cajun. There's no way I'm doing it."

"No, no. Listen, I'm not crazy. See, defense lawyers always be doing it."

"Doing what?"

"Like making up something so the jury has an alternative suspect, like on television. You know, like, *yeah he coulda done it, but so could that cat over there*. You dig?"

I didn't even have a shovel. What I heard was that we could be making some serious enemies if we fucked with the Satans. "Do you have any idea what the Satans would do to us if they knew we set them up to take the fall for Winona's murder? Do you have any idea?"

The waitress arrived with the waffles.

Sweets ordered more toast. When she left, he said, "Look, I know there's nobody at the clubhouse because the assholes are cruising the coast. We place an anonymous call. Bad boys return, cops arrest them. All's cool. Sure, they'll be upset, but how will they know who did it?"

This was not the help I'd been expecting from Sweets. But given Sweets' shaky moral character, I don't know what kind of help I expected. Speaking of moral character, I was wondering about my own, and feeling depressed.

Sweets kept eating, and I kept telling him he was insane, and he persisted, through mouths full of bacon and pancakes, and waffles and toast. It was disgusting. This was the only way he could avoid being sent to prison, he explained. He reminded me that he'd saved my pop.

Low blow. I told him so. I'd pay for a lawyer. Finally, I got fed up with all his whining.

"Look, Sweets, this is it. I'm taking the Impala back to where we found it and leave it. You do whatever the fuck you want getting an alibi." *Vincent would be proud of me.*

That's when Sweets confessed. No, he didn't admit to killing his ex-girlfriend, but he explained that there was an outstanding warrant for his arrest in Louisiana, pronouncing it Loosyana.

"I've been very careful since I moved here," he said.

Sweets was a burglar, so how careful could he have been, I wondered. "That's your story," I said, but I could tell by Sweets' eyes that he was scared. He started describing what the inside of a maximum-security penitentiary in Louisiana called Angola looked like. His voice trembled when he described some of the atrocities that happened there. Half way through his sad tale, I held up my hand, took a deep breath and said, "All right, stop. We'll do it your way." Pop, I thought, this decision is on you.

"It's a solid plan, Victor. The Satans are a bunch of muthafuckin killers anyway. You have any idea how much dope they're personally responsible for putting on the street, killing our children?"

Saint Sweets, give me a break.

Besides, they'll all have alibis," Sweets said. "Our plan will misdirect the cops, you know like in football, fake right, run left. Sheeet, they'll get around to me soon enough, but by then I'll have my story in place. Been in Santa Cruz the last four days, Mr. Po–liceman. I'll have at least three witnesses."

I nodded. The lies kept coming. Sweets was the kind of guy who believed his lies. Lots of politician like that. Still, agreeing to his plan seemed the only way the Brovelli boys' used car business would not take a hit financially, Pop's precious honor would remain unblemished, I wouldn't lose my Impala, and Sweets might have a chance to survive the atrocities of Louisiana's prison from hell. Anyway, after tonight the Brovelli Boys would be out of it. It occurred to me that no matter how air-tight Sweets' alibi, since this was a homicide case, I couldn't imagine the cops not discovering his priors. If that happened, I promised myself the Brovelli family would send care packages to the prison in Louisiana. It was a rationalization, but necessary to convince myself. I heard my pop's voice: *Ci si può lavare le mani, ma non la coscienza, You can wash your hands, but not your conscience.*

I fingered the medal of Saint Anthony hanging around my neck and said a little prayer. Sweets and I made plans where to meet and at what time. I paid the bill because Sweets never had any money. I left the burglar to finish his breakfast. As I walked out the door, I heard him calling for more waffles.

Now I had to explain Sweets' plan to my brother and hope he wouldn't freak out.

CHAPTER 3
ONE SCREWED UP GOOMBAH

Lasciate ogne speranza, voi ch'intrate.
Abandon all hope, ye who enter here.
Dante's Inferno

My twin and I both drive by the proverbial seat of our pants. You'd think this would make us compatible, but it doesn't. Consider comparing us to classy cars - that is to say we're not just ordinary vehicles. I'd be a Porsche, and he'd be a Rolls Royce; it's a matter of style. I'm for the back roads; he sticks to the highways. Neither of us lets up on the throttle once we feel we've got the right of way. Both of us have been labeled stubborn, which I have to admit is true. Vincent claims I'm more aggressive. Still, I've never met a man more fearless than my twin. *Oh, the stories I can tell you about him.* The one constant in our lives is this, if we're not arguing, something's wrong.

I was half way through explaining Sweets' plan to Vincent before I noticed snoopy Sylvia on the office steps pretending she wasn't listening. I waved her back into the office, and continued. At any moment I expected my brother to punch me, but he held his temper. Finally, after assuring him that there was no way this would come back on us, he agreed to Sweets' plan for disposing of the beautiful Winona. Against his better judgement, he added.

The first thing I did after we'd settled things was drive the Impala behind our office. Vincent and I pulled on gloves so we wouldn't leave fingerprints, wrapped the body in a couple of blankets we had in the storage unit and tightly duct-taped the shroud, transferring it to the back of a 1960 International Harvester Travelall. I kept reminding myself that this was only flesh, Winona's soul was in purgatory. We're Catholics. In our religion sinners are sent to purgatory, which is like a waiting room in a doctor's office where they hang out and suffer a little before they're allowed into heaven.

Even though Winona was wrapped as tight as an Egyptian mummy, I brought a pillow from my car and tucked it under her head. Vincent was having a hard time, sighing and mumbling about what happens to young good-looking guys in prison, so I told him to go home. He'd married his high school sweetheart, a delectable Italian beauty, Gloria Mancuso, two years ago, which kept him from the possibility of being drafted. That Gloria reminded me of Mom was something I'm sure drew my twin to her. Gloria was pregnant. If there was any trouble at the Satans' clubhouse later I didn't want my twin involved. For once, he didn't argue.

After wiping the car clean of fingerprints and ripping out the carpet in the trunk, I took the Impala, which Vincent kept referring to as the death-mobile, to our detail man, Jack Swan, who went by Swanee, for the Sewanee River, which is close to his birthplace somewhere in the state of Tennessee. Swanee has small eyes, centered in a round bald head, wears bib overalls over a beer belly, chews tobacco, and speaks with a drawl that's often hard to understand. But he's no redneck cracker. He's a member of the Sierra Club, votes Democrat, and is married to a Korean woman he'd brought back with him after the Korean War. I asked him to replace the carpet and give it his primo A-1 cleaning job. I was already in so deep, I figured an additional obstruction of justice charge wouldn't make much of a difference. I walked the four blocks back to our lot. Vincent was getting into his car. He gave me a doleful look and drove away. An hour later, at five o'clock, Sylvia left the office for home, unaware her bosses were committing a felony. Our cousin, who attends mass every Sunday and takes communion, would have been shocked if she'd known what was happening. I watched her drive her yellow VW Bug off the lot in the direction of downtown Oakland, leaving me alone to handle any evening customers.

Our company sign reads: *Open Weekdays 8 A.M to 7 P.M. Saturday and Sunday 9 A.M. to 6 P.M.* These are Vincent's and my hours. On Sundays Pop never opened until after attending ten o'clock mass with Mom, eating his midday lunch and taking a *pizzolino*, an afternoon nap. Do my brother and I take any days off? Not many. We're 26 years old and aspiring to be millionaires by the time we're thirty, Vincent because he wants stability and comfort for his family, and me for the glamor, which of course comes with chicks.

I wasn't hungry, but I knew I'd better eat something to keep my strength up for tonight.

I called out to the Hong Kong Buffet for their five-buck special. As I waited for the delivery,

I walked around the lot making sure all the cars were locked. In the center of the lot, on a raised platform, sat a 1951 Ford Country Squire with a hard-rock maple frame, mahogany paneling, fat-man front end, red leather interior and a Merc dash with power steering and brakes. The sight of it almost gave me a hard-on it was so sexy. Even though we'd marked up the price beyond reason, it drew lots of people in off the street. This was Vincent's idea. You know, he'd explained, it's like when owners of casinos employ shills to get gamblers to the tables. Vincent is a shrewd business man. Trouble was no one was buying. On either side of the Ford, Vincent had placed the more affordable black and white '62 Ford Sunliner with low mileage and an equally fine '55 Ford Victoria with turquoise and white exterior and interior, priced to sell. If all of this craziness hadn't come down, I was scheduled to pick up a 1950 Packard Super 8 convertible for a great price that I was sure I could turn around for a nifty profit. I'd called the owner and told him I couldn't pick it up until tomorrow. By then I hoped all this *cazzata* would be behind us.

I went back to our office, a small rectangular building located at the back end of our lot with parking spaces in the back for our cars. Facing the building, the entrance was to the far left, one wooden step to the door. Directly inside was Sylvia's work station. To the right, set against a large picture window, looking out onto the lot, were Vincent and my desks, facing each other. On the wall directly opposite our desks was a red leather couch with gray metal file cabinets on either side of it like bookends. Above the couch hung Pop's 3 x 4 foot enlarged photograph of houses in the city of Naples. Pop had drawn a red circle around a yellow house with a red front door to the left of a steep sidewalk staircase that he said he grew up in in the neighborhood of Vomero. Black rotary phones, the tall kind with the hanging receivers, stood on each of the desks. Sylvia and I liked the look of these old-fashioned models. Vincent hated them. *Majority rules.* Vincent and Sylvia had photographs of family on their desks. I had a photograph of the Saint Mary's College rugby team that Vincent and I played on, the

Galloping Gael team that almost won the WAC Championship in our senior year.

I sat down at my desk, couldn't get comfortable, stood up, paced the room, stared out the window, and sat down again, my nerves frayed, a tension headache beginning to throb. I checked out some invoices, pretended they were sales contracts, but the lie didn't help to calm me. The coffee pot was still warm, but it was too muddy to drink. I swallowed a couple of aspirin, and looked longingly at the shelf behind Sylvia's desk where a bottle of 15-year-old, 107 proof Pappy Van Winkle Family Reserve straight bourbon whiskey stood, a prize our pop won at a national Lion's Club convention. Since Pop only drank wine, he'd given it to us with the instruction to take a sip on those occasions when we made a substantial profit. I asked Ozzie Averbuck, the owner of A & B Liquors down the street, whether this booze was any good. He'd responded in hushed, reverent tones. "Victor, you are holding one of the finest, if not *the* finest straight Kentucky bourbon in the United States, only to be outdone by its 23-year-old brother. I'll buy this bottle from you right now, five hundred dollars, cash on the barrel-head." Since it was Averbuck talking, I knew the bottle was probably worth double. So I'd brought it back and placed it gently on the shelf. The day Vincent and I took over from Pop, we'd opened the bottle, taken a sip each, toasting our futures, after which we marked the bottle against future incursions. No worthy successes followed, and the marker had dropped only once, the day I stupidly left Sweets alone in the office. So there it stood, waiting for us to get our financial shit together. I needed something to smooth over my completely whacked out nerves and was tempted to take a taste. One shot, who'd know? Thankfully, I was restrained by the arrival of my chow mien and pot stickers. I paid the kid, and he raced off on his motor scooter. Instead of the whiskey, I settled for the Coke that came with the meal. Better I should be clearheaded tonight.

Thinking about tonight's gruesome task cost me whatever appetite I thought I had. After a few bites, I gave up, tossed the food in the garbage and left the office. I walked around the lot again. I was tempted to leave early, but decided to keep to our normal business hours. At quarter to seven I switched on our night lights and hung the chains that blocked our driveway. It wasn't much protection, but we'd had very little trouble with theft or vandalism since the Amigos had left us alone. The businesses along the street watched out for each other. Across from us was Discount

Furniture, owned by an Armenian and an ancient Iranian, which stayed open until ten. In their front window, they'd placed a sign saying they supported the Brown Berets, The Chicano Revolutionary Party and the La Raza Unida, an obvious kiss-ass move to attract the business of the neighborhood's growing Chicano population, particularly in Jingletown, an area south of East 14th along the Oakland estuary and bordered by the Park and Fruitvale bridges. North of us lived mostly middle-class Italian, Irish, and Jews, but things were changing and many of the locals were moving further into the suburbs to escape the influx of the "coloreds." These were troubled times. The Vietnam War was ratcheting up, Negros were fighting hard for civil rights. In Oakland, The Black Panthers and student activists were making the Oakland city fathers extremely uncomfortable, not to mention J. Edgar Hoover. Recently, a group of UC female students took off their bras in front of the Rexall Drugstore on Sproul Plaza and burned them. Now that was the kind of protest I approve of.

To the right of our lot was Stokes Chevron gas station and garage with 24-hour service owned by Calvin Stokes, but everybody called him Jitters because of his twitch. He also stuttered, a condition he swore he never had until he spent a year in a North Korean prison camp. Jitters was short, spidery-thin, and of an undetermined racial mixture. He is our unofficial mechanic, a genius with engines. To the left of our lot was an Irish tavern called Flynn's owned by Body Flynn, who had red hair, a freckled John Wayne face, and a body like Jackie Gleason. Although Body arrived from Ireland at the age of thirteen, thirty years later, he still spoke with a broad Irish brogue. Body was a patriotic American, but he held strong views about a unified Irish republic and didn't think very kindly about the British. All the guys in the neighborhood liked Body and so did I, even though he had the annoying habit of making me suffer his stupid Italian jokes. Flynn's was a popular watering hole on East 14th. It served Anchor Steam on tap. His lunch menu was Irish stew on Mondays and Wednesdays; Body's notorious I-Dare-You-Chile on Tuesdays and Thursdays. And being a good Catholic, clam chowder on Fridays. Most week nights at Flynn's you could find a friendly game of poker or an intense game of darts. On Saturday nights Body held team darts competitions. The night manager, Stuart Tamberg, lived above the tavern. He had pitch black hair combed straight back and pale skin. He was an insomniac and looked it with weary, red-rimmed eyes. When Stuart took the job and moved in upstairs a year ago, he'd offered to keep a look-out for any late hour trouble. Vincent and I had given him our telephone numbers, and he promised to call us if he saw anything suspicious on our lot. Next to Flynn's was the DoNut Hole owned by Larry Hughes, a First Team All-American football player out of Grambling State University, who'd played second string defensive tackle for the Oakland Raiders for two seasons before his knees gave out. Larry's head was shaped sort of like an eggplant and about the same color and sat atop wide shoulders and an even wider body. He is the most optimistic and generous guy I've ever known.

Driving the International Harvester Travelall home with Winona's corpse in the back made me nervous and unhappy. I thought maybe it would have been better to have left the Travelall on the lot and come back for it. I'd decided not to because Stuart, the insomniac, would probably be sitting by his window tonight peering out over the terrain like a bat, as he does most nights. He'd wonder what I was doing there that late.

On the way home, I got to thinking that this is what the driver of a hearse feels like. Being around death as much as they are, morticians must think of dead bodies as products, like watermelons or furniture. I turned on the radio to take my mind off the corpse. The news came on. More political stuff. It was a Presidential election year. Hubert Humphrey was the front runner for the Democratic Party, but Eugene McCarthy and Robert Kennedy were also in the race. The Elephants were offering Richard Nixon, one time California senator and Eisenhower V.P. I'm not gung-ho about politics. The rest of the family gives me shit about it, calling me unpatriotic. That's not true. I'd registered for the draft like all 18-year-olds and would have gone if I was called up, but the gods of our local draft board luckily missed my name. Either that or our pop knew someone on the board. I never asked. Government is nothing to be excited about, not when our country's smartest minds never run for office. Who's left? See what I mean? You can't get fired up over mediocrity, at least I can't. I switched to a music station. "Light My Fire" by Jose Feliciano didn't improve my mood. So I switched again. "Mony, Mony" by the Shondells cheered me up a little. But the next song, the Four Tops singing "If I Were a Carpenter," brought me back to Winona. There'd be no marriages, no babies, and no tomorrows for Winona. Since I wasn't into marriage or babies, I don't know what I was depressed about, just the sudden absence of life, I suppose. One minute you're here, the next you're not. I reached the Fruitvale Avenue Bridge that spans the channel connecting Oakland to the island city of Alameda where I live. The drawbridge was up and I had to wait for a sightseeing boat to pass through. I remembered Winona having a sweet smile. I snapped off the radio. The bridge came down and I drove the rest of the way home in gloomy silence. I parked in my slot and entered the lobby of my apartment building, a five-story structure that had once been a hotel, but converted to apartments. Park Street, the principal shopping street for the east end of Alameda, was only a few blocks away. Alameda is divided into east and west business districts, the west end being close to the bay and the Alameda Naval Air Station, a busy part of town these days with the Vietnam War accelerating.

The lobby of my building has oak floors covered with fake Persian rugs, doors on the left that open into two street-facing business: Four Seasons, a florist and The Fireside, a smoke-your-lungs-out piano-bar that I never go into because the owner, Marilyn Delmar is forever fumbling at the ivories, crooning Broadway tunes in a voice gone raspy from too many Phillip Morris cigarettes. I'm not a big fan of Broadway musicals. At Flynn's, guys keep their smoking to a minimum because they know Body is allergic to smoke. And nobody wants to mess with Body.

I took the stair to the fourth floor, keyed the door to my apartment, and snapped on the hall lights. Inside was stuffy, so I opened the window in the living room that looked out onto a billboard advertising Pabst Blue Ribbon Beer, the bottle in the hands of a gorgeous looking blonde chick with droopy Marilyn Monroe eyes. I've christened my billboard blonde, Marilyn, in honor of the actress whose death six years ago I was still not over.

"Marilyn," I said. "You're looking at one screwed up goombah."

I thought you were smarter than this.

My billboard babe doesn't really talk back, but today I was feeling crazy enough that I thought I saw her lips moving.

"Thanks a lot," I said. I undid my tie, got out of my coat and slacks. After I hung my clothes up and pulled on sweatpants and a T-shirt, I headed for the kitchen for a glass of water. I took it to the couch, flopped down, drank, and spaced out. I needed rest. I put my legs up and laid back, propping my head against a cushion. I knew I wasn't going to be able to sleep, but ten minutes later, my eyes grew heavy.

Whatever the dream was, it startled me awake, sweating, with a crick in my neck, the room dark except for a faint light coming from the open window. I reached up, turned on a reading lamp and looked at my watch. Two in the morning. *Madonna*, I'd slept for close to six hours. In an hour I was scheduled to meet Sweets in front of Lenny's. I went to the bathroom, splashed water on my face, brushed my teeth and ran a comb through my hair, which does hardly any good with my tight curls. I dressed in black sweat pants and a black long-sleeved T-shirt. I stuck my feet into an old pair of black Converse shoes like the Boston Celtics wear. On my way out, I grabbed a black hooded sweatshirt hanging by the door that I wore for my morning runs on the Alameda beach. For a moment I considered rubbing charcoal on my face, then said, "Fuck it."

At half-past-two I was in the Travelall and driving. Vincent and I had done a good job sealing the body, but I was pretty sure I was smelling something unpleasant; it could have been my imagination or it might have been a guilty conscience. I took Santa Clara to Broadway, crossed back over the Fruitvale Bridge into Oakland, merging onto the Nimitz heading south. Sweets had assured me no one would be in the Satans' Clubhouse after two a.m. But we would do a couple of drive-byes to make sure. All the way to Lenny's I was arguing with myself over the effectiveness of Sweets' plan. That I wasn't worrying about the moral implications of my actions demonstrated how desperate I believed the situation was for the Brovelli Boys and family. I exited the freeway onto 98th Avenue, pulling to a stop in front of the restaurant. Sweets was standing in front munching on a Snickers bar.

"How the hell can you eat?" I asked, as he got in, but I knew the answer and waved off any reply. I said, "Let's get this done."

"Hey, I thought you dagos all had killer genes, your family being from Sicily and all."

"Screw you, Sweets. We're from Naples and there's no mafia in our family."

"Oh, yeah, Sylvia is your cousin, and she's a Vitale, right?"

"Come on, so her dad's from Sicily and might know a few mobbed up people." I didn't want to think about my cousin's family on her father's side being mafia. " They have nothing to do with us Brovelli's."

"Right," Sweets said, giving me a conspiratorial wink, which looked more like a twitch.

I pulled away from the curb. This part of Oakland in the wee hours is a scary place. Every dark side street off East 14th contains some imagined urban horror. Sinister shit lurks in every doorway. An approaching car could spell trouble: Mexican gangs mostly, the Amigos being the worst. You drive around here at night, you keep your car doors locked. I checked our door locks. Sweets, a denizen of these nether regions, chuckled. It seemed like it took hours to reach the Satans' Clubhouse, but my watch told me we'd been on the road barely five minutes. I drove by at regular speed, made a U turn a couple of blocks later and drove by again a little slower. At 3 a.m. there was little traffic, but I was wary.

"You see the alley?" Sweets asked.

"Yeah, next to the sign that says abandon all hope, ye who enter here."

"You're joking, right?"

"Right," I said. I didn't think Sweets would be impressed that his co-conspirator knew the inscription to the entrance to Hell in *Dante's Inferno*, which I'd read in my sophomore year.

As we drove past the clubhouse, the memory of Dante's dire warning made me shiver.

"Get us back in front of the alley," Sweets ordered. "I'll tell you if there are any cars coming. When I give you the go ahead, you pull in and dowse the lights."

It was cold, but I hadn't turned up the heater, for obvious reasons. Still, by the time I got us back to the alley, I was sweating. Sweets hollered, "Go, baby, go," and I cut the wheel. I turned off the lights and rolled slowly down the alley until I was parked parallel to the backdoor. We jumped out. Sweets proceeded to do his burglar thing, and soon we were inside. Sweets turned on a flashlight to low beam.

"Go make sure all the drapes and blinds are closed."

Finished, I came back and saw Sweets standing in front of a long leather couch, that I assumed would be Winona's temporary resting place. I made the sign of the cross.

We hurried to the car. I took the shoulders. Sweets took the feet. *Don't think about what you're doing.*

"On three," Sweets whispered.

I nodded.

"One, two, three."

We lifted, carried her inside and placed her gently on the couch. I cut through the duct tape and we slid her body out of her plastic shroud. I tried not to look at her, but couldn't help it. If anyone ever tells you dead people look like they're asleep, don't believe them. Dead looks dead. As

I was considering this, her arm slid off the couch, exposing the Mickey Mouse watch strapped to her slender wrist. There was something so pathetic about that watch. I felt tears.

"Oddio," I said, hoping God could hear me. I closed my eyes and lifted her arm onto her body.

"Sweets left and returned with a blanket. He tucked a throw pillow under her head and placed the blanket over her. I crossed myself again.

Sweets drawled, "Rest in peace, dahlin."

I felt the building shake. Oakland sits on the Hayward Fault Line. I felt hands grab me and a voice whispering, "Victor, Victor. Let's get out of here."

"It's an earthquake," I said.

"It's nothing, man. You're wiggin out."

He shook me, and I came to my senses. We hurried out of the building and scrambled into the car, started the engine and shifted into reverse. I was almost to the end of the alley when a truck pulled across the entrance, blocking our exit.

"Shit," Sweets muttered. "Take it back out of sight, fast."

I put the car in reverse and eased it back into the shadows

"Cut the engine, man."

"It's cut, it's cut."

Sweets said. "Unless the driver walks back here, he can't see us, but we better get down anyway."

"Can you see anything?" I asked.

"Nothing so far." He was peeking over the top of the front seat. "I take it back. He's coming into the alley."

"*Merda*," I said.

"Shit is exactly right," Sweets said, giggling.

"What's so funny?"

"Dropping his drawers, man, going to take a dump."

Disgusting I thought, like the jerk couldn't hold it to a gas station.

Sweets announced the guy was through and heading back to the truck. Soon, the engine turned over and the truck pulled away. I backed out slowly. This time we made it and turned on to East 14th. I hit the headlights and accelerated, trying not to speed when every bone in my body was telling me to stomp on the gas. Sweets told me to drop him off at Jitter's gas station so he could buy beer and some hard candy. I looked up at the billboard atop the pottery store.

ETERNITY...
WHERE WILL YOU GO?
NO SECOND CHANCES...
Call: 415-665-7134

What rung of Dante's hell was I destined for, I wondered.

I dropped Sweets off. He told me he'd walk home, wherever home was. I didn't ask. As I pulled out, I saw, Jitters, the owner, walk out of his office, his head twitching waving at Sweets. What the hell was he doing working at this hour? Damn, I thought, once the body was found, and the cops asked around, Jitters could place us in the area at 3 fucking a.m.

On the drive to my apartment, I kept looking in the rear-view mirror just in case Winona's ghost suddenly rose out of the back. I made it safely home, without being haunted and went to bed exhausted and slightly sick to my stomach. I closed my eyes. I heard Pop's voice, muttering, "*Vutu nun sidisfettu e comu nun s'avissi fattu.*" An unfulfilled vow is as if it had not been made. *Yeah, well, I fulfilled it all right.* I went to sleep feeling like original sin.

CHAPTER 4
CONFESSION

If you forgive anyone his sins, they are forgiven;
If you do not forgive them, they are not forgiven.
John 20:23

The basic form of confession in the Catholic Church has changed over the centuries. In the early days, confessions were made publicly, not only before the priest, but before the congregation. Today, confession is a one-on-one, sinner-to-priest event and is practiced under a strict seal of secrecy. Lucky for me, I thought, as I stepped into the dark of the confessional and closed the door behind me.

Forgive me, Father, for I have sinned. It's been three months since my last confession.

I'd hardly slept at all after getting back from the gruesome task of delivering Winona's body into the care of the Satans. I woke up filled with remorse. For Catholics, Saturday is considered the best day to go to confession, which allows the least amount of time before Sunday communion to commit another sin. I'd driven across the Bay Bridge to San Francisco to Saint James Church in the Mission District, far away from our family church in Alameda. If I'd gone to confession to our parish priest Father O'Quinn at Saint Joseph's, all I'd have to do was kneel down and open my mouth, and I knew what he'd say: *Okay, Victor, what poor woman have you compromised this time?*

If I thought the Guerrero Street priest, not knowing who I was, might give me a break. Ten minutes later I was proven wrong. The padre was a priest straight out of the inquisition. He even had a Spanish accent. When he realized I was not going to take his advice and discuss my grievous fault to the police, he gave me absolution and sentenced me to a Stations of the

Cross, done the old-fashioned way, on my knees. I think I said something like you gotta be kidding, Father. He wasn't. Do you have any idea how long it takes to get around the nave of a church on your fucking knees, stopping at each of the fourteen reliefs of Christ carrying the cross to his crucifixion while reciting six Hail Mary's and six Our Fathers at each station? Usually my sexual peccadillos only cost me a couple of Hail Mary's, kneeling in a pew. I guess this priest, better known as The Grand Inquisitor, Torquemada, believed I'd committed a mortal sin, which is a grave violation of God's law, and what I remember from my elementary catechism, requires full knowledge and complete consent. I couldn't argue that point. I'd covered up a murder and maybe helped a murderer, although I didn't believe Sweets was one. So there I was soiling the knees of my trousers, rosary in my hands, competing with an old woman draped in black to see who'd get around the Stations the fastest. I wondered who she'd murdered to warrant this penance. She had a head start, but I caught her after the fourth station and passed her on the fifth, made the turn, genuflected my way past the altar and down the other aisle, with the checkered flag in sight.

By the time I got out of the church, it was ten o'clock. I stopped off at my apartment to change into my work clothes – a light blue Oxford button-down shirt, blue and red stripped college tie, gray wool slacks, and a blue blazer. Vincent would be wearing the same blazer and tie. Slacks and shirt, his choice. I stopped on the way to work to buy a *Chronicle*. I looked through the paper for any news of a body in the Satans' clubhouse. Nothing. Had fucking Sweets forgotten to call? A half hour later, I parked the Travelall on the lot.

On Saturdays, the Brovelli Boys barbeque chicken and hot links for the neighborhood businesses and residents. The three grills were already in place, and Vincent, his red and blue chef's apron on, was pouring in the briquettes. I took a Double Discount sign off the Rambler and stuck it on the window on the Travelall. I'd take below cost to get rid of its resident ghost, which I was sure would haunt me as long as the car remained in our possession.

Brovelli's Barbeque Saturdays – Open to All.

I came up with this idea last year. Vincent wasn't initially sold on the cost of feeding the multitudes for free, but bought in after the first Saturday when our lot filled up with people, and by the end of the day, we'd sold six cars. That we had to repo four of them later was not relevant at the time. We were basking in early success. Vincent's suggestion was to add Italian sausage to our menu. We don't do soft drinks, but provide water from a cooler. Sylvia contributes by adding lemon slices to the water. Her other job is to hang our alma mater's red and blue college Galloping Gaels pennants above our office door that is the signal that the barbeque is done and the festivities can begin. According to Sylvia, the pennants were like waving red flags at hungry bulls. The minute she put them up, the bulls would come charging.

Our outdoor speakers were pumping out Otis Redding's "Sitting by the Dock of the Bay". Sylvia was setting up the folding tables. Vincent lit the briquettes and was watching the flames, ignoring me. Sylvia waved. I let them finish up while I went into the office to do some paperwork. A little later, Sylvia joined me. She didn't say anything, but I could tell from the look on her face, she knew there was something going on. *I say nothing. I know nothing.* That's what Sergeant Schultz says on *Hogan's Heroes.* I finished what I was doing and went out on the lot, steering clear of Vincent. A minute later Sylvia was out, holding a package of chicken and sausages. I helped her sort the meat for the grill. She asked me if I was okay. Why wouldn't I be was my reply, hoping she couldn't somehow sense how guilty I was still feeling.

It was close to noon and the chicken was almost ready before Vincent finally spoke to me.

"There's nothing in the paper this morning," he said. He sounded uptight, but not angry.

"That fucking Sweets," I said, "He was supposed to tip off the cops."

"Oh, man," he moaned.

"Sylvia left a note that Pop called." I said. "He's taking Mom shopping in Oakland, then they're stopping by for lunch."

Pop calls our Saturday barbeque, Trattoria Brovelli.

I could have told Vincent that I went to confession, but I'm sure he would've just sneered. I'm a believer, Vincent, not so much. Vincent told me he thinks of confession as a junior college where you could raise your grades before being admitted to university.

I took a quick walk around the lot, pretending to check cars. The fog receding in the distance left behind a sunny day cooled by a slight breeze. You can't beat the Bay Area for general mild weather year-round.

Sylvia appeared at the open door of the office.

"Victor," she yelled, call for you."

A year before we took over, Pop hired our cousin Sylvia. She's a whiz at automobile financing, having worked for her father, the owner of a number of Volkswagen dealerships. He's got showrooms all over California, his biggest one in San Diego. Give me a solid American car any day over those weenie German Bugs. Sylvia maxes out at five feet and can't weigh more than a hundred pounds, half of which are her tits. If she weren't so top heavy, she'd be attractive, with wide penetrating dark eyes, porcelain skin, and a Cupid's bow mouth. Her hair is black, cut short like that Carol Heis chick who won the figure skating Gold in the '60 Olympics at Squaw. Why did Sylvia leave her daddy's business to come work for us? According to her, to learn from the bottom up. Vincent believes it was because she's had a crush on me ever since we met as kids at a family wedding.

As I entered the office, Sylvia whispered, "It sounds like that louse, Sweets, but he's trying to disguise his voice." She shook her head.

"What, what?"

"Nothing."

But the look she gave meant something. I said, "He told me you called him a *chiuccio*."

"Well, he is and you know it. After you get off the phone, we gotta talk."

She gave me her version of the evil eye and handed me the phone. I turned my back to her and moved away from her desk. "Yeah," I said into the phone.

"It's me, man. I'm in the telephone booth across the street from the clubhouse. Six Satans just cruised in. They parked their hogs in the alley."

"I thought you'd said they were out of town."

"Well, they're back."

"Yeah, and why the hell haven't you called the cops?"

"I just did."

"Day late and a dollar short," I said. "If you don't want them to recognize you, you better get your ass gone from there. And, just so you understand, don't call me anymore. Don't come by here anymore. I don't want to see your Cajun face again. Disappear. Get lost. Go to Santa Cruz. Drown in the fucking ocean. Make a shark's day. Aren't you supposed to be working on. . .?"

I hadn't meant to speak so loudly, so it was lucky I caught myself before I said the word, alibi. Sylvia turned from her filing cabinet and frowned. I slammed the receiver down. Sylvia reached to grab my arm, but I was out of the office.

I almost made it to the grill when Sylvia yelled. "It's Sweets again. He wants to know if he can come get some chicken."

"Tell him if he steps on the lot, I'm going to get Vincent's baseball bat and club him to death."

Our cousin raised her eyebrows. "It will be my pleasure, but Big Sal's not going to like it." Using that sing-song voice kids use in a classroom to terrorize other kids – *but Sister Mary Rose ain't gonna like it.*

"And you're not going to tell Pop," I fired back.

She flipped her thumb against her front teeth, the Italian equivalent of get stuffed, and returned to her desk.

"Up yours too," I hollered.

Outside, Vincent was putting on the hot links and the Italian sausages. I asked if he needed any help. He waved me away with the baster. Blobs of red sauce flew through the air in my direction. I ducked out of range. Vincent was going to stay angry with me for a while.

Sylvia came out of the office holding a big pot of *Maccu*, a thick Sicilian style fava bean soup that was more like a stew. We pay for the ingredients, and Sylvia makes the side dish for our barbeques.

Redding had finished sitting *on the dock* and was singing "Shake". I began moving cars around, placing certain ones in strategic locations so customers could spot them easier. We had two 1960 Buicks: a LeSabre and a purple Invicta that were priced low enough to attract a buyer. I moved one close to the driveway and the other one near the opposite driveway. I shifted a few more cars around to make room so I could place the '61 Cadillac DeVille close to the grill. Pimps in Oakland love Caddies. I moved a few more cars around in order to separate the makes and models. Chevys from Fords; Pontiacs, from Oldsmobiles. It was my theory that car buyers become confused if two of the same make of automobile are parked next to each other. It was not a theory easily proven.

The aroma of chicken grilling wafted out on to the street. One whiff of Italian sausages grilling, and you'd faint dead away with pleasure. A friend of Pops makes the sausages from scratch. Nick Parsegian, one of the partners of Discount Furniture from across the street waved and gave us the thumbs up. A couple of cars honked as they drove by. We'd cook until we were out of meat. I was beginning to feel better, ready to sell a couple of classy pre-owned vehicles.

Feeling better didn't last long. Three cop cars roared by, sirens wailing, lights flashing. I grabbed a buffer rag from the hood of a Ford Crown Victoria and began polishing. I sighed with relief as I watched them disappear down the street in the direction of the Satans' clubhouse. I looked at Vincent. He looked back at me, a pained expression on his face.

• • •

By the time Pop arrived, we'd already served a bunch of neighborhood freeloaders, as well as a dozen walk-on and walk-off customers. We were used to the pretense, the feigned interest in a car. The so-called customers would walk around, pat a few hoods, open doors, check the engines, like they knew what the fuck they were doing, sit inside, hold on to the steering wheel with both hands and stare out the windshield as if they were looking down that long dusty road. Then, mumbling something about the need to talk to the Missus, they'd head for the grill, which was their original destination.

Pop placed a bag of tomatoes on the table next to the grill. He grows vegies year around in a fancy backyard greenhouse with fancy new temperature controls and other gadgets without which he'd have to suffer the Bay Area's short growing season. In southern Italy growing tomatoes is traditional. Pop's tomatoes have won prizes. In Northern Italy, tomatoes are fed to pigs.

"You make salads. The Early Girls are ripe," Pop said, touching three fingers to his lips and kissing them. "I give to your mama this morning. She starting sauce for pasta best in all America."

"And you are the best eater in America," Mom said. "You see his stomach?"

They were both smiling at each other. *Talk about two old people still in love.* They were a worthy model for how to have a long, happy marriage, something my twin and other sibs were trying to emulate, except for Mario who'd just returned from Vietnam, and me. My time would come, I thought, but hopefully not before I was middle-aged. That's when I'd bring over a beautiful twenty-year-old from Italy who looked like my mom, had her same sweet disposition, and could make the best pasta sauce in all America. Okay, so that sounds a little idealistic. And totally macho, which is okay with me too. Being around Pop and Mom usually put me in a good mood. Today, however, looking at Pop, I kept flashing on that damn Sweets.

"No need, Pop," I said. "We got plenty of food." We fixed paper plates for our parents, and went inside the office to eat, leaving Sylvia behind to handle the grill. With our bosomy cousin working the grill, the two dirty old men from across the street and guys next door at Flynn's would be over any moment.

Pop had brought a bottle of Chianti. We sat around my desk. I did the honors, and we toasted to Brovelli Boys' Used Cars as we always did on these Saturdays, with Pop making the toast in Italian and going on a little too long about Italian manhood and Mom rolling her eyes. After the toast, Mom took over, pumping Vincent about his wife's pregnancy and how the baby's room was coming, which was a family joke since Vincent's wife redecorated every week. Pop feigned interest. Finally he cocked his head to the right, and we walked out on the lot. I brought Sylvia a glass of wine. I showed Pop the new cars I'd just mortgaged our souls for. He approved of the cars. He was particularly impressed with the 1931 Ford Model-A Hot Rod with red side flames. Even more so when I told him what I got it for it, and what I intended to sell it for. I didn't mention the loan I had to take out.

Pop clapped me on the back. "You did good. Will make nice profit."

But not enough, I thought. Pop had no idea his sons were having some very bad sales months. In the used car biz, you don't want to go too many months in the red.

He said hello to a couple of old timers who'd been customers when he ran the lot by himself. He asked after their families. I showed him a few more cars and a terrific1958 Mercury that Sylvia found for us from her father's San Diego dealership. He'd taken it in on a new Volkswagen. With a little pressure from his daughter, the old man had wholesaled it to us. I'd flown down to drive it back. Sylvia couldn't because she was driving a car her dad sold her. Daddy's little girl had a good gig going. Once a month, her father would sell her a nice-looking low mileage car below wholesale, which is often the price a new car dealer pays for a trade-in. She'd fly south, drive it up, sell it, and pay her father the wholesale price and keep the rest for herself. Occasionally, as in the case of the Merc, she'd find a car for us. Since she's worked here, there's no telling how much money she's earned. It's a strong possibility that Sylvia is making more money than the

Brovelli Boys. I suggested one time that she show me her books, and got nothing but a sneer in return. To say Sylvia is a focused business person is an understatement. The story goes that in one of her religion classes at Holy Names College, she'd written an essay on Moses, and spelled Prophet, Profit. She keeps bugging us to let her buy into our business, claiming to have lots of good ideas about selling cars. It's not that we don't believe her, but this car lot is all about the Brovelli's. A Vitale on her dad's side and a Rizzo on her mother's side; her mom is our mom's younger sister. Pop had agreed that it was good we didn't let her buy in. In his words, "She buy in, smart girl, she buy you out in no time. Better you pay her salary." *So much for a vote of confidence.*

Walking back to the office, Pop asked about Sweets.

It was the question I was dreading. "Got me, Pop. He's usually here the minute the banners go up. He's never missed a Saturday. Maybe he's out of town."

"I worry for that boy."

Hardly a boy, I thought. "Look, Pop, I know Sweets saved you, but you know he's a crook."

"*Anche la legna storta da fuoco diritto.*"

"Yeah, I know, crooked logs make straight fires?"

"*Bene.* You don't lose the Italian. You don't forget Sweets."

"I won't Pop."

"You tell Sweets to come see me, stay for dinner. I make pasta con le sarde. Maybe you come over too, one of these days. Your mama don' see enough of you," he said cuffing me on the back of my head. If Hollywood advertised a casting call for an old-fashioned Italian father, our pop would get the role hands down.

"I don't think Sweets like sardines, Pop. I don't like sardines either."

"Sweets is a good man, have strong soul. Mama make cannoli, Sweets likes."

'If I see him, I'll give him your invitation."

"He saved my life, you know."

"Come on Pop, that was years ago. You've paid him back plenty. Don't you think it's time we stopped letting him have any car he wants for nothing. It's not good business." The second the words came out of my mouth, I could tell they were not going to fly. Pop growled, "*Non, assolutamente non!* A man pays his debts. *Capisci?*"

I raised my hands in surrender. "I understand. Just thinking aloud, Pop, that's all."

Pop called for Mom, and they walked with her on his arm, to his silver '65 Chrysler Newport Town Sedan that he cares for with the same meticulous detail he does his vegetable garden. We waved goodbye and relieved Sylvia at the grill. The line for food had thinned out. So far, only lookers. No buyers.

I placed the few remaining chicken and sausages in cartons and put them in our refrigerator. Vincent began scraping the grill, while Sylvia bagged the trash. When we were finished, Sylvia took down the Gael banners signaling the end of Brovelli's Saturday lunch. Vincent headed for the office. Sylvia went back to work, and I stayed on the lot with nothing to do, which often happens in the used car biz, standing around in the event a customer arrives. Vincent and I take turns. It's called "ups." Twenty minutes later, Vincent was leaning out the door calling my name.

"With all that's been going on, did you forget something?" he asked as I approached.

I couldn't think of anything.

"Dobbs."

"Ah shit," I said. I'd forgotten.

CHAPTER 5
REPO MAN

The best armor is to keep out of range.

Repossessing cars is an essential part of a used car salesman's life. Repo'ing in the projects, a West Oakland neighborhood of rundown apartment buildings, meant risking that life, particularly these days with the Black Panthers strutting their stuff. Stuff often meaning automatic rifles. We'd carried paper on Charles Dodd's 1961 Olds Super 88 convertible, and he hadn't paid us in three months. Three months was the extent of the Brovelli Boys financial patience.

"Give me the address and the extra keys, and I'll get Mr. Converse," I said. Mr. Converse is a large leather gym bag that holds jumper cables, hot wiring equipment, and a couple of different length door-lock openers. It also holds a blackjack and a tire iron just in case. It takes two of us to repo a car, one to drive to the location, and the other to retrieve our car. It was my turn to do the retrieving, which was the dangerous end of the operation.

We keep Mr. Converse in the shed behind the office. I returned lugging it over my shoulder. We left Sylvia in charge and took off in the direction of West Oakland. We were always a little worried as we approached the architecturally bland buildings that marked this part of west Oakland. It was never a good idea for two white guys to be driving through this part of town, even in daylight. If it had been night, we'd be two bulls' eyes for any black gangster with a hard on for whitey. These days especially. But a repo is a repo. Business required a little courage.

"I think the apartment complex is that way," I said.

Vincent turned the corner and ran into a dead-end street. "Next guess," he said, backing out quickly. In the projects, you don't want to, God forbid, stall out in a dead end no matter what color you were. . We drove two more blocks and this time I guessed right. I low-geared to a slow roll down the street hunting for our Olds. Hoping to trick the repo man, deadbeats never park their cars close to where they live. Another of their tricks is to hide the car under a full-sized car cover, gray being the color of choice as it's less noticeable. Not for two eagle-eye Brovelli boys.

"There it is," I said. "What's he think, I don't recognize the shape of an Olds?"

"You sure?" Vincent asked. "Could be a Buick."

"Nah, trust me. That's ours. There isn't another car in the entire neighborhood with a cover over it."

Vincent stopped, and I got out. I lifted the cover and gave Vincent a thumbs up. Vincent brought me Mr. Converse. Opening the door was a snap. I popped the hood. Vincent placed the battery in front of the car, and I attached the cables.

"Hey, you, what the fuck you doing to my car?"

It's not hard to recognize the voice of a very angry man. The voice was coming from down the block and coming fast. Dobbs. When he wasn't drinking, Dobbs was a good enough guy. Given the tone and the epithet, I was betting he was plenty juiced.

"Time to split," Vincent said.

I was in the Olds and cranking the motor over, praying it would start on the first try. It didn't.

The angry voice got closer. "That you Brovelli pricks?"

"Crank it, crank it," Vincent yelled.

"You get your ass out of here," I yelled back.

"I'm staying. If it doesn't turn over, you'll need help with elephant man."

My twin, what a guy.

It finally caught with a loud roar just as a shot rang out. "Mavaffuncullo," I yelled. Vincent peeled off the cables, slammed down the hood, and scampered back across the street to his car, holding Mr. Converse in front of his face for protection. He peeled out, and I slammed the car into gear. As I hauled ass, the rear window of the Olds exploded. I ducked but not before a couple of pieces of glass embedded themselves in the back of my neck. *Hurt like a sunavabitch.* I leaned over the wheel and kept driving. Ahead, Vincent had already turned the corner. Full throttle to the cross street, I looked back at fucking Dobbs aiming a six-shooter like in a cowboy movie. I swung the wheel to the right and fishtailed around the corner. I took my foot of the gas, re-corrected. down-shifted, and stomped on the gas, laying a patch. Ahead of me, Vincent was doing his Cale Yarborough Daytona 500 impersonation. Doing my Mario Andretti thing, I caught up and passed him, pushing eighty. My neck was bleeding, and I was pissed.

Back on the lot, Sylvia dug the shards out of my neck and applied iodine and Band-Aids. Vincent was outside looking morosely at the shattered window. Not that costly to replace, but Dobbs had trashed the interior of the Olds. Swannee would charge us a couple of hundred to get it back up to Brovelli standards. We'd have to add on the cost to the asking price. I joined my brother.

"No more cars for Dobbs," Vincent said. "He's 86'ed."

"No fucking kidding. Did you see the back seat? It's like he used it as his personal lunch counter. I'll drive the Olds down to Swanee for a cleanup job and walk back. I'm going to stop in to Flynn's for a quick brew. I'm still shaking."

"My turn when you get back," Vincent said. "That darn Dobbs."

By now you probably figured out that Vincent doesn't swear like I do. He's much more of a gentleman. But if my twin *does* swear, you better watch out.

"Next time it's your turn to repo," I said. "And I'm the driver."

As I headed for the door, Sylvia grabbed my arm. "Vittorio, I really need to talk to you."

"Not now, Sylvia. I'm wounded and badly in need of a brew." Talk to Vincent.

"It's got to be you."

"Then you got to wait." I walked out the door, leaving her fuming.

• • •

The lights are always turned down in Flynn's. Ambiance, Flynn says; cheapskate, I say. The maroon faux leather booths against the wall opposite the long bar were empty. Beer ads and dim lights hung on the wall above the booths. Two men I recognized as salesmen from Montgomery Ward's auto parts were sitting at the bar nearest the door, shaking dice. The back of Flynn's opens up into a large room in which there are two pool tables and a couple of dartboards. A local pool hustler by the name of Cash – that's his real name - was sharpening his game, the sound of ivories cracking against each other. The jukebox was playing Frank Sinatra doing it his way.

Even though Body Flynn stocks a number of tasty Irish beers, I stick to our local Anchor Steam on tap, which he poured into a frosty mug. He wouldn't dream of putting a bottle in front of a customer. I sat down at the bar next to Jay Ness. Jay is a detective sergeant in the Oakland Police Department. We met at one of Body's poker games and became friends. He's about my height, not quite six feet. If it wasn't for his pot belly, you'd mistake him for a weight lifter. He's pumped iron so much that it's difficult for him to button his ubiquitous corduroy sport coat. His Jimmy Durante-size nose dominates his round face and small mouth. Bags below his eyes make him look sad all the time. His brown hair never seems to be combed. I heard some people remark that Officer Jason "Jay" Ness is the ugliest man they know who seems to convince really gorgeous women to marry him. I felt a little self-conscious, as he slapped me on the back, since it was conceivable at some point in the future Jay would have to arrest me for screwing up a crime scene, or being an accessory to a murder or whatever other frightening criminal activity Sweets would involve me.

"You okay?" Ness asked. "You were sighing."

"Bad day. Had to repo a car. Dobbs took a shot at us." I pointed to the bandage on my neck.

"Hell you say. You want me to arrest him?"

"Nah, he was drunk."

Body placed the frosty mug in front of me, and smiled. "Tell me, Victor, me-boy-o why do so many Eye-talians have mustaches?"

"Haven't a clue, Body, but I'm sure you're going to tell me."

"So they can look like their mothers."

The smirking Irishman slammed his hand on the bar and began laughing. Ness joined in.

"Got to run, Victor," Ness said, standing up. "Town's in crises mode."

Before I could ask, the door was closing behind him.

Flynn was still laughing. All the years I'd been drinking here, Body never failed to come up with an Italian joke. I could have countered with an Irish joke, like what's the difference between a smart Irishman and a unicorn? Nothing. They're both fictional characters. But, then, Body would have had to retaliate, and I'd have to counterattack. See what I mean? So I suffered the stupid jokes, like it was a cover charge to drink in his joint. We moved on to sports, our favorite subject. We talked while I drank my beer.

Body Flynn is one hell of a good guy, and we'd been through a lot of boozy nights together. His parents brought him to America and settled in San Francisco when he was nine years old. Body grew up rooting for the USF Dons, who I always managed to point out hadn't won a basketball championship since the Bill Russell era in the early fifties. From 1958 on, the Galloping Gaels of Saint Mary's have dominated the sport. That too, I never failed to point out. *Fooking Gaels*, he calls us, which, considering the accent, makes the adjective funny rather than insulting. When I'd pointed out Gael derived from Gaelic, he responded with, "Saint John Baptiste de la Salle was a *fooking Frenchie*." The Saint was the founding father of the Christian Brothers whose teaching order runs Saint Mary's College. Lately, neither team had been doing any winning. Body and I are both Giants fans. I was finishing my second brew when Vincent walked in and told me it was his turn for some suds.

As I walked back on the lot, Sylvia was waiting for me in the door baring my entrance, scowling. "Okay," I said. "So what's so important?"

"Vittorio."

Whenever Sylvia starts with my Italian name, it's trouble. I sighed.

"Vittorio, listen to me. I overheard some of what you and Vincent were saying. The whole neighborhood probably heard you. What have you guys got yourselves mixed up in with that nut job Sweets?"

Sylvia was tapping her foot like some exasperated grade school teacher.

"I need the truth here. If Brovelli Brothers' Used Cars is going down in flames, you got to give me a heads up. You know I've been making plans to be part of this business someday."

"Not a chance, cousin," I said.

"You wait, but that's not the point here. I'm still your business manager. I need to know what the hell's going on, and if you don't tell, I'm going to quit, *capisci*?"

"I hear you, but you wouldn't quit. You're making too much on the side with your daddy's gift cars."

"Not enough to get in trouble with the cops. I heard enough to know you guys might be taking up space in the slammer. Then where would I be?"

Sylvia had a point. "Give me a minute," I said, walking away from her, trying to figure how to deal with this problem. What the hell, I thought, there could very well be a time when we'd need Sylvia's help, perhaps as a witness or a person to vouch for our good character in a court of law.

Vincent might brain me, but the look on Sylvia's face told me she wasn't bluffing about quitting.

"All right," I turned to her. "But you're not going to like it." I started with Winona's dead body in the trunk of the Impala and ended with Sweet's plan to dispose of Winona's remains."

"*Che cazzo,*" What the fuck, Sylvia exclaimed, throwing up her hands. "What is wrong with you? Are you completely out of your minds? This is murder, and your Pop's so-called savior, that *chooch*, Sweets, is probably a goddamn murderer."

"I know, I know, Sweets is a dumb ass," I sighed. "We should've told you from the start."

"You Brovelli's," she said. "What am I ever going to do with you two?"

"It's done deal, cuz, so what you *can* do is keep your mouth shut. Pretend this never happened. There is no way this can come back on us." Sylvia's large bosom heaved. She shook her head a couple of times. The look in her eyes told me I was one pitiful soul.

"Okay, Victor, whatever you boys need. I'll cover your asses, but you have to keep me in the loop."

I promised.

"I don't want to be visiting you boys in San Quentin." She said, turned, and walked into the office.

I remained on the lot, talking to the cars. "San Quentin, did she say San Quentin?"

Not one fine pre-owned automobile responded to my question.

A half hour later, just as I was contemplating jumping off the Golden Gate Bridge, the Asian couple Vincent had been talking to returned, and I sold them a gold Pontiac Bonneville. We made a decent profit since we didn't have a lot of money tied up in the car, which lifted my spirits some. Vincent returned from Flynn's, and gave me the old I-told-you-so about the Asian couple. When I told him about telling Sylvia, he clenched his fists and squared his jaw. We stood facing each other, breathing hard, moving right, moving left, feeling each other out as to who'd throw the first punch. Mario, our middle brother, used to call us bantam roosters circling for an advantage. Finally, I turned away, and he didn't follow. We managed to avoid further confrontation by staying at opposite ends of the lot.

By closing time Saturday, we'd sold two additional cars. That surprised me even more. Perhaps things were going to pick up. I could only hope. The young Asian couple were both employed, made a strong down payment, and selected an automobile the bank had signed off on, so Sylvia was able to write them on a non-recourse contract, which meant the bank paid us and took responsibility for the balance of the contract. Aside from cash, that was the best possible deal for us. The second buyer was less financially stable, so Sylvia wrote him up on a recourse contract. In that case the bank will loan on a car, but if the buyer defaults we have to pay the bank back, then hustle to repo our car. The third buyer, a grad student at Hayward State, bought a Volkswagen van with a bumper sticker on it that read, *If the van's rockin, don't come knockin*. He was too risky for a bank, so we had to carry the paper at a percentage rate for which we would have been charged with usury had we lived in the Middle-Ages, and been denied the sacraments and a Christian burial. Considering the past six months of slumping sales, today turned out to be a fantastic sales day. The three of us, Sylvia, Vincent and me split the left-over chicken and hot links between us to take home. I was putting up the chains when a police car came flying down the street, its siren on, flashing red light. A moment later another cop car roared by, then another. I watched them speed down the street. I knew where they were going; it put a knot in my stomach.

"You Brovelli Boys are in soooo much trouble," Sylvia yelled from the office door.

CHAPTER 6
PERSONS OF INTEREST

Compassion is a two way street.
Frank Capra

Our parish priest looked at me skeptically as he placed the wafer on my tongue, like *how come I didn't see you at confession yesterday?* I left the church feeling better, not an unfettered soul, but one for whom the stain of guilt was not as dark as before. I bought a copy of the Sunday Tribune and drove to Ole's for breakfast. I was relieved to be driving my own car again, an apple-red 1965 Ford Mustang luxury coupe, sporting an all-wine red leather interior, loaded with a 289 cubic inch V-8 engine. It has only twenty-one thousand miles on it. I take it to the airport and challenge airplanes to a race.

Just kidding.

I sat down at the counter and ordered my usual of three eggs sunny-side up with crispy bacon on top of a waffle. The front page of the Tribune was all about President Johnson's decision not to run for a second term in office. Who gives a shit, I thought. As far as I could tell, he'd fucked things up pretty royally in Vietnam. I thumbed through the rest of the paper. Mostly, it was same-o-same-o: the war, flower-children, economy, segregation, and Congress. On the fifth page, however, I spotted what I was looking for, an article that an anonymous telephone call had led the Oakland Police Department to the Satans' Clubhouse on East 14th Street, where they discovered a dead female. Her name was given as Winona Davis, There were few details. Sunny Badger, head honcho of the Satans stated that the woman was unknown to any member of the club, and this could be a set-up by a rival motorcycle gang. He wouldn't name the gang, but we all knew he was talking about the Mongols. I felt a twinge of guilt, but shook it off when I reminded myself that I'd gone to confession, been absolved, and taken communion. The article explained that the woman had yet to be identified, except she appeared to be in her early twenties and had a tattoo of a red and blue parrot on her left shoulder. It said nothing about a white Mickey Mouse watch. The death was reported as a homicide. Four of the membership of the Satans, including their leader, were being detained for questioning as persons of interest. I finished my breakfast, paid, and set out for work.

I was an extremely interested person. So was my brother, and Sweets, of course, wherever that numb-nuts was. I knew Vincent was not convinced of Sweets innocence. According to my twin, this whole thing was going to turn to crap. Me, I couldn't see how Winona could be traced back to the Brovelli Boys, unless Sweets was arrested. Even so, considering we'd gone the distance to protect him, I found it hard to believe he'd fuck us. But no matter how often I reassured Vincent, he only shook his head morosely.

There was business to consider, cars to sell. At the lot, I said good morning to Vincent. He didn't reply. Fuck him, I thought. He stayed in the office, and I took first-ups on the lot. According to Pop, Sundays were good days for buyers. It was his theory that after church people were more inclined to spend money. They'd opened their mouths and accepted the Body and Blood of Christ. Their souls were saved, why not buy a new automobile for the soul to travel in? You might not believe this, but Pop was dead serious. He didn't take into account non-Catholics and Atheists. He wouldn't have. In Pop's belief system there were only Catholics. As for those that weren't, *eh, they were missing out on the fun.* I often wondered what fun being a Catholic Pop was talking about, not the fun I'd just gone through in the dark of the confessional as the priest quizzed me about my mortal and venal sins, that's for sure, or the fun I received on my knuckles in the fourth grade by Sister Mary Immaculata. No priest had ever tried to grope me, but I'd heard stories. Or I could site examples from history like the inquisition, but that wouldn't mean zip to my pop. Sal Brovelli was a big-time Catholic with an abiding belief in all its tenets. Vincent follows in Pop's footsteps. As for me. I'm a believer, but with less enthusiasm for the tenets. I remember telling my religion teacher in high school that churches would be better places without the people in them. That got me a one-day suspension.

For as long as Vincent and I'd been in the business, Pop's Sunday theory of car sales had never proven true, but by noon today we joked that the old man might have been on to something. We sold the Model-A Hot Rod for better than Vincent and I had imagined. By the end of the day, the purple Invicta was gone, and a 2-door Olds Cutlass. All three were cash sales, which thrilled Sylvia, who caresses money the way other women caress infants. The three of us agreed that it would take more than these sales to get the Brovelli Brothers' Used Cars business out of its fourteen-month slump. Still, our bankers would be pleased. Ironic, I thought, that after committing a crime, we'd been rewarded rather than punished. I didn't share the thought with Vincent, as he doesn't believe in irony the way I do. My theory is that all the events of the world are in some sense governed by irony. You know, like shit happens when you're thinking of a beautiful woman. Vincent is a cause-and-effect kind of guy. He dug that whole Saint Thomas Aquinas causality bullshit we studied in Philosophy 101. Not sure how he managed to hear the lectures while slumped on his desk asleep.

Around noon, Sylvia, who was back treating me normally and not like a guy preparing for life behind bars, drove me to San Leandro, a town south of us, where I picked up the 1950 Packard Super 8 convertible. I parked it in a slot next to the '61 Impala that Swanee had detailed. Unlike the Travelall I refused to place a discount price on the Impala, even if its trunk *had* contained a dead body. It was just too pretty.

The afternoon proved less profitable. But around closing time, a guy walked in off the street and bought the '55 3100 Series Chevy Pickup and put half down. Any bank would love that contract, and we'd be happy to take the bank's money, which made Sylvia happy. And, since the entire day passed without any blowback from the "event", for the first time in two days my twin was no longer frowning at me.

I volunteered to close up. Sylvia's VW Bug was being serviced, so she hitched a ride with Vincent. "Say hello to the bambino," I said.

"It might be a girl," he said. "But I'll pass on your choice of gender to the carrier."

"Yeah, her too," I yelled as he got in his car. We gave each other the Italian fuck you-sign. It always feels better when my bro and I are getting along. With us, and maybe most twins, the fundamental personality question is always: *we got along in the womb, why can't we get along now?*

The two of them were barely off the lot when my smile turned dark. What happened to sour my mood was a telephone call from Sweets.

"Hey, dude, I'm in the slammer."

"Call your lawyer, why call me?"

"I don't know any lawyers."

"There's something called the public defender's office. They provide legal services free."

"No way Jose," he said. "Has-beens, never-was's and kids just out of law school. We need real help, see what I'm saying?"

How the hell do you see words, I thought. Sweets had some kind of nerve. "I'm not sure what you mean by we, Sweets. Where does "we" come into it? There's no "we" *capisci* I helped you the best I could. I agreed to your stupid plan. That's as far as I go. Do not involve me or my brother."

To say I was not feeling compassionate was an understatement. I slammed down the phone determined I'd no longer have anything to do with Sweets Monroe, even if he was a direct descendant of Jean Lafitte. That determination didn't last long. The phone rang again, and Pop's voice was on the other end of the line.

"How you not get lawyer for Sweets, huh?"

How in the hell did Sweets finesse a second telephone call, I wondered.

"You listening to me Vittorio?"

Pop's angry voice is cross between a 16-wheeler downshifting and a lion growling. The more I listened the more my resolve turned into squishy filial obedience. I lied to Pop that I'd just gotten off the telephone with Harvey Innis, our lawyer and one of Pop's pals from the parish church. When I hung up I immediately made good on my lie, and placed the call. Harvey said his son Carter would get right on it. Carter had graduated from Saint Mary's a class ahead of us and recently passed the California State Bar Exam on his third try. I always thought he was sort of dim. Fine, I thought, a rookie lawyer who's not very bright. Serves Sweets right.

Before I could leave I checked all the cars to see if they were locked. Then I cleaned the office. Sylvia was a great accountant, but had something against brooms. At seven, I grabbed the case holding our ignition keys, locked the office door and set the alarm. I went behind the office for my car, drove it off the lot and parked. The slots where the cars we sold today had stood needed to be filled. I knew where I could pick up a clean 1960 Caddy for a reasonable price, thinking what's a little more debt? I locked the chains in place across the driveway and headed to Flynn's for a couple of cold ones.

Two steps inside the bar, I was greeted by a loud Irish voice. "Hey, Victor, how do you know you're Italian?"

"I give up," I answered as I sat down at the bar. "How *do* I know I'm Italian?"

"When you're 5'4", can bench press 325 pounds, shave twice a day, but you still cry when your mother yells at you."

"My laugh-needle is not budging," I said.

Body was laughing so hard, he was crying, bent over, holding his stomach. When he stopped, I ordered my usual.

A couple of Anchor Steams turned into three and lots of arguing with Body, over why the Giants should fire their manager, Herman Franks. I was pro, Shaun was con. My reasoning went like this: with a team that had Jim Davenport, Jesus Alou, Willie McCovey, and Say Hey Willie Mays with pitchers like Juan Marichal and Gaylord Perry how come they messed up last year? Flynn argued that a 91 and 71 game season was hardly a screw-up. He wasn't wrong, but I like to play the devil's advocate with Flynn and watch his white cheeks puff up and turn pink like he's holding his breath. Before I left, I bet him fifty bucks that the Giants would not win the National League crown. We gave our money to Stuart Tamberg, the night bartender, who'd just walked in, to keep for us, not that we didn't trust each other, but fifty dollars will pay for the cover charge to see Carol Doda at the Condor Club and enough drinks for sustained appreciation of her.

I drove carefully, not that I was drunk. I can handle three beers, which was about what the guys of my class partook of most weekday nights for four years in college, leaving the weekends for six packs and shots, a tradition that I'd decided to forego after graduating. I don't need booze to get me fired up. I kept both hands on the wheel and concentrated, so by the time I reached my apartment I was completely sober, but suffering from a tension headache. I pulled into my slot in the back and walked around to the lobby. My headache turned into the all-purpose, all-cranium kind when I spotted Sweets sitting on the lawn chair next to the entrance. I made a quick about face, hoping he didn't see me and headed for the back entrance. If I could just reach the staircase.

No such luck. I managed to make it up two steps when I heard Sweets.

"Yo, Victor, I've always been a fan of your Mustang. That color red is boss."

"Should I check out the trunk, Sweets? See if you hid one of your girlfriends in it?"

"No need to be like that, mon ami. It's not my fault someone is trying to mess wit me."

"What are you doing here?"

He ignored the question, reached into his pocket and withdrew a couple of wrapped candies.

"You want one? Cherry on the outside, gooey chocolate in the center."

I shook my head. "You said you'd have an alibi in place. How come the cops nailed you so fast?" I continued climbing the stairs, Sweets following me.

"Ah, man, I forgot to mention that Winona had a no-fly zone against me."

I turned around and looked down at him, incredulous. "An injunction?"

"We got in a few fights, know what I'm saying."

This was way too depressing. "Look, Sweets, I got you a lawyer, you're out of jail. That's it, man. No more. You're on your own. You don't hear very well. I told you, the Brovelli boys are out of the picture." I stopped talking and waited for his reply. I didn't like the way Sweets was looking at me, like he had a grip on my balls, and was about to squeeze.

"Well, I wouldn't say you're *completely* out of the picture," he said, popping a candy into his mouth.

"I knew it, I knew it. Okay, tell me what you did, Sweets."

"I told my lawyer the whole story."

"You got to be fucking kidding me. You told that *cretino* about what we did?"

"He's actually not that dumb. I didn't tell him every teeny bit, but I had to tell him something. I wasn't going to sit in jail, man. Jail gives me the hives. Besides, right now all the evidence the cops got is circumstantial. I told Carter you guys are working on finding out who the killer is."

"We're not working on anything except selling fine pre-owned automobiles."

"Let's discuss this in your apartment, Victor. I'm cold and hungry, and you always have some good grub your mother cooked for you in the fridge."

We reached my floor and started down the hall.

"I need a crash pad," he said.

"No way. Not a chance. Absolutely not."

"That's not what your father said. He offered his house, but I couldn't impose. He told me you'd be happy to put me up while you guys straighten things out."

"Jesus Christ, Sweets, you didn't tell Pop we found the body. Tell me you didn't do that."

"Of course not. I wouldn't want to worry your parents."

"Well, what the hell did you tell dumb-ass Carter?"

"That we found the body in the alley, and we put it the Satans' clubhouse."

I thought I was going to have a heart attack and die. It might be a better fate than what I imagined lay ahead for me. "Carter can't possibly have believed you."

"Oh yeah, he was cool. Said it showed compassion. Don't worry dude, it's all lawyer client privilege thing, like mums the word. Unless, of course, in the course of the trial. . ."

"What trial? We're not going to any fucking trial." We reached my apartment. I keyed the door and stomped inside. I turned on the lights and pulled down the shades, trying to control my breathing. The Brovelli boys were in deep shit. Of our own making, I grant you. One of Pop's many proverbs came to mind: *Chi ha fatto il male faccia la penitenza*, which translates loosely into you made your bed, now lie in it. I didn't see any way out of the frigging bed unless we joined forces with Sweets and figured out who was setting him up. Moreover, the mess was pretty much on me. If I'd taken my brother's advice – *oh man, if only* - and called the cops right away, none of this would be happening. God, I hate it when my twin is right.

"Cool crash pad you got here," Sweets said. He toured the living room, then walked into my bedroom.

"Stay out of there, Sweets, that's private."

He ignored me. I was ready to throw his ass out when I heard a crash and a grunt. He came out holding a book in his hands.

"Tripped over this goddamn book. How many pages it got? Hit somebody over the head, it keel 'em dead."

"Give me that," I said

"Whoa, dude, all you got is bed and books in there. Where are the cool posters of chicks? I can't sleep with all those books. Reminds me of school n' shit."

He was holding *War and Peace*. Two walls of my bedroom were bookshelves. I wasn't happy that he knew I read books.

"Get the hell out of there," I said. "What makes you think you're sleeping in my bed, anyway? What're you thinking? You're on the couch,

Birdman, and that's just for tonight. After that, you find a nice warm spot under the freeway, capisci?"

Sweets shrugged and tossed me *War and Peace* and strolled back across the living room to the kitchen. I followed him holding the book that at 780 pages and perfect bound was a suitable weapon with which I was thinking of bashing Sweets upside his head.

"Sweets, who posted your bail?"

"Your daddy," Sweets said as he opened the refrigerator door and looked inside.

Of course, my pop. Who else? The burglar with a perennially empty pocketbook had removed a container of Mom's lasagna and put it on the kitchen table. He pointed to the pasta. "You want me to set two places?"

I was hungry driving home, but I'd lost my appetite. "No, you go ahead. I got a date."

I didn't have a date, but I needed to get away from Sweets. "You got the couch. There are blankets in the closet. "I'll be back in a couple of hours."

"You're totally groovy, Victor. I really appreciate this. I'm counting on you, ma man."

As I was leaving, a question occurred to me. I returned to the living room. "Sweets, how come when you got arrested, the cops didn't find out about the outstanding warrant for your ass from Louisiana?"

Sweets was busy chewing, and I waited. He was about to take another bite.

"No, no before you feed your face, answer the question. If there's an out-of-state warrant on a person, the cops don't let him post bail."

"True enough, Victor. True enough." He hung his head. "You caught me in a lie. What can I say? I needed you to feel sorry for me, man. It was all I could think up on short notice."

"That figures, that goddamn figures," I said and stalked out of my apartment, mad as hell – at Sweets, but mostly at myself.

CHAPTER 7
MILLS COLLEGE FOR WOMEN

Danger – a word that instills fear into some, while in others there is nothing quite so arousing.

The Fifth Dimension was singing "Stoned Soul Picnic" as I parked in the visitor's lot of Mills College. On Sunday evenings Mills College campus was quiet, all the resident students back from weekends at home and preparing for bed, but the dorms were still open for visitors. I got out of the car and headed for Andrews Hall. After being blackmailed by Sweets and feeling taken advantage of, I needed some female company. Renee Sorenson was as close to a girlfriend I had. Well, not as in steady or future relationship. Certainly not marriage. I'm not prepared to settle down with wife and family just yet. I'll leave that to my bro. My in-the-moment girlfriend has honey-blonde hair, hazel eyes, and a gap between her two front teeth, called a diastema which, according to my theory of flaws, increases a woman's beauty. I developed this theory based on what Edgar Allan Poe said: *There is no exquisite beauty without some strangeness in the proportion.* In my sophomore year in college I dated Mary Ann Majerus who had a wandering left eye. It was totally sexy. Renee is at least four inches taller than me and reminds me of Ingrid Bergman who was also tall and Nordic. Renee's a music major in her senior year at Mills, a college known for their music department. She brags that Dave Brubeck had once taught at Mills. I don't listen to a lot of jazz, a little too abstract for me, but I knew who he was. Renee plays first violin in the Oakland Junior Philharmonic. I attended one of her concerts and was proud of myself for not falling asleep.

I called up to Renee's room. Soon she was down, and we were walking to the Mustang arm in arm. We got in and she flung herself across the seat into my arms. Our mouths sprung open and our tongues collided like we'd both turned a street corner and weren't paying attention. We laughed and she bit my neck. Who ever said, northern women are cold? Probably a Sicilian. We went at it for a while and then backed off. Steering wheels and gear shifts require creative adjustment when involved in sexual groping. Tonight, however, we both recognized the front seat action as hors d'oeuvres. The main course would come later.

I drove into the Berkeley hills and parked off Grizzly Peak Road at a turnout overlooking the Bay, a place I like to go to from time to time for thinking and pleasure. I turned off the engine. Below us were the bright night-lights of Oakland and in the distance the glitter of San Francisco, a solitary light winking atop Coit Tower. That Coit Tower has been considered San Francisco's phallic symbol had nothing to do with my choice of a make-out location.

As much as I needed to talk to someone about my dilemma, confiding in Renee would be a mistake. She was a girl of the Sixties, which meant that her standards were a mixed bag of convoluted philosophies. Sex was cool. She referred to cops as pigs and had been arrested at a sit in at the Alameda Naval Air Station. In January, she'd traveled to Washington D.C. to be part of the Jeanette Rankin Brigade Anti-War March on Congress. On the other hand, she also attended the Lutheran church regularly and played the organ for the choir. When dating high-minded, brilliant women, it's my policy to avoid controversial subjects such as the murder of Winona Davis. When I mentioned Vincent's name, her eyes lit up. She has a thing for stories about our brotherly predicaments we get into, the used car business being surprisingly dangerous. They turn her on. My musical genius is aware of and embraces this inclination whole heartedly and bodily. My first thought was to tell her about our repossessing a car from a 260-pound drunk with anger management issues. I weighed the possibility, but tonight I needed some real heat, and Vincent's scrapes tended to be even more dramatic and hair-raising than mine, for reasons only a psychologist could explain because my twin is mostly a stable and logical person.

At this point, you might ask why the lookout and not some place more comfortable like my apartment, which was not an option this evening with Sweets in it. But that's not the reason. Even if my apartment were available, I prefer making love in an automobile. There's a creativity required of a man and a woman having sex in an automobile that leads to a different, perhaps heightened, sexual experience than the one you have in a bed, particularly one's own bed. It is my theory - one I've proven to be true - that automobiles are like aphrodisiacs. Two bodies lusting after one and another packed into the back (or front) of an all-leather Mustang, breathing the same confined air made musky by pheromones firing off like pistons, well, you get the picture.

A bedroom doesn't have the same primal atmosphere. Not that I have a whole lot against making love in a bed, it's fine if we're both in the mood for a more laid-back experience. If that's the case, I offer the damsel in question, a bedroom in the remarkable Claremont Hotel, nestled in the Berkeley hills or a suite in the Mark Hopkins on Knob Hill in San Francisco where I have a working arrangement with two night managers, both Saint Mary's grads. We alums stick together. Autos at cost is not too high a price to pay. At all costs, hah, hah, I avoid taking a woman home to my apartment. It is my theory that love-making in one's home bed tends to give a woman ideas about stability, long-term relationships, image of walking down the aisle, bambini, and a life time of togetherness. Get the picture.

Renee has never once hinted that she required a bed. Tonight she curled her legs under her, smiled wickedly, and asked, pretty please for a story about Vincent, preferably one I hadn't told her before. Something new and daring.

I had just the story in mind.

"Okay," I said. "Here goes. There was this time a crazy person wound up sitting under Vincent's desk. I mean a real nut case." I could tell by the eager look on her face that this was new to her. "It happened a couple of months ago, the way Vincent told it to me." I begin in my best imitation of my twin's voice:

You see, Victor, I'm on the phone talking to Jack about this and that, and I look out the window. Across the street, I see a big guy with no shirt and muscles like Arnold Schwarzenegger. This guy looks mean and he's holding a baseball bat and swinging it into the palm of his hand, snap, snap. Nothing happy about the way he's doing it, like he's itching to crack somebody's head.

I say to Jack. "There's a nut across the street swinging a baseball bat, looking right at me."

"Get your ass out of there," Jack says.

I agree, but before I can get out of the chair, the dude starts running across East 14ᵗʰ, cars blaring their horns. He almost gets run over by a bus. He's paying no attention, his eyes fixed on me. Jesus, I don't know what to do. I know Sylvia keeps that old Second World War pistol her daddy gave her in her desk, but the guy's already inside, standing in the door, staring at me. I put up my hands. He doesn't do anything just stares.

Renee had her left arm around my shoulder; her right hand had moved to my thigh. "What in the world did Vincent do," She asked, breathing heavily.

"Nothing, he didn't need to do anything."

"Don't keep me in suspense." She was snuggling, her hand on my thigh now on my crotch.

"You won't believe it. According to Vincent, the guy drops the bat, falls on the floor, crawls under his desk, wraps himself up into the fetal position and starts blubbering like a baby. The baseball bat wasn't even wood; it was made out of plastic."

"So?"

"So, nothing. Vincent calls the cops. They come over and haul the poor bastard away. They tell Vincent since Governor Reagan closed down the mental hospitals, the streets have been full of crazies."

Renee removed her hand from my crotch, which I took to mean she was disappointed in the story. I thought it was pretty damn tense. Perhaps I should have embellished it.

"Why does your secretary have a pistol?" Renee asked. "Isn't that dangerous?"

A rational question, one that I'd asked Sylvia when we took over the business from Pop. Her response was that a good Catholic girl had a right to protect herself, given the nature of the neighborhood. Renee said that sounded logical. She'd thought about buying a pistol herself, considering Mills College was not in one of the better sections of Oakland, just north of the Fruitvale Ave neighborhood, the home turf of the Amigos, one of a growing number of Hispanic gangs in Bay Area.

"What kind of a gun does Sylvia have?" Renee asked.

"Sylvia says it's a Beretta her father brought home from Italy after the Second World War. It's a scary looking thing."

Renee placed her hand back on my crotch and said, "I'd love to see it."

I took that as a hint and moved my hand over hers.

Keeping her left hand in place, Renee reached for the dash with her right hand, snapped on the radio and tuned in to a classical station. A violin something, a little sad, a little passionate.

I suggested a move from the front bucket seats to the back, and Renee agreed that would be wise because she could see my gun better.

Talk about a sense of humor. I recalled my brother Mario telling me about when he went through boot camp that a sergeant holding a rifle with one hand and his crotch with his other hand kept yelling: *This is my rifle, this is my gun; this is for shooting, this is for fun*

I got out, walked to her side and opened the door for her. We *Italians are known for being gentlemen.*

Driving back to drop Renee off, I asked her what the name of the music was. Her dreamy response was Felix Mendelssohn's *Violin concerto in E Minor, opus 64.* Given the results the concerto produced, I vowed to get a lot of the guy's music.

I returned to my apartment with three hickys, a depleted sperm count and a smile on my face. I imagined Renee back in her dorm room equally satisfied. The theory I have developed about Renee and me is we're two people who should never be married but should meet once or twice a year for the rest of our lives to engage in fabulous sex. Such a relationship would allow us to marry partners for worthier reasons than sex, such as love, friendship, and bambini.

The light was off in the living room. I tipped toed in hoping not to wake Sweets, but the only thing on the couch were a bunch of hard candy wrappers, no Sweets. He was, however, in my bedroom, laying on my comfortable king size Sealy mattress curled up under my comforter, snoring lightly. For a moment, I thought to wake him and point him in the direction of the couch, but the bum would probably want to start talking. I was feeling pretty blissful and didn't want to be reminded that tomorrow I'd have to figure out how to solve a murder. I grabbed a pillow and blankets from the closet and headed for the couch. I was almost asleep when I heard a rustling and looked up, expecting to see Sweets. Instead, standing by the window was Winona. I leaped from the couch, tripped over the coffee table and fell on the floor. I scrambled to my feet. The window was open and the Venetian blinds were rattling. Nothing there. The rest of the night, I stared at that window, falling asleep at first light.

CHAPTER 8
THE SATANS

Mildred: Hey Johnny, what are you rebelling against?
Johnny: What've you got?
The Wild One, 1953

After a fitful night on the couch, my back was aching, and my mind was filled with apparitions. I remembered my father saying to us kids, "If you start seeing ghosts, don't blame my side of the family." According to Pop, there were *Stregoneria*, witchcraft on our mother's side of the family. Pop would remind us that our mom's great aunt, Maddalena, communicated with the dead. The old man got a kick needling our mom about her strange family. Our mother was very patient with him. Sometimes if he got too loquacious, she'd slap him across the head. Then, he'd chase her around the room, and she'd let him catch her, and they'd hug and kiss. What can I say? Even today they're still a couple of old romantics. They're Italians. What else could they be? What if I had inherited seeing ghosts from my mother? It was not a thought I wanted to contemplate. I put apparitions out of my mind.

It was Monday, April 1st. If the end of March was any kind of a predictor, it wasn't looking good for April. This was not a good thought to start the month. Stay positive, Victor, I thought to myself.

Before going to work, I drove to the YMCA, worked out in the weight-room and took a steam bath. Refreshed, I headed for the lot, all thoughts of Winona's ghostly appearance gone from my head. Given what was happening, I figured I was allowed a bad dream.

Renee had suggested I listen to jazz more and told me to tune in to KVIE MORNING JAZZ. I gave it a try, but couldn't handle the improvisation. I switched channels. Soon, Dione Warwick was showing me the way to San

Jose. When I pulled into the driveway, Sylvia and Vincent were already hard at it, and the reduced-price signs on the cars we'd determined could be sold cheaply were on their respective windshields. I hadn't figured out how I was going to tell Vincent that Sweets had blackmailed me into helping him find out who murdered Winona. To avoid getting a broken jaw, I'd have to be at my persuasive best. I was at my desk thinking about it, when Vincent hurried into the office, a startled expression on his face.

"Victor, it's the Satans. I can't deal with this. It's on you."

"Don't give me any April Fools crap," I said.

"No, no, I'm not fooling."

That's when I heard the rumble of motorcycles. "Ah, *minchia*," I said. "What the fuck. The sun's barely up. Those bad asses should be sleeping off hangovers."

Sylvia didn't look too happy either. The Satans' notorious leader, Sunny Badger, had been sending her flowers. She looked up from the invoices. "Maybe one of those bozos wants to buy a car."

She thought they were here to buy a car. I thought they were here to dismember Victor Brovelli and feed the lions at the zoo with my parts. I'd have to convince them Vincent had nothing to do with it.

I took a peek out the window and shook my head, "They don't look like prospective customers to me." Sunny Badger was the first off his motorcycle. Sunny spelled his first name as if he brought light into the world, an irony his parents probably couldn't have anticipated.

"Here comes Sunny," Vincent whispered.

"Why are you whispering?" Sylvia asked

"Looks like bad weather to me," I said. "You take this sale."

"Bad joke, bro," Vincent said. "I'm sure he wants to talk to you."

"Sunny wants to ask Sylvia out on a date," I said, hoping for that to be the case.

"He knows better. He's got the look of a customer. Get your butts out there."

"You're a better salesman than me." I said to Vincent.

"You look tougher, Vittorio. These guys respect tough."

"You two are pathetic," Sylvia said. "I'll sell them a car, and I'll take the commission."

"The commission's all yours," I said. "I'm going to the john."

"I'm right behind you," Vincent said.

"I don't know what I'm going to do with you Brovelli boys," Sylvia said as she walked outside. "And if that bozo Sunny Badger says anything about my breasts I'll kick his butt all the way back to their clubhouse."

"He loves you Sylvia," I crooned as Vincent and I hurried to the toilet.

In the bathroom, I told Vincent about Sweets and what I promised to do. Luckily, he was peeing in the stall when I broke the news; otherwise, we might have duked it out right then and there. It's sort of low class fighting in the toilet. I suggested we go back to the office.

"Not until the Satans are gone," he said.

"Look, the Brovelli Boys have never backed down from trouble in our lives. Why should we start now?" I was starting to feel more courageous. "Besides, we can't leave Sylvia out there on her own."

"Right, but we never involved a bunch of frigging killers in a murder investigation. I knew this was not going to work out. I knew it. I knew it."

Vincent's face was flushed like he was about to have a stroke.

"If you'd only listened to me in the first place," he yelled. "You and Pop and all that *onore* bull pucky. Honor, my *behind*."

Vincent never swears, but he throws a mean punch.

I didn't see it coming. Next thing I knew I was sitting on my fanny under the sink. I tried to get up, but hit my head on the basin. My stomach hurt where he punched me. It took a moment for me to catch my breath. I closed my eyes, thinking of what I was going to do to Vincent. By the time I staggered to my feet, Vincent was long gone. I stumbled out of the bathroom. *Dead meat, that's what he was.* Through the office window I saw Vincent, transformed from angry brother to confidant salesman, hands in his pockets, a smile on his face, standing next to Sylvia talking to Sunny Badger. *Oddio.* Oh God, Badger's henchmen were off to the side by their bikes, smoking cigarettes, looking like they'd just walked off the set of *The Wild Ones*. Badger, himself was no Marlon Brando's Johnny who was sort of a violent idealist. Sunny boy was idealistically addicted to spreading fear and drugs. The office window was open, and I heard Vincent tell Badger how sorry he was about all the trouble they were having with the police.

"'Preciate it," Badger replied. "I'll tell you something, if we ever find out who put that little lady in our clubhouse, sumbitch better leave the country; otherwise, we'll cut his ass up and feed him to the crocodiles in the zoo."

Great, I thought. I'd better see if my passport has expired. The hell with Sweets. People call him the birdman. *Bene.* When Sunny throws him off the bridge, he can prove it.

Vincent pointed in the direction of the office, motioning Badger to follow him. I was poised to split back to bathroom when I saw that my brother and Sylvia had veered off and were escorting Sunny to the rear of the building. What the hell was Vincent up to, I wondered. The answer came back in an image of lost profits, and I was out of the office like a flash. Satans or no Satans, Vincent was not going to do this. What was that saying, nothing to fear but fear itself? I leaped down the stairs, but the trio were already around the corner. I got there in time to hear Badger.

"Well, I'll be damned. You weren't kidding. These are two bitchin looking vee-hee-cles."

Up close, Sunny looked even more dangerous than his reputation because his back was noticeably curved forward. It gives him the appearance of a cougar or some kind of wild cat about to pounce. He was wearing his usual leathers, his huge, tattooed biceps poking out of his sleeveless vest. A red and black bandana encircled his forehead. His face was weathered from too much wind. His eyes were hidden beneath wrap-around shades. Word was he slept with his shades on.

Sunny was talking about a 1963 Studebaker Avanti and a 1963 Powder blue Buick Riviera that I'd managed to convince a dealer in Lodi to sell me at a price we could afford. I was keeping them in the back away from the main lot for the right customer, one who would pay top dollar. I had in mind a couple of my college classmates with lots of family money and the will to spend it. I didn't think Sunny Badger was interested in top dollar.

"These cars are not for sale," I announced as I approached.

They turned around. Sunny cocked his head and gave me the stare, like *You talking to me, that kind of look*

"Why not?" he asked with nothing close to friendly in his voice.

"Yeah," my brother said. "Why not? If Mr. Badger finds one of these two automobiles to his liking, I'm sure we can offer him a reasonable price, him being a good neighbor and all."

What kind of good neighbor? Badger was the only Satan that had ever set foot on our lot, and he'd come to hit on Sylvia, not buy a car. They'd never shown up even for our Barbeque Saturdays. They were probing. That was it. This was a recon maneuver. They were on to us. Anyway, I knew what my brother was doing, and it wasn't going to work. It didn't matter what the Satans thought they knew, giving Sunny a discount was not going to happen.

"Tell me about the Avanti," Badger said, turning his attention away from me as if I didn't count and back to my brother, but not before scowling at me. Was that a growl, I heard?

Vincent started in, "It's got a 289 cu in engine with a Paxton supercharger. 240 horses. It's a 4-speed manual. That's custom, not standard. Take a look at the interior; it's wood and leather. I bet you've never seen a front-end design like that. Looks like an airplane, right?"

Sunny's head was bobbing. I edged around Sylvia, so Vincent could see me shaking my head.

"What are you asking for these wheels?" Sunny asked tapping the hood of the Avanti.

"For you, Mr. Badger," my twin said, "$3,000.00 dollars even. Tax and license not included."

My heart missed a couple of beats. I'd never heard my twin being so obsequious. "No, no, sorry," I said. "My brother has that price confused with the Riviera. We can't let the Avanti go for less than five grand. Now, five thousand in the condition it's in, is very fair." It wasn't the top dollar, I'd envisioned, but I could live with it.

Sunny turned to my brother, "This guy looks just like you, but I like you a lot better."

Sylvia said, "They're twins."

"I can see that little missy," Sunny said, looking at her breasts and smiling. "You are looking fine today, Miss Sylvia. I hope you don't mind my saying."

Sylvia growled.

Badger touched his heart, like she'd just said something endearing in the language of animals. Then he turned to me. "How'd you get that scar buddy-boy?"

The lie popped into my head like salvation. "Nam," I said. "A slope got me with a bayonet, but I got the bastard in the end."

Vincent and Sylvia looked at me as if I'd just entered the continent of insanity?

"Good for you soldier," Sunny said, slapping me on the shoulder. "The government ought to round up all those chicken-livered anti-war radicalmuthfucking-Commie bastards that was marching yesterday and ship all their asses over to Nam. See how long they'd last."

"Hoowah!" I yelled.

Sylvia mouthed, "Are you nuts?" But Vincent's quick smile told me he knew the game I was playing. It's called thinking fast on your feet, a Brovelli family talent. I figured Sunny was too dumb to pick up on it.

"What unit were you in?" Sunny asked.

"101st Airborne," I said, naming the one my older brother, Captain Mario Brovelli, West Point graduate, had served in before he'd had his right hand blown off a year ago, which earned him a Purple Heart and an exit visa out of the war. I was flying by the seat of my pants. It was obvious Sunny was a real gung-ho, pro war kind of guy. I was betting that Badger had never been to Vietnam, so I could bullshit him. Get him on my side, so to speak, you know, *mano a mano*, make a higher price on the Avanti easier for him to swallow. From the letters Mario wrote to us, I knew enough about the war to sound convincing. "Got this baby," I said, pointing to my scar "during Operation Hump. You know just north of Bien Ho. You were in Nam, right?"

"Oh, yeah," Sunny said. "At the beginning. I'm a little older than you."

He was a lying, but that was good because he knew I knew he was lying, which gave me an advantage. "Brothers in arms," I said. We smiled at each other.

"No doubt," he said. "You done good, soldier. Now how much you say this Avanti is worth?"

So, I thought, this was not a fact-finding mission. He was really here to buy a car. I took a deep breath. There was no way the brothers-in-arms-strategy would wash completely. I looked Sunny Badger in the eyes and said. "For a vet like you, Sunny. I'll let it go for $4,500 and I'll pay the tax. License is your responsibility, but that's pretty standard."

"How about for cash?"

"For cash, I'll take $4,000 even, and you pay tax and license." I felt like a father giving away his lovely daughter to a felon with a record of spousal abuse. I wanted to cry, but at least the car would be going out the door for a little profit, be it ever so goddamn humble. And, perhaps, the Satans would think kindly of the Brovelli Boys.

Sunny Badger bent at the waist and drew up his leather pant leg. Out of the top of his boot, he withdrew an envelope from which he pulled a bunch of greenbacks. It had been a long time since I'd seen five-hundred-dollar bills. According to our bank, they were going to be discontinued next year. I accepted the William McKinley's suspiciously, raising them up to check to see if they were counterfeits.

"They're good," Sunny said. "Just got them off a couple of Banditos that owed us. They know what would happen to them if they tried to pass off funny money."

"I understand," I said. The Banditos was a Mexican motorcycle gang.

"Let me get you the keys to the car," Vincent said.

We walked to the office and Sylvia led Sunny Badger in so he could sign the paperwork. Badger was walking real close to Sylvia, talking up a storm. He looked like a man in love, and I wasn't talking about the car. An hour later Sylvia, Vincent and I were waving goodbye as Sunny Badger and his men motored off the lot. He'd left the car, that was to be a gift for his father with us and said he'd be back for it. His return was not something I was looking forward to.

"Can you believe that guy," Sylvia said. "He keeps asking me out on dates, like I'd date a dirt-bag like him. All the time I'm making out the papers, he's staring down my blouse."

"Hey, good looking fellow and a Vietnam vet. Why not?"

"Vet, my buttinski," Sylvia said. "Those cruds are nothing but trouble."

CHAPTER 9
SUSPECTS

Everything begins with choice.
S.J. Wardell

It had taken the better part of the morning for Vincent and me once again to get back on speaking terms. I was suffering from severe vehicular post-partum. Sylvia had returned to the office, but before leaving us, she'd remarked at the strangeness of our behavior, calling us *bisheri,* which means jerks in Italian. Looking back on it, I'm sure we'd been jerks that day, but we had cause, which was what I told my brother once Sylvia was out of hearing range.

"If we're ever getting out of this *cazzata,* we've got to do what Sweets wants."

"And how do two used car salesmen go about finding the killer, assuming it's not Sweets himself? Are you some kind of private detective? Been taking criminal investigation courses in your spare time?"

In his spare time, my brother can be a real asshole, but he had a point. Neither one of us had a clue how to proceed. "There've got to be other suspects besides Sweets."

"How do you know? We don't know anything about Winona except that she was part-time clerical and that Sweets said she used to ho. He could have been lying about that. She didn't look like a whore to me when she worked for us."

"Right. How many days was Sylvia out gone for her father's birthday?"

A week, but she took an extra day to drive up that cherry silver Mercedes 190 SL her father gave her. She told me she had a buyer already lined up."

"Yeah," I said, "that girl's a real go-getter."

"Altogether, Winona filled in for eight days," Vincent said.

"Winona worked for a lot of other companies around here," I said. "We could start there. She might have met someone at work. Like she and someone had a little *tresca*." I gave Vincent the universal hand-sign for getting-it-on. "Maybe that someone was married. You following me? She puts pressure on him. He can't take the pressure and knocks her off."

"You been watching too many episodes of *Dragnet*."

"Come to think of it. *You* were alone with Winona plenty of times and *you're* married, that makes *you* a suspect."

"Up yours, Victor, You were alone with Winona as often as I was."

I was only kidding and told him. Vincent would never cheat on his bride. Neither would I. It may not sound like it, but I believe in the sacrament of marriage. Still, I suppose I might lust in my heart from time to time.

I continued explaining. "We got to identify all the people Winona came into contact with, on the job and off the job. Friends, boyfriends, co-workers."

"It's a start," Vincent conceded. "How do you want to do it?"

"I'll get the ball rolling. You stay on the lot. Sylvia will go ape-shit if we leave her alone. I'll talk to Sweets. He can probably give us a few names. I'll start with them." I slapped Vincent on the arm, told him not to worry, and that I'd check in with him later.

Even with Bay Area traffic building up to its noon gridlock, I managed to get to the Fruitvale Bridge and across it without swearing too much. There are two bridges and a tube that runs under the Oakland estuary that connect Alameda to the city of Oakland. Its southern shore fronts the bay, the northwest part of the island is mostly military. My apartment is only six blocks from Saint Joseph's High, the school the entire Brovelli children attended. The Victorians on my street, the last ones before the business district begins, are graced with elaborate turrets and wide wraparound porches. In the middle of a block filled with these stately homes, sits my building, which has some architectural integrity, unlike many of the rectangular duplexes sprouting up all over Alameda. The city council is proposing a permanent halt to such construction in the hope of preserving the original architecture of our island city. My mom and a bunch of her friends are leading the charge.

I drove into my parking slot and locked the Mustang. Inside, I waved at the florist whose first name was Flora. Trust me, Flora the Florist.

She waved back. When I reached my apartment door, I hesitated before inserting the key. There was loud music coming from inside. I entered. My coffee-table was covered with an assortment of colorfully wrapped candies. Sweets was sitting on the couch, his head bobbing up and down, his mouth sucking. The music coming from my record player was a mix of accordions, harmonicas, snare drums, something like a dog whistle and maybe a kazoo and sandpaper being rubbed together. "What the hell is that noise? I asked.

He looked at me aghast. "That's Zydeco, daddy-o. Rosie Ladet singing "Eat My Pousiere."

"Tell me you're kidding."

"La Pousiere means dust, you horn-dog. It's good Cajun music. Brought a couple of albums in my backpack. You want to hear Clifton Chenier? "Tout Le Ton Son Ton," he crooned.

"You sound like you've got a sore throat. Turn it off. We got things to talk about."

"You want a hard candy?"

I shook my head. He turned Rosie off, and placed her among a bunch of 45's laying on the floor. I explained what I wanted. I found a pencil and paper and waited for Sweets to get it together.

"I told you already. I'm not sure anyone knows where Winona came from. She ho'd for a pimp named JR, hangs out at the Oasis just off Fruitvale Avenue, you know, near the Mexican bodega."

"That's Amigo country."

"You better believe it, brother. The Oasis is their headquarters."

"Girlfriends? Winona must have had girlfriends?"

"Only one I know is Arabella, a waitress at the Golden Dragon. At least she was a couple of months ago. Her last name is something Asian."

Arabella didn't sound Asian to me. I'd heard the name before, in a novel I read in college, but I couldn't place it.

"Winona used to drink at Flynn's every once in a while. She might have gone out with that night guy. I can't remember his name, Tambourine, something like that."

"Tamberg," I said. "First name's Stuart."

"Yeah, that creepy dude. Say, you think he might be the one killed her. Sometime I see him walking the streets after the tavern's closed, just walking around like he's looking to suck someone's blood."

"He's an insomniac," I said.

"Like I said, fucking vampire."

Come to think of it, Stuart did look a little like Bella Lugosi. No pointy ears or fangs, but slicked-back black hair atop a thin face with bloodshot eyes.

"He *is* kind of pale," I said.

"We better check him out," Sweets said.

It was curious how Sweets managed to sneak in the "we" to remind "me" what I was supposed to be doing. "All right. So far we got some suspects: JR, the pimp and Stuart. Can you think of anybody else Winona dated?"

"She might have let that Greek furniture store guy bang her. She worked part-time for him some. He's a horny bastard."

"Parsegian. He's Armenian."

"And how about the other partner, the raghead?"

"You mean Ron Sharifi? And he's not a raghead. He's Iranian." Sweets didn't pay much attention to political correctness. To be honest, I couldn't say I did either. "I can't see Sharifi getting it on. He's too old and real religious."

"What, like getting down on his knees on his little rug and praying to Mecca? Sheeet, lots of Black Muslims do that and be getting it on ten minutes later. As for old, you're never too old."

Armenians are Christians, but I didn't bother to explain that to Sweets. "So Sharifi goes on the list of suspects. Anybody else?"

"Well, except for you guys and Discount Furniture, far as I know she took a bunch of one day jobs. I used to pick her up after work when I had an automobile."

He looked at me accusingly before listing them: Hyatt Hotel, Marbles Stationary, A dental lab on Broadway he didn't know the name of, and Hayward Printers, that wasn't located in Hayward but in San Leandro. I wrote the names down.

"Man," he said, leering at me. "Did you ever taste a little?"

"Cut it out," I said.

"Yeah, well, she told me that you were giving her the eye."

"So? She had a hell of a body." All good female bodies deserve the eye, which is the first part of a theory that I've developed. The second part is that the more eye you eye the more body you get. But there's a difference between the eye, and The Eye. I don't look at a Cadillac in the same way I look at a Porsche, or a Maserati the way I look at a Bugatti. I explained this to Sweets.

"So? Your name should still be down on that list," Sweets said.

"You want my help, or not?"

He grinned.

"Then stop fucking with me," I said. "This is going to be damn impossible anyway, you know that."

"Solid," Sweets said. "I got all the confidence in the world in you."

Confidence is one thing, producing is something else. I had work to do. Once I had a final list of suspects, my first move would be to check on alibis. Any guy who watched Dragnet knew that. I'd start with the one-day jobs and see if any likely suspects turned up. Then, I'd check employers for whom she worked longer periods of time. I called Vincent and explained what I was up to. He cautioned me to watch my butt at the Oasis. I told him no worries."

"I remembered something," Sweets said when I got off the phone.

"I can use all the help I can get."

"Winona wrote in her diary all the time. I mean she put down everything, like what she had for lunch and who she talked to on the telephone. She said she'd been doing a diary since she was twelve years old. The way she wrote every little crappy thing down, like what she had for breakfast or the color of her lipstick. I bet there'd be something in there that would help."

"Okay," I said. "That's good." Then, I thought, or not. By now the police must have found the diaries. "Have you thought that maybe she didn't exactly rave about you."

"Oh, man, we were just love spatting. There's got to be something in her diary about JR. She hated that fucker."

True, I thought, but if the cops had her diaries, and JR was in there threatening her or something, the cops would have hauled him in along with Sweets. Maybe they didn't have the diaries. "Where does Winona live? I'll go by and see what I can find."

"I don't know, man. I think she was bunking with Arabella for a while. But that was a while back.

"See if you can remember an address. I'll check with this Arabella chick. In the meantime, I'll start with the list we have." I hauled out my telephone book and began leafing through the Yellow Pages. After I let my fingers do the walking, I got up and announced that I was off.

"You want me to go with you?"

"Nah, Sweets, I need to be real subtle."

"I can be sub-tel."

"Your personal appearance would be a distraction."

"There's nothing wrong with the way I look."

I opened the front door. "Check the mirror lately," I asked. Before he could reply, I closed the door. What Sweets would have seen in the mirror was a shirt that matched the candy wrappers and a pair of zebra stripped bell bottom trousers. Even the hippies in Height Ashbery would have trouble with that outfit.

• • •

A half tank of gas, and two hours later, I'd visited six businesses. All of them had secretaries that once I hit them with my dimples were happy to help me. They hardly remembered Winona, except to say that she hadn't made any mistakes, which most temporary hires did. None of the bosses or supervisors I talked to seemed remotely like murderers, two were women, the other four were men that my gut told me were too wussy to be killers. But how could I know, having no experience in the detecting business. Trusting my gut, I checked them off my list. That left the owners of Discount Furniture, the Oasis where she'd tended bar on and off, and JR, the pimp. But first, I'd talk to Winona's friend Arabella, who might be able help. Good friends confide in each other. I called The Golden Dragon and asked for Arabella. The voice on the other end of the line replied that I was talking to her. I hung up. I wanted a face to face. After Arabella, I'd visit Discount Furniture, then hit the Amigo's bar, the Oasis last, maybe catch JR alone while it was still too early for the heavy hitters. Sort of kill two birds with one stone. I'd finish off my list at Flynn's. By then, Stuart would be behind the bar. I was pretty sure Stuart had not dated Winona, but I had to check him off my list.

CHAPTER 10

A VERY PRIVATE INVESTIGATOR

Every man at the bottom of his heart believes he is a born detective.
John Buchan

On the way to the Golden Dragon, I stopped at Walden's Pond, a used bookstore on Grand Avenue and found a book imaginatively entitled. *How to be a Private Investigator* published in 1961. The author's name was Oscar Medford. His bio on the back cover stated that he'd been a private investigator for twenty-five years in Los Angeles and a consultant to Warner Brothers Studios on their detective movies. His photo showed him dressed in a trench coat with a Fedora pulled low over his eyes. Before that, he'd been an FBI agent. I didn't think you could claim to work for the feds unless you actually had, so I was impressed. The book cost a buck and had a bunch of loose pages. I didn't care. I was looking for tips on how to interview suspects or witnesses, if I came across any. Witnesses to what? Like the murder? I should get so lucky.

The introduction was a history of Private Investigation. I learned that the first agency was started by a French criminal gone straight, Eugene-Francois Vedoq in 1811. In the United States the first private cops were the Pinkertons, famous for hunting down train robbers in the late 1800's and strike-breaking in the early 20th century. I skimmed and turned to the first chapter that started with a list of attributes amateur private investigators possessed, with a lot of stress placed on the word amateur. That was me, I thought, very private and very amateur. I read, looking for attributes I could lay claim to.

Attributes of Amateur Detectives:
Independent, Adventurous Sensible, Likeable snoops, Careful observers of human nature, Distrustful of the surface appearance of ordinary people,

Possessed of keen powers of observation and deduction, Committed to uncovering the truth, Ruthless on behalf of the innocent.

I was okay with the first two. Was I a careful observer of human nature? As a salesmen, maybe. Was I committed to uncovering the truth, or was I simply trying to save the Brovelli Boys' hide? I had no answer to that question. It required delving into one's personal ethics. Could I be ruthless? On the rugby field, you bet. Off the field, maybe. If I had a tire-iron in my hand.

I closed the book and browsed some more. I bought a paperback mystery entitled *Harper* written by Ross Macdonald. I'd seen the movie with Paul Newman and liked it. There was a comfortable old armchair located at the end of the bookcase. I sat down, put aside *Harper* and opened *How to Be a Private Investigator.* The first chapter dealt with the licensing authority of each of the states. California's looked complicated. In our state the applicant had to eighteen years old, submit to a background check, have three years or one thousand hours of mentored experience working for a detective agency, and pass a two-hour multiple-choice test. Since I wasn't planning on a new career, I skipped to chapter two. This chapter was dedicated to disillusioning the prospective PI. It emphasized that the majority of the private investigator's work consisted in public and private records research, basic background checks, skip tracing, and report writing. The chapter contained multiple examples of various methods of writing reports. Skip tracing seemed interesting, so I read up on the section called Methodology.

Skip-tracing was also known as debtor and fugitive recovery. A skip was a person who was sought by law enforcement for a number of different reasons, but primarily for not showing up for his court date, thus leaving the bonds dealer liable for the public debt. In such a case, the bondsman would hire a skip-tracer to find where the runner was hiding and haul his ass, or possibly her ass, back to jail. It was sort of like hunting for repos, which my brother and I had a lot of experience with, so I figured I would qualify, so I read on for a while but got bored with the details.

The next chapter was about law firms. Seventy-eight percent of private detectives worked for law firms, doing research mostly. Salaries for private detectives were not impressive. High end agencies got $50.00 an hour plus expenses. I skipped to the next chapter, which was about the process, more what I was looking for. There was a list:

1. *Get all the facts.*

2. *Analyze the facts and come up with at least three hypothesis.*
3. *Each hypothesis should include names of people related to suspects in the case.*
4. *Follow the hypothesis to their natural conclusions.*
5. *If your case involves a homicide, always begin with family members or relatives.*
6. *If your case involves robbery or fraud, always begin with employees.*
7. *Follow the money.*

The list went on and on and included detailed explanations. I read for a while – interesting -then flipped pages to the next chapter: "The Outward Appearance of the Private Investigator". This was more up my alley. It started with this sentence: The private detective should never draw attention to himself by acting or dressing conspicuously. *Like wearing a blue blazer with a Saint Mary's College logo on it.* Got it. I thumbed ahead a couple of pages, then continued reading about researching your environment. Example: If you need to be in Las Vegas, study street maps, know the locations of important facilities, police stations in particular. Since a private investigator is usually licensed to carry a concealed weapon, people should not be able to recognize he is carrying. I thought, well hell, why not have the gun exposed? That way the bad guys know they better not fuck with you.

There was a chapter on how to conduct interviews. I skimmed through that. A lot of the advice was simply common sense. I paid and left with my books.

The one thing I'd noticed when reading was that most of the investigators mentioned in the book were middle-aged men, many of whom had previous careers in some sort of law enforcement. I wasn't even thirty and had no experience with the law. How the hell was I going to have a chance to uncover Winona's murderer? Maybe I should just murder Sweets. I spent the rest of the drive to the Golden Dragon thinking of foolproof ways to knock off the birdman.

The sun was in my eyes as I dropped down off the Nimitz Freeway and drove into the concrete sprawl of downtown Oakland to Eighth Street and Webster where I found a parking space not far away from the Golden Dragon. Oakland's Chinatown is smaller and a lot less architecturally interesting than its counterpart in San Francisco. But, like Pop says, why bother going across the bay when we have our own Chinese food right here, all Chinese food being alike, to his way of thinking. That's Pop for you. He feels the same about all other kinds of cuisine. If they're not Italian, no matter how good, they're inferior. I knew the difference between the Good, the Bad, and the Ugly of Chinese cooking. The Golden Dragon definitely fell into the good classification. By the time I reached the door, I realized I was very hungry. I checked my watch. The big hand was heading for five, and I hadn't eaten lunch.

The inside of the restaurant was dark. To my right, a back-lit waterfall fell into a round rock-rimmed pool of water in which lily pads floated like small white islands. To my left, hung a tapestry depicting a ferocious Golden Dragon. The hostess greeted me and showed me to a booth. Take her back ten years, and she would have been a beauty. Except for a couple in the farthest table, there were no other customers. I slid in the booth and placed my detective book in front of me. She looked at the title and smiled. I smiled back the way I remembered Paul Newman smiling at Lauren Bacall in *Harper*. The young hostess handed me a menu and left.

The cover of the menu contained a brief history of the restaurant, the usual story of a mom-and-pop enterprise that blossomed into gold. Toward the end of the story, it mentioned that Bruce Lee, the famous martial artist and film star frequented this restaurant. Sure enough, above my booth hung an autographed photograph of Lee with his arms around mom and pop. It was signed to his second parents. It wouldn't be a good idea to start any trouble in here, I thought.

My waitress arrived, a young Asian woman with long black hair with a narrow streak of silver dropping like a waterfall down to her shoulder. Could this be Arabella, Winona's friend? At that moment I recalled where I'd heard the name before. Arabella was a sexy and not too bright farmer's daughter in *Jude the Obscure*, written by the British writer Thomas Hardy, voted by the business majors in our senior year as the second most depressing novel we'd been forced to read in our four years in college. The woman standing in front of me didn't look anything like the character from the novel. I didn't see any other waitresses, so I ventured, "Arabella?"

"Do I know you?" she asked in a throaty voice. *Oh, boy.*

"No. My name is Victor Brovelli. My brother and I own Brovelli Boys' Used Cars on East 14th." I paused so that she could say she'd heard of us. When she didn't, I continued, "Winona Davis worked for us as a temporary clerical worker." As I spoke I was staring into mahogany eyes too wide for an Asian, so I suspected a racial mix of some kind. She had an oval face with moist red lips. The ear on the left side of her head that was exposed came to a point like Spock on Star Trek. I was a big fan of the TV series, and was secretly in love with Uhuru, but a little unsure whether I should reveal my infatuation with a woman of color. The fellows I ran with were not prejudiced, but neither were they enlightened by The Sixties. Not that I was necessarily, but I didn't think a fantasy counted as the real thing.

At the mention of Winona's name, tears sprung into Arabella's eyes, and I rose out of my seat. She brushed her hand through the air and over her eyes. I expected her to say something, but she didn't.

"I know Winona was a good friend of yours," I said. "I'm sort of working with the police department helping them gather facts about her."

"Police don't work with civilians. What are you up to?"

It had been a weak lie offered in a hurry. "You're right," I said. "I shouldn't have lied. The police don't enlist civilians. My brother and I are working on our own. We want to find out who murdered Winona."

"Why?" She was looking down at me, pointing her pen at me. "You one of her boyfriends or something?"

I took the word, something, to mean something to do with Winona's prior career. "I never dated Winona. She worked for us for two weeks and became friendly with our secretary, Sylvia. Winona dated a regular customer of ours. He's being questioned by the police as a person of interest."

"Not Sweets?"

A moment of truth. She'd either like Sweets or hate him. That's the way he affected people. "Yes, Sweets."

"Sweets wouldn't hurt a mosquito if it was biting him."

I breathed a sigh of relief. Arabella would not be a problem. "Sweets is in real trouble," I said, "unless we can find out who the real killer is."

"Go ahead and order. When I come back, if there're no more customers, I'll sit down and talk."

I ordered egg drop soup, orange beef, Szechwan green beans, fried rice, and a bottle of Tsing Tao. Arabella walked away. Tall for an Asian. Nice ass. No, not nice, damn nice. As I waited for my meal, I thought through the events of the last couple of days beginning with discovering Winona's body, trying to formulate a hypothesis like the book on detective's had explained was a good way to start an investigation.

Hypotheses are suggested ideas which are then tested by experiments or observations.

Once the hypothesis was settled on, the author explained, my job was to disprove it. The more evidence I could come up with to disprove it, the more likely it was that I could discard the suspect. A process the author called negative elimination. As I waited for my food, I gave it a try. Guess number one: Sweets killed Winona. Guess number two: JR killed Winona. Guess number three: Parsegian killed Winona. Guess number four: Stuart Tamberg killed Winona. I guessed this wasn't exactly what the author had intended. Perhaps a little too simplistic? I began thinking about motives. Maybe I could come up with a hypothesis based on motives. Did Sweets have a reason for killing his girlfriend? I couldn't think of one except a lover's quarrel that went bad. In that case I figured Sweets would have beaten her up. She might have fallen and hit her head. Something like that. Being shot in the head with a small caliber pistol seemed too premeditated. Somewhere I'd read that hit men use a small caliber pistol because it's more efficient and less messy. As for J.R., no doubt the *cholo* was violent, but like all pimps he was more likely to use physical force or, in the case of a weapon, a knife or razor. If Winona and Parsegian had been getting it on, and Winona was blackmailing the Armenian, premeditation was more likely. But, again, why a pistol? Wouldn't he strangle her? As for Stuart, I only had Sweets' word that he'd dated Winona. Stuart was such a weird guy, I couldn't see drop-dead gorgeous Winona having anything to do with him. I tried to imagine what Winona could have done to JR that would have required getting rid of her. Being a pimp, he was definitely into a lot of drugs. Winona could have found out about some drug caper he was involved in. If he thought she'd rat him out, he'd have no problem killing her. After that, stuffing her in one of our cars made sense, since he was pals with the Amigos. He'd earn some brownie points with them for screwing up the Brovelli Brothers' Used Cars.

I was imagining other scenarios involving my list of suspects when my food arrived. Arabella placed the plates on the table and scooted onto the seat opposite me.

"I don't mind if you eat and talk at the same time. I need to know why you're so anxious to help Sweets. He's a burglar, you know."

I told Arabella about Sweets and my pop's relationship, ending with the concept of honor, that Pop held so dear, the relationship that we'd promised as sons to uphold. She told me that she understood completely because her father was from the old country and maintained such old-fashioned beliefs - the old country being Taiwan. I asked about her mother. She was Eurasian, half French and half Puerto Rican.

"I'm a racial trifecta," she said.

Sticking to the horse racing theme, I said, "You look like a gorgeous filly to me." *Okay, so I was flirting. There's no rule against flirting while investigating a murder is there?*

She gave me a smile that made me glad that I was reasonably handsome, unmarried, and possessed of a strong libido. Then, she waved her hand as if to say enough with the compliments and began questioning me about the murder. Did I have any suspects in mind? I told her and provided some information about each of them. According to her, JR was a dangerous guy. She agreed with me; however, that he'd be more likely to kill someone with a knife than a pistol. She remembered Winona telling her about Nick Parsegian that he was a good boss, but that the other owner, the old guy was always trying to look down her blouse. She never heard of Stuart Tamberg.

"Did Winona say anything to you about coming into some money, an inheritance, something like that?"

"You think she was blackmailing someone?"

"It's a thought. If she was having an affair with Parsegian, she could have threatened to tell his wife."

"Maybe," Arabella said. "Winona had a hard edge. I might have been her only friend. But she never really opened up to me, except to tell me the basics. Her childhood was rotten, and she was on the street by the time she was fourteen. When she came here from LA, JR found her and turned her. I'm not sure how she got free of the asshole, but she did. For the last year, Winona was into changing her life. She was taking classes with me at Laney College."

"Sweets told me Winona always wrote in her diaries. Did she ever let you read her entries?

"Yeah, she sure did. But she was real secretive, so I never saw a word she wrote."

"No, Winona kept her diaries real secretive. Do you think she had something on JR? Maybe that's why he let her go?" You know, pimps don't give up their whores willingly."

"Especially beautiful ones," she said. "So, yes, it's possible.

"You don't by any chance know where her diaries are?"

"Not off hand, but I'll look through some of the stuff she stored in my closet."

"That would be great. Call me if you find them. If I'm not there, leave a message. Tonight, I think I'll pay the Oasis a visit and talk to JR."

"Are you out of your mind? What are you going to do? Walk up to him and ask him if he killed Winona?"

"No, no. I'll be cool. I'm a salesman. Persuasion is my game."

Arabella laughed. The sound was soft, sensual. If it had been tactile I would have opened my mouth and taken a bite.

"I have to get back to work," she said. She wrote out her full name Arabella Duan and phone number. "Call me, I want to help."

With that, Arabella slid out of the booth, gave me another 300-watt smile, and departed. I watched her go, my blood pressure rising with each movement of her hips. I finished my meal, paid, and left. Next on my list of suspects was Parsegian at Discount Furniture.

CHAPTER 11
THE TEMP

Fail again, fail better.
Samuel Beckett

The sun was low on the horizon by the time I got back to East 14th street and Discount Furniture. Nick met me at the door with his hand out. No man in the history of sales stuck his hand out faster than Nick. He was looking at me as if I had dollar signs on my forehead.

According to Nick Parsegian, there was nothing more manly in furniture than a leather

La-Z- Boy. He pointed to black, brown, and a tan one. He had one arm around my shoulders.

"Think of it, Victor, my friend. You're in front of your television. The 49ers are playing. John Brodie is in the pocket preparing to pass. The coffee table in front of you is filled with Bowls of chips and guacamole and bottles of Schlitz."

"I can't afford this chair Nick. Besides, Schlitz tastes like piss."

"We can make a deal. My daughter, Sarah, is looking for an automobile. You sell her a good low mileage vehicle at cost, I sell this Cadillac of easy chairs to you for cost."

I should have known Parsegian was up to something. He almost ran toward me, grabbing my arm, steering me in the direction of the La Z Boy section of his store, which is more the size of a warehouse, probably because, at one time, it *was* a warehouse. It was so big, voices echoed. The building was divided into sections for different types of furniture. When I moved out of my parents' house, I'd bought a bedroom set from Nick. The bedroom section and the mattress section took up the entire back of the store. Nick Parsegian was the salesman. Ron Sharifi his partner, was the business manager. Sweets called Ron, Abdul, which the Iranian resented because Abdul is an Arab name and Sharifi is a Shiite Moslem, a sect that believes the Sunni brand of Moslems from Arabia are heretics, information Nick had explained to me one time in Flynn's when the subject had turned to a less than sober discussion of world religion. When I'd passed that information on to Sweets, he'd said it was gross to name their religion after shit. Sweets, who looked as if he was the long-term result of the blending of least three different races, never passed up the opportunity to slam Moslems. When I asked him about it once, his only response was crazy people. I thought this was pretty damn hilarious since Sweets was the craziest fucker I'd ever known.

From what I could tell, the owners of Discount Furniture have done very well. Nick lives in Kensington, which has some of the highest priced real estate in the Bay Area. I didn't know where Sharifi lived, but he drove a brand-new silver Cadillac Coup de Ville.

As for the deal Parsegian was referring to, 'cost' means different amounts depending on the business. Vincent and I keep our costs per car a secret except from Sylvia. And there's so many ways to hide true cost that whatever Parsegian would sell me the chair for - for his so-called cost - would most likely have a profit playing hide and seek with the IRS somewhere in their accounting system. And, more power to him. Profit is profit. I'm not a Communist, which is what Vincent accuses me of when he thinks I sold a car too cheap.

Parsegian slapped me on the back. "What do you say to that, Victor?"

"I say I'll be happy to sell your daughter a car, Nick, but I really don't need a chair. That's not what I came in here for."

"You want a new mattress? That Sealy you bought is passé. I brought in some firm ones you'll love. Any back pain, poof, gone."

"My mattress is perfectly fine." Before he could go on to another item, I held up my hand. I'd prepared and rehearsed my story. "I'm trying to track down a car Winona Davis bought from us. She temped for you, remember a couple of months back. The address she gave us was a phony. I've asked the police. They have no known address. Her friends tell me she moved around."

He screwed up his face, thinking. "Winona, you mean that poor young Negro lady that was murdered?"

I nodded. "She worked for you for two months, Nick. You were the one who recommended her to us." I wasn't about to let him off the hook.

"In fact I saw you two in Jack London Square. Seemed as if you were real friendly." It was a lie. I'd never seen them there, but if they were having an affair, Jack London Square had a lot of bars and restaurants they could very well have frequented. The minute I saw Nick's mouth open and close, the set of his jaw, I knew I'd hit a nerve.

"Victor, Victor," He finally said. "Victor, my friend, Victor."

"I'm right here, Nick, standing in front of you."

"It was a business lunch."

"With a temp?"

"She was very good with accounting. A surprise to Ron and me. You know how meticulous Ron is with our books. He couldn't believe Winona discovered such errors."

Aha, I thought. Well, people don't really say aha, but possibly detectives do when something is revealed. Errors, in this case might be the hidden profits I was explaining. Maybe Winona's murder had nothing to do with an affair, but was about money. Didn't my detective book instruct me to follow the money? I took another shot in the dark.

"So Winona found out some irregularities. And what? She said she'd overlook them if you guys paid her a bonus. Like that?"

"Victor, my boy, what are you suggesting? That Winona was blackmailing us? Don't be ridiculous. The fact is Winona saved us a ton of cash. Ron is getting a little old, you see. He overlooked a number of factory discounts that we could have taken advantage of. We got in just under the wire for application. The factory kicked back 10% on all the items we bought for the last six months. It added up. When you saw me with Winona I was taking her to lunch at Fisherman's Grotto. I gave her a check for two hundred dollars. So you see you have everything mixed up."

Easy enough to check. Pop knew Tony, Michael and Andy, the owners of the Grotto. There was still a problem in my mind. "How in the world did a temp get her hands on your books?"

"Now that did constitute a bit of dilemma. Ron keeps the accounting in the bottom drawer of his desk. It's clear she was snooping. But once we learned that her snooping had made us a bunch of money, we overlooked the rest. Of course, we never used her again. Snoops don't stop snooping, in my opinion. Ron wanted to keep her on."

"Why was that?"

"She always wore these low-cut neckline blouses. It gave Ron an erection. Not healthy for an old man like that. In any case I put my foot down. No more Winona."

It was hard to imagine old Ron, who had to be pushing eighty, with a woody. The conversation was going nowhere. There was no way I could prove or disprove Nick's version of events without talking to Ron. Ron wasn't in, and by the time I got a hold of him, Nick, if he was lying, would have persuaded his partner to back him up.

"You weren't suggesting that I had anything to do with Winona's murder, were you Victor?"

I didn't answer, let him sweat. "Did she give you guys an address?"

"Temps don't do that. The temp office does all the personnel work. We fill out the W-4's. We pay the temp office, and they pay the temp. But you know that, since she worked for you."

"Yeah, all right. Look, we're trying to find where she stashed our wheels. Vincent is on my ass. When in trouble, I blame my twin. He does the same to me. "Sorry to bother you."

"You sure I can't convince you to purchase this La Z Boy?"

"Nah. Maybe in another year."

"I'll send my daughter to see you, okay? A car with a good engine. Something low mileage. A good price would make her poor father very happy."

"You're rich as Midas," I said as I headed for the door having discovered nothing that would help me solve the murder of Winona Davis. My next stop was the Oasis and JR.

CHAPTER 12
THE OASIS OR HOW I ALMOST LOST MY LIFE

I think the eyes flirt most. There are so many ways to use them.
Anna Held

The club's florescent sign on the outside of the Oasis was a shimmering green outline of a naked woman holding a martini glass standing next to a yellow palm tree with the letters OASIS blinking atop the tree. The street light had just flickered on as I stepped inside. It was so dark that you'd need night-vision glasses to see through the gloom and low-hanging cigarette smoke. I took my time adjusting my eyesight before finding a seat at the horseshoe shaped bar that filled the middle of the room. In the center of the bar was a long liqueur well with a circular platform about four feet in diameter, rigged for pole dancing. Red and green painted wooden booths hugged the walls with a row of tables standing between the booths and the bar. The walls above the booths were decorated with paintings of palm trees and Arabian maidens dancing with Mexican men in sombreros, an artistic nod to multi-culturalism or Arab/Aztec schizophrenia. The back of the Oasis was taken up by three pool tables, two in use and a dozen or so pinball machines, all with players standing in front of them.

I'd figured the Oasis would not have a lot of customers yet, but I was wrong. Half the stools were filled and most of the booths. I didn't see any Amigos, thank God. I recognized a couple of guys who dropped in for barbeque on Saturdays. They waved to me, then returned to talking to the woman sitting between them. I felt a little better that I knew someone. As long as there weren't any Amigos, I believed there wouldn't be any trouble. After a silent Hail Mary, I took a seat at the horseshoe turn, closest to the door in case I had to make a dash. I'd concocted a story on the way that I was looking for the car that Winona had bought from us, and now that she was dead. . .etc. . . and she couldn't make payments, etc, etc. . . something like that.

The cute, petit bartender, with a blond beehive hairdo, who looked under age, asked me what I wanted. I ordered an Anchor Steam. She shook her head and pointed to choices over her head. I asked for a Pabst on tap. She poured and brought me a glass. This was not a frosty mug kind of place. Bowls of peanuts dotted the surface of the bar. I munched, sipped, and thought. In order to eliminate JR as a suspect I needed to talk to him. Sweets said he was a regular, which meant he could be here. Sweets had described him as tall, greasy looking, pock-marked face and ugly. No one fitting that description was sitting at the bar. No greasy looking guy occupied the booth directly to my right and left. I was sitting at a wrong angle to see into the rest of the booths.

I waited a while, then asked the bartender where the restroom was. She pointed to the back. As I walked I checked out the rest of the customers. I went to the toilet. It was surprisingly clean, except for a red Amigo graffiti taking up the entire back wall above the urinals. When I left, I pretended to examine the unused pool table like I might be interested in playing. No JR among the players. I returned to my seat via the opposite side of the bar, checking out the booths on the other side of the room. No guy fit JR's description.

I'd try the bartender. I finished my beer and held up one finger. She nodded and took my mug, filled it, and set it in front of me.

I said, "I'm looking for someone."

"I've been looking for someone for years, but I've never found him," she countered.

Funny, I thought. "Maybe you haven't been looking in the right place."

"Are you saying the Oasis is not the environment in which I'll find my future husband?"

Her dimples were showing. So were mine. But it was her eyes that told me we were in a flirting contest.

I said, "Not a husband, but how about the next best thing."

"And would that be you, Mr. Brovelli?"

"Wow," I said. "Do we know each other?"

"You sold my brother a neat MG. I was with him. You asked me if he was my boyfriend. When we drove off, my brother said to stay clear of you because you were a total womanizer."

I wanted to ask, is that the same brother who allowed you to tend bar in this place frequented by gangbangers and drug dealers? But that would have ended the flirtation. Instead I said, "Womanizer, in my case has a more dignified definition. It means a man who totally respects females. And, now that you mentioned the MG, I do remember you. Your hair was a couple of shades darker, more honey blond. Right?"

"That's right, as sweet as honey." She batted her eyelashes.

"That MG was in mint condition," I said.

Sometimes I remember people, sometimes I don't. But I never forget a car. Once I focus in, it pops up onto my memory screen along with the person who bought it. In this case, her, but not her brother. "It was a red convertible with a regular top plus a tonneau cover. Black leather with red piping interior. Twin carbs. And that day *you* were flirting with *me*."

"That's not how I saw it Mr. Brovelli."

"Call me Victor." I stuck out my hand. We shook. Soft hand boded well for the rest of her body.

"You can call me Fredericka but everybody calls me Freddy."

"I like Freddy. It's cute like you. Your brother still have the car?"

"Nope. It's mine now. He bought a new Jaguar."

"Ugh," I said. "He's going to make his mechanic a rich man. He should have come back to the Brovelli Brothers."

"I'm ready to trade up. You got anything for me?"

"You'd trade in the MG?" I asked incredulously. "That's a fine automibile."

"I want something with a front and back seat."

Our conversation was interrupted by someone from the other end of the bar calling her name. She left, promising to return. I watched her walk away, slender hips. Petit but athletic looking thighs and calves beneath her butt-tight mini-skirt. Gymnast came to mind. This was good. She liked me, which would make it easier to ask about JR and bring up the subject of Winona. I might even ask her out. She was pretty cute. I wasn't sure about the beehive hairdo with the tiny pearls decorating it like a wedding cake.

The Oasis was beginning to fill up. A male bartender entered the horseshoe from the other end. He and Freddy exchanged words. She gave him a brush kiss on the cheek, and he headed to the opposite side of the liqueur well.

When Freddy returned I got down to business. I went through my story about looking for the car we sold Winona.

"I'd never seen you in here before," Freddy said. "I wondered why you were here."

"I hang out in Flynn's mostly," I said. "Right next door to our dealership."

"I don't like the place. All the TV screens, guys yelling about football. I tried the joint on a Saturday night and it was full of Irish guys straight off the boat throwing dice and singing about Good Old Emerald isle." She paused, shook her pretty head. "I usually drink for company at the Embers at the Hilton near the airport. Nice piano bar. Classy guys."

"So, how about this place?"

"The Oasis is where I make a living." She looked up at the stage. "Stick around. I'll be dancing soon."

"I wouldn't miss it," I said.

"Sorry I can't help you about the car. Winona hasn't been in here for at least six months. You might want to ask JR. He might know about the car."

"I was looking for him earlier, but I didn't see him."

"He just walked in."

I turned in my seat toward the door.

"He's bartending," She said, pointing to the bartender mixing a drink, close enough that I could see him in profile.

The only part Sweets got right about JR was that the man was tall. The real JR had wavy black hair, a straight nose, over a thin mustache, and strong jaw. Not ugly. From where I sat, he looked like Dick Tracy in the cartoon. So much for Sweets' description.

"Hey, JR, get over here," she called.

JR served his drink and came over. He stood next to her and looked at me. He would have been handsome, except for small eyes that were deep set.

"This guy giving you trouble, sis?"

Ah shit. In my mind's eye I saw the MG, top down, brother and sister driving away from our lot, and me waving them on their way, money hard-earned by his whores in my hand. JR was not my picture of a pimp, but the more I looked at him, I decided just because he was white and didn't wear outrageous clothes didn't mean he wasn't a sleezeball. Maybe I shouldn't ask Freddy out on a date. Like brother, like sister.

"You remember Victor Brovelli, JR? You bought the MG from him."

"Yeah, a good car, good price. What can I do for you?"

He was smiling, but he wasn't showing any teeth. Pretty creepy.

I began my story about Winona's car, but a couple of minutes into my explanation he interrupted me.

"What the fuck's your deal, Brovelli? Winona never owned a car. She didn't know how to drive and didn't have a drivers' license. So what's all this bullshit?"

JR was tall but not that husky and there was a sturdy looking bar between us, so I felt relatively safe for the moment. I'd already measured the distance between my seat and the door and calculated getting out of the joint was doable unless the sonavabitch had a gun under the bar. The question was what was my next move, now that my cover story had been blown?

I didn't believe honesty would work with a pimp, so I needed a story he'd buy into, a whopper of a lie. I took a swig of beer and began, giving him my best worried look.

"Winona stole some money from us when she temped. We found out about it, but we didn't turn her in when she promised to pay us back. But then she got herself killed, and, naturally, we'd like to find out if there is any left. We thought if we could search the place where she lives, she may have hidden it there. Our business has run into a little cash flow problem and we've been trying to call in all our outstanding debts." I finished. Looking at JR, I could tell he wasn't impressed.

"No, no, I think you're still bullshitting, Brovelli. You know what I think? I think you're trying to hook me up in some way to Winona's murder, like it was me who shot her. Well, I got an airtight alibi, and you can ask the pigs, you dago prick."

"JR," Freddy said, touching his arm. "The word is Eye-talian."

"So, what do you say, you Eye-talian prick? You trying to fuck me up?"

Damned if he wasn't smiling the whole time he was cursing me out. I held up my hands in surrender. "Cool down JR. It's nothing like that." Of course, it was everything like that. Time for honesty. "Okay, okay. Here's the real deal. I'm not accusing you of anything. I'm trying to help a friend out. The cops have arrested him for the murder, and I know he didn't do it. So I'm helping him out."

"It's that goddamn Sweets Monroe," Freddy said, turning to her brother. "He's helping that scuzzball."

That did it. I would *not* be asking Freddy for a date. Although her face remained pretty, all the sweetness had disappeared, replaced by something ugly.

"Sweets is not that bad a guy," I said. By now our raised voices had attracted the attention of the men at the bar, looking our way, not looking happy.

"Sweets Monroe can kiss my ass," a voice behind me said.

I turned. There was a behemoth wearing leathers, looking down on me with his one good eye. Ah, shit. A frigging Amigo. I stood up and as I did, Freddy, transformed by her anger into Fredericka, raised her hand to her beehive and withdrew one of the pearls. Attached to it was a vicious looking five-inch needle, which she pointed in the direction of my left eye. At the same time JR whipped out a switchblade. It sprung open. *Great, a brother and sister killer act, just great.*

"You're a lying muthafucka," JR said.

Fredericka hissed, "And to think I was considering you to be that special someone." She jabbed her needle across the bar.

I fell backward. The big guy caught me, wrapping his huge arms around my chest. I might have one chance to get out of here alive, I thought. With a little luck, I could kick back and catch him in the balls, then make a dash for the door while he was flopping around on the floor.

Another prayer to the Blessed Virgin might be in order. Just as the prayer entered my mind, the prayer was answered.

"I got a very large pistol barrel shoved inside your big ear, you understand, *stronzo?* I'll blow your turd brains out if you touch my brother."

And that's how I escaped death in the Oasis.

CHAPTER 13
WHAT A GUY

Help your brother's boat across and your own will reach the shore.
Hindu Proverb

After we hustled out of the Oasis, I followed Vincent's taillights to East 14th. Both of us needed a drink. I pushed open the door to Flynn's and was greeted by Tom Jones singing "Delilah". There was a darts tournament going on in back. Jack "Swanee" Swan was shaking dice at the end of the bar with Jitters. As we pulled out stools and sat down, Stuart Tamberg, the night bartender, placed a frosty mug of Anchor Steam in front of me and a mug of an Irish brew called Smithwicks in front of Vincent. We asked for a couple of shots of Jack Daniels. We dumped the shot glasses into the beer and watched them sink to the bottom, turning the beer a darker amber. The beer went down smooth and fast, and we asked for seconds. It took a third to settle our nerves.

I asked Vincent how it turned out he was at the Oasis in time to save my ass. In some ways it was a rhetorical question. Since their zygotes split into two embryos, all twins understand that one of their missions in life will be to cover each other's butts. Vincent explained that he'd had a bad feeling ever since I'd told him I was going to the killer bar to talk to JR. Vincent excused himself to go to the bathroom. What a guy, I thought as I watched my twin head for the back of the tavern, walking a little funny like maybe he'd pissed his pants, which I wouldn't have blamed him, what with having to hold the muzzle of Sylvia's Beretta in the ear of the monster Amigo guy, probably one of JR's pimp friends, then smacking the dude on the head with the gun butt so he'd think twice about following us.

When I say what a guy, that doesn't always refer to times Vincent has backed me up in fights or got me outta dilemmas. Despite Vincent's conservative approach to business and politics and culture, he's a man who never fails to seize the moment. It doesn't matter what the moment is either, from jumping out of airplanes, to agreeing to box in a charity match against a guy twice his size, to swimming into a riptide to save a drowning child for which he received a San Francisco Mayor's commendation for bravery. I can come up with a lot of examples. There have been some doozies, some that have to do more with his stubbornness than his bravery.

There was the time the Oakland Police Department called Vincent at two in the morning to inform him that our lot had been broken into, and would he come down to assess the extent of the robbery and damage. Vincent was in his car and down there in a flash. The window to our office had been broken, the interior ransacked and our petty cash box stolen, no big deal since it only had seventy-five bucks in it. However, one car, a 1961 Buick 88 convertible, one of Victor's favorites, was missing. The thieves had used bolt cutters on the chain guarding our driveway. We've since installed double chains and reinforced the posts and locks. To say the least, Vincent was not a happy camper as he drove home a couple of hours later after boarding up the window. His unhappiness turned to shock when he came to the stoplight on the corner of Broadway and McArthur Boulevard. Facing him, coming from the other direction on Broadway, also waiting for the light to change, was our Buick, driven, according to Vincent, by a man of Polynesian extraction the size of a volcano. He was so huge, that Vincent said if the top of the convertible had been up the dude wouldn't have been able to get his head in. So, there my brother was, faced with the question, what to do? The wisest thing would've been to find a phone booth, call the cops and tell them the direction from which the robber was traveling. But, Vincent was worried that the car thief might turn off onto another street. Here's where my brother's stubborn gene kicked in, the way he described it to me later. In his words. I can still hear his voice.

"I tell you Victor, there was no way I was going to let that asshole, no matter how big he was, get away with our wheels."

This may be hard to believe, but it's the God's honest truth. You couldn't make up this story if you were a prize-winning novelist. Vincent drove through the red light, blowing his horn, hooked a U, slamming over the street divide, almost destroying the rear-end of his own car, and began tailgating the robber as he pulled away from the light. After that, the chase turned into a scene out of a Keystone Cops movie. By the time the asshole hit the freeway, both cars had run every red light on the way and were doing eighty plus. The thief must have thought a crazy person was chasing him. Vincent said he kept blowing his horn, leaning out the window, waving his fist and cursing at the top of his lungs. The car thief's mistake was thinking that if he got on the freeway, he could outrun Vincent. Bad decision. Vincent was driving a 62 Thunderbird with a 454 cubic inch, 500 horse power Pro Street Chevy engine that Jitters, our mechanic and part time drag-racer, had recently rebuilt.

"The sunavabitch thought he could get away. Not a chance. I stayed on his ass up to the Caldecutt Tunnel. And guess what, on the other side as we came barreling out of the tunnel, there was a highway patrol car pulled off the side of the highway. The sheriff snapped on his lights and siren, and it was all over in a couple of minutes."

Word of the chase made the papers, and Vincent became a local hero, especially lionized by our fellow used car dealers along East 14th who'd been suffering a bunch of robberies by the same gang of Samoans that hit us.

That's my twin brother for you. What a guy.

As Vincent returned from the john, I waved to Tamberg to bring us another round. Vincent called for a club soda. The vampire brought our drinks along with a plate of hardboiled eggs and a bowl of pretzels and returned behind the bar.

"You think that big *ciuccio* will come looking for me?" Vincent asked.

"I doubt it. The fool doesn't have much between the ears." I laughed. "He did look a little like a donkey, didn't he?" I downed my shot, and called for another. Tamberg made a face, but poured one half full. I was beginning to feel it warming my body. "Clear as a bell," said, pointing to my head.

"I could have fit the whole pistol inside that ear of his," Vincent said, pulling the Beretta out of his jacket and waving it the air. "I'll stick it in his ear again."

I grabbed his arm. "Jesus, put it away before you give Stuart a heart attack."

As he put the weapon back, I said, "Those ears were so big you could have shoved a shotgun barrel in."

"A machine gun."

"A fucking bazooka."

Vincent started laughing and so did I. Soon we were both laughing hysterically and pounding the table. Behind the bar, Tamberg also started laughing, which caused the couple sitting at the other end of the bar to start laughing. Our laughter I'm sure had more to do with an intense sense of relief than with anything really humorous.

When we calmed down and caught our breath, Vincent asked what I'd accomplished tonight. Were we any closer to identifying Winona's killer?

"I don't believe JR had anything to do with it. He was pretty upset about her death, and his reaction when he thought I was accusing him of the murder was convincing. On the other hand, I'm not sold that Parsegian was telling the truth." I explained about Winona looking through the stores accounting and finding a way to make the company more profitable. "I'd like to get into the company books and see if he really did cut Winona a bonus check."

"I can't see how you can manage that," Vincent said. "When it comes to money, those two are lock-down secretive."

"Sweets has a special skill," I said.

"*Merda.* You're not thinking about having Sweets break into the store, are you?"

"Just thinking," I said. "Nothing wrong with doing a little thinking."

"I'm not going for a burglary."

"I never said that's what I was *going* to do."

The minute the thought popped into my mind, I knew that's exactly what I *was* going to do. Vincent didn't need to know. In this case, I'd keep him, as they say in the spy thrillers, on a need-to-know basis.

From the bar, we heard Stuart announcing, last call. I signaled for another shot. I leaned toward my brother. "Vincent, stick around. I want to talk to Stuart. That way we'll have gotten our three suspect out of the way."

"I personally can't see Stuart having anything to do with Winona's murder. What motive could he possibly have?"

"Sex," I said.

"You go ahead and talk to him. I need some fresh air. I'll wait for you outside."

Vincent walked away, looking at his watch and mumbling about how Gloria was going to clobber him for coming home so late. Pussy whipped, I thought. Vincent's wife, Gloria, was the youngest of six Mancuso girls, each one of them known in the Bay Area for their beauty and their fiery tempers. Gloria attended Holy Names College, when we were in Saint Mary's. I dated her a couple of times, but once she set eyes on the unmarred handsome face of my twin, I didn't have a chance.

Once Vincent left, the bar was empty except for me and Stuart, who was washing glasses. I poured my shot into my beer, took a long swallow and walked a little unsteadily to the bar.

Stuart looked over at me. "Hey, Victor, closing time. Finish it up."

"Give me a minute here." I said, "I'm still recovering."

"From what? You two were laughing so hard, it must have been something really funny."

Trying not to slur my words, I gave Stuart the short version.

"I know JR from the neighborhood," Stuart said. "He doesn't look like a pimp, but Winona told me what the real deal was with him. Not a nice guy."

Stuart broached the subject of Winona, I followed up. "I didn't know you knew Winona."

"When she was temping for Furniture Discounts and you guys, she'd come in after work. I was just starting my shift. Not a lot of people around. She and I'd talk while I cleaned up and got ready for the night crowd."

The week night crowd was composed mostly of men playing pool or darts. Team dart competitions were held on Saturday nights. It was also the night the tavern turned into a meeting place for a bunch of Irish guys Body had explained were IRA, raising money for the cause of freeing Northern Ireland from the British. Once a fellow had mistakenly walked into Flynn's on a Saturday night wearing a University of Syracuse orange sweatshirt and damn near got himself killed.

"When was the last time you saw Winona?" I asked.

"Oh, I don't really remember, maybe about a month ago."

"Were you getting it on with her?" The question obviously surprised him. His narrow eyes widened.

"Not my style, Victor."

I don't know what I expected him to say, but not my style was not it. Winona Davis was every uncastrated male's' style. "You can't be serious," I said. "Winona was a hundred on a scale of ten."

"Not my gender," Stuart said.

What the hell? That Goddamn Vincent. Stuart, gay. Jesus, H. Christ, who else in the neighborhood knew? How come I didn't? Not that I gave a shit if he was homo.

"You mean?"

"Yeah. I don't keep it a secret, Victor, but I don't go around advertising my preference."

A gay vampire, I thought. I scratched Stuart off my mental list of suspects. I didn't know what else to ask him, so I placed a ten on the bar. He gave me change. I left a dollar tip. "Gay," I muttered as I walked out, shaking my head.

"Don't worry Victor. It's not catching," he yelled.

"I'm not stupid, you know," I yelled back.

"Yeah, but you'll be stupid if you try to drive."

"Sober as Sister Mary Louise," I said, thinking I sure must be stupid about gays. Which didn't make me lonesome cowboy. The vast majority of men I hung around with got real up-tight when the subject of homosexuality came up. Italians who have a psychological stake in maintaining strong macho images were particularly threatened by gays. Okay, the Irish, Poles, and Latins too. Perhaps it was all Catholics. Catholic men's colleges were notorious for female bashing and gay bashing. Ninety percent of the jokes in our dorms were about pussy or queers. My response to the gay issue was that it left more females for me. Okay, so I was a moral coward. Maybe, I reasoned, something in the future would happen to raise my consciousness. Until then, I had cars to sell and a murderer to catch.

The fresh air slapped me in the face, and I reached out for the telephone pole to catch my balance.

"You leave your car here," Vincent said. "I'll drive you home."

The telephone pole was moving like a stripper's hips. The day, the night and six shots and beers had caught up with me. Vincent helped me to his car, and I was asleep by the time his engine turned over.

CHAPTER 14
BREAKING AND ENTERING

Oh yes, It's obvious to my trained eye, that there is much
more going on here than meets the ear.
Inspector Clouseaau

My hangover was not as bad as I expected. By the time I was through showering, shaving, and dressing, I felt close to normal. And, I knew what I wanted to do. I went to the living room and shook Sweets awake.

"It shouldn't be any problem," Sweets said after I'd explained. "When do you want to do it?"

"Tonight," I said. "I'm sure there's something bogus going on with Parsegian. I don't buy his story about giving Winona a bonus for uncovering some kind of accounting error. First of all, how good were her accounting skills anyway? And second of all, those two cheap bastards would rather have their balls cut off than part with two hundred dollars."

"Agreed," Sweets said. "I've watched Parsegian in Flynn's enough to know he's always the last guy to buy a round."

"Settled. They close up around ten o'clock. We wait until two after the bars close and go in. You're the expert, you figure out how we do it."

"Let me use your wheels, and I'll go scout the place out right now. Like I'm looking to buy a bed set, or something."

"You'll have to take your motorcycle," I said. I left my car outside Flynn's."

"Yeah, mon frere, your eyes tell me a sad story."

"I am not your brother and there's no sad story. I just drank a little too much." I looked at my watch. It was nine a.m. Go pick it up for me. Then you can check out Discount Furniture. But you better rethink your strategy. Parsegian's not going to believe you're interested in buying anything."

THE CASE OF THE '61 CHEVY IMPALA

"You hurt my feelings. I have a bank account."

"How much is in it?"

"Little short this month," he said. "Anyway, the hog's on the fritz."

He popped another hard candy into his mouth and made a disgusting sucking sound. It was a wonder Sweets' teeth hadn't rotted to the gums. "You'll have to take the bus" I said.

"When I get to the lot, how about I pick out a new car? You know I haven't had wheels since the Impala."

"You have some big *coglionii* asking for a car. Just use my car and get your ass back here."

He shrugged. "What's the problem, Victor? Have I ever missed a payment?"

"You never *made* a frigging payment," I said. "You want a car. Sylvia will write up the Travelall. She'll put it on lay-away."

"Argh, man, that car's haunted. I'd probably get in a wreck and die. Winona and I didn't break up under the best of circumstances."

"For Christ's sake, Sweets, I was only kidding about the Travelall. Just bus it."

He interrupted, "How about the Cady El Dorado?"

"Not a chance."

"Okay, then, the Olds Cutless. The blue 1960."

"Are you fucking deaf? No car. Get your ass in gear. Make sure you tell Sylvia what you're doing, or she'll think you're stealing my Mustang." I threw him my keys.

"Sylvia and I are buds."

"Sylvia hates you. You come on the lot the first thing she does is lock the office and hide the cash drawer." Not to mention hiding the Pappy Van Winkle from Mr. Thirsty, I thought. Sweets headed for the bathroom to clean up. Ah, hell, I thought, I'd better call the office and warn Sylvia Sweets was on the way. She picked up on the first ring with a cheery "Brovelli Brothers' Used Cars." Cheery voice changed to pissed off voice once I explained the reason for my call. A number of colorful Italian adjectives followed, decorating Sweets name like a Christmas tree. I told her that I was expecting a call from Winona's friend, Arabella.

"What's this about, Victor? You promised to tell me what you're up to."

"Winona kept a diary." I explained Sweets' idea that, considering Winona's penchant for writing down every tiny detail of her life, there was a good chance she'd have written something in this year's diary that would lead to her killer. Miss Grumpy sniffed, good luck with that. I told her to tell Vincent that I was taking the day off and that he'd understand. She grumbled and hung up.

Sweet joined me in the kitchen for a cup of coffee. I told Sweets that either Sylvia or Vincent would have my car keys. "I'm taking the rest of the day off. I'm going to spend some time reading my detective manual, get some tips, then maybe take a nap before we bust into Parsegian's store. When you get back, wake me when you're ready." Sweets nodded, and I left the kitchen. On the way to the bedroom, I stopped off at the living room window to say hello to my Billboard Marilyn. The sun was on its westerly decent to the Pacific, highlighting her golden hair with rays of sunlight. I pictured Arabella, the lovely waitress, she with the mahogany eyes and skin, the color of a sandy beach. My revere reminded me that I already had a girlfriend – well, kind of - a Nordic beauty, who I should telephone. Renee didn't have morning classes, so she could be in her dorm room. I should set up a date so I could tell her about my recent adventure, certain that it would warm her heart, so to speak. The thought of Renee with a warm heart, made me wonder if my day would be better spent with her in the back seat of my car than in bed reading detective stuff. I headed to the bedroom and dialed Renee's number. There was no answer. I left a message at the college switchboard. Just as well, I thought. I swung my feet up onto the bed. I closed my eyes and was instantly asleep.

The telephone rang and woke me. It was Renee returning my call. I looked at my watch. It was close to noon. I hinted about what had happened to me, sort of setting the stage for a more detailed account. She said she couldn't wait to hear the whole story. There was a lecture she had to attend but would be free after ten. Renee at ten meant Renee for most of the night, which precluded a planned burglary. I told her tonight was out. She made mewing sound that was a definite turn on and told me she was going to take a hot shower and imagine danger. I almost convinced myself to put off the burglary and the danger that it entailed – almost.

After hanging up, I gave myself a pat on the back for having the willpower to resist temptation. One less trip to the confessional. I took my investigators books to the couch and read until Sweets returned around five with booze on his breath and my keys in his hand.

He threw himself on the couch and closed his eyes. He was asleep and snoring before I could ask him what he'd discovered in Parsegian's store. I left him for my room, closed the door so I couldn't hear his boozy snoring that sounded a lot like a braying donkey. I opened *War and Peace* to where I'd left off. A chapter later, I too fell asleep. When I woke up, it was close to ten, and Sweets was still sound asleep.

• • •

After coffee and a couple of omelets Sweets made, we left my apartment at midnight. Hardly any traffic. As usual the neighborhood after the bars close was empty and dark. I pulled in behind the store and cut the lights.

"I don't want any burglar alarms going off," I said.

"No worries mon frère. We're in, we're out like a boy's first piece of ass."

The alley behind the store was dark. Sweets cautioned using the flashlight was not a good idea until we got inside. I had on black Levis and my navy pullover wind jacket. Sweets was also dressed in a black, tight-fitting bodysuit. He handed me a black ski mask, and I pulled it over my head. He pulled his on and withdrew a small backpack from the back seat. Once the mask covered that obnoxious blond comb of hair, it was like a streetlight had gone out. I stumbled through the dark behind Sweets. I guessed being a burglar for so long, his eyes has evolved so he could see in the dark like night monkeys or opossums. Somewhere I'd read that a little monkey called a Tarsier that could see splendidly in the night had eyes bigger than its brain.

Could be the same for Sweets I thought. Sweets stopped in front of a window. "Here we go," he whispered. Dressed the way I was, I felt like one of the Japanese Ninja warriors in last year's James Bond flick, *You Only Live Twice*. There was a sticker on the glass. I stepped forward and read: **Alarm System Armed after 10 P.M.** Sweets reached into his back pack and pulled out an object that looked like some kind of space machine I'd seen lately on a new TV series called Star Trek.

"I modified this Stripmaker 50060 series. It'll get the job done."

"Which is what?" I asked.

"I'm going to cut a hole in the glass, reach in and open the window. Voila, we climb in."

"Are you, nuts? Can't you read that sign?"

"No worries. I told you those two guys were cheap. One of the things I found out when I reconnoitered was that their system was so old, I knew right away it was bogus."

He pressed the tripod in the center of one of the panes, slid the cutter out along the bar attached to the tripod until it reached six inches. Taking the handle, he began moving the cutter slowly and without a lot of pressure around the tripod until he'd completed a full circle. Satisfied, that the blade was in place, he started the circle again, this time applying pressure, around and around. He stopped and gave me a thumbs up. Carefully, he pulled back the tripod toward him, with the glass stuck on it, leaving an empty hole through which he placed his hand, unhooked the latch and opened the window. It took about five minutes. Sweets beckoned.

"I'll go in first, then you follow." He placed his equipment into his backpack and dropped it through the window. He eased in. I followed. Inside was coal-mine dark. Sweets handed me goggles.

"You'll need night Vision glasses," he said. "I'm cool."

I slipped them on. The showroom turned a sickly green, but I could see clearly. Clearly enough to see a large shadow slowly approaching. "Sweets, what's that coming toward us?"

We both heard the sound at the same time, a long, low growl that sounded a lot like the werewolf in the movie, *Hour of the Wolf.* The shadow and the sound moved towards us.

"It's a goddamn guard dog," I whispered.

"You're goddamn right, daddy-o. That's the biggest fucking dog in the world." He yelled, "Move your ass."

My ass was moving. We hit the window at the same time. Sweets is not very heavy, so I grabbed him by his shirt collar and the back of his trousers and pitched him through. I was halfway out, when I felt a sharp pain in my ankle that could only have been the devil dog's teeth. It hurt like hell, and I screamed, kicking back with my other foot as hard as I could, but the leverage was not sufficient, and I missed. The brute was growling while feasting on my flesh. Desperate not to turn into dog food, I kicked again and heard the growl turn into a yelp. With my ankle free, I flopped onto the ground outside and slammed the window shut. I looked back. The dog's front paws were on the window sill and his gigantic head was sticking through the circle Sweet's had cut. I didn't wait for him to decide to bust through the glass. I hopped like the gimpy deputy in *Gunsmoke* after Sweets. We were halfway to the car when I heard glass shattering, and I knew the hound from hell had made up its mind.

"He's coming," I yelled. We slammed the car doors closed just in time, as the beast flung itself against the Mustang, trying to eat the passenger side window. I started the engine, punched it and fishtailed out of the alley, tires squealing. As I was about to turn onto East 14th, I looked back into the alley and saw the figure of a woman standing behind the snarling dog. Winona's ghost.

Who was she trying to protect?

I did not believe in the paranormal, although on my mother's side of the family I'd grown up with ghost stories, scary variation of the Neapolitan Cult of the Dead, *Malocchio,* the Evil Eye and *Masciare,* women healers. I thought such superstitions foolish, but on that night, terrified, I spun out onto the street, burning rubber, downshifted to third and yelped at the pain in my ankle. On East 14th, I brought the Mustang under control and slowed in the event a cop car suddenly appeared. *Madonna, I was having visions. Not a good sign, not a good sign at all.* Reaching with my left hand, I felt my ankle. My hand came away bloody. "I'm bleeding. Son of a bitch, I'll need a tetanus shot."

Sweets was mumbling, "Muthafucka, muthafucka."

The cracked window on the driver's side looked like a spider web. "Jesus Christ," I said. "No wonder they didn't have an alarm system."

"The dog might have been one of those Irish wolf hounds," Sweets said. "I could have put a saddle on him."

"How come I've never seen that dog in Parsegian's store, huh? You can't keep a dog that size hidden. Ten years they've been across the street from us, and the only dog I've ever seen inside was their cleaning lady's Shiatsu."

"If that was a Shiatsu," Sweets said, "it was on steroids."

"Did you see those fangs?"

"I was too busy hauling ass. Say, that was bitchin of you, Victor, to shove me through the window first, real thoughtful."

"You were frozen to the floor. The dog would have eaten you."

"I was hauling."

"You were frozen with fear."

"Was not," Sweets said.

The pain in my ankle was pretty intense. Driving to the emergency was risky. If Parsegin reported a break in and his dog with my blood on its teeth, I could be arrested. Or I could die of rabies.

"You need to drive me to the emergency before I bleed to death, and I need a rabies shot."

"You go to emergency and Parsegian reports a break-in cops be checking emergencies."

"Just get me there you *Stugats*."

"Stewed guts back at you, man," Sweets said.

I almost laughed, but I hurt too much. *Stugats* in Italian translates into a lot of different expletives. In this case, I meant dickhead.

Dickhead drove me to the emergency at the Alameda general hospital, perhaps far enough away from the crime. I got ten stitches and a rabies shot.

CHAPTER 15
ARABELLA

Oggi in figura, domani in sepultura.
Today in person, tomorrow in a grave.

The pain in my ankle kept me up most of the night. It was still hurting like a bitch when I limped into the office on Wednesday morning. Vincent and Sylvia were already there, drinking coffee and talking. Vincent had a guilty look on his face. I asked Sylvia if she'd give us a moment. She crossed her arms and refused.

"What did you tell her," I asked.

Sylvia said, "I can't believe you took my Beretta and hit some pimp with it. It wasn't loaded. Did you even check?"

"Ah, man," I groaned, smacking Vincent on the shoulder.

"What good is an unloaded gun, Sylvia?" Vincent asked, looking startled, probably wondering what would've happened to him had the Amigo known the gun was empty.

"You guys are always leaving me alone on the lot. There's cash and inventory, so my daddy gave it to me. I keep it just to scare some *ciuccio* off, anybody give me any trouble."

"Like Sunny Badger," Vincent said with a smirk.

"You damn right, I'd shoot the bastard," Sylvia said, "he keep coming around asking me out."

"That gun is a World War Two relic," I said. "What'd your daddy do, hide it from the allies after they captured his ass?"

"Up yours, Vittorio. My father warned me not to get hooked up with your side of the family."

"What does that mean?" I asked. "Just because your father owns all

99

those weeny little German cars stores, he's some kind of *Capo di tutti i capi* of automobile dealerships? And how come he's got these great German connections?"

"Are you saying my old man is Mafioso?"

"Why not, and maybe he was one of Mussolini's boys."

"Oh, you've gone too far this time, Vittorio, too far."

"*Basta, basta,*" Vincent cried.

"Don't tell me to stop it. Your brother just insulted my father."

I could tell by the hurt look on Sylvia's face that I really *had* gone too far. She *was* our cousin, and she had feelings, but sometimes we could get up each other's noses. I took a deep breath. "Sorry, Sylvia. I take back what I said about your father. He's not a Fascist."

"Or mafia."

"Or Mafioso. He's a simple Italian-American successful businessman, okay? Let's kiss and make up." I held out my arms and made kissy sounds.

She sighed. "What am I going to do with you, Victor?"

I shrugged.

"Breaking into Discount Furniture. What were you thinking?"

"I guess I shouldn't have relied on Sweets."

"You can't rely on Sweets to tie his own shoes," Sylvia said.

"He's a successful burglar. You should have seen how fast he got into that building."

"Who says Sweets is successful? I don't see him living like he's got big bucks."

Sylvia had a point. No one really knew whether Sweets' rep as a burglar was legitimate.

Since he gave free groceries to single moms, the neighborhood took it as a matter of faith. Vincent had pointed out that groceries wasn't exactly the same as giving away free washing machines. Jitters said it was kind of cool, like having one's own Pink Panther, which I now thought was prophetic given last night's Peter Seller's performance.

"Look, can we get to work selling cars and stop with Sweets." I said. "I woke up this morning thinking that maybe we don't even have to do anything. Sweets is out on bail, and there's not enough evidence to take him to trial. No gun, no fingerprints, no nothing. I'm going to talk to Ness and see if I can get an update before I continue with my investigation."

"Continue with my investigation," Sylvia mimicked me. "Like you're some kind of Joe Friday. You think Sergeant Ness is going to risk his job to give you insider information, just because you guys play cards together? Not a chance."

"I'm ignoring you, Sylvia. See, I'm walking away. Notice how one foot is moving in front of the other. Going to work, to the office where my desk is waiting for me. And you should be at your desk doing invoices." I limped a couple of steps and turned around. "And as far as the business goes when our ship comes in you're either going to be on board or over board. You can tell your daddy that Brovelli's Used Cars has hit the bottom and is on its way back up, up, up and away." I turned and headed for the door. Behind me I heard Vincent and Sylvia laughing. Good, getting back to normal. What would normal be without a little fighting with each other.

I couldn't wait to sit down and take the weight off my ankle.

A couple of minutes later, Sylvia joined me. Vincent stayed out on the lot, walking from car to car being a salesman.

From her desk, she said, "I'm sorry I ragged on you, Victor. I felt you guys were keeping me out of the loop. You know I'm behind you all the way, I only wish I trusted that damn Sweets more. Your father sees something in the raggedy-ass burglar that I sure don't."

Ragged was not the most accurate description of Sweets wardrobe that consisted of clothes that were the latest fashion from the Salvation Army, but always clean with nary a hole or a loose thread.

"You don't think Jay will tell me what they've got on Sweets?"

"I doubt it. Maybe if you can get the good sergeant drunk."

Not likely as my friend's drink of choice was a shanty gaff, a mixture of beer and ginger ale, and most card nights never drank more than three. It occurred to me that if I could convince Sylvia to go out on a date with Jay, he'd probably tell me everything I wanted to know. That wouldn't happen. Before Sylvia would date Ness, she'd probably date Sunny Badger, who also had the hots for her, and refused to take her many version of "no" seriously.

"Well, it won't hurt to ask Jay," I said, returning to the list I'd been working on, a list of automobiles new car dealers had taken in on trade and didn't want to keep as part of their used car inventory. Selvy Chevrolet was one of our better sources. They were very picky about keeping trade-ins, which left some pretty decent wheels for us to pick from. We always got the first call because the owner's son, Chris, was a Saint Mary's Alum.

I finished checking off a few cars that might fit our budget, be it ever so humble, and called the dealership to see if I could drive over and take a look. As I was about to leave, I noticed a yellow message slip next to my phone. It was from Arabella. Sylvia had written 6:46 P.M. 4/2. I turned to Sylvia and waved the message slip."

"Damn, sorry, Victor. She called just before I closed up last night. Got into it this morning with Vincent and completely forgot about it."

"Why didn't you call me?"

"I tried, but there was no answer."

"Did she give you an idea what she wanted to talk to me about?"

"No, only that you should call her."

I dialed the number. I let it ring a dozen times then hung up. I called the Golden Dragon. She was not on schedule for today. I'd drive by her apartment. Face to face is always a better way to talk to a beautiful woman. On the way I kept seeing Arabella's high voltage smile. The address on the message was in the Lake Merritt district, up in the hills behind the lake. I found the apartment building and parked. She lived on the fourth floor. It was a little after noon. Maybe she'd agree to go to lunch with me. I limped to the elevator. As the doors were about to shut, a young woman rushed in, breathing heavily, apologizing. When I saw her face I knew she was related to Arabella. Her features were not as refined, but all the rest of the "wow" factors were in place.

"You must be related to Arabella Duan." I said.

She hesitated, giving me a quick once-over, probably to assure herself I wasn't an ax murderer.

"I'm her sister."

"Younger, no doubt," I said, hoping for a smile.

"Older," she said, unsmiling.

I stuck out my hand. "My name is Victor Brovelli." She didn't respond, keeping her eyes lowered and fidgeting nervously with her handbag.

The elevator made its slow ascent. When we arrived at Arabella's apartment, her sister, pushed the buzzer. No answer. She knocked, once, then again. She looked at me.

"Mr. Brovelli, I don't know who you are, so I'm going to ask you to step way down the hall, okay? I'm going to open the door with my key. I'm worried about my sister. I haven't been able to get in touch with her, and she may be ill."

"Fine," I said. I took a few steps back. "I'll stay out here. Call me if you need any help."

Two minutes later, a scream froze me in my place. Another scream propelled me forward. The door was unlocked, and I ran into the living room. The reason for the scream was sprawled on the couch, Arabella Duan, with one arm draped along the couch, her beautiful head titled to the side with a bullet hole just above the ear. Arabella's sister was on her knees sobbing.

"*Madonna*," I whispered and pulled the woman away from the body. "Where's the phone? We gotta call the cops."

• • •

The Oakland Police Department arrived in three waves. The first to arrive were two uniformed officers, followed by two homicide detectives, one of whom was Jay Ness. The last to arrive I guessed were the forensic specialists, carrying a whole bunch of medical-looking equipment.

By then, Arabella's sister - her name was Mirabella - and I were in the hall having been asked to wait there until an officer could talk to us. She'd slid to the floor and had wrapped her arms around her knees. I sat beside her. I explained to Mirabella, who answered to Mira, what my business was with her sister. She hadn't known Winona well, she said, between sobs.

"My poor baby sister," she wailed.

How do you comfort a woman who's just seen her sister with a bullet hole in her head? She was shaking and her sobs had turned to hiccups. I took off my sports coat and placed it around her shoulders.

"My poor baby sister," she kept repeating, between hiccups, "My poor baby sister."

When her tears stopped and her breathing returned to normal I questioned her about Winona. Mira began talking about her sister as if she were alive, about their life together growing up. I figured she was in some kind of shock. Jay saved us from a longer painful trip into her memory.

"Excuse me Ms. Duan, I'd like to speak with this gentleman," he said, his voice rising slightly sarcastically at the word, gentleman. I stood up - like a gentlemen.

He took me by the arm and pointed me down the hall out of hearing distance.

"You got a bum leg, Victor?"

"No, I limp like this because it attracts beautiful women who feel sorry for me and immediately want to hold me in their arms."

"I should have known better. A Victor Brovelli response to any question or subject would have to do with sex."

"Romance," I said. "Romance. Your mind is always in the gutter. Is that something they teach you in the Police Academy?

"Whatever, Brovelli," he said, smiling. He opened his notebook and took down my statement.

When I finished, he said, "Your being here isn't a coincidence, Victor, is it? Your friend Sweets being investigated in the death of Winona Davis and here you are at the apartment of Winona's best friend, Arabella, shot in the head in the same manner as Winona, and it looks like with a similar small caliber pistol." He caught his breath and continued. "Not confirmed, but I'd bet on it."

"Before you go on. Sweets is not my friend. He's a valued customer."

"I hope for your sake you're not sticking your dago nose into police business because if you are I'm going to have to write you a ticket for impersonating a private investigator without a license."

"Ha," I said.

"So, what gives? Straight talk."

I decided to tell Jay the truth, not the whole truth and nothing but the truth, but the truth about my pop and Sweets' relationship and how Pop had made Vincent and me promise to help prove Sweets had not murdered Winona.

After I'd finished, Jay shook his head and said, "Your father is a pretty sentimental old guy."

"Old fashioned," I said. "Old country."

"Victor, you're a smart man. Don't get involved. Tell you what, I don't think we've got enough evidence to bring Sweets to trial. But now this comes along," he said, pointing back into Arabella's apartment, "We're going to have to bring in your valued customer again."

"Come on, Jay. What reason would Sweets have to kill Arabella?" The question was answered immediately in my mind: Diary. I wondered if I should tell Jay about the possible diary. I wondered, but I didn't.

"The investigation is just starting, Victor. I've got your statement. Take off. If I need to talk to you some more, I'll come by the lot."

"I'll be there."

"Tell Sylvia hello," he said as I walked down the hall.

"Absolutely," I said. "She'll be happy to hear from you." I recovered my sport coat from Mira, said, goodbye, and kept walking.

Usually I enjoyed putting my friend on about Sylvia, but all I was feeling was a terrible sadness that Arabella, the beautiful, was lost to the living. I didn't know her well. Her beauty could have concealed an unattractive soul, but I doubted it.

I returned to the lot and told Vincent and Sylvia what had happened. Sylvia crossed herself. "I will light a candle," she said.

Vincent shook his head. "What the heck is going on?" he asked.

As if I knew.

CHAPTER 16
JAILBIRD

*The origin of the word "jailbird" can be traced back at least
to Medieval England, where convicts were often placed
in iron cages suspended several feet above the ground. These
cages were generally visible to passersby, who were routinely
inspired to refer to the caged occupants as jailbirds.*

It didn't take the police long to find Sweets and stick him back behind bars in the Alameda County jail, accused of murdering Arabella Duan. Thankfully, they'd picked him up on the street and not in my apartment. This time there'd be no bail for the ancestor of Jean Lafitte. Carter Innis, his lawyer, called right after I got to work in the morning to tell me that Sweets fingerprints had been found in the apartment and there was other physical evidence pointing to his client. He hadn't received all the information from the District Attorney's office. Arabella had been Winona's friend and ex roommate, so the police had jumped all over that connection. When I got the news in the morning at work, my first thought was Sweets could save us all a lot of trouble by hanging himself in his jail cell. I'd no sooner hung up talking to Carter, than my pop called telling me he'd just heard about the terrible tragedy that had befallen Sweets.

"*E un peccato,*" he said. "This thing they do to an innocent."

I wasn't sure about innocent, but agreed it was awful. "*Figurati,* Pop, I'll think of something."

"*Magari,*" he said.

Not a great vote of confidence. What he was hoping for and what I could accomplish seemed to me to be wildly limited by my infinitesimal investigative skills. Things were getting completely above my pay grade.

"Yeah, Pop, let's hope so." I hung up the receiver, stress tightening all the muscles of my body into one head to toe Gordian Knot.

"Was that Pop?" Vincent asked.

"Who else?" I said. He knew better than to ask me why Pop had called.

"He can't possibly want us to continue trying to help Sweets."

"He can and does," I said. "All the lawyer's fees are coming out of his pockets."

"Our pockets, too, you realize."

"*Onore*," I said half-heartedly.

"Yeah, frigging honor," Vincent said, sighing.

We stood looking out the office window onto East 14th, saying nothing, thinking about frigging *onore*, until Sylvia spoke.

"The reality is that Sweets might very well be the killer," She said. "You know I've never liked the guy. I'm guessing that the only way he was able to save your father, back when, was because he's friends with the Blacks."

"Sweets is hardly a Negro," Vincent said.

"Bi-racial," I said.

"He thinks he's a Frenchman," Vincent said.

I remembered a year ago during a series of burglaries in the ritzy residential township of Montclair that bags of food began showing up in the morning at the doorsteps of families in West Oakland. Lots of basic stuff: macaroni, bacon, bread, milk, vegies, and fruit. And always a bag of hard candy. Sweet had an alibi for the burglaries and denied care packages. That was Sweets, saint and sinner. Maybe mostly sinner, occasional saint.

"Saint Jean Lafitte," I said.

CHAPTER 17
BLACK PANTHERS

All Power to the People.

Sylvia looked out the office window, took her rosary out of her purse and said, "We've got company."

I did not like what I saw. "Is that who I think it is getting out of the car?" I asked.

"Terrance Bowles, in the flesh," Vincent said.

"*Madonna*," I said. "He's Huey Newton's right-hand man."

"Panther's Minister of Education," said Vincent. "I see his picture in the papers all the time."

At the mention of the Black Panthers, Sylvia went back into the office, no doubt to get her Beretta.

I followed her into the office. I put on my sports coat that I left hanging on the back of the chair. It was my new double-breasted blue blazer with nautical buttons. I slipped it on over an open-collar Oxford dress shirt and returned to Vincent's side. In the event of my sudden homicide any person inspecting my body would be able to see I was a gentleman. Unless, of course, my sports coat was riddled by bullets.

The minister had paused and was talking to his men, body guards, I figured. The Black Panthers Party, BPP, originally the Black Panthers' Party for Self Defense was founded by Huey Newton and Bobby Seale a couple of years ago, its goal being to monitor police behavior in Black neighborhoods. That the Panthers advocated armed resistance did not sit well with the Oakland Police Department. The Panthers were a frightening bunch dressed in black leathers with matching berets. But as Vincent succinctly pointed out, it was the guns they carried that elevated the ensemble from frightening to terrifying. He got no argument from me. The guns had to do with a statement made by Franz Fanon, *"The people have to be shown that the colonizers and their agents are not bullet proof."* How did I know this? Recently, a couple of Black Panthers attended one of Brovelli Brothers' Used Cars Saturday barbeques and treated me to the entire history of their party, its inception greatly influenced by Fanon's writings. My pop would have called Fanon a Commie. At the time, I didn't mention that to my friends in black leather, one of whom later bought a clean 1961 Ford Falcon. Who was I to turn down a cash sale, commie or no commie?

Huey Newton's trial for murdering a police officer in 1967 was set for this July and things were tense, particularly in West Oakland. The Brovelli Brothers' Used Cars had established a good rapport with the growing Negro community in Oakland. Still, I didn't know whether I should be pleased with the arrival of one of the Panthers top brass or be scared shitless.

"How did we get so lucky?" Vincent whispered. "First the Satans and now the Black Panthers, all in two days. I'll tell you what it is. We've been jinxed ever since we agreed to help Sweets. That's what this is."

I nudged Vincent, "No discounts."

"You gave the Satans a discount, you want the word to get out you're prejudiced?"

"I'm not laughing, Vincent. You see me laughing, huh? I've got enough problems."

The approaching Black Panther Minister was NBA tall and slender with a neatly-trimmed slightly graying afro. Behind granny glasses, his eyes were piercingly black. The glasses were perched on a long thin nose. There was a thin line where his lips should have been. His skin was the color of nutmeg. He wore a black leather jacket over a powder blue shirt, black leather pants and black beret. The thin line spread into a surprisingly warm smile as he held out his black gloved hand. Over his shoulder I could see that his body guards and driver standing by the car and not smiling were holding automatic weapons. One of them had a bandoleer across his chest. I flashed on a photograph my older brother Mario sent Vincent and me of him in Vietnam standing in a rice paddy holding a rifle the size of Wisconsin, with a similar looking bandoleer across his bare chest. A couple of Mario's platoon were squatting on the ground sucking dope through the barrels of their rifles. Mario was an officer, but it looked to me that he was hanging with the enlisted men. The photograph was inscribed to us with a note: *Don't show Pop or Ma.*

"You gentlemen were recommended to me by a couple of our members," Minister Bowles said. "They told me they purchased a car from you, and you gave them an honest deal. Is that true?"

His voice had the same deep timbre as our Pop's, and he pronounced each word as if every syllable was important. I hadn't forgotten the 1961 Ford Falcon we'd sold a member of the Panthers. You don't forget selling a car to someone who looked like he had anger management issues. I shook Bowles' hand. "We have a lot of excellent vehicles," I said. "All of them have been evaluated by our mechanic and fixed if fixing was needed."

"I'm looking for a specific kind of vehicle that I can transport things in, a wagon of some kind.

I looked quickly around the lot. There was the International Harvester Travelall that I'd toted Winona's body in, and a Ford Country Squire that was a beauty: Hard-rock maple frame, mahogany paneling, red leather interior, and a Fatman front end. Oh, man, if I could get rid of the Travelall. He shook his head at Winona's hearse. He took a little more time thinking about the Country Squire and nixed that too.

"A commercial van would be the more desirable," he said. He pointed to a 1964 Dodge A-100 Sportsman Van.

I thought the bright orange paint job would call too much attention to itself if they were planning to use it as an assault vehicle, but I wasn't about to broach the subject.

He asked for a test drive. I went to the office and grabbed the keys. Vincent whispered, *"Buona fortuna."* I'd need it, I thought. Out of the corner of my eye, I saw Sylvia crossing herself.

Terrance Bowles drove out of the lot, a nervous Victor Brovelli riding shotgun. I noticed that the car Bowles was driven to our lot in was tailing us. We reached the Nimitz, hit the onramp, and sped down the freeway, Bowles maintaining a nerve-wracking silence. I was trying to relax, to pretend this was just another car sales. Bowles exited on 5th Street. It didn't take me long to guess that we were headed for West Oakland, not a neighborhood in which an Italian Caucasian would be welcomed, especially not these days. All of the Bay Area was stressed over the Vietnam War with race riots erupting throughout the country, but since the March 16th My Lai massacre had been exposed, tensions were running particularly high. A great many African-Americans agreed with Mohammed Ali on the day he refused to be inducted into the army, when he stated, *I ain't got no quarrel with those Viet Cong.*

"Don't worry," Minister Bowles said, as if he was reading my mind. "You're safe with me. I'm taking the wheels to our community center to see if the cadre think it fits our needs."

"This van used to belong to a guy who ran a catering service. We removed all the shelves from the back, so it could be re-fitted for any use."

"Like to carry grenades and rocket launchers," he said.

"You're kidding," I said.

He began laughing and pounding the steering wheel, obviously delighted he'd frightened Whitey. I didn't think it was all that funny, but laughed anyway, forcing myself to enter into the black humor, a pun that would not have been found humorous in present company. The way I figured it, I was taking my life in my hands just driving with Bowles.

"You should have kept the shelves in," he said, after he'd stopped laughing. "If you can put together a fleet deal, we'd be interested in three more. We need large vehicles to deliver free breakfasts for school kids in our neighborhood, and we're going to start a food bank and delivery service to feed our hungry elderly brothers and sisters. I like the way this van drives, real smooth for a truck. We wouldn't want to have it break down. It would be an embarrassment."

An embarrassment that might get my ass kicked. "Got it," I said. "You don't have to worry. If you want the van, I'll have our mechanic give it another complete inspection. I'm sure we can discount for that many vans." It looked like the Black Panthers were doing some good stuff, and weren't the scary revolutionaries the papers made them out to be. Breakfast for kids, deliveries for old folks, and money in the Brovelli Boys' pockets. A quick prayer of thanks was in order. Who was the patron Saint of car salesmen, I wondered. If there was a saint for chefs, there had to be one for salesmen.

Bowles turned onto Grove Street and drove to 45th. At the corner he slowed down. "Ah, fuck me," he said, pulling suddenly to the curb.

"Did I say something wrong?" I asked, preparing to grovel if I had to.

"Pigs," he said, pointing out the windshield.

Sure enough, three Oakland Police Department cruisers were parked in front of a building that bore the Black Panthers' logo and slogan, **All Power to the People**, below which was a banner announcing a Free Huey Newton Defense Fund Barbeque to be held at DeFremary Park on April 7th. Newton had been arrested for murder in October of 1967. Eight Panthers and four of their women were standing outside the store being questioned by the police. It looked like trouble. The Black Panthers' minister of education parked the van and got out. I checked to see if the doors were locked. No way was I setting foot on the sidewalk. If bullets began to fly, I could duck under the dash. A car skidded to a halt behind us. Bowles' driver stepped out and followed his leader toward the confrontation. I was relieved to see that he'd left the carbine and bandoleer in the car.

My relief didn't last. Suddenly the six officers of Oakland's finest, none of them black or even remotely brown, pulled their pistols and began yelling for everyone to drop to the ground. *What the hell?* It didn't seem to me that anybody had done anything to warrant guns. I looked at the ignition to see if Bowles had left the keys in. He had. If I pulled out real slow, the cops might not notice me. Probably not a good idea since they'd seen us drive up. In the meantime, as I was thinking of how to make a break for it, Bowles was arguing with the officer in charge and waving his hands like he was conducting an orchestra. The cops were clearly not enjoying the tune. The buildings in the neighborhood were mostly empty, abandoned warehouses and storefront so there were not many witnesses to what was going on. The few passersby who stopped and protested found themselves joining the Panthers. The men in blue were attempting to handcuff all the people on the ground, but they were refusing to cooperate, which caused more yelling and swinging of batons. The women were covering their heads with their hands and screaming. Jesus, I didn't like them beating on the women. Bowles was now shaking his finger in the face of the head honcho officer, his own face twisted in anger. It was clear the cop did not like what he was hearing because he suddenly twisted Bowles into a choke hold.

My mind was torn between trying to help or getting the hell out of there. What could I do anyway, one guy? Maybe being white would help, I thought. But how? To my right just behind the van was a sidewalk telephone booth. Maybe I should call Vincent. He'd only tell me to get my sorry ass out of there. He'd be right of course, but for some reason I stayed put. The telephone booth gave me an idea. There was a chance it could work. I had to do something, didn't I? I couldn't just sit in the van like a lump and watch the cops beat up on people who, as far as I could tell, had done absolutely nothing wrong. I crawled over into the driver's side and opened the door to the van. You can do this, I said to myself. *Myself responded, no you can't. Yes I can. No you can't.* Back and forth we went.

Meanwhile the screaming went on. I closed the door. Then I opened it again. Fuck it, I thought. I stepped out onto the sidewalk, hunched over and moved slowly around the van so the cops couldn't see me. I checked my attire, straightened my college tie, and ran my fingers through my hair. I made it to the telephone booth unobserved. I lifted the receiver off the hook, quickly reviewed in my mind what I was going to say and stepped out on to the sidewalk, holding the receiver to my ear, stretching the cord as far as it would go. Above the screaming and cursing coming from down the street, I heard myself yelling. Or was it someone else, a braver person I didn't recognize or a more foolhardy person. Take your pick. There are times in a person's life when one decision can change everything. I didn't know it at the time, but as I look back, I was doubling down on game changing decisions, one already behind me, another about to happen.

"Officer, officer, hey, officers," I yelled at the top of my lungs.

The big cop holding Bowles swung around to face me, still choking Bowles.

"Officer, officer," I repeated. "I'm not armed."

He yelled back, "This is a police matter, mister. Don't interfere. Sir, you better get out of here."

"Well, you see, I can't," I yelled back. "I just made a telephone call to the Oakland Tribune. I thought you'd like to hear what I said. Maybe if we talked about it face to face, I could call back just in case I got it wrong. You know tell him there's no story, that I was mistaken."

"What the hell are you talking about? What story? Drop that phone and get over here."

I leaned into the booth, pretended to say something into the mouthpiece and hung up. I took my time walking toward the officer, who threw Bowles to the ground. As I approached, he withdrew his pistol and pointed it at me. With each step the needle on my fear tachometer rose. If I made it out of here alive, I was heading straight for Mills College and Renee and hustle her into the back seat of my Mustang. There is no way any of my brother's stories could top this.

As I got close, I said, "Hold on, I'm not armed," sticking out my hands, like my hands were presents he'd have to accept. "Let me introduce myself. My name is Victor Brovelli. I own Brovelli Brothers' Used Cars over on East 14th." The way he looked at me I thought that at any moment he might make my twin a singleton. When he didn't shoot, I said, "Officer, the man you've got on the ground is a customer of mine. You see that beautiful van over there?" I pointed behind me. "He was bringing it here to see if his friends approved of the sale."

The officer's face said what was going through my own mind: Are you fucking nuts? Bowles was on his back looking up at me. I think he was thinking I was nuts too. But I noticed he had a slight smile on his lips. The cop had his pistol trained on my salesman's heart. Surprisingly my fear had disappeared. What the cops were doing was just plain bullshit.

"What's your reason for being here?" the cop asked. He was a huge guy, with ruddy complexion and a square jaw. "This is police business. You better start making sense, and fast."

"I just explained, officer. This is all about purchasing an automobile. Mr. Terrance Bowles there, the guy whose chest your foot is on, is about to purchase that Dodge delivery van from me. It's a fine truck, perfect for the service that this organization is starting. You're aware of the Black Panthers' project to feed the hungry people of Oakland. Can you imagine what good this will be for the community?"

"Are you out of your mind, son?" the officer asked. He stepped off Bowles and stepped toward me. When he did, Bowles sprang to his knees. The cop whirled back, his pistol in a two-handed grip. "Get the fuck back on the ground, you mothafucking, ni . .."

Bowles' hand shot into the air, palm out like he was bringing traffic to a halt. "Don't say it, cop or you'll have a war on your hands."

Brave, I thought, but not smart. This cop was no lover of Bowles' race and seemed to be itching to pull the trigger. Pop would have called the cop a *babbo*, Italian slang for a totally stupid person. Pop simplifies his prejudices to communists and fascists. Black, brown or yellow people are fine as long as they're car buyers and don't interfere with his life. Sweets complicated racial mixture doesn't faze him.

I was looking at the barrel of the pistol, but I needed to deflect the heat from Minister Bowles. "Officer, I'm a member of the city of Oakland's Chamber of Commerce and a member of the East 14th Street Lion's Club. I don't know the mayor, but I do know the Deputy District Attorney. We play cards together at Flynn's. You know Flynn's? Best Irish stew and chili in town. You know Detective Sergeant Jay Ness, well, he eats there. Great guy. Good friend. Anyway. . ." I stuttered "Anyway, like I was trying to explain. I put in a call to a reporter friend of mine for the Tribune. I told him I might have a story for him" Thinking of Bowles, I said, "See what I'm saying?"

Big cop's eyes squinted like a rattlesnake's.

Oddio, I might be in trouble.

I heard Pop's voice, *Quando si e in ballo, bisogna ballare,* which has sort of the same meaning as in for a penny, in for a pound. I forged ahead, "I'm trying to decide if I should follow with a call. If I'm not mistaken, I've heard your fellow officers use a bunch of racial slurs. I can't imagine you'd say something like that, you know, with the times changing the way they are, but if they did. Mind you, I'm not *saying* they did. But just *supposing* they did? As a citizen, I'd have to do something about it, right? And once it hit the papers, well, your supervisor probably doesn't like bad publicity. No, no, I wouldn't think so." I was on a roll, but I was also close to pissing my pants. *Have you ever done something totally out of character in your life, without a clue as to why?* That's what Victor Brovelli was doing.

By now the rest of the police officers, having finally managed to cuff all the Panthers, were staring at me as if I was one of the loonies panhandling on the streets. The commanding officer's ruddy complexion was turning ruddier as he stepped threateningly toward me. I took two steps back. With his free hand, he grabbed my sport coat and pushed me until I was backed up against a telephone pole, his nose very close to my face. He had a big nose and bloodshot eyes. His breath smelled like a cheap cigar. I pulled away and saw one of my coat buttons tear off in his hands. He threw it on the ground and grabbed me again. Another of my buttons bit the dust.

"You mind not mauling my sports coat?" I said.

"You better wipe that grin off your face, punk," he said, sounding like Father Barry, the principal of my high school who used to say the very same thing to me every time I was hauled into his office, minus the "punk."

"You wouldn't be related to Father Augustus Barry would you?" I asked.

"Are you messing with me, punk?"

"I'm sorry officer. I meant no disrespect. I smile when I'm nervous." The next thing I knew I was on the sidewalk holding my stomach, definitely not smiling, definitely gagging. Through the pain I could hear Bowles yelling for him to stop kicking me. I was struggling to catch my breath when I felt my left ear explode. I tried to look up, but the dark closed in around me.

CHAPTER 18
YOU'RE AN ANGEL

Night and day when united bring forth the beautiful light.
Victor Hugo

When I woke up, I was on a couch lying on my back looking up at the most beautiful face I'd ever seen. "Angel" I whispered.

"Say what?" the voice came from above but seemed from far away. I remembered being kicked. I touched my ear. It hurt. Then the voice again.

I shook my head. *The eyes, man oh man, those eyes,* two shades of green, the one on the left with a speck of amber in the iris. Her full lips curved like a bow. Skin, the color of caramel. Honest to God, it shone like a mirror. For a moment I thought I could see my face reflected in her complexion. Her afro looked like a dark halo.

"You're an angel," I said.

"Cop kicked you upside the head."

Whoever she was pressed something very cold and soothing against my ear. In my hazy memory I tried to recall if I'd ever seen a depiction of a non-Caucasian angel. Never an angel with an Angela Davis afro.

"Only angels look like you," I said.

She laughed and called out, "White man's awake and talking stupid."

From the next room, Terrance Bowles and a couple of Panthers about the size of Bekins moving vans appeared. Bowles was smiling; the moving vans were not.

"Pig hit you hard," Bowles said. "I'd go see an ear doctor just to be on the safe side. I got it in the ear once. Never did hear well out of it after that. How else you feeling?"

I didn't want to know about hearing loss. I told him that I'd had better days. He said welcome to the club, adding that black men hadn't seen better days for a long time. I didn't respond. What the hell did I know being a young Italian white guy talking stupid. Anyway, I guess he didn't care to hear what I knew about the conditions of America's Black community because he didn't elaborate. From the inside of his jacket pocket, he removed a checkbook and a pen.

"I'm ready to write you a check for the van. How much are you asking? I forgot what with all the action."

Nothing like a sale to shake the wobblies out of a car salesman's brain. "$1,600 plus tax and license," I said. "You come in tomorrow and sign all the papers."

"Deal," he said. "I'll be at your lot by ten a.m. to get the papers for the DMV. If you can find two more like this one, we'll buy them for fifteen hundred. Fleet price."

"Deal," I said. I was starting to like the Black Panthers Minister of Education.

"You know, I'll tell you a secret," Bowles said. "You screwed up a well-thought-out plan, but we won't hold it against you. What you did was stupid but brave, threating the po-lice like you done. They backed down and even apologized."

I wasn't sure I wanted to know about the plan, but asked anyway.

My angel, who Bowles had introduced as Sister Agbo, answered. "We'd been warned ahead of time that the Station Defense Team was going to hit our office today. We was all planning to be arrested. We also figured the pigs don't pay any attention to the rules and would smack us around some. The newspapers wouldn't believe us if we accused them of brutality. We could have stashed a newsman with a camera on the roof but news folks get written off as liberals. We decided a white upstanding civilian, you know, Lion's Club and all the shit, would be better. Plus, we was pretty sure that you'd mention what the van was going to be used for, right? Good publicity on every level. Can you dig it?"

Talk about being manipulated, I thought. "So you didn't really want to buy the van?"

"Not true," she said. "We *were* looking for transportation for our Feed the Hungry project. To do it this way made it seem more natural just in case the newspapers started poking around. Like, hey, we didn't bring whitey in as a witness, he was here on legit business."

"Anyway, it's all done with," Bowles said. "Not exactly the way we planned, but what the hell. Couple of my men tell me you make good barbeque on Saturdays. Maybe I'll swing by for some chicken."

"From an old Italian recipe," I said.

Bowles laughed. "One more thing, Brovelli, The Black Panthers owe you one." He lifted one finger in the air, so I couldn't mistake one meant one and no more. "You need help, you give me a call. The Black Panthers are men of honor."

My pop would have loved to hear that. But some of the guys down at the tavern, who didn't have a lot of good to say about the Panthers, would definitely be skeptical.

"Call me Victor," I said.

He nodded, "Victor it is."

My stomach was aching, and there were Bells of Saint Mary's ringing in my ears, but what the hell, I'd sold a car, made a nice profit, and it couldn't hurt to be on the good side of the Black Panthers, at least as far as a white guy could be in Oakland during these racially troubled times. I thanked Terrance Bowles for his business. Bowles wrote me a check. He removed the glove on his right hand and held it out. We shook, then he and his men left the room.

Once they were out of hearing range, I looked at my angel and blurted out, "Is there any chance you date white guys?" She shook her head like I was crazy. The way things were going, I was beginning to believe I was.

• • •

It took me a while to shake the cobwebs, and the ringing in my ears began to subside. I figured I wouldn't need to go to see an ear doctor. I called Vincent from the BPP headquarters and briefly explained what happened. His reaction was, "You can't be serious." I told him that I needed to rest and wouldn't be coming back to work. When I got off the phone, I thanked my ministering angel. She told me her first name was Adila, but Dila would do. I said that Victor would do. I thought I recognized the beginning of a smile. I was about to leave, when she asked me how I was getting home, since the van was now the property of the Black Panthers.

"Is there a bus stop nearby?"

"You better let me give you a ride, Victor," she said, putting a little emphasis on my name. "The way things are shaking out in these parts, you might run into a few resentful brothers. And you're not big enough to back anybody off."

"You might be surprised," I said, raising my right arm and flexing my muscle.

"Yeah, well, best not to find out. Let's get a move on," She drawled. "Some of my male co-workers be getting nervous 'bout you being here. You don't want to over-stay your welcome."

Heaven forbid, I thought.

She handed me my sports coat with its missing nautical buttons. Damn, I loved those buttons. She grabbed a shawl and threw it over her shoulders. She was wearing a purple dress that modestly covered her knees. Her legs I could tell were long and slender. There were red scrapes on the side of her legs that had probably happened when she was knocked down by the cops. Purple toenails peeked out from her leather sandals. As we left the office, two Panthers got out of a Yellow Cab, and headed our way. They hailed Dila and kept walking past us and into the office. Not a nod in my direction, as if a white man strolling out of their headquarters with a black woman was an everyday occurrence.

"Wasn't that Bobby Seale and Little Bobby Hutton?" I asked. Their photographs had been all over the papers recently.

"Yep," she said casually like they were just a couple of next-door neighbors dropping in for lunch instead of arguably two of the most polarizing men in the United States.

Dila led me around the corner where her car was parked, a 1964 two-tone red and black Ford Galaxy. The paint looked a bit faded. I opened the door on the passenger side. Staring at me was a rifle propped up on the seat. It looked like it belonged in the hands of a Viet Cong guerrilla fighter.

"Put it on the back seat," She said. "Be careful; it's loaded."

"Really, you want me to handle a loaded weapon?"

"Oh, for goodness sake," she said.

She reached over, lifted the cannon with one hand and placed it on the back seat. I got in.

"What kind of rifle is that thing?" I asked.

"An M1 30 caliber carbine."

"You know how to use that?"

"Why not? It's light weight and easy to handle."

My Angel suddenly felt a little less like a ministering angel and more like an urban guerilla angel. She started the engine, shifted into low and took off.

"What is the Station Defense Team, anyway?"

"Po-lice hit men, as far as I'm concerned. For the record, they're highly trained rapid response unit, go anywhere there's trouble sometimes on their own, sometime to help other pigs. Whole idea started with the LA fuzz and caught on."

Giving all the chaos going on, it sort of made sense, but what they were doing, beating up on women didn't sound like good law enforcement. They looked like a bunch of thugs to me. We drove for a while in silence. On the floor at my feet was a copy of *Plato's Republic*. I picked it up.

"Interesting reading," I said, thinking how weird – Plato and a loaded rifle.

"Required reading. Huey gave all of us copies. He explained reading it saved his life. I'm struggling."

"Huey Newton read *The Republic*," I said incredulously.

"He was illiterate as a teenager. He learned to read by reading Plato."

I felt myself frowning.

"What?" she said. "Are whites the only people with intelligence?"

It was said as a challenge, but I didn't bite. I figured, Dila Agbo was not someone I'd wanted to tangle with verbally. I was also thinking that her grammar and vocabulary had improved since we left the Panther office, but thought it best to keep this observation to myself.

"No, that wasn't what I meant at all," I said. "I went to college with a lot of Negros." Which wasn't exactly true. Most of the black guys at the college during my four years were members of the basketball team.

"Negroid is a race like Caucasian," Dila said. "We don't talk about you whites, like, you know, I went to school with a lot of Caucasians. You're a White; I'm a Black. You understand? If you want, you can refer to us as African-Americans, you know, like you're an Italian-American."

I felt foolish because I knew that. In my senior year in college, I'd attended a forum about cultural diversity and racial sensitivity. Vincent had said it would be a snore but do what I wanted. Our star basketball player Ty Manning, who lived in our dorm and I liked a lot, had spoken. I remembered he was very specific that the only way to say the N word, which was highly offensive to people of his race, was to call it by its first letter. It made sense to me. If someone in those days had called Vincent and me dagos that was fighting talk. I didn't think I'd changed, so why wasn't I bothered by Body calling me a dago all the time and driving me crazy with his stupid Italian jokes? Perhaps because I countered by calling him a fucking mick. As if it balanced out. Ty hadn't been as adamant about the use of the word, Negro. Ty had explained it pretty much the way Dila had. As far as I could remember, the N word had never crossed my lips, even when I was young and didn't know better. And I certainly wouldn't want to be called a Caucasian.

"I understand completely," I said. "You won't hear Victor Brovelli use the term again."

Dila made a *hrumph* sound and flipped on the radio. Stevie Wonder came on singing, "Hey Love" . I wasn't familiar with the song, but Stevie Wonder's voice was an original. I opened *The Republic* and a theater playbill fell out. It listed four performances of *Othello* at the Wee Globe, a little theater on Shattuck Avenue. Adila Agbo was playing the role of Emilia, the wife of the villain, Iago. A *Black Panther chick?* Interesting, I thought. I folded the program and stuck it in my pocket.

On an angelic scale of 1 to 10, Dila was a 12. Her broad cheekbones were divided by a straight nose below which were full, sensual lips. Her chin was strong. She wore a gold link necklace around a long slender neck. Her Afro was fashioned in the style made popular by Angela Davis, a political activist whose picture seemed to be constantly in the news. Davis was attractive but couldn't hold a candle to my chauffeur.

Then, there were those eyes. "You into acting?" I asked.

"Yes, how'd you know?"

"Saw the playbill for Othello."

"Yeah," she said.

That's all she said. "You sure you don't date Italians?" I asked.

"I said I didn't date white guys, didn't I, and unless your mirror is telling you something different, guess what color your skin is?"

It occurred to me that I was making a fool of myself trying to hit on a black chick, a Black Panther chick, for God's sake, who probably loathed the white race. But something inside me said: *Go on, Brovelli, when it comes to women, you're an expert at making a fool of yourself; it's part of your DNA.*

For a couple of minutes I listened to Stevie sing, then I said, "Most Italians are hardly white, you know. My Mom and Pop are from Naples in the south. They're more brownish." I pulled up the sleeve of my jacket and held my wrist up so she could see without taking her eyes off the road. "Look, that's not a tan; that's original skin color."

"So, can I tell the brothers Italians from the south of Italy are descended from Africans?"

I hesitated enough that she gave a little snorting laugh. "I thought so. How'd you get that scar on your face?"

"Got hit by a baseball."

"Do you know that the Betamaribe tribe in Benin scar their children to insure their ancestors' protection and good health? That's the tribe my daddy's family came from."

"I don't see any scars," I said.

"And you won't," she said.

I was suddenly feeling encouraged, her talking about family. Maybe I was getting somewhere. "Scarring you would have been a tragedy," I said.

"Not if you were an African male."

"I'm an American male, and your face couldn't be more beautiful," I said.

"Hrumph," she said.

I thought the hrumph sounded friendlier than the previous hrumph, so I ventured, "Back to the subject of skin color. Now that I've proven Italians are brown, how about a date?"

"Brown is also the color of bullshit, too, you know," she said.

So much for feeling encouraged. "I give up," I said.

But I really hadn't. This was not a woman I'd give up on without exerting greater effort. The Brovelli boys are nothing if not stubborn. In this case, I should say Brovelli boy, singular. I couldn't see Vincent ever dating a black chick. As for Pop, even with his simplistic idea of race, if he thought I had *una raggazza nero*, a black girlfriend, he'd go ape-shit.

Stevie Wonders' song ended. The broadcaster came on reminding the radio audience that Doctor Martin Luther King Jr had spoken to sanitation workers in Memphis. Dila turned up the sound. We listened as the guy behind the mic tried his best to do justice to Doctor King's voice. I'd heard the *I Had a Dream* speech. If Father O'Quinn had that kind of a voice, I might have paid attention to his sermons. The broadcast ended, and Dila turned off the radio. "Oh, dear," she said. I had a feeling she wasn't looking for any commentary from her white passenger.

Vincent and I had spent some time in this part of Oakland repo'ing cars, but never paying too much attention to the surroundings. I stared out the window at the houses, some in dire need of repair, some well-kept, many of them with bars on the windows and chain link fences around the yards, some of them with lawn and flowers, others overgrown by weeds. Graffiti decorated fences and walls of buildings none of which I could decipher. Some looked ominous, with black curlicues and angles and arrows, and others looked more benign, artistic even with swirls of primary colors that reminded me of a botanical garden my uncle had forced me to see when I visited him in Florida. There were lots of anti-war posters and recruiting posters for SNCC, the Black Panthers and the Nation of Islam, more commonly called Black Muslims. On the same wall with the Nation of Islam poster was another one that was clearly old, dating back to 1967 of the Cassius Clay vs Sonny Liston Heavy weight title bout. Clay was now Muhammed Ali and a member of the Nation of Islam. Ali had been banned from boxing in 1967 for refusing to go in the Army. This neighborhood was familiar to the Brovelli Boys. We sold cars to people who lived here. I shouldn't have been surprised by its crummy condition, but I found myself wincing at the numerous signs of poverty and neglect. When I was little and my father wanted me to pay attention, he'd grab me by the ear, and say, "You listening, boy." I suddenly felt like someone was holding me by the ear. We passed a large sign board that read YOU DON'T HAVE TO LIVE IN THE DARK TO BE COLORBLIND.

"You know," I sighed. "I'm one of the people too."

My Angel laughed - more like a scoff, "You're a rich college kid, what do you know?"

"In Italy, my pop was poor as dirt."

"In Benin, my ancestors were rich traders."

That shut me up. I went back to looking out the window at a neighborhood the city of Oakland had forgotten, trying to remember if I knew where Benin was located on a map of Africa. *Madonna*, how many people in the United States knew anything at all about Africa? I sure as hell didn't. We drove past McClymonds High School. Any sports fan in the Bay Area was acquainted with McClymond's legendary athletic history, having produced the likes of Bill Russell, the great Boston Celtic star and a number of major league baseball greats, like Vada Pinson and Curt Flood. I recalled the time my high school played a baseball game at McClymonds and how nervous some of our team was including me as our bus stopped in front of the school and all around us were black faces.

At the Fruitvale Ave turnoff, I directed Dila to my apartment. She parked, and I hesitated getting out. Maybe something would happen. A kiss would be too much to hope for, but maybe a handshake. She didn't move. I thanked her for icing my ear and for driving me home. She looked at me and arched one eyebrow as if she didn't know what I was talking about. I got out of the car. Before I closed the door, she said, "Good luck," then drove off.

I didn't know why she'd wished me good luck unless she knew something I didn't. Considering the times in which we lived, given that I'd probably made enemies of a bunch of mean-ass cops and consorted with a black urban terrorist organization, I'd take any luck that came my way. I keyed my front door, took off my sport coat and trudged exhausted up the stairs to my apartment. Inside, I headed straight for the couch.

I thought of Dila. I closed my eyes.

In my dream I was surrounded by women, each one had a different skin color: white, brown, black and yellow, but also blue, red, green, and orange. They were dancing nude, their arms twisting like snakes. The motion and color was hypnotic, as if I was staring into a kaleidoscope. I asked a beautiful chartreuse skinned babe what planet I was on. She said something that sounded like chlorophyll. I asked her if she dated Caucasians. I woke up before her answer.

CHAPTER 19
AMATEUR GUMSHOE

April is the cruelest month.
T.S. Elliot

The next morning, driving to work, I was still puzzling over Dila. *So, Brovelli, you'd been hitting on a Chinese chick just a couple of days ago, why not a black chick?* I didn't have a good answer for that. It couldn't only be race. No male in his right mind would turn down a date with Dorothy Dandridge, one of Hollywood's' beauties. Beautiful is beautiful. Perhaps it was the times. For a lot of white people, blacks seemed dangerous, particularly activist ones. I'd dated a Japanese girl in college and taken flak from my buddies. My mother had cautioned me nicely that perhaps the young woman's family would object. I think Mom meant our family. I wasn't being a liberal when I told her I could think for myself. But soon after, I broke up with her. I'd always worried that I did because she was Japanese.

Italians are not known for being racially progressive - not the descendants of the Roman Empire that at one time ruled the known world. Pop held a unique view of races. Pop had taught us to think of people as customers. There were good customers and bad customers. Good customers you treated well. Bad customers you shunned. We Brovelli boys bought into Pop's stripped-down view of humanity at a young age. It was not profound and, had I expressed it in college in my Philosophy class, the professor would have laughed me out of the room. The question remained, however, if was to become engaged to a good customer who happened to be black, I knew how Pop would feel about that. How would our mom feel? I wasn't certain.

I drove on to the lot and parked the car next to my brother's wheels. I was excited to tell Vincent about the Black Panthers willing to buy two more vans. Should I tell Vincent about Dila, I wondered. Probably not. Vincent's view of Negroes had become more negative lately. I stopped my thoughts and reversed gears. I could hear Dila scolding me: *Blacks or Afro-Americans, but not Negroes.* No, I thought, better to keep Dila to myself. And I wouldn't mention her to Flynn or Ness either, even though they were close friends, and in the past we'd shared problems and conundrums. Flynn's jokes were equal-opportunity racist, and Ness' views on race were liberal, but being a cop these days, I wouldn't blame him if he was feeling a bit overwhelmed by the subject of race. Maybe I could talk to Larry Hughes. Being African-American, Larry might give me some tips how a white guy could approach a black woman. Nah, Larry might take offense. I would have to figure out this *complicazone del coure* on my own. Maybe I should just cool it for a while. It might not even be a complication of the heart. Not yet, at least.

I turned the corner to the office. Vincent was standing at the door pointing toward one corner lot where an old man was inspecting cars and to the opposite corner at a couple standing by a 1955 Pontiac station wagon. I nodded, and headed in the direction of the old man, slipping on the blazer I was carrying over my arm. I straightened my tie, a navy blue one with little gold fleur-de-lis. Vincent, already attired in his blazer, took the couple. We were wearing the same white shirt, gray wool slacks, and loafers. Same tie, if you can believe it. Believe it. It's not unusual that we show up to work wearing exactly the same clothing. The blazer is a sort of uniform, but the rest of the wardrobe choices are the result of the vibe twins share. The only difference is Vincent accessorizes better. Today, he'd opted for a shirt with French cuffs. The cufflinks were small gold fleur-de-lis.

I introduced myself. The potential customer said his name was Marvin Rothstein. His face was wrinkled, and he wore spectacles with thick lenses. He was wearing a dark blue and silver checkered sports coat over a crisp yellow shirt, tucked into sharply-creased charcoal wool slacks. At his neck was a powder blue silk ascot. His shoes were black loafers with tassels. Very spiffy, if a bit loud. It occurred to me that maybe selling him a car might be risky, considering his age. I figured him to be somewhere in the eighties. I wouldn't want to be arrested as an accessary to a vehicular homicide. If I'd voiced this concern to Vincent, he'd have said, "*Che cosa?* You're already an accessory to murder."

And I would have answered, *What's this "you"? It's about "us."*

And he would have said, *Oh yeah, oh yeah.*

The old man was too busy inspecting the interior of a 1967 Ford Fairlane sedan, so he didn't hear me laugh for no apparent reason. I asked him what kind of car he was looking for, which led to a long explanation of his automotive needs. He knew a lot about engines, so I decided he was a legit buyer and turned on the old Brovelli charm. It took an hour and three test drives before he settled on a 1960 white Chrysler Imperial with Alaska Blue interior, a car he said would impress his dollies. I handed the ancient Don Juan over to Sylvia for the paperwork.

In the meantime, Vincent sold the International Travelall to the couple. Can I tell you how relieved I was to get that reminder of Winona's dead body off the lot? *Bye, bye ghost.* Now all we needed to do was sell the Impala.

I'd missed breakfast, and I was starving. By eleven-thirty I told Vincent I was going to Flynn's. It was Friday. Flynn would be serving Boston clam chowder with crusty French bread. Traffic on East 14th was moving at a snail's pace. Over the last couple of years, I'd noticed drivers were becoming increasingly impatient. A newspaper article recently had predicted that the Bay Area by the turn of the century would be more difficult to drive in than New York City, something I found hard to believe. As if to prove me wrong, a Dodge D-100 pickup slammed into the back of a Sunset Garbage truck, blocking traffic. Horns started blowing and people yelling and cursing. It was turning into a fight. This was not just about traffic. It was the times. I swear, average people without a cause, right or left, were frustrated and on edge, frightened of losing their dependable middle-of-the-road lives to hippies. I ducked into the tavern. Flynn's was empty except for two guys in overalls, sitting at the bar drinking beer and shaking dice. I asked Body if the chowder was ready. He nodded and disappeared into the back. He appeared carrying a bowl and a mug of Anchor Steam. He stood back from the bar, withholding my food and drink, looking at me, smiling his half-ass smile.

"Tell me the Goddamn joke and get it over with Body. I'm hungry."

He placed the bowl and mug in front of me. "Victor, me boyo, what do you call an Italian with his hands in his pockets?"

I shrugged.

"A mute."

I usually don't laugh at Body's stupid jokes, but this one was pretty right-on. I told Body and he expressed regret that he hadn't offended me. He promised to do better next time.

The chowder looked delicious, creamy with a tab of butter in the center. I'd just started my meal when my friend Detective Sergeant Jay Ness showed up, slapped me on the back and sat down next to me. Jay had made sergeant and been transferred to our precinct about the time Vincent and I took over Pop's business. He and a few other cops were regulars at Flynn's.

"How's the amateur gumshoe?" he asked.

"I'm waiting on my license, then you might as well look for a job since I'll be solving all your homicides for you."

Jay gave a fake ho, ho, ho and said, "Your buddy, Sweets, has got his dick in a wringer this time for sure."

"You're telling me. My pop is very concerned." Jay never liked Sweets, but unlike Sylvia, he had a valid reason. Before being promoted to homicide, he'd been assigned to the Oakland PD's robbery division, and Sweets was a burglar who'd avoided being caught. Robbers that get away with robbery are not popular with the robbery dicks. *Dicks, that's P.I. slang for detectives.* Jay always told us that Sweets would finally do something stupid, and they'd put the Birdman in a cage.

Jay ordered chowder and said, "I would never have pegged Sweets as a killer, but I've been a cop long enough to know better than be shocked by human behavior."

"Nobody in the neighborhood believes it," I said, "except Sylvia."

"How *is* your fair secretary?" Jay asked.

Sunny Badger was Jay's rival for the affection of our fair secretary, not that Sylvia would consider either one of them. Sergeant Jay Ness, twice divorced and presently single, had been making moves for the last month or two. Sylvia explained it wasn't that he was ugly, it was that he was a cop. I figured her disinterest was caused by an allergy passed down from mafia family to mafia family. If I'd told her that, she'd have slapped me. For as long as I can remember, our family has been joking around about Sylvia's daddy being Mafioso. It really pisses Sylvia off.

I said. "You know, Sylvia doesn't wear any panties?"

"Why are you telling me this?"

"Because she was just talking about you. You should ask her out one of these days."

"You asshole," Jay said, "I've asked her out a dozen times, and she's turned me down flat and you know it. You Brovelli's like to stir things up. I should write you a ticket for being a trouble maker."

Body brought the chowder and his usual beer mixed with ginger ale. Sounds disgusting, but it's not too bad. We ate and drank quietly. Body repeated his Italian joke. Jay said he'd have to write him a ticket for telling bad jokes. Saying he's going to write somebody a ticket is one of Jay's favorite witticisms.

I ordered another beer and a second for Jay. He took a long drink and sighed.

"I know you can't talk about open investigations, Jay, but just between you and me, you know, old poker mates and all, what's the evidence you guys have on Sweets for Arabella's murder."

"We have his prints in the woman's apartment."

"On a gun?"

"We haven't recovered a weapon. But ballistics confirmed it's the same caliber as the one that killed Winona, a 22. And the bullets that killed Winona and Arabella were fired from the same gun."

"How the hell do they know that?" I asked.

"Since you're a hot-shot P.I., I figured you'd know," Jay said.

"I'm a car salesman, Jay, damn it. Come on, stop being a jerk."

Body leaned across the bar. "I'll tell you, Victor. The inside of every pistol barrel has its own kind of scratches and marks that are left on the bullet as it's fired through the barrel. If the scratches and marks on the bullets are identical that means the bullets were fired from the same gun."

"How come you know that?" I asked.

"In Ireland, me da was a cop."

"Is he still a cop or retired?" Ness asked.

"Himself took a bullet when I was seven trying to stop a robbery. After that me and ma came to America."

"Where did you live?" Jay asked.

"Dublin. It was a big city, lots of crime in certain parts."

"Getting back to the subject, aren't .22's sort of weeny guns?" I asked.

"Ladies and contract killers," Jay said. "Bullet goes in, doesn't come out, bounces around making mashed potatoes out of the brain."

I gagged on my chowder. "Okay, so bullets came from the same gun, but you still don't have the gun. What else did you find besides Sweet's prints?"

Can't tell you, but forensics said the fingerprints were crystal clear."

"So what? All that proves is Sweets was in Arabella's apartment."

"We've got other evidence."

"Like Winona's diaries?"

Jay looked surprised. "What are you talking about? What fucking diaries?"

I'd blurted it out, so I had to fess up about the possibility of Winona keeping a daily diary, and that I'd been at Arabella's apartment hoping she'd found it.

"Of for Christ's sake, Victor, you can't just go around withholding information. That's obstruction. I could arrest you. I *should* arrest you."

"Look, I didn't ask for the information. When I talked to Arabella at work, she said she'd call me if she thought of anything important."

"And you didn't think of informing me, you stupid dago?"

"I would have, I promise." In the world of lies, it was a mere venal sin and confession would easily take care of it. "So, did you find the diaries?"

"Diaries? More than one? Come on, Victor. Cough up the truth."

"According to Sweets, Winona has a bunch of diaries. You haven't found any?"

"No, we haven't, but I guess we'll have to start looking. Jesus, Brovelli, you're such a screw up. You've put me on the spot, you know."

"Look, I'm sorry, what can I say? Go ahead and arrest me."

"Fuck you, Victor. You know I'm not going to do that."

I did know that, so I pushed our friendship a little further. "You said you guys have other evidence against Sweets?"

"You have some nerve. Don't ask me to reveal shit, Victor, my lieutenant would kick my ass back to walking the beat. He's so stressed out anyway with what's happening to this town. Ask Sweets' lawyer. The DA has to share all evidence with the defense, but as a bona fide PI you'd have known that."

"Of course I knew. I was just testing you."

Jay gave me the old ho, ho, ho. He signaled Body to give him his check.

"It's on the Brovelli Boys' Used Cars," I said.

"Thank you kindly, Victor, but you can't bribe more information out of me."

"Right," I said. "Good luck." For you and me, I thought.

"The way things stand in the Bay Area," Jay said, "It's total chaos.

There's a march being organized at Laney College, and you all know what's happening on the Berkeley campus. I'm actually getting used to the smell of tear gas."

Body said. "Almost as bad as the *fooking* Orange Men."

Jay, and I and the rest of the guys sitting at the bar groaned.

"We're going to start putting all the trouble-makers in the slammer," Jay said. "That means cat burglars as well as pinko demonstrators."

"Sweets is not a cat burglar according to my P.I. manual. He doesn't go into house where someone is home, creepy shit like that."

"Cat or not," Jay said, "The Commies will be joining your buddy in prison."

"You got it right, Jay," a disembodied voice out of the dark end of the bar hollered, "Goddam Commies."

Another voice chimed in, "Deport all the fuckers to Russia, that's what I say."

"Yeah, love it or leave it," another voice chimed in.

With the Vietnam War going, there were lots of those bumper stickers around. I didn't doubt that things were coming to a head in the Bay Area – and just about everywhere else in the country. You could feel the tension in the air. Berkeley, home to the University of California, Oakland, San Francisco, South Bay, all the way to San Jose, cities and suburbs were smoldering with civil unrest. Our Hollywood actor turned Governor was talking about placing the California National Guard on alert. In other states, the guard had already been called out to help local law enforcement contain some of the larger anti-war protests. The previous day there'd been the national draft-card-turn-in and burning in Boston. Fifteen thousand protestors showed up. My older brother Mario had flown out and thrown his Purple Heart into the fire. His picture was in the paper front page. Pop saw it and stopped speaking to him. Mario lost his hand in the war, which gives him credibility to protest despite what our pop thinks.

Anti-war sentiments were not limited to the United States. Two days ago, I read in the paper there'd been a firebombing in Frankfurt, Germany, and all sorts of violent protests in merry old England. Lately I'd been avoiding reading the newspaper because all the news seemed to be either about the war or civil rights. It's not that I'm uninterested, but Vincent and I have other priorities. The front page of this morning's Tribune was all about Doctor Martin Luther King Jr's speech to the sanitation workers of Memphis, in which he'd said he'd been to the top of the mountain and seen the other side, or something like that. Was he predicting his death? Maybe I should have read the whole speech, so I could impress my black angel how *au courant* I was when the next time we meet. And I'd be damned if we wouldn't meet again. This last thought came to me out of nowhere. Yeah, by God, I thought, there was something special about that woman.

"I wouldn't mind sending Sweets to the Soviet Union," Jay said, interrupting my thinking.

Lumping Sweets in with all the radicals was a little on the extreme side, and I told him.

"He killed a woman; they're killing America," Jay said. "Killing is killing."

Madonna, I thought, Jay was losing it.

"Hell, Jay, Sweets is way too much of a coward to shoot anybody," Body said.

"Yeah," I agreed. "He cut his finger once and fainted at the sight of his own blood."

"True enough, boys, but everybody has a dark side. It just requires the right set of circumstances to trigger the violence. Let me give you bleeding hearts an example. Last week, we got a call from the Christ the Savior Lutheran Church. The good padre had stabbed his music director ten times in the heart."

"I guess he got to the heart of the matter," Body said.

"Ha, ha, and ho, ho, you dumb Mick. You wouldn't be making jokes if you saw the body. The minister was sitting calmly in his study, reading the Bible. He offered us tea, tea, for God's sake."

"Some of those Prossi hymns would drive a music lover crazy," Body said. "Give me a good Catholic boys' choir any day."

"I don't want to hear about boys choirs," Jay said. "We got a Catholic padre behind bars for fiddling one of his choir boys." He shook his head sadly. "I got to get going. Thanks for picking up the tab, Victor. I'll see you tonight for poker."

There was a playbill laying in the top drawer of my desk. "Sorry, Jay, I'm going to see *Othello* at the Wee Globe."

"That's about the black guy married to a white chick, right?" Body asked.

"About sums it up," I said, deciding not to be sucked into discussing inter-racial relationships. "Since I won't be playing, Jay, it'll give you a chance to win some money finally."

"Oh yeah, I should arrest you for being a wise ass."

• • •

Carter Innis, Sweet's lawyer, Gaels' class of '62 told me to be at the Alameda County jail by two-thirty. I made it exactly on time. The visiting room was divided in half by a long table with benches running down both sides of it and a foot-high bullet proof glass divider running lengthwise down the center of the table. Visitors and prisoners talked by telephones. At the end of the table was an attorney whispering to his client. The muscles of the inmate's arms bulged and stretched the sleeves of his shirt. I didn't like thinking of Sweets locked up with such behemoths. We moved to the other end of the table and sat down. I'd never seen a place so dismal. There were cracks in the puke green walls that looked like webs spun by stoned spiders. A guard sat on a stool next to the door reading a newspaper.

Sweets was escorted in by a guard that looked like he was an understudy for King Kong. Jean Lafitte's ancestor was looking decidedly un-pirate-like in his oversized faded blue prison garb that hung loosely on his slight frame, his hands cuffed in front of him. I listened to Carter explain the legal procedures he and Sweets would be going through in the near future. According to Carter, it looked as if Sweets might as well get used to his jail cell. There were so many arrests going on these days that judges were not inclined to be generous. Sweets' past record, his general rep, and the fact that he was under suspicion now for a double homicide was enough to keep him inside without bail. Carter apologized. Sweets nodded morosely. Carter laid out the facts working against his client, the evidence that Ness had refused to tell me. First, there were candy wrappers. Second, the candy wrappers had his fingerprints on them. Third, the cops had found a water glass half filled with vodka with his fingerprints on the glass. While Carter was talking Sweets kept shaking his head, his lips shaping round NO's like he was blowing smoke rings. Fourth, and most damning, Carter said, was that Arabella's neighbor across the hall, an old women with a rep for spying on her fellow residents, had peered through the peep hole in her door and seen a person in a raincoat, with odd looking blondish yellow hair, knocking on Arabella's door. Once Arabella let the person in, the old gal returned to her armchair in her living room and her TV. She was positive about the

odd scruff of blond hair sticking up on top of the cranium, the rest of the
golden locks hanging to either side. When Carter explained that the old gal
would place him at the scene of the crime, Sweets hung his head. Since no
murder weapon had been found, Carter explained to his despondent client
that fingerprints alone would not be enough circumstantial evidence, but
the old woman's description of him on the day and time of the murder was
extremely harmful. Sweets raised his head. He looked like he was about to
cry. I couldn't help feeling sorry for him. While Carter finished discussing
his next legal steps - mostly legal jargon - I tuned out and thought about Dila.
I replayed our conversation in the car. Those eyes. The way she looked at me
when she wished me good luck. I felt a hand of my shoulder. Carter was
looking down at me. "I'm done, Victor, He's all yours. I'll meet you outside."

The first thing I said to Sweets was, "You were lying to Carter when you
said you've never been in Arabella's apartment, weren't you?

"As God is my judge, Victor, I wasn't there. It wasn't me the old woman
saw. I swear."

"But you have been in her apartment haven't you? You dated her, and
you never told me. Tell me I'm wrong."

"Wrong, wrong. I was with Arabella only one time, and Winona was
with me."

I frowned at him and said nothing.

"Okay, maybe I was in her apartment a couple of times when I was
dating Winona, but that's it man. I never dated Arabella. I swear to God."

"So how do you account for all the candy wrappers? Those can't be
from some past visit. Arabella would have cleaned up your mess, unless
she doesn't do house cleaning."

"I have no idea how those candy wrappers got into her apartment."

"And tell me how do you account for the old gal describing you the way
she did?" I asked. "What other person do you know has bright yellow hair
and wears it sticking up like a cockatoo?"

"You don't have to be insulting, Victor."

"Answer the question you *ciuccio*."

"Look, everybody in Oakland knows what I look like. It would be easy
to make a wig."

"Ah, man. The police aren't going to buy that. It looks like the same
caliber bullet in Arabella's head is the same caliber bullet found in
Winona's head."

"You're not going to give up on me, are you Victor? I beg you, man. On my honor, I didn't kill anyone. Killing is gross." He paused for a moment, then leaned closer to me and whispered, Victor, I gotta tell you man, sometimes I see Winona."

I almost said, me too. Instead, I told him to calm down.

"No, no, mon frere. It's her fuckin ghost. She's all pale and shit."

"She black," I said.

"Yeah, but pale black."

"Jail is getting to you," I said. I wasn't about to admit to him Winona's ghost had haunted me too. Now that the Travelall was sold maybe she'd switched her haunting to Sweets.

"I'm telling you man, it's no fun sharing a cell with a criminal and a ghost."

"What the fuck, Sweets, you're a burglar. Doesn't that qualify you as a criminal?"

"It's a hierarchy thing," Sweets said.

"Yeah, I don't get it."

"The bottom rung of the ladder of crime is reserved for the pedophiles, the lowest of the low, a step up are the mass murderers, followed by other strata of murderers, after murderers going up the ladder come armed robbers. You see what I'm talking about?"

Sweet's logic was upside down. "Right, so you burglars are high up the ladder, close to heaven. I understand now."

"You're a smart dude, Victor. You're a college graduate. I'm counting on your smarts to get me off."

"Sweets, you need a real professional, a private investigator that knows what he's doing. I'm not licensed. All I know about detecting I'm learning out of a book and a novel."

"You know I can't afford a PI, Victor, and neither can your father."

The implication was clear. If I backed off, he calls Pop. Pop, of course, would come up with the money for a private investigator who'd suck his savings dry. And, there was always Sweet's threat to reveal our part in disposing of Winona's body. I sighed and threw out my arms.

"All right, all right. I'll keep on it." I sighed again. "I'm going to leave now, but you better not be lying about Arabella."

Sweets crossed his cuffed hands across his heart and swore on the grave of his saintly mother that everything that came out of his mouth was the absolute truth. "By the way," I said, "Detective Sergeant Jay Ness is going to be talking to you about Winona's diaries."

"I bet the killer was after the diaries. Why else would anyone want to kill Arabella?"

Sweets had to be right, I thought. I signaled to the guard that I was finished. I watched Sweets being led out, thinking of one of my Pop's Italian sayings: *There are three sides to every story, mine, yours and the truth.*

CHAPTER 20
NO WAY!!

Why must we always kill our prophets before we listen to them?
Jame Thompson, Pastor, West Branch, Iowa

It was four-thirty when I left the county jail. Friday traffic, which at this hour would normally be building up to serious congestion, was surprisingly light. I pulled into the lot and parked. Vincent was not in sight, so I went to the office. He and Sylvia were standing in front of the small black and white TV on the top of our file cabinet. They didn't turn around when I came in.

"What the hell's so important on the boob tube?" I asked

Neither of them moved, but Sylvia said, over her shoulder, "Someone shot Doctor Martin Luther King."

"No way," I said.

Vincent said. "Truth, bro. King was on the balcony of his motel in Memphis and some whacko from somewhere across the street shot him. Just happened. It's like the whole country has gone nuts."

I moved closer to the TV and the three of us watched and listened. Commentary after commentary, speculation after speculation. The news kept flashing back to earlier scenes on the motel balcony of Doctor Kings' entourage, some kneeling beside the fallen body, some pointing, some yelling, some weeping.

"Switch channels," I said. Vincent did. All the stations' commentators with their serious faces, their astonished faces, their grieving faces. Cameras occasionally switching from Memphis, panning to crowds of people in cities across the country looking confused or shocked or both. In Black neighborhoods already a gathering anger. One broadcaster said, it was like a shadow was cast over the country. I thought of Dila yesterday after hearing of Doctor King's speech and saying, "Oh dear." The way she'd said it, so surprisingly sad. Was she having some kind of premonition? For her sake and mine, I guess, I wished that I spent more time listening to his speech or reading about his movement. I felt suddenly ashamed.

Vincent kept repeating, *Mi fa cagare, mi fa cagare.*"

"It's awful," I repeated. The word *awful* seemed too slight to express the horror of Doctor King's murder. In Italian it sounded more tragic. President Kennedy and now Martin Luther King, Jr. I was surprised to feel tears welling in my eyes. Not that I didn't feel the tragedy, but, like a lot of young white guys, I wasn't into the social upheaval going on. The white dudes that did had beards and long hair. I never volunteered to do community serVictore. Up to now, life for Victor Brovelli was selling cars and maximizing pleasure. So, from where did this grief originate?

Vincent and I went back to work, but with little enthusiasm. We took our ups on the lot. Sylvia worked on the finances. I came back to the office and found Vincent sitting on the couch, his eyes closed, a rugby magazine from Australia open on his lap. Sylvia was standing by the coffee machine. I closed the door, sat down beside him, and slapped his knee, "Your ups."

"Not asleep, just thinking."

The sound of knocking startled us. The door opened, and Black Panther Minister of Education, Terrance Bowles, flanked by two men carrying rifles at port arms, entered. I imagined at any moment they'd swing the rifles into firing position. I imagined bullets erupting from the barrels. I imagined my flesh being torn apart. I imagined Vincent and me bleeding to death beneath Pop's poster of Naples, all because of some white Tennessee fucking racist. Because on this day vengeance seemed to me to be completely logical. There was no way I could make it to Sylvia's desk in time to get her Beretta before they shot us, if the frigging antique even worked. My voice stuck in my throat. Next to me, I could hear Vincent breathing heavily and Sylvia whispering the Hail Mary.

For a moment Bowles looked at us, perhaps rethinking his position vis-a-vis ducks in the gallery, then he said. "We stopped by to give you a little advice."

I could hear Vincent sigh with relief.

Sylvia whispered, "Jesus, Mary, and Joseph."

"I'm not going to ask you how you are, Mr. Bowles," I said.

"Good, and no need to offer condolences or crocodile tears. I just want to tell you that it would be a good idea if you white boys closed up shop for the day and headed home. And I mean this minute. If you get my drift."

And that is how Vincent wound up at the Oakmont Golf Course teeing-off, and I wound up parked in front of the Wee Globe Theater, looking up at the marquee that read **Closed Due to Death in the Family.**

to tell you that it would be a good idea if you while boss closed up shop for the day and headed home. And I mean this minute. If you get my drift." And that is how Cyrus wound up at the Oakmont Golf Course going off at ... I wound up parked in front of the War Globe Theatre, looking up the ranqlize ... at Chos ... all in the family,

CHAPTER 21

IN THE MIDST OF CHAOS

Love is the greatest healing energy.
Sai Baba

On the night of Doctor Martin Luther King Jr's assassination, with so many cities around the country rioting, I wound up in the arms of Renee Sorenson, which proved my theory that, in the midst of chaos, men and women seek simple comfort in acts of love. It also occurred to me later that I was with Renee to cushion my disappointment at not seeing Dila Agbo. But on that night I let thoughts of Dila go and concentrated on Renee.

Instead of the back seat of my Mustang, we had agreed on the Clairmont Hotel and its comfortable king-size bed. We spent the night together, practicing the art of comforting. It was not our usual passionate lovemaking. It was quiet and gentle. It was also necessary and, yes, it *was* comforting. Between us, there was a sweetness I'd never felt before. I don't recall why I was so in need of comforting. I was in college when JFK was shot, and I didn't remember my tears over the president's death. Perhaps it was all the violence of the last few years rushing together like speeding traffic at an intersection towards the inevitable collision in Memphis. I saw myself standing in the middle of the intersection holding up my hands like a traffic cop, even though I knew it would be no use.

When Renee woke up, she went straight for the TV. I preferred she not turn it on, suspecting the news would be grim, and I had just experienced enough grim.

The faces of the two newscasters, a man and a woman who looked as if they'd been up all night, could only be described as grim. The Bay Area, for the most part, remained free of the violence that was erupting all over the country in other cities. Numerous outbreaks of violence ranging from window breaking, fire bombing, looting, and fighting. Police were on the streets, and the National Guard was on alert. In Washington D.C., Chicago, and Baltimore and in many other cities around the country, Blacks were rioting. In Memphis, where the assassination had taken place, the riots were widespread despite Stokely Carmichael and SNCC's call for peaceful demonstrations.

The bad news drove us back to bed and into each other's arms where the news was always good. Surprisingly we didn't make love but fell asleep. Perhaps it was just the touching we needed. We woke up a couple of hours later. Stretched out on the bed, Renee smoked a cigarette. She sent a perfect white fluttery ring toward the ceiling. Pop's voice entered my mind: *Remember, Vittorio, goood sex makes bad troubles not so bad and leettle troubles disappear. I* couldn't remember how this goes in Italian. He'd given me this advice the day I graduated from high school assuming, perhaps, that I was a now a man and needed to know such manly things. As I looked at the dissipating smoke ring that was turning into separate Impressionist clouds, I recalled asking him if there was anything like bad sex? He'd laughed loud and hard, and I'd taken that to mean no.

Thinking of Pop reminded me of Sweets in jail and the promise I'd made to take care of the problem. I must have dozed off because when I opened my eyes, Renee was already dressed and in the front room, the T.V. back on.

"Robert Kennedy made a speech in Indianapolis," she yelled. "He quoted Aeschylus."

All the Greek playwrights blurred together in my mind. I couldn't remember anything he'd written. I remembered Plato's *Republic* in Dila's car. Where was she right now?

"I got to get to work," I yelled and climbed out of bed. I had to get to East 14th and see if our cars made it undamaged through the night.

By the time I was showered and dressed, Renee had ordered up coffee from the restaurant.

She handed me a cup. We sat of the sofa and watched the T.V. while we drank. I forced myself not to think of the tragic event of the previous day. There was no mention of riots in the Fruitville area of Oakland, but we'd been warned. The last bit of news we heard before we left our room was that the Siege of Khe Sanh, where over six thousand marines had been surrounded by the Viet Cong, had finally been broken. It was news my brother Mario, although a Vet Against the War, would be particularly pleased to hear.

I dropped Renee off at her dorm, got back onto Fruitvale Ave and drove south. It was a bright Sunny day, trees blossoming, flowers blooming, cheerful if it wasn't the setting for so much violence and grieving. Natural beauty in the midst of man-made ugliness reminded me of an afternoon on one of our family trips to Italy driving into Naples from the airport and having to slow down for an accident. There were people lying on the pavement bleeding and the vehicles looked like metal pretzels, and the lights of the ambulance were flashing, people walking around in a daze, and people weeping, but my vision was diverted to a field of sunflowers behind the wreckage extending as far as the eye could see, golden and full of life.

It was close to noon when I arrived at the lot expecting to see our office windows broken and cars missing or vandalized. Instead, there were Vincent and Sylvia standing outside drinking coffee as if it was a normal business day, our office was untouched, all our cars in place and unscathed.

Our neighbors had not fared as well. The picture windows of Discount Furniture were boarded up, so were the windows of Flynn's Tavern and the windows of Jitter's gas station.

The DoNut Hole next to Flynn's also had its windows broken and its siding covered with graffiti. Larry was outside sweeping up the glass. He waved his broom at me and gave me his usual broad smile, then continued sweeping. I wondered how he could smile with his store front damaged. When I had time, I'd drop by his place, buy him a beer, and get his take on what was going on from a black business man's perspective.

"It could have been worse," Sylvia said. "Not like in other cities."

"Parsegian came over when I got here," Vincent said, "wanting to know why the vandals had left our place alone. It was like he was accusing us of something."

"Fuck him," I said. "It's none of his business."

"The frigging liberals are going to destroy America," Vincent said.

"When did you become a Conservative?" I asked. "The liberals didn't touch our place, did they?"

"Not a good argument, bro. We lucked out. You helped the Panthers, and they owed you. Otherwise, my guess is we wouldn't have any inventory left. Carlton Motors lost five cars and six damaged beyond repair, good only for scrap."

"*Damn*," I said. "Bobby Carlton is a nice guy."

"Yeah, a broke nice guy," Sylvia said.

"Are you a fucking Republican too?" I asked.

"I've always been a Republican. My daddy is Republican. So are my uncles."

I was tempted to say something about Republicans deserving the support of the Mafioso, but held my tongue. "Yeah, well good for them," I said. "We're still in business, so let's get to work."

"That's what Sylvia and I have been doing while you've been running around being Pop's little helper, if you haven't noticed," Vincent said. "This morning despite all the crap I sold a car, and Sylvia got rid of the car her daddy gave her last week. She's rolling in dough."

"Really, you sold something in the middle of this chaos? Which one did you sell?" I asked.

"The '57 red and black Olds Fiesta Wagon.

I turned to Sylvia, "Good contract."

"Well. . ."

"Could have been better." Vincent said. "But Carl's good for it."

Carl's Sherz was a finance officer at one of our banks, and if Vincent vouched for a buyer, he always took his word. I don't know what Vincent has got on Carl, but it must be something juicy

"You want me to make the deposit?" I asked.

"No need," Sylvia replied. "I gotta make a deposit in my account too."

Sylvia went into the office and emerged a couple of minutes later holding her purse and our leather deposit pouch. She got in her Bug and drove away. I told Vincent I'd take the lot if he needed to catch up on paperwork. Before he left, I asked him how his golf game had gone.

"It was crap. Bogeyed six holes."

"Back to the grind." I said.

Vincent pointed to the office. "I've got to review our floor plan to see if we can buy more cars. I wouldn't be considering any more spending except we've had a pretty damn good three days of sales despite what's been going on. Might be a trend we should be paying attention to."

Like Rome burning down while the Brovelli boys fiddled?

I put the image out of my mind. Our flooring - meaning our line of credit - was two-hundred thousand dollars and Vincent was looking to increase it to half a mil. That sounds like a lot of money for a small used car lot, but it really isn't. One's inventory is collateral. The bank can't lose its investment as long as the cars we buy with their money are good cars. To insure that end, the banks send an inspector once a month to check the cars that we've bought using their line of credit. The inspector is very thorough. He checks under the hood and the odometer. He gets under the car and checks the drive train. He inspects the frame to see if there are any signs of an accident. A newly painted car always causes suspicion. The inspector would sign off on the cars that the bank would finance on a non-recourse contract and the ones they'd finance on a recourse contract. As many cars we'd been buying the past month, we were due for a visit.

I was walking among our cars, checking to make sure the storm of protest that had struck last night hadn't ruined any. Whether the Brovelli Brothers' Used Cars could survive future storms was another matter. For the time being, at least, the Black Panthers had marked the door posts and lintel of our office so that the fury passed over us and left us untouched.

CHAPTER 22
ANIMAL CONTROL

One good act of vengeance deserves another.
Sicilian adage

An hour after Vincent called the bank, he got the word that our line of credit was increased but only a hundred grand. Good enough. But it made me nervous. Perhaps the Car Gods might be playing a trick on us. The day we found Winona in the trunk of the Impala, the Brovelli Boys' business was in the red. Suddenly we were heading for the black, and the banks were looking upon us favorably.

As I was pondering the reasons for this good fortune, Sylvia returned, walked into the office and threw our bank book on her desk, then her own.

"You want to bet which has more money in it?" She asked, smugly. You want to increase sales, all you got to do is let me buy in. My daddy's connections can really help us."

"No offense, cousin, but we're not interested in partners."

"Is it because I'm a woman?"

"Not at all, Sylvia. Women can be good salesmen, but they're better off selling cosmetics."

If looks could kill, I'd be keeping company with Winona.

"Only joking. Only joking," I yelled as she squinted her eyes and balled her fist.

• • •

It had been some time since the Brovelli twins had spent any time together on the lot. We took off our blazers and pulled on cover-alls. I put on some Carpenter tunes and cranked up the loudspeakers. We took an hour washing our cars and wiping them down, ever mindful of Pop's belief that first appearances, like a business man's wardrobe, was an important part of salesmanship. I took one side of the lot, Vincent the other. We met in the middle. Jitters came over from the gas station. We started talking about carburetors, but switched to the riots and damage to businesses along East 14th and elsewhere in the Fruitvale neighborhood. Most of the damage had occurred below MacArthur Boulevard. Jitters went back to work and so did we. I took the lot, and Vincent took the paperwork. The weather was a typical non-weather Bay Area day, fog in the early morning, followed by skies of pastel blue, followed by pastel gray, followed by a scattering of blue in the afternoon. Temperature somewhere in the 60's. But the day had a different feel, like our cities by the bay were experiencing a hangover. I couldn't imagine we'd get any paying customers, but surprisingly toward the end of the day, Vincent sold one of our best, a midnight blue 1966 Olds Toronado with custom rims. It had a 425 cu in V-8 engine with 385 horses and was one of the first cars with front wheel drive. 1966 was a historic safety year in the auto industry. Lots of new government requirements like non-rupturing gas tanks and hoses, collapsible steering wheels, four-way flashers, and standard bumper heights and a bunch more that raised the price of cars. As used car dealers we didn't have to worry about the cost of new technology, but new car dealers were grumbling about socialism.

Vincent and I were happy for the sale, but were a little sentimental about the loss of the Olds, a car that we'd often placed on our center platform to attract passersby, kind of like good looking chicks' casino owners provide free chips to attract guys to sit down and lose their money.

After helping with clean-up, I told Vincent that I needed to go to Alameda County jail before visiting hours ended. When he asked why, I told him I needed to talk to Sweets. He shook his head sadly. I left without going into details. I wouldn't need much time with Sweets to get what I needed.

The guard brought Sweets in. The burglar looked worse than the last time I saw him. "You look like shit," I said.

"I feel like shit. The food is shit. I'm surviving on candy."

Sweets asked me if I had anything good to report. My answer was you gotta be kidding. "You don't get the news in here?"

"Yeah, Martin Luther King was murdered, and my people are rioting."

"Your people? When have you ever acknowledged your African heritage, you dickhead?"

"Doesn't matter, Victor. The brothers in here have accepted me as one of their own." He paused, gave me a wink. "In here, Blacks are in the majority. Prison is an entirely futuristic social order."

I reminded him first that this was not quite San Quentin and, in any case, the wardens and guards were mostly whites.

"Don't be naïve, dude; it's the inmates that control what really goes on in here, you dig?"

I dug all right, like maybe his grave, and changed the subject. I explained what I needed. He thought awhile, then thought some more.

"I'm getting old waiting," I said.

"Patience, my man, patience. A master brain at work here." He paused and looked at me to see if I was going to make a snide comment on the status of his brain.

"Okay," he said. "The glass removal won't work, but there is a way to get in through a sky light, so that's your best bet. You'll need one of my tools. My tool kit is in your apartment under the sink. You'll find a couple of half inch and quarter inch wide metal bars of different lengths about the thickness of a credit card. Take all of them with you and use the one that will extend from the edge of the skylight where there's a rubber seal. You can jiggle the bar through the seal. Once you get it through, move the bar so you can hook the latch. We already know that Parsegian doesn't have a burglar alarm system. Drop the rope and shimmy down."

"How about the dog?"

"No problem. If I'd only known, I could have taken care of him. Get a couple of pounds of ground beef. In my tool kit you'll find a package of sleeping powder I got from a veterinarian friend. Mix it with the meat. Before you shimmy down dump a pound of the meat and wait for the dog to pass out. Keep the other pound with you in the event the dog wakes up unexpectedly."

That didn't sound comforting. Given the size of the beast, whose name I'd decided should be Rex for Tyrannosaurus. I'd probably need the entire cow to pacify him. I rubbed my ankle that still hurt and wondered if mixing in a little cyanide might be the better idea, nothing like a little doggie payback. Cancel that, I thought. There's little satisfaction in revenge against an animal. People, on the other hand. . .

"Make sure you poke holes in the meat wrapper. Dogs have a high regard for a person holding food.

"What if I can't get the skylight to open?" asked. "Any other way I can get in?"

"The old disappearing act works well in a department store."

"What's that?"

"It's simple. You go into the store about twenty minutes or so before the store closes. Find a hidey hole. When they start announcing that the doors will be closing, you hide and wait until all the employees are gone and the place is locked down. You exit your hiding place and do what you got to do. That's the way I always get my wardrobe."

"You burglarize the Goodwill?" I asked.

"I'm strictly a Nordstroms' man," Sweets said. "Steal from the rich is always more fun."

I couldn't imagine Nordtroms or any other department store carrying clothing as eccentric as the kind Sweets wore.

"How the heck can I hide in Discount Furniture? Parsegian follows his customers around like they were planning to shop lift one of his couches."

"Know what you mean," Sweets said, smiling. "Stick a coffee table in a pocket and walk out."

We both laughed and the guard looked up from the *Sports Illustrated* he was reading and frowned. I said, "Sorry."

"Lighten up, Victor, there's no rule against mirth in jail."

Mirth, did he just say mirth? How does a Cajun burglar come up with a word like mirth, I wondered.

"All right," I said. "Plan A or Plan B. I'll figure out some way to hide in the store if Plan A doesn't work."

"This is not the Hilton, Brovelli. You got to get me outta here. There's one big bozo who's been smiling a lot at me lately and checking out my butt."

"Don't succumb to the temptations of the flesh," I said as I stood up and signaled to the guard that we were finished.

"Ass hole," Sweets said.

"That's exactly what I'm talking about," I said.

"Jerk," Sweets said.

As I left the building, a woman walked past me and through the doors. I did a double-take. She was the spitting image of Winona Davis. I rushed after her, but she'd disappeared. *Che cazzo*, I said to myself. Helping Sweets was one thing, dealing with apparitions was not part of the bargain. Back in my Mustang, I sat for a while, both hands on the steering wheel, getting a grip. It was my mind playing tricks. *You make one mistake in your life, and your life can be fucked. One selfish little mistake to protect your business, help a friend, be a good son, and see what happens. You start seeing ghosts.* I turned the engine over and slammed the Mustang into first. I'd have to talk to my mother about this, in case I'd inherited some kind of supernatural gene.

But later; I had things to do.

• • •

Midnight had come and gone and East 14th was quiet. I was crouched on the roof of Discount Furniture, dressed in my burglary duds. It was a clear night and in the distance I could see the tops of the buildings in Downtown Oakland and further in the distance the glow of San Francisco. It was a cool, but I was sweating. The burglary was not working. No matter how hard I tried, I couldn't get the damn bar to unhook the skylight latch. I sat atop the roof feeling that burglary was not a career I should consider. I climbed down with my tools and two-pound bag of hamburger. Time to activate Sweets' Plan B, which meant I had to enlist the help of my twin.

CHAPTER 23
PLAN B

Just because people are liars is no reason for us to be fools.
Erle Stanley Gardiner The Case of the Ginning Gorilla

Sylvia, and Vincent were standing in front of the office, when I drove in the next morning. The news around the country was of more violence. So far, Oakland and the Bay Area remained relatively calm. We went into the office. Vincent and I sat at our desks facing each other. Sylvia went to the coffee machine. I leaned forward and explained Plan B.

I said, "All you have to do is make like you're having a heart attack."

"Not a chance," Vincent said. "I'm not making a fool of myself. I'm twenty-six years old. How many men my age have heart attacks?"

"Clap, maybe," Sylvia said, looking down at us with a smirk.

"Not interested in your humor, Miss Nosey," Vincent said. "Don't you have some invoices or something to do?"

"What I'm doing is listening to you two fuckups."

"Vincent, please. Pop is calling all the time." I imitated our pop's voice, "You boys, what you doeeg no helping Sweets Davis? In jail again. Your mama worries, I worries. Get offa you ass."

"*Merda,*" Vincent said, "You sound just like him."

"You guys," Sylvia pleaded. "I swear to God you two are the most foolish. . .."

I interrupted her before she could assign us a proper insulting name. "You wanted to be kept in the loop, I'm keeping you in the loop," I said. "But no comments from the peanut gallery."

Sylvia made a face.

What I was describing was my pop's not-so-obvious parental-appeal-to-filial-obligation-strategy. It worked on me all the time. You'd think since we were twins what guilt I felt, Vincent would feel, but Vincent was more immune to our pop's old time Italian sensibility than I.

I kept after him.

"All right, all right," Vincent finally moaned. "Run this insane plan by me again."

"I know there's something hinky about Parsegian. The book I've been reading on being a private investigator says that good PI's trust their gut feelings. Well, my instincts tell me that Parsegian is guilty of something. May not have anything to do with Winona's murder, but it may. I've caught him in lies before, like big sales he's made and didn't. I need to examine his accounting ledgers. From what he said the last time we talked, they're in Sharifi's office in the old man's desk. If Parsegian was lying and Winona found out something illegal they were doing instead of the cock-and-bull story he fed me, then we can offer Carter a legitimate alternative suspect to build a defense around."

Sylvia sneered. "That only works on Perry Mason."

"Perry frigging Mason," Vincent moaned. "Why don't you go smoke a cigarette, Sylvia. My brother gives me enough grief."

"I think I will," she huffed, grabbing her purse and stomping out.

"Forget Perry Mason," I said. "This is a real possibility. Do you want to get Pop off our butts or not?" I was also thinking of getting Winona's ghost off my butt. Her reappearance was making me question my sanity. "You know how stubborn Pop can be."

"I said I'd do it, didn't I?"

"Yeah, but I need a little more enthusiasm. And, a little appreciation wouldn't hurt since I'm the one doing all the leg work while you're playing father knows best at home with the little missus."

I ducked the punch and grabbed him. We jostled, banging into our desks, knocking over the telephones, but both our hearts weren't in it. There've been times in our lives when a good free-for-all was like medicine. As we grew older, however, our fuses became longer and today we are more likely to hug than fight. But we were not anywhere near the hugging stage that day. I spun Vincent around into his chair, expecting another charge. He came up laughing, his fists at the ready, but just to prove a point.

"Start from when Sylvia interrupted," he said gulping for air.

After I explained for the second and third time, Vincent said he got the picture.

Sylvia returned. She stood in the door, tapping her watch. "It's Barbeque Saturday, and we're late setting up."

Thankfully, Pop and Mom were visiting Carlo and the grandchildren and would not be joining us. We rolled out the grills from behind the building and started the coals. It was my turn on the fire. When the coals were ready, I put on the chicken, slathering on sauce. Sylvia and Vincent took care of the folding table and accessories. When the chicken was almost cooked, I threw on the sausages. We kept our eyes out for customers. When Sylvia hung the blue and red college pennants announcing chow was on, the first people over were Body and some of the guys from the tavern, with beer in to-go cups. They were closest to the aroma of barbeque. Jitters and two of his mechanics came next. Then, Swanee and his crew. Before long our lot was filled with the usual hungry crew: Larry Hughes from the DoNut Hole, Nick Parsegian holding an extra plate for his business partner, Ron Sharifi and two homeless guys who made their home somewhere down by the estuary, Korean vets they claimed. Hughes' plate of chicken and sausages looked like Mount Everest. He looked at me sheepishly and explained when he was stressed he ate a lot. I figured broken shop windows would certainly be cause for stress.

Saturdays at Brovelli Boys' Used Cars always meant good food and lots of laughs. The food was there but not the laughs. All the conversation was about Doctor King, the war, and the mess the Bay Area was in. By the time Sylvia took down the pennants, friends and neighbors had devoured all the chicken and sausages, not one car had been sold, but a bunch of political and social problem had been resolved to no one's satisfaction. We put away the grills and stored the tables and chairs. Sylvia left us on the lot and went into the office.

I'd been too busy serving to eat myself, and I was thirsty. I could use a nice cold frosty mug of Anchor Steam before Vincent and I performed Plan B later in the afternoon. Vincent said he'd watch the lot.

The moment I walked into Flynn's, I knew I'd made a mistake. Sitting at the bar were three officers of the law, one was my pal Jay Ness, but the others I thought I recognized. One of them turned to see who had just entered and yes, indeed, it was one of the officers from the Black Panthers' Headquarters - clearly no pal of mine. I was about to make an exit stage left when I heard Jay call my name.

"Victor, get your ass over here. Couple of guys want to meet you."

This was not going to be fun, I thought.

"How goes it, Jay. Cleaning up the city?" Sometimes I just can't help being a jerk. Besides, a good offense is better than a good defense.

"With the help of my fellow police officers and without the help of a certain used car salesman," he replied, calling my sarcasm and raising it. "I'd like you to meet Mark Halpern and Wilson Bennett. They're part of the OPD rapid response team. It's called. ... "

I interrupted. "I know. We've met."

"So I've heard?" Jay said. "Was that when you screwed up a perfectly righteous weapons bust recently and never mentioned it to me? I didn't know you were friendly with the Black Panthers."

The two cops were looking at me. They weren't smiling. Neither was Jay. "I guess you didn't win at poker, huh?" I said, hoping he'd let the subject of the Panthers go, knowing it wouldn't happen.

"Poker is not high on my priority, lately Victor. We've been too busy putting out fires."

"The fires your liberal friends, like the fucking Black Panthers, have been setting all over the city," the cop named Halpern said.

Well, what the hell, I thought. In for a penny, in for a pound. "You know damn well Jay, I'm not friends with the Black Panthers or any other radical group, but your fellow officers here were out of line. I just stepped in and saved their asses from being sued. So, fuck you very much."

Halpern and his buddy, Bennett were looking at me as if I was some kind of sub species of cockroach. I didn't like it, and I didn't appreciate Jay, who I considered a friend, doing this shit to me.

Halpern stood up. I'd forgotten how big he was. "You some kind of Communist, Brovelli?"

"You guys are off duty, right?" I asked.

"You bet I am, fuckhead," Halpern said. "And I wouldn't mind taking care of that other ear for you."

The day that I'd run home from elementary school with a bloody nose and tears streaming down my face, my pop told me, "Vittorio, the guy who gets the first punch in has the first punch in." Sound advice I thought as I swung and landed a perfect right hook on Halpern's nose. I probably should have mentioned I did a little boxing for the CYO, the Catholic Youth Organization. I could feel the squish of cartilage. Halpern fell back against his barstool. Holding his nose, he staggered sideways, cursing, blood oozing between his fingers. I was in a boxer's stance, fists up, dancing back and forth on the balls of my feet like my favorite middleweight, Sugar Ray Robinson. *I was ready, bring 'em on.*

"You crazy dago," Jay yelled and jumped between me and the other cop who'd leaped from his stool.

"You can't punch a cop," Jay yelled.

"Who says he's a cop?" I screamed. "And damn straight I can if he's an off-duty dirt-bag cop threatening me. You heard him threaten me."

"I'm hauling his ass in," Halpern, growled from under the shirt tail he was pressing to his bloody nose.

He'd have a couple of terrific shiners by tomorrow.

The other cop, Bennett, was standing behind Jay glaring at me. I was hyperventilating. "Yeah, you go ahead and try," I yelled, showing off my footwork, followed by a short, left-hand jab at the air between us. "And I'll be filing a lawsuit by tomorrow morning."

"Cool it, Mark." Jay ordered. "You too, Halpern."

"You don't outrank me, Ness, and I'm cooling nothing," Halpern said. "The whole country is going berserk. A couple of our men are in Merritt hospital with bullets in them. This wop is going to jail."

"That Italian-American is going nowhere except to his own home." The voice came from behind the bar. "Mr. Brovelli, here, is one of our best customers, and I'll testify that you were threatening him."

Over Halpern's shoulder, I saw the pale presence of the nighttime bartender, Stuart Tamberg, who'd just become my favorite nighttime bartender, looking every bit a vampire with his pale skin, slicked back black hair in his customary form fitting black T-shirt and black Levi's.

Halpern looked at Tamberg. "You're interfering with the law."

"Brovelli has a second witness."

This time the voice came from behind me. I turned my head and saw Larry Hughes squeeze his gigantic body out of one of the booths and stretch to his full six foot four inches.

"I own the Donut Hole next door," Hughes announced. "You want my full name and address? I heard lots of name calling against a good Italian-American voter. See what I'm saying?"

"It's a goddamn conspiracy of Communist liberals in here. Go ahead and call your goddamn ACLU lawyers," Halpern hissed and spit on the floor.

From the dark at the end of the bar, "Hey, no Communists in this bar, buddy. Flynn's is red, white, and blue all the way."

"Yeah, Halpern said, "Bunch of jungle. . ."

"Jungle what?" Hughes interrupted menacingly.

The silence that followed was its own menace. Hughes rep as an NFL football player was that he took no prisoners. I could see the two *batardi* thinking it over.

"Commies, bunch of commies," Halpern grumbled. "You haven't heard the last of this. Let's get out of this nest of pinkos." He motioned to his partner. "Officer Ness, you coming."

"Think I'll stick around with the wop and pinkos," Jay said. "And it's detective sergeant Ness to you."

That made me smile. Maybe I'd let Jay buy me a beer.

• • •

Three hours later, Vincent grabbed his heart and keeled over onto the sales floor of Discount Furniture. Parsegian's face went pale, and he started hollering, "Oi, oi, oi" clasping his hands together and repeating, "Oi, oi, oi." I yelled for him to get to a phone and call the fire department. The moment he turned his back, I sprinted to the other end of the store, looked to see if he was out of sight, then popped into an antique armoire, closed the door behind me, settled my beating heart and listened. The plan called for Vincent to be on his feet by the time Parsegian returned from making the call. I knew when Parsegian was nervous, his English deteriorated, so he'd fumble around trying to explain to the operator, providing enough time for Vincent to logically recover and escape being carted off to the emergency. *Yeah, pretty smart, Brovelli, if I do say so myself.* I cracked the door open slightly so I could peek out.

It worked. I could hear Parsegian loudly imploring Vincent to lie down, to take it easy, not to worry, help was on its way, while my twin - the academy award winning actor - very convincingly explaining that he was feeling much better and to cancel the ambulance. He'd go to our family doctor, and Parsegian continuing to be obnoxiously solicitous. I closed the door, placed the briefcase I was carrying, that held some of Sweets' tools and two separately wrapped pounds of ground beef on the floor of the armoire. By my watch, it was a quarter to ten, fifteen minutes to wait before their normal closing time. I slid down on my butt and drew my knees up. I hoped Parsegian was not planning on staying later for any reason.

I still had no idea where that monster dog could possibly be in the building, unless they had some storage units attached to the showroom floor where they kept him penned. While I waited for Parsegian to close up his store, I tried to nap, but wasn't sleepy. My thoughts to family in general, and then specifically to my brother Mario. I hadn't seen him for a while. I wondered how he was doing. What he was doing. I knew he'd been going through rehab at the Veterans Hospital. His missing hand had been fitted with a metal prosthesis that looked like two small lobster claws. Because of Mario's stance against the war, Pop was not talking to him. *Onore, again.* You honor the country that protects you was Pop's way of looking at it. *Come back a big hero, then turn into big coward.* I wanted to slug the old man. I promised myself once this stuff was over, I'd take Mario to lunch.

I checked my watch. Quarter to eleven. I nudged the door open a crack. The showroom was dark. I couldn't see the office. There was a better view of the office from the sofa section. I moved quietly out of my hiding place and dropped to my knees. On all fours I crawled down an aisle until I was behind a leather couch with matching recliner. The offices were dark. Bending low, I hurried back to the armoire and removed the packages of beef from the briefcase. I tore a couple of holes in the wrapping. This dog had nostrils the size of a baseballs, so I figured it wouldn't take long before the aroma would be having him salivating. I picked up my briefcase and began walking toward the office, listening for the galloping of the hound from hell. I was feeling like maybe I was home free as I placed my hand on the door knob of the office. Perhaps the dog was taking a night off. That's when I heard the growl. I wish I could say I did not panic, that I stood my ground and calmly placed the ground beef on the floor, all the while saying, "Good doggie, good doggie." Good doggie was not going for it. The animal dropped his head. If he had horns he would have made a good bull. I dropped everything and lunged into the office, slamming the glass door behind me. I made it just in time. The dog's front paws were resting on the glass, his huge mouth open, fangs exposed. I prayed the glass would not shatter. For a while, the beast stayed in that position, frothing at the mouth, then it dropped to all fours, and I heard him whining. I hoped it was getting a whiff of the meat. When I got up enough courage to look, sure enough the dog from hell was feasting on the meat as well as the paper wrapping. A couple of minutes later, the animal was on its belly. Then, it rocked onto its side.

"Rock-a-bye, baby," I whispered. I waited until I was sure, then stepped out and retrieved what was left of the briefcase. The tools were covered with slobber, but they looked useable. There were a number of them to pry open file cabinets and desk doors, but I hoped one of Sweets' keys would work, so evidence of a break in could be avoided.

I tried the desk first. Locked. One by one I went through each key on the ring. Finally one worked. The accounting books were in the first drawer. I opened my flashlight and sat down at the desk and began to read, keeping an ear out for any sound from the sleeping brontosaurus.

I'm not an accountant. Sylvia takes care of our books. She's whizz. I looked around the office just in case they owned one of those fancy Xerox machines. They didn't. I continued reading.

About an hour went by before I came to a page that had a note attached to it. I read the note with a sinking feeling. It was a receipt, scrawled in Sharifi's shaky handwriting.

$200.00 to Winona Davis. Bonus for services rendered.

$26.80 to Keegan Florist. A dozen roses for Winona

$52.00 Reimbursed. Lunch for Winona at the Red Sail.

Services rendered could have been a payment. But Sharifi wouldn't have given a blackmailer a bouquet of roses. Parsegian was telling the truth. Damn it to hell. I replaced the accounting ledger, locked the drawer. I looked out at sleeping beauty, still sleeping. I left the office, cleaned up whatever remained of my briefcase, put the remains in a paper bag. I went to the front door and looked out onto East 14th. It was still reasonably early and cars were firing down the street, but there were few people on the sidewalk. I looked through the glass door. No one around. Home to bed, and much needed sleep.

CHAPTER 24
OUT OF SUSPECTS

The center will not hold.
W.B. Yeats

It was barely sunrise when I woke up, still tired. I made coffee and opened the Sunday Oakland Tribune. The previous day in the evening while I was hiding inside Furniture Discount, there'd been a shootout between the Oakland police and some of the Black Panthers. Little Bobby Hutton, one of the Panther leaders, had been shot and killed. I flashed on Dila and me walking out of the BPP office and passing Hutton. The paper said that the Oakland Police officers had stopped to question the occupants of several parked vehicles. When one of the officers stepped out of his cruiser, he was shot. The officers returned fire and the men in the car fled to a nearby building where a standoff proceeded until the police lobbed tear gas inside. According to the story, Hutton exited the building acting strangely and was told to get down on the ground. When he didn't, the police opened fire. Another leader of the Black Panthers, Eldridge Cleaver, was wounded. The Oakland Police and Alameda Sheriffs were out on the streets in full force. Until now the Bay Area had not experienced the kind of violence other cities had. The killing of Little Bobby Hutton was definitely going to increase the tension. All over the U.S. there continued to be fallout from the Doctor King assassination - angry mobs roaming the street of the cities' black neighborhoods. President Johnson had ordered the regular army into Chicago. The United States was in a state of chaos. I took my second cup of coffee into the living room and called Vincent at his home. He answered with a why-are-you-calling-me-so-early-yawn.

"I'm taking the day off, "I said. My twin didn't argue. He can tell when I'm feeling down. The same goes for me. It felt as if everything in the world

I knew was falling apart. As for Sweets, I'd run out of suspects and didn't have a clue what to do next. The word incompetent came to mind. I'm kind of a compulsive guy, and hate it when I can't get things right. I told Vincent I intended to do something constructive. I told him I was going to find our brother Captain Mario, Brovelli, Vietnam War vet, recently turned radical hippie, and take him to lunch before the FBI put him in prison for his Anti-War activities. After that I'd maybe play a round of golf. Or not. I wasn't passionate about golf like Vincent was. The phone rang. It was Renee asking me if I wanted to go to a candlelight vigil for Little Bobby Hutton tomorrow night. Lots of the Mills College co-eds were going. I tried to imagine all those white chicks, mingling with the radical crowd, mostly blacks but lots of the usual anti-war folks. Personally I could see no point being jostled by people carrying candles, listening to speeches condemning the United States, singing "We Shall Overcome", while being fumigated by weed. Pot made my eyes so red I looked like Wile E. Coyote after the roadrunner had lured him off a cliff. I declined her offer, telling Renee that as a local business man, I certainly didn't need to be arrested, and there was a good chance things could get really out of control. She sounded disappointed. After I hung up the phone, I changed my mind.

Dila Agbo, my Black Angel, would be among tomorrow night's throng. It would be a natural way to see her. And being there, showing her I was sympathetic to the cause wouldn't hurt my personal get-a-date cause. I wondered where among the throng Dila would be. How would I find her in what Renee had described as five thousand candles? The odds were good that Halpern and his fucking Station Defense Team would be roaming the fringes like a pack of hungry wolves. After the afternoon when I socked him in the nose, wouldn't that asshole love to finish what he threatened to do to my remaining good ear? What the hell. I was about to live dangerously.

I rinsed out my coffee cup and went to the bedroom. I pulled on Levis and my light blue V-neck alpaca sweater over a white polo shirt. I slipped into brown tasseled loafers and went to have breakfast at Ole's. On my way out, I grabbed my detective manual to read while eating. Maybe it would give me some ideas.

The waitress gave me a big smile as I sat down at the empty counter. She brought me coffee. As I waited for my breakfast to arrive, I opened "How to be a Private Investigator". I'd read chapters one and two. Chapter three was on surveillance vehicles. Since it had to do with cars I read on. It

started with this question: *Is your surveillance vehicle completely forgettable?*
I looked out the window at my candy apple red Mustang with white walls
and shiny wheel covers. The answer was no way. The chapter went on to
say, a P.I.'s automobile should be.

Beige and brown. Such colors tend to be the least noticeable and,
incidentally, get the fewest tickets. Red, yellow and custom paint
jobs make your vehicle memorable.

Beige and brown, not a chance in hell, I thought. My three sunnyside
eggs over a waffle arrived. While I ate, I continued reading about
surveillance. It had not occurred to me because I wasn't sure who I should
watch. Or for what reason. Nothing else in the chapter seemed useful to
me. I paid my bill and left. I threw the manual in the back seat, and drove
off to find Mario, but before Mario, I decided to go to nine-o'clock mass.

Morning traffic on Park would usually be slow. People heading to
work, students trudging to school, walking across the pedestrian crossing
intentionally slowly to frustrate drivers. Just like Vincent and I used to do.
In Alameda pedestrians have the right of way and the traffic cops strictly
enforce the law. One day some impatient crazy would slam on the gas and
bodies, books and futures would go flying into the air. But being Sunday,
the streets were close to pedestrian-free.

If I wanted to take communion, I'd have to get into a confessional before
mass started and confess my recent sexual activities with Renee. Pass-a-
robles on that, I thought. I wasn't feeling guilty enough to be preached at
about the sanctity of sexual intercourse in the confines of a good Catholic
marriage. I drove to Saint Joseph's. To be on the safe side I checked the
parking area for Pop's car, even though our parents normally attended the
early bird, seven o'clock mass. His Chrysler Newport was not in the lot or
parked on the street. Coast was clear.

I genuflected my way into the last pew, knelt briefly then sat. Saint
Joseph's is a beautiful old church with some fabulous stained glass depicting
the life of the church's patron Saint. The organ introduced the choir. They
began with one of my favorites: "Alleluia Sing to Jesus". First came the male
voices, then the females and then they joined forces. It was not Saint Peters
Boys Choir, but not bad for a bunch of amateurs. I once attended a Protestant
service with a girl I was dating, and the inside of that church was artistically
ho-hum. And the choir was pathetic. All the clergy spoke English. Where
was the mystery in that? There are a lot of the Catholic Church's doctrines

that bother me, but Catholicism handcuffed me at an early age, and I've never found the keys to unlock myself. I drifted off during the homily. I felt a slight twitch of guilt through the Eucharistic prayer and communion. I hurried out of church before dismissal to avoid having to say hello to people I knew. Although I hadn't confessed and taken communion, I felt good, not holy or anything like that, just good. Mass once a week only takes an hour out of your life, and it's better than a session with a shrink, and costs a hell of a lot less. The trouble is that spiritual goodness doesn't last long. By the time I got to my car I was thinking of the crap going on in the country, not to mention the mess the Brovelli Boys were in.

Mario was not in his apartment. Charley Radley, his roommate, a Vietnam vet like Mario, wearing a Eugene McCarthy for President Button the size of a dinner plate, told me I'd find him at the Robert Kennedy Presidential Campaign Headquarters in Berkeley that was also the office for PeaceLinks. Two liberals, supporting different candidates. Me, I couldn't see an ounce of difference between McCarthy and Kennedy. I was registered as an Independent, leaning to Hubert Humphrey, an old-school union kind of guy, which was the way Pop and Mom were going to vote. I know that doesn't seem as if I think for myself. *You don't mess with me, I don't mess with you* could be the motto of a political party I'd support. Perhaps in the future somebody would start one like that. Vincent told me he wasn't going to vote Democrat this year. His guy was Richard Nixon, who looked to me like he was trying to sell you the Golden Gate Bridge at a cut rate price.

Traffic on the freeway was light. I took the University exit to Shattuck Ave where the Robert Kennedy for President Headquarters was located. Being on Shattuck reminded me of the Wee Globe, Dila Agbo and Othello. Maybe when I met her at tonight's event, she'd invite me to see a performance. But if she didn't, there'd be no reason I couldn't go on my own. I spotted the headquarters, a huge portrait of Bobby Kennedy was fixed about a sign for PeaceLinks, a new organization devoted to peace and harmony. I parked across the street. When I entered, I saw Mario right away. At six feet four inches tall, he's the only one of us sibs with height. Pop jokes with Mom that she was naughty with the basketball-player-size butcher at the local supermarket. The rest of the family do not aspire to great heights, so to speak, although the time I wore cowboy boots. I once reached the nose bleed height of six feet.

Mario was standing next to a long table talking to five seated women stuffing brochures into envelopes. I felt a tug at my heart. Mario was more than an older brother to me. He was my pop when Pop was away working his tail off to make the car business work and had no time for two rowdy twins. He was by my side at the hospital when my baseball accident almost cost me my eye. Both of us looked up to him. He waved me over with his black-gloved prosthetic hand. As I approached, a woman with an ivory complexion, jet black hair and large baby blue eyes, stood up. Her lips were full and red. Wow, I thought, maybe I should reconsider my candidate choice. She was wearing one of those formless Earth Mother dresses. I would have guessed a hammer and sickle insignia on her beret, but instead there was a peace symbol around which was a circle of chains - whatever that meant. I was suddenly struck by the notion that recently I'd been encountering a lot of beautiful women, some of them alive, some dead, and some ghosts. What that meant, I couldn't tell you either. Were all these women omens? Like Odysseus, in his travels, being constantly hindered from going home by some crazy beautiful chick.

My brother embraced me and introduced me to his co-worker. The beauty's name was Grace O'Conner, co-founder of the Peace-Links. *Aha, peace sign plus chain-links, got it.* We shook hands. I had to look up. The black hair and blue eyes combo were common to the Black Irish, descendants of Cromwell's invaders, unlike Body Flynn whose coloring marked him as a descendant of the original blonde Celts. Her shoulders were broad and her breasts were large. The rest of her was hidden beneath the ankle-length tie-dye dress. When she spoke to me it was with an Irish lilt. I could tell by the way she looked at my bro that they had a thing going. Good, I thought, he needed someone to help him lose the bad memories he'd returned with from Vietnam.

"What brings you down to hostile territory, Victor?" Mario asked. "I thought the family's voting for Humphrey."

"Not that committed. I'm thinking of changing over to the Republican Party and voting Nixon."

All the stamp lickers, including my brother's girlfriend, looked up from their envelopes with horrified faces. Mario smiled. He knew I was bullshitting.

"Another registered Republican in the family," he said. "I can't take it."

Our first family Republican was our corporate attorney brother, Carlo. Mario was talking about my twin, whose recent defection had more to do with throwing out the party that got us into the war, than with ideology. I've never doubted my twin's sincerity when he took a stance. Vincent was a rock solid *cumpa* or as they say in the gangster movies, goombah. Me? Well I had some cracks in my rock.

"He thinks Nixon will get us out of Vietnam," I said.

"He won't get a chance. Bobby Kennedy is going to get the Democratic nomination and beat Nixon's pants off."

"In the meantime," I said, "Do we have time for some lunch?"

Mario looked at his watch. "Sorry, bro. We've got pizza ordered for a working lunch. Lots of work, not much time. But let's go get some coffee and catch up."

It was good to see Mario acting normal, like he had a purpose. My mom worried about Mario's sullen and moody behavior since returning from Vietnam. As we walked, we passed Mario's parked Mustang. I asked him how it was holding up. Vincent and I, with help from Jitters, had fixed up a 1966 navy and white Ford Mustang for Mario as a coming home present. We'd added a steering wheel nob so he had better control with one hand.

"Runs like a dream. I changed steering wheel nobs. I didn't want Grace to see the picture of the naked dancer you jokers stuck under the glass."

"That nob's a classic. That was Carol Doda, if you didn't recognize."

"Who's she?" Mario asked.

"Man, you sure you didn't get a head injury in Nam?"

Mario chuckled and slapped me playfully on the side of my head. We found a small café with linoleum-everything and ordered coffee that looked like oil, but tasted pretty good once I doctored it with sugar and cream. Mario drank his black. He lit a cigarette. One sniff and I started coughing.

"Gaulois," he said, pointing to the blue pack on the table. "I got addicted to them in Nam,"

Along with a bunch of other shit, I thought.

As if reading my mind, he said, "I got a handle on the hard drugs, Victor. Can't seem to shake the grass and the ciggies."

"I'm not judging." I said. "How's the rest of your life? Vincent and I haven't heard word one from you in a month."

"Well, I've heard of you," Mario said, "the savior of the Black Panthers."

"*Oddio*," I moaned. "Tell me this isn't getting around."

"Word on liberal-street is that certain boys in blue are on your case. I was going to give you a ring and warn you."

"When? Next month, next year?"

"Cool down, little brother. I just heard."

The hell with it, I thought. All my life, I'd never worried about authority, I wasn't going to start now. Was I or was I not, an upstanding member of the community. Wasn't my twin the sergeant of arms of the local Lion's Club, the youngest to have ever been elected?

"Let's get back to what's happening with you, Mario. You and that fine looking Amazon for peace. You two got the hots for each other?"

"That obvious, huh?"

One mug of coffee was spent talking about Grace. She'd grown up in the city of Dublin. She'd arrived in the United States in 1966. I could tell how impressed he was with her that she'd become a leader in the Anti-Vietnam War movement in such a short period of time. He spoke admiringly of all her accomplishments. I could tell he was truly smitten. We spent another cup of coffee just being brothers. Mario looked healthy for the first time since he returned from Nam. He didn't even seem as self-conscious about his prosthetic hand, which he'd kept hidden in his lap the last time I'd seen him. Now, he was waving it around like a conductor's baton to make his point. I spent our third cup of joe explaining Sweets. Mario said that Pop's old country view of life was nuts, and I should drop the whole thing. I promised I'd try, although I figured it would be difficult. When I drove off I felt as if I'd reconnected with Mario.

For a while, I stayed on Shattuck, then turned east into the hills until I came to Grizzly Peak Road and followed the twists and horseshoe turns of the ascent, enjoying the rhythm of shifting gears. At the summit, I pulled into a turnout, turned off the engine and got out. At the edge of the drop-off, I sat down on a log. In front of me was a panoramic view of most of the Bay Area, the Golden Gate Bridge to my far right, the metallic gray erector set called the San Francisco/Oakland Bay Bridge to my left. The Bay Bridge was separated in the middle by Treasure Island, with a tunnel running through its hump. Beyond the island was the skyline of San Francisco, and the white phallus of Coit Tower topping Telegraph Hill. The sun was just about overhead. A long line of linked barges moved slowly across the tinseled bay. The view reminded me of how much I loved living in a city. My twin's big plan is to get out of the city as soon as he can afford it and move to the suburbs surrounded by meadows and trees. He likes nothing better than to drive into the Sierras and go skiing in the winter or camping in the summer. He belongs to the Sierra Club. Not this goombah. Give me a little park tucked into a neighborhood with a bench and a few squirrels and some Live Oaks or an artificial pond in the center of a lawn, a few ducks paddling, surrounded by high-rises, within hearing distance of car horns and skidding tires – the music of city life. I don't mind exhaust fumes as long as it's not pouring out of some eighteen-wheeler directly in front of me. I appreciate a sunset over the peaks of the Sierra, but it doesn't compare to the moon balanced like a yellow beach ball on the peak of the TransAmerica building.

I turned away from the view and cast my gaze inward to the frustration growing in my gut. I needed to think. So far, I'd done my best for Sweets. Surely he and my pop would understand. The only detection skills I had were coming out of a used book that was laying on the back seat, a first and only edition, not a sign that it had attracted a lot of readers.

A half hour later I was still thinking and drawing blanks. I needed to think more deeply. Sitting here wouldn't do. It was time for open road driving. Often that's when I could think best. Which meant a change of vehicles. I apologized to my Mustang and drove to a small, detached garage I rented not far from my apartment where I kept my 1965 silver gray Porsche 356 Cabriolet hardtop coupe that I bought from a guy who'd had it shipped over from Holland. He'd promised me that it was one of the twenty or so Cabriolets assembled for the Dutch police force. The car had been driven hard, so maybe he was telling the truth. It took Jitters, our mechanic, and me, about a year to get it in shape.

I pulled off the tarp and slid in. Seated, holding the wheel, I inhaled the manly aroma of aged leather. Okay, baby, let's head for the road. I dropped it into first, moved out of the garage, and turned onto the street. I didn't mean to burn rubber; it's just that it's difficult not to when shifting this baby from first to second. I drove to Oakland and up-ramped onto the Nimitz, the four cam Carrera engine throbbing as I worked through the gears. I hit seventy, dropped it into fourth and punched it. In no time I was crossing the Bay Bridge heading west. I zipped past San Francisco through Daly City and on to the Coast Highway, the Pacific Ocean on my right, keeping an eye out for cops. The further south I drove, the greater the drop-off to the ocean. Manzanita dappled the hillsides on my left. Driving the curves in the Porsche was like waltzing with a beautiful woman. I do know how, so I'm not just talking. I had seen my Pop and Mom floating around our living room floor on those special occasions when they got into their best finery and turned the clock back to their youth. The girlfriend I was dating at the time and I tried it out and got pretty good at it. So how does it relate to driving? It's a visual-sensual thing a leaning into and leaning out of, if you get the picture.

Just before Half Moon Bay, I slowed down and turned into a spot overlooking the ocean. I parked and retrieved my detection book from the back seat. I opened it to a chapter entitled "Intake Sheets".

Start by gathering as much information as you can from the
client and/or suspects up front. This sounds pretty obvious but
you'd be surprised. Many clients simply want to give you the
subjects name, age and address and leave it at that. A detailed
intake sheet draws together information above and beyond the
industry standard: information such as doctor appointments,
therapy appointments, marital status, number of children,
hobbies, etc. This allows for a clearer picture of the subjects
routine and helps you avoid re-inventing the wheel out in
the field. This information, together with a search of public
and proprietary data, will save you time and allow you
to provide your client a more cost-effective investigation.

Opening to this chapter was fortuitous. Not that it contained the "ah ha" moment I was seeking, but it could possibly provide me with a way to kick-start my lagging investigation. *My investigation?* Why not? I had to admit to myself that I liked the excitement of detecting. It really got the juices flowing, that was for sure. A ridiculous notion struck me that I could take a couple of classes and actually earn a private investigator's license. Wouldn't Ness faint at the thought of me as a bona fide private eye? I'd sell cars during the day, solve crimes at night. We'd call our dealership, *The Brovelli Brothers' Used Cars and Detective Agency.* I laughed out loud. It had been a long time since I'd had any fantasies other than the one I was having lately about dating Dila Agbo. Growing up, our three older sibs were allowed to dream big. Mario got to attend

West Point. Costanza became a fashion designer, and our oldest bro, Carlo, top of the sibling ladder, received his law degree from Boldt Hall at the University of California and was working for a prestigious law firm in San Francisco. But Pop raised his twin boys to be car salesmen. The apex of our dreams. End of story. Not that I'm complaining. The P.I. fantasy didn't last long. It was way too stupid.

On the return trip, I put on a classical station in honor of Renee. Lots of violins. Not too bad, kind of soothing. I waltzed those curves over the hills as the brass section joined the violins followed by the wind instruments. When the drums joined in, I dropped below seventy and switched to the pop station. I drove the speed limit into the city of San Mateo to the sound of the Temptations, "I Wish it would Rain", and was driving east on the San Mateo Bridge to Oakland as the Bee Gees began "Words". Hit the freeway going north toward Oakland and gunned the Porsche to "Dance to the Music" by Sly and the Family Stones. Cruised at eighty to "Carpet Man" by the Fifth Dimensions, and "I Wish it Would Rain" by the Temptations. All the while I was thinking. I'd decided to create an intake sheet for Winona and Arabella. The question was how could a civilian such as myself gather the kind of information the author of the book recommended? I'd begin on the telephone. I reached Alameda and pulled the Porsche into the garage, covered it with the tarp, locked the garage, got in my Mustang, said, "hi cutie," and drove home. My Mustang is definitely female, while the Porsche is a total male experience.

My livingroom carpet was covered with Sweets' candy wrappers, his dirty dishes still in the sink, as reminders of his slovenly and unwelcome presence in my life. I called Sylvia and asked her to telephone one of her buds at DMV when she got to the office in the morning first thing and get the driving skinny on Winona and Arabella. She grumbled something about Sweets, but agreed. I made a note to myself to call an ex-girl friend of mine who worked for Wells Fargo Bank for as much financial info as there was on the two dearly departed.

It was still early in the afternoon. There was nothing I could do until tomorrow. For the first time in a while, I felt like I had nothing pressing. Perhaps a call to Renee. But I didn't pick up the phone. It didn't seem right to call her while I was thinking of Dila the way I was. There always seemed to me that Renee's sex was like a gift, and I'd be an ungrateful asshole if I didn't treat it with respect. As for Dila, I shook my head over the realization that I could not get Dila out of my mind. In todays' society, aside from a few hip liberal enclaves around the country, a mixed-race couple would have to suffer some hard times. If Dila would actually agree to date me, we'd more than likely run afoul of a lot of unhappy folks: her parents, her friends, the Panthers, my pop and mom, my sibs, my extended family. So, what the hell was going on with me? *Ah, fanculo. Screw it, Brovelli, you're thinking too much. Let it flow. Trust your instincts.*

I went to my bedroom and picked up *War and Peace* from the floor next to my bed. I had the place marked where I left off at the Battle of Borodin. Tolstoy's tome served two purposes: it would either entertain me, or it would put me to sleep. Today, either result would be fine with me.

CHAPTER 25
MONDAY, MONDAY

"Monday, Monday, can't trust that day,
Monday, Monday, it just turns out that way."
Mamas & the Papas

Nobody buys cars on Mondays. This may or may not be true for other used car dealers, but it's been true for Brovelli Brothers' Used Cars. So, I took my time getting to work. *War and Peace* had put me asleep about seven o'clock, and I slept through the night, waking up about as refreshed as I'd been since the whole Sweets fiasco happened. A long, very hot shower made me feel even better, after which I pulled a pair of gray wool slacks off a hanger. Finished dressing in a white shirt, knotted my Gael rugby tie, and donned my blue blazer. Vincent would be in his blue blazer, but he'd have found the right accessory to tie his wardrobe together. Vincent considers me a wardrobe failure for failing to pay attention to the little things.

There was fog as I drove, but the kind that would burn off and leave behind a sunny April day. Traffic was light as I crossed the Fruitvale Bridge and turned right onto East 14th. I was met at the office door by a distressed Sylvia.

"Victor, you have *got* to help me."

Her anxiety was definitely a mood changer. "If I can, cuz," I said. "What's the problem?"

"When I arrived this morning, this was on the office steps." She turned to the open door and pointed. Standing on the floor was a huge vase with what looked like enough red roses in it to supply florists for a couple of decades of Valentine's Days.

"It's not Valentine's Day," I said.

"I counted them, twenty-four long stem beauties," Sylvia said. "Guess who from?"

"Got to be someone in love," I said. I only knew of two people in love with my cousin at the moment, but I didn't say anything.

"That *ciuccio from the Satans.* Can you believe the nerve? I don't know how many times I've told Sunny to back off. Jesus, Victor. You got to do something."

"Sylvia, why me? The man's crazy for you. It's *amore.* How do I get in the way of a man's obsession without him killing me?" That brought back the memory of Sunny threatening that he'd throw whoever put Winona's body in the Satans' clubhouse over the Golden Gate Bridge. I saw myself flying over the railing and turning into shark bait.

"Sometimes you can be such a dick, Vittorio. Enough with the love thing. I need support here not the needle."

"Sunny's a stone killer, and he doesn't like me."

"He *does* like you. He thinks you're old soldiers in arms."

"Look, write the guy a nice thankyou note and tell him you're donating the roses to Saint Joes."

"Some help you are."

I stepped past her and the roses into the office and reached my desk. Sylvia followed me, carrying the vase and placed it on top of her filing cabinet where it stood looking like a volcano eruption.

"Don't forget to make the call I asked you to do yesterday."

"Maybe I will, maybe I won't," she said, pouting.

"Okay, okay, you write the note to Sunny, and I'll take the damn roses to the church for you and deliver the note to Sunny. *Please*, make the call."

Sylvia squinted at me, then moved to her desk and telephoned her contact at the DMV. She hung up and told me it would be take some time. While I waited, I placed a telephone call to my ex-girlfriend, Dolores, and asked her to get as much credit or financial information as she could find on the two dead women. Since she and I had parted friends, she was happy to oblige. She'd get back to me, and I owed her a drink. Not a problem. Dolores is a looker, and it never hurts to be seen around town with a beautiful dolly on your arm.

Vincent's pulled into the lot driving his wife's '67 Ford Country Squire she'd convinced my twin to buy anticipating the dozen children they were bound to have, being good Catholics. I'm kidding, but only by half. The

Squire had a Magic Door-gate that allowed the tailgate to drop down or swing open to the side. The body of the car was robin's egg blue, and I wouldn't have been caught dead driving it. He pulled in behind the office. A couple of minutes later, he walked in, complaining that Gloria was so uncomfortable she couldn't sleep, which meant she wouldn't let him sleep. I told him to go relax, get breakfast, read the paper, drink some coffee. The twin wardrobe vibe was right on, but he'd selected a blue hanky that definitely did work with the blue blazer. He checked out the explosion of roses, and gave Sylvia a thumbs up. In return, she gave him the finger. He walked out the door, grinning. I watched him heading down to the DoNut Hole. I hadn't eaten breakfast. Bring us a dozen glazed, I yelled at his back. He nodded. I sorted through old files, not really paying much attention, killing time. A half hour later, Sylvia got the call from DMV. She took notes and hung up the phone.

"Here's the deal," Sylvia said. "Winona had a driver's license in California, but it expired long ago. Her first driver's license, before her Cal one, was issued by Louisiana, with an address in New Orleans. . ."

Sweets, you lying piece of shit. You knew Winona from the Big Easy, didn't you?

"As for Arabella," Sylvia said, "her driving record was clean and in good standing. Is that all you needed?"

"Yeah, thanks, Cuz."

I remained seated at my desk, pretending to do paperwork, but thinking about Winona and Sweets in New Orleans. There was no way the cops could have missed this connection, but in the event that they did, it was not up to me to give them a heads up was it? As I was mulling over this ethical question, the phone rang for me. It was Dolores with more information that I wrote down. Normally, she said this would have taken much longer to find out, but she had a good friend who worked in banking in Baton Rouge. I thanked Dolores and told her I'd call her back to set up a time to get together for a cocktail.

Vincent returned with a box of donuts, placed it on Sylvia's desk and went out on the lot to wipe down the cars. Staying in my chair, I rolled over and picked out two orange-glazed and rolled back to my desk. While I munched, I read through my notes. In New Orleans, Winona had co-signed on a home mortgage with her husband, a guy by the name of Jordan Fournier. The house had been repossessed for lack of payments.

Her husband had appeared in court and blamed everything on his wife. His testimony was that she'd disappeared with their savings, and that was one of the reasons he'd failed to pay his mortgage. Winona showed up in California five years later, where she legally changed her name back to her maiden name Davis. I figured by then she'd been a prostitute. She applied for one of the new BankAmericards, apparently using a bunch of phony data. The card had been issued and revoked six months later, also for lack of payments. Her attempt to get a Macy's credit card had been denied. There was no divorce on record. Apparently, Winona had still been legally married when she was killed. For the last three years, there was nothing. Except for a checking account and payments to City College.

All right, I thought. Most of this information didn't seem to me to be of much use, except the part about Winona having a husband. I needed to find out more about this guy, Fournier. What if he'd found out where Winona was living and come to settle accounts. If this was so, Fournier would be a reasonable suspect.

I checked the lot from the window to see if there were any potential car buyers. Just empty space disguised as customers and my twin spit-shining hoods. Winona's ghost was hovering above the Impala we'd found her in. I'd thought I'd been rid of her when the Travelall was sold. I was getting sort of used to her presence and annoying habit of tapping her Mickey Mouse watch to remind me to get a move on. I turned back to my desk. I placed a call to the employment agency where I was told that Winona had worked as a temp employee for the last two years. Evaluations from her employers were all positive. I figured that, having already talked to some of her past employers. The lady at the office wouldn't give out any personal information, but she did offer that Winona had an accounting degree from a small business college in Baton Rouge. This was new, and I didn't know what to make of it. Why, with such a degree, had she worked as prostitute?

Next I called Jay at Police Headquarters. Luckily he was at his desk. After calling me an authentic pain-in-the-ass, he confirmed that Winona was from Louisiana, which according to him would not help Sweets. I agreed. Jay went on to say that Winona had not committed any crimes in Louisiana, but had failed to show up at a bankruptcy hearing with her husband. I asked him about Arabella. Ongoing investigation, he told me. He said I owed him for the info he'd given me. I told him in my best James Cagney voice, "Fat chance, copper." and hung up.

Neither Vincent nor Sylvia liked it that I took off to visit Sweets, but I'd said it was urgent. On the way, I dropped off the note to Sunny Badger at the Satans' clubhouse in person, which I considered foolhardy, but she *was* my cuz, and I *do* like her even if I give her a bunch of shit. Sunny read the note, and I swear the killer teared up. He thanked me from one troop to another. Son-of-bitch, I thought, as I drove out, the guy really had the hots for Sylvia. Sylvia was going to owe me big time. From the clubhouse, I drove by Saint Joes and gave the roses to Sister Mary Louise who takes care off the altar. I got to the lock-up in Oakland and checked in. Sweets was escorted in to the visitor's' room. As I suspected, Sweets did not appear surprised when I mentioned Jordan Fournier. Nor was he contrite that he'd failed to mention the guy, or that he knew Winona and Fournier were still married.

"Why would I bother?" he asked, sucking on a piece of hard Italian candy called Sorrento Spicchi that my pop had delivered to him yesterday. "It weren't my business. Married pussy no different than the unmarried kind."

"Yeah, I get it, but what if this Fournier character is the jealous type and followed her out here. Hell, he could be the one who killed her, did you ever think of that?"

His face brightened. "Damn straight. I knew Fournier back when. He was a small-time hood a couple of shrimp short of a jambalaya, running errands for the D'Agostino family. I bet that fucker killed his old lady. No doubt, man. Can you believe that shit?"

Speaking of small-time hoods, I wanted to say but instead said, "Slow down, Sweets, Slow down. We have no proof he's ever set foot in the Bay Area." Sweets stopped smiling.

"What does he look like?" I asked.

"French Cajun, but got some Mex in him. Skinny, black hair, bushy eyebrows, kind of pouty lips. Not handsome like Sweets. His nose is sorta crooked. It's been close to, I don't know, ten years since I've seen him. He could have changed for the worse."

Sweets started giggling at his attempt at humor, and the guard looked at us over the top of the *Playboy* he was reading.

"Are you sure," I asked, reminding him of the last description he'd given me of JT, which had turned out to be completely wrong.

"Yeah, I'm, sorry about that. But I'm right about this dude. "

"If Fournier is not a possibility, Sweets I've flat run out of suspects. I talked to Jay, and he says they've got you by the balls, so they're not even trying to look for anyone else. You're it, man."

"Once a cop, always a cop," Sweets said. "You'll prove him wrong, bro."

"Jay's just doing his job. Really, I don't know what else I can do."

"You'll think of something. You know, we family, we stick togetha, dig what I'm saying?"

I left Sweets, sucking on his candy, complaining to the guard that his cell mate wouldn't let him listen to his Clifton Chenier records. I walked out of the jail into the late afternoon sunlight, wondering how Sweets had managed to get a record player into his cell. "Nothing's easy," I said aloud as I got into my Mustang. I started the engine and pulled out into lunchtime traffic. I'd give Sylvia and Vincent the rest of the day off. Both of them had been pulling my share of the load for the last couple of days while I tried to be a detective. I'd go directly from the lot to the Bobby Hutton memorial candlelight vigil.

CHAPTER 26
WHAT A COINCIDENCE

*When coincidences begin to happen, it means you're on
the right track.*
Detective Sergeant Jay Ness

I was driving to Oakland City Hall. The Fifth Dimension was singing
"Up, Up and Away", and I was thinking that if I joined the army, I could
be in Vietnam sitting in a cozy foxhole out of reach of Sweets and the
possibility of joining him on San Quentin's death row. With the Viet Cong
all around me, I wouldn't have time to worry about Pop's convoluted idea
of honor. What's a few Viet Cong anyway compared to the pressure an
Italian father can bring to bear on an Italian son.

Given the police were mired in so much political strife, I wondered
if they were even concerned with the death of two young women, one of
them an ex-prostitute. They'd pinned the murders on Sweets. Why bother
looking elsewhere? Well, there'd have to be a trial first, of course. But the
way my poker buddy, the good sergeant, colorfully put it, "Sweet's going to
fry", which could no longer be the case since executions in California were
performed by lethal injection.

I'd left the lot in a foul mood, not one car sold all day. I needed a drink.
I needed something to eat. I needed Sweets out of my life, and Dila Agbo in
my life. We'd figure out the race thing. Across from City Hall was Romano's
that served some of the best linguine con gamberi e pomodorini, prawns in
a thick tomato sauce, in the area. Even Pop occasionally took our mother
there on special occasions. *E nufesso chi dice male di macaroni*, Pop would
say. It means one would be an idiot to speak badly of macaroni. A couple
of years ago, Vincent and I tried to enumerate the number of maxims
proffered to us over the years by our pop. We'd stopped counting at fifty.

The traffic was not moving, while my hunger was growing. I was in the right lane heading to the Bridge, only a few yards away from the Broadway exit. "If I had the wings of an angel, over these cars I would fly," I improvised. The Fifth Dimension didn't have to worry about me competing with them. I inched the Mustang to the right and flashed my turn signals. Ten minutes went by before there was enough clearance for me to hit the gas pedal and drop down to Broadway and freedom. I shifted into second, turned right onto 12th Street. Third gear took me a couple of blocks to City Hall where I luckily found a parking place. It was still light, but purple shadows were falling. At the bottom of the City Hall steps was a group of police officers in helmets and riot gear. Some were setting up a perimeter of sawhorses. Some were fanning out and taking positions along the sidewalk adjacent to the building. By the look of the gear, they were expecting trouble. I looked around to see if there were any Black Panthers or their women. I checked my watch. Time for some pasta

I entered Romano's and adjusted my vision to the dark interior. Black upholstered leather booths lined the wall facing a long bar behind which hung a bar length mirror encased in an ornately carved frame. Chandeliers hung from the ceiling. It was the kind of place where the waiters dressed in black and white and wore bow ties. I found a booth in the back, ordered the linguini with shrimp and little tomatoes and a glass of their house red. Each of the booths were fitted with a music selection box. I flipped through the songs until I found "Broken Hearted Melody" and inserted a dime. My choice of songs did not mean I was broken hearted. I can't ever remember having my heart broken. The odds, however, didn't favor this string of good luck to last. On one of our visits to the old country, my mother's great aunt Maddalena, a woman bent like an olive tree, read my fortune with tea leaves. She took my tea cup and drank the remaining tea. Turning the cup over, she shook the leaves onto the saucer, poked around a bit and announced a broken heart was in my near future. I was twenty-one at the time and just graduated from college and had been the heart breaker. Playing along, I gasped. She poked around some more. Looking up at me, she scowled. "Molti fantasmi," she muttered and limped away, leaving me wondering what she meant by many ghosts.

The waitress brought my linguini and wine. I tucked right in. The prawns were perfect, the linguini cooked slightly il dente, the way it should be, the tomato sauce not too overpowering. The wine was so-so, and I regretted not ordering something a little better quality.

Romano's was a favorite watering-hole for city officials, but there were no official-looking people in sight.

Perhaps, I thought, my Black Angel would be the one to fulfill the old woman's prophecy. *I frutti probiti sono I pui dolci.* More of Pop's homespun philosophy came to mind, and I hoped that it was not true that I was only interested in Dila because she was forbidden fruit. Besides, who said she was forbidden? Who makes up these rules about human relationships?

While eating, I thought about the prospect of meeting Dila Agbo at the vigil. Then, it occurred to me that I might bump into Rene? I'd have to do some quick thinking. I was pretty good at improvising. My watch read quarter after seven. Romano's was filling up. I figured most of the customers were part of the press corps. A couple of men had cameras slung around their necks. I finished my meal, leaving my wine glass half full. Time to explore the possibility of meeting my Angel. I paid my check and headed for the door. What was that song the Temptations sang? "Earth Angel, Earth Angel". Something about would you be mine. . . If only I could sing I would serenade my love. *Mama mia*, this Sweets thing was making me weirder by the day. I stepped outside.

The setting was expanding and the atmosphere was ratcheting up. A podium and sound system had been installed on the steps of City Hall. Just below the steps, unarmed Black Panthers were standing in single file. Next to each of the Panthers were members of the Brown Berets, a militant Chicano nationalist organization that had begun in Los Angles and last year opened a branch in Oakland, its headquarters in the Fruitvale District, not far enough away from our lot as far as I was concerned. I suspected that some of them were members of our family's nemesis, The Amigos. I searched the growing crowd of people for Dila and spotted her handing out candles. I edged forward in her direction. I had no idea what I'd say.

The best I could come up with was, "Well, isn't this a coincidence."

She looked up, her one emerald eye sparkling. She was frowning like she didn't remember me.

"Victor Brovelli," she finally said, her voice rising into a question.

"Dila," I said, smiling.

"What in the world you doing here, boy?"

"Looking for you."

"Hrumph," she said. "You better take a candle. The people refusing candles are being noticed." I looked around, remembering the novel *1984* and the thought police. Dila nodded in the direction of a group of somber looking Panthers strolling the perimeter of the crowd.

"I'm all for candles. We Catholics light candles all the time. My mother lights a candle for each of her five children every Sunday." I took a candle and a printed handout with a smiling photograph of Little Bobby Hutton on it, looking like an altar boy.

"We're not going to start the rally until it gets dark. Lot's more people on their way."

"I didn't know the Brown Berets and the Black Panthers had joined forces."

"We haven't. But they're harboring the same frustrations we have."

"I was looking forward to seeing *Othello*, but I understand why it didn't go on after Doctor King's murder."

"Good of you to understand."

"Come on, Dila. You know what I mean."

"Touchy subject, Victor. Look, I gotta get to work."

She took a couple of steps then looked back. "You can walk with me, if you want," she said, handing me some candles and pamphlets. "Make yourself useful."

"You got an extra dashiki I can wear?" I asked. She was wearing a long red, green and black striped African dress that reached her ankles. Her Afro was hidden under a similarly patterned turban.

"Wouldn't work with your coloring."

I was thinking of a come-back, when a huge Black Panther loomed in front of me blocking my way and anything that was left of the sunlight.

"This white man giving you trouble, sister?" he growled.

He didn't actually growl, but it was a fearsome voice.

"No trouble. Helping me out."

"Why?" he asked.

Time for some quick thinking. "Church said to come down here and support the cause," I said. "We Unitarians are on the side of racial brotherhood."

"You fuckin-wit me, man?"

"That's the truth, James," Dila said. "Didn't you get the memo about the Unitarian Church volunteering to help us? Like the Brown Berets."

James shook his large head. "Sorry," he said to me. He looked chagrined, probably for missing the alleged memo.

"No problem. We're in this together," I said. The big man gave me a stare and walked away.

"You lied," I said.

"You lied first," She said. "I was only covering your butt. James is naturally mean, but if you make him mad, his mean-self turns vicious."

"You've never seen an Italian in action."

"Why you so cocky, Victor? You think that helping us one time gives you a pass for all time? I'm warning you to be careful. As far as race goes, things are about as tense right now as they've ever been since Selma. If push comes to shove, your white skin will wind up with a bullseye on it."

Being a target was not an appealing image. But I wasn't going to let a little thing like a bullseye on my chest get in my way. "I'll be careful," I said. "Now, how about that date?"

"White boy, you have *got* no shame," she said. Then she started laughing, a delightful, soft, bubbly sound like water from a fountain. When a couple of Panthers looked our way, the fountain dried up. "What about society," she asked. "Yours, mine. There are rules governing who we love, who we marry, hell, who we sit down to have coffee with. Are you saying you're not aware of those rules?"

"I never paid attention much to rules. I was the kid that was always sitting in the principal's office. And, by the way, isn't this supposed to be like the Age of Aquarius?

"I wouldn't have figured you for someone who is interested in Hair."

I wasn't sure what she meant by hair, but didn't want to sound stupid. "Yeah, I'm all into the hair stuff. Does that mean you'll go out on a date with me?"

Dila shook her head. "Why do you want to date a black woman? Even though it's 1968, there's still a color barrier the height of the Berlin Wall. You Eye-talians don't have the greatest rep for racial tolerance, you know."

"Untrue," I said. "Italians are colorblind compared to Norwegians."

"Norwegians? Are you teasing?"

"Absolutely not. How many black people do you think live in Norway?"

"That's stupid," She said, "You're not one of those white boys got kinky ideas about how hot black women are?"

The question pissed me off. In my mind I'm a simple paesano. I love my family first, then come cars, and women. Or women and cars, depending on the woman and the car. I explained this to Dila, and she told me that was completely sexist and not funny. We continued walking and handing out candles and brochures. I loved the way she walked, her hips swaying like she was skating. I had to raise my voice above the din of the growing crowd.

"This may sound strange to you coming from an Eye-talian, but I've never worried about skin color." I wasn't sure if I was lying or not. If my twin had heard me, he'd have laughed and said I had to be kidding. I didn't think I was. In my mind, all women are hot, particularly the ones with those sexy little flaws." I explained my theory of flaws to Dila, mentioning the different color of her eyes. She looked at me as if was nuts, but wound up smiling. I felt I was making progress and blathered on about the nature of flaws.

After I finished talking, she turned to me and said, "Oh, my goodness, I need to put some distance between you and me, Victor Brovelli, you might be dangerous to my health."

I hung my head and did the little boy routine that always gets the chicks.

Before I could say another word, she shouldered her way through a group of people holding signs. Her back was turned away from me, but I heard the laughter, the fountain bubbling again. I tried following her, but by the time I caught up, she was already talking to a black version of Bruno Sammartino, Pop's favorite wrestler, who looked as if he could crush me to death just by flexing his bicep. Where the hell did the Black Panthers find these behemoths?

Patience, I thought. Race relations being what they were, I didn't want to be pushy. I eased back toward the door of Romano's, hoping to escape inside for another drink before heading home.

That's when I saw Jordan Fournier.

From Sweets' description, I knew it was him. Holy coincidence, I thought.

CHAPTER 27

THERE'S A RIOT GOING ON

A Riot is the Language of the Unheard.
Doctor Martin Luther King

Fournier paused outside Romano's, looked around, then walked in. My investigator's manual warned me that in the detection biz there were no such things as coincidences. Not even luck. Good detectives made their own luck, the author wrote. I'm not a cause-and-effect kind of guy. For me, life's more of a gamble and coincidences are part of the mystery. And mysteries make life interesting.

However, if the author was right, I thought as I stood looking at the door of Romano's then Fournier's appearance represented something of significance. How about this: *the sonavabitch hates his wife so much that it finally reaches the boiling point, and he hops a plane to the Bay Area and shoots her. Then, for some reason – perhaps Arabella recognizes see him committing the deed, so he shoots her as well.* There it was, Sweets' alternative suspect theory. He'd be elated. I was elated. I felt like throwing up both my arms signaling a touchdown. I'd call Carter and tell him, so he could put his weenie legal brain to work organizing the defense. And, best of all, I'd be off the hook with Sweets and my pop. I touched my Saint Christopher's medal that I wear under my shirt and said a little thank-you prayer. I pushed through the door and adjusted to the light.

Fournier was sitting the end of the bar with a glass of red wine in front of him. He stuck a cigarette in a gold holder and lit it. *Wussy,* I thought. *I'm going to nail your ass.* In order to do that I'd need proof of his ass being in the area at the time of the murders. I needed a camera, but mine was at home. If I left, I'd risk losing him. Where would I find a camera fast? Sylvia. Yeah, Sylvia lived near Lake Merritt, Ten minutes max if she was home.

There was a sign pointing to a pay phone in the back. I dialed her number. She answered on the first ring.

"*Pronto,*" she said.

"We're you expecting a call from Italy?" I asked.

"As a matter of fact, yes. My cousin. What do you want Victor?"

I explained.

"Winona had a husband?" she said, her voice rising into a question.

"You don't believe in husbands? "

"Of course not, I just. . . never mind. I'll bring my camera." She rattled off a few choice Italian expletives to demonstrate how she felt about Sweets, which included *stronzo,* turd; *pigrone,* lazy bum, and my favorite, *babbo,* slang for imbecile.

"*Subito,*" I said. "Right now."

She said, "Keep your shirt on."

I took a seat at the end of the bar close to the door and furthest away from Fournier with a clear view of the killer. Yeah, I thought, killer sounded right to me. I was feeling very much the P.I. I might have to invest in a trench coat, like the one Humphrey Bogart wore in *The Big Sleep* an oldie but goody I saw recently on TV.

The dude who might have done it was going on his second glass of wine and I was sucking on my second Anchor Steam when Sylvia tapped me on the shoulder. She slipped a small camera out of her purse.

"Where's your guy?" she asked, handing the camera to me.

"Be cool, Sylvia, okay. He's the *stronzo* sitting at the end of the bar, the one with the crooked nose." Sylvia stepped to the side and looked over my shoulder.

"*Oddio.*"

"What," I asked.

"Nothing, nothing. You think he killed Winona and the other chick?"

"How do I know? But he could have. He'd have motive and opportunity." I explained Sweet's Other-Dude-Did-It-Defense, adding that Carter Innis believed it to be a perfectly reasonable legal maneuver and not some cockamamie idea Sweets had seen on television.

"Got it Sherlock."

I said. "I'm Sherlock the Second. As soon as I get these developed, Carter will take them straight to the D.A."

"You see how well we work together." Sylvia said.

"Don't start, Sylvia," I said.

She shrugged. "Bring the camera to work tomorrow. Gotta run."

I thanked her. She stomped out the door before I could offer her a drink, looking mad. No problem, I thought. Sylvia often stomped and often looked mad.

The camera was a Kodak Brownie 44 point-and-shoot. Not complicated. But I'd have to wait until Fournier was outside. Outside, it was getting dark. The flash might attract his attention, but maybe not as there were lots of people with cameras. Anyway, I didn't have a choice. I couldn't take his picture in the bar. I finished my beer and went out to the sidewalk to wait for him. I felt relieved to have a bona fide suspect.

While I'd been in Romano's, the space in front of City Hall had filled up with people, so many that moving in any direction was difficult. Lots of shouldering, and shuffling as people tried to position themselves for a better view of the speakers' platform on the steps. From somewhere came the strains of music and a chorus singing a hymn about reaching the Promised Land. People were sitting on top of a couple of old school buses with rainbows painted on their sides, parked to my left. A guy next to me, standing on a milk crate, jumped off, and I leaped on ahead of a woman who gave me a nasty look. Over the top of the crowd, I saw lots of signs saying, "R.I.P. Bobby," "Bobby, You'll be Missed," and "Oakland Gestapo." Standing on the City Hall steps were groups of men and women, mostly Blacks wearing black armbands. I recognized a prominent Afro-American clergyman from San Francisco who'd been in the news a great deal lately that Jay Ness and his fellow police officers always referred to as a shit-disturber, recognizable by his white ropes of hair jutting out at all angles from his head like Medusa's snakes. I knew him as Reverend Quincy Davis, proud owner of a 1961 Cadillac DeVille purchased from the Brovelli Brothers. The car had made us a neat little profit. Behind him was Ron Dellums, newly elected to the Berkeley City Council whose photo had been making front pages the last couple of months. Mario liked the guy, which meant he was real liberal. I couldn't identify any of the other speakers. Certainly his honor, John H. Reading was nowhere close to this site, no doubt sitting down to dinner in the safety of his home complaining to the wife and children about the country going down the tubes. Whoa, I thought, was I getting cynical. I was surprised how many whites were in attendance. I probably shouldn't have been. This *was* the Left Coast.

Even so, you wouldn't have found any of Pop's Lion's Club buddies here. And probably not many of my own friends and acquaintances from college or Flynn's. There was no great appreciation of the Black Panthers, among the white middle class that were not impressed by all of the social services the Panthers performed in their own neighborhood, something the newspapers never wrote much about. Black neighborhoods resembled small foreign countries, not worth writing about, unless they were about to go to war, which was the present case. Guerilla war, I thought.

Although it was still twilight, some candles were already lit, their flames flickering in a light breeze, the sun's last shadows forming a tableau vivant. It reminded me of a scene three years ago when I'd visited relatives in Naples, standing in a crowd, holding lit candles in front of the Basilica of Santa Maria della Sanita built over the spooky catacombs of San Gaudoso. Being a Catholic is important to me, but some stuff my brethren buy into is totally ri-dic-u-lous, something I'd never say to my parents for fear the old man would punch my lights out.

I hung the camera around my neck and withdrew the candle Dila had given me from the inside of my jacket. There were a number of newscasters with their accompanying cameramen. There were singletons with cameras at the ready, probably freelance reporters. Spread through the crowd were Black Panthers and Brown Berets, guardians of order. Or chaos, I wasn't sure which. As I scanned the crowd, I kept my eye on the front door of the Romano's. It occurred to me that given the number of reporters and cameramen, Fournier wouldn't think it was unusual if I snapped his picture. *Just getting some background shots, mister.*

A turned to the sound of my name and looked into the eyes of my brother Mario with his gorgeous girlfriend towering next him. Either he'd shrunk since this afternoon or she'd grown. I hopped down off the box. I checked out her feet to see if she was wearing six-inch heels. No such luck. Flats. I wanted to ask her how tall she was, but that would have been impolite.

"Don't ask," Grace said, reading my mind. "I'm six feet four inches."

"I bet you played basketball," I said.

"Ballet," she said.

"You're kidding," I said.

"Gotcha, little brother," Mario said. "I'm surprised to see you here. You growing a conscience?"

"You can't grow a conscience like you grow a zucchini." I said. "What I'm doing is making a conscious effort to get a date with a woman who just happens to be here."

"The only women here are liberals, unless they're undercover cops or FBI agents," Grace said.

She spoke with a rising inflection in her voice the way Body and his Irish friends spoke, but in her case it sounded musical. My goodness she was breathtakingly beautiful. Mario, you lucky devil, I thought.

"I already know the woman's politics," I said. "I've a theory that only a fool would let politics get in the way of romance."

"I know a lot of the women working today," Grace said. "What's her name?"

"Dila Agbo."

"Oh, my," she said, turning to Mario. "Your sibling sure knows how to pick them."

"Well, she's not quite my girlfriend yet, but I'm working on it."

"A Black Panther sister," she said. "The brothers won't be happy with you Victor."

"This brother will, but Mom and Pop won't," Mario said. "Victor, I'm proud of you. I never thought you were prejudiced, but dating an Afro-American, that I wouldn't have guessed."

Before I could explain, over Mario's shoulder, I saw Jordan Fournier exit Romano's, stop and look both ways as if trying to figure out which way was the best direction to go. I removed the camera from its case.

"Hey, guys," I said. "On this historical day, I'm going to take your picture. Right? Right. Now get close together." Mario and Grace looked confused. I pushed them together and stepped back, so I could get a clear shot of Fournier in the background. Before Mario and Grace could say a word, I was snapping photographs. I reckoned I got at least three good shots before Fournier began walking. I'd managed to get a couple of Little Bobby Hutton signs in the background that would authenticate the date the photographs were taken. I'd read that in the chapter on surveillance.

"Hey, bro. I got to split," I said, "I'll explain later. It's about Sweets, okay. Nice to see you Grace." I pointed at Mario, "He's a keeper." I slipped the camera back in its case and followed Fournier into the herd of people. Behind me, I heard Mario cautioning me to be careful. Did he know something? I didn't have time to find out.

Fournier maneuvered his way across the street toward the City Hall steps where he stopped to talk to one of the Brown Berets, a big guy I'd seen before, but couldn't remember where. I snapped a photograph of them. It might come to me later. A loud crackling sound came from the podium speakers. Then a voice calling, "Testing, testing."

"Little muddy at the bottom," someone hollered.

More testing went on back and forth until there was a consensus that all was a go. The sun had dropped and flood lights were turned on. In the Bay Area, when the sun goes down, so does the temperature – rapidly. Through the soft twilight glow, I watched as Black Panthers' Minister of Education Terrance Bowles appeared at the podium, and tapped the microphone. He called out to the crowd to settle down. Loud voices turned to hushed voices. All around me, people were holding burning candles. Bowles introduced the first speaker, Reverend Davis. As the old man stepped to the podium, an object flew out of the crowd and hit the preacher in the chest. From where I was standing I wasn't sure what it was except that the reverend's gray suit coat was covered in red goop. Not blood, Tomato, maybe. Next thing I knew, the air was filled with more flying objects. *Miiiiinchia*, one landed at my feet and splattered. Definitely a tomato. Another landed, did not break and rolled next to the guy standing to my right. An Heirloom. Pop's heart would break at the sight of his favorite fruit being used as a missile. A barrage of tomatoes followed and other vegetables; celery, carrots, and potatoes filled the air. Damn, I thought, potatoes could do some damage if you got hit on the head with one. This was clearly an organized attack. Black Panthers and Brown Berets began pushing through the crowd of people, yelling into walkie-talkies. I pivoted in all directions, trying to spot the throwers. I thought of Dila, and bullied my way through the crowd to one of the cement lions guarding the city hall steps and swung up like a cowboy onto its back, trying to locate her in the middle of the growing chaos.

It was only a matter of time, I thought, before a fight would break out. Sure enough, right in front of me some dudes began punching each other. That started a chain reaction. *Fucking Domino Effect*. A couple of Panthers were hammering their way toward the fight, only to find their way blocked by another fight. Then, it became their fight.

From my saddle, I kept looking for Dila, but by now with the melee going full blast, it became increasingly difficult to identify anyone. I zeroed in on all the women with colorful turbans. Finally, above the noise of people screaming, I heard Police sirens. Strangely, as far as I could tell, there were no officers on the ground to help maintain order. At the start of the vigil there'd been plenty stationed in pairs around the perimeter of the area. Their absence now was peculiar, to say the least. I began snapping photographs. Other photographers were snapping shots. One reporter and his camera man were pushed to the ground by a guy in a black sweat suit who stomped on the camera. I yelled, "Hey," and snapped his picture. He turned in my direction, but looked past me, to the top of the steps where, suddenly a troop of police officers in riot gear emerged from the entrance to City Hall. The hooded attacker whirled away and pushed into the turmoil, swinging his fists at anyone in his way. I spotted Dila. She was helping a group of older women inch their way up the stairs. I didn't think she realized the police were poised to march down the stairs in her direction. I leaped from the back of the lion and bounded up the stairs two at a time, just as the phalanx of police, rifles at port-arms, began descending, a second line following the first, and a third on its heels.

Shit, shit, shit, I thought.

From the midst of the crowd, a shot rang out. *What the fuck else could happen?* I reached Dila, grabbed her arm, and hustled her down the stairs, her struggling all the way. Holding her tightly with one arm, I swung around behind the cement lion and pushed her to the ground then knelt beside her. She bucked and twisted, trying to get up.

"What the hell you doing, Victor?" she screamed. "Those are my sisters. I gotta help them."

"You got to be safe. The cops are holding rifles if you didn't notice, and there are people shooting."

"We have weapons too," she screamed.

"Are you nuts? Look what's happening. No don't look," I said as she tried to rise. "It's out of hand."

It was. There was screaming and shooting and bullhorns blaring for people to disperse. Nobody, it seemed, was paying attention. I wondered where Mario and Grace were in this turmoil. The lines of cops kept slowly marching down the steps. They weren't in any hurry, but they looked determined.

Shit like this was being played out in cities, big and small, all over the country. The anger on both sides was palpable. You could damn near taste it.

"No, *you* look," Dila grabbed my arm. "I can't stay here cowering behind a lion when I could be helping."

"The cops were bearing down on you."

"I know, I know. A couple of sisters were frozen with fear. I was trying to convince them to move to safety. Let me see what's happening. Come on, you can take your hands off me. I promise I won't run away."

"Promise?"

"Yeah, yeah. Ease up, Victor. You're hurting me."

I released her. Rising up, she pivoted and slammed into me, knocking me backwards into a row of prickly bushes. By the time I struggled to my feet, Dila Agbo had disappeared into the curtain of tear gas enveloping the collective madness. From behind the lion, I put a handkerchief over my nose and mouth and continued to take photographs of the Little Bobby Hutton Candlelight Vigil gone to riot. The phalanx of the police had reached the action and were now methodically and violently dispersing the crowd. The last photograph I took before I ran out of film was of two officers carrying Dila Agbo to a paddy wagon. Above the din, the loudspeaker continued to send forth the voices of a gospel choir singing:

Life will be pleasanter, sweeter,
Stony no longer the way;
Enter the fullness of favor,
Cross over Jordan today.

CHAPTER 28
CROSSING OFF JORDAN

Dai nemici mi guardo io, dagli amici mi guarda iddio.
I can protect myself from my enemies, may god protect
me from my friends.

I wasn't home more than ten minutes before the phone rang. It was Renee excited, breathlessly explaining what happened at the Little Bobby Hutton Candlelight Vigil. Thank God she hadn't seen me. Her emotions were raw, she said, and did I want to drive over. Normally Renee with raw emotions would have propelled me out the door and into my Mustang, but tonight, after what I'd just seen, I would have felt. . . I wasn't sure exactly, maybe a cheat, someone who'd take advantage. For sex, and from a woman who was always straight up with me. And there was more I was feeling. While I was playing at being an amateur sleuth, all around me Americans were going completely berserk. My familiar life: selling cars, playing poker with the guys, driving my Porsche, my relationship with Renee seemed less familiar.

Promising Renee I'd call tomorrow, I hung up the phone, my head spinning, and went to the kitchen. I grabbed a bottle of Anchor Steam out of the fridge, chugged the bottle, then a second. After the third beer, I went into the bathroom for a shower. Finished and dried off, I picked up my brand-new woolen slacks that now sported a brand-new hole in the knee. I tossed them from my bed onto the floor and crawled under the covers. It took me a while, but I finally fell into a troubled asleep.

In the morning, I awoke, my sleep shirt sweat-damp, but clear-headed, thinking the first thing I needed to do was have the film developed and deliver the photographs of Jordan Fournier to Carter's law office, so Carter could begin building the Other-Dude-Did-It-Defense. The second thing I had to do was write Sweets a letter. Carter could deliver it. I found paper and pen and sat down at the kitchen table.

Dear Sweets,

Vincent and I are finished with the detective business. I have provided your attorney with the alternative theory that will save your pathetic, skinny ass. We are extremely happy for you. Pop is delighted. Mom is delighted. All my brothers and my sister are delighted. The entire city of Oakland is delighted. I'm explaining this so you to let you know that I take great delight in severing our relationship with you. Capisci?

The end. If you beat these charges, and I think you will, there will no longer be a car for you from the Brovelli Brothers unless you want to buy it the same way all our customers do. With money. I know you will go whining to Pop. But Pop can do what he wants. Vincent and I have fulfilled our pledge to him. As for any other form of blackmail you might try, it's our word against yours.

Sincerely, get stuffed,
Victor Brovelli

I cannot begin to tell you how relieved I was after I finished writing. It felt almost as good as selling a car or ending a relationship with a woman who was hinting that her biological clock was ticking. With a friend like Sweets, who needed enemies? The books about being a private P.I. I'd donate to the library for the next amateur sleuth to read, *and good luck to him.* I'd keep the Ross McDonald novel, which I'd finish one of these days now that I would no longer have to spend all my fucking time trying to save a burglar's life. I re-read the letter to make sure it said everything I needed to say. Questo e tutto, I mumbled, which means that's it, done, over. I felt as if I was at a crossroad in my life. I dressed for work. On the way I dropped the film off at the photo lab we used for some of our advertising. Since I was the first customer of the day, I was assured by a cute clerk whose nose looked charmingly askew that she'd have it ready for me by noon. I drove to Ole's for a celebratory putting-Sweets-behind-me breakfast.

Three cups of coffee and the best breakfast I've ever had warming my stomach, I drove to work, making a quick tour of the neighborhood first. The broken window of Furniture Discount and Flynn's had been repaired. The Donut Hole's front window was still boarded over, but there was a long line of people waiting to get in. A huge white canvas sign hung above the door read:

Solidarity = No Cost
All donuts = 50% off.

I parked the Mustang behind the office and went in. Sylvia and Vincent were drinking coffee and eating the DoNut Hole's famous rhubarb muffins. On Sylvia's desk was a vase of yellow long-stem roses with a card attached to the vase in the shape of a motorcycle. The wheels were red hearts.

"Doesn't look like I convinced Sunny," I said.

"If he doesn't stop sending me flowers, I going to kill the sonavabitch."

"Means more flowers for the altar," I said.

"You're welcome to them," Sylvia sneered.

Clearly Sunny Badger didn't understand the word, no. I almost started laughing, but seeing the look on Sylvia's face I thought better of it. I took the roses and put them in the bathroom out of sight.

When I returned, Sylvia said, "You know you were on television."

"What're you talking about?"

"CBS News," Vincent said. "Got a shot of you running down the city hall steps hugging a black babe."

"She's a friend."

"Friend?" Sylvia sneered

"Yeah. You gotta problem with that?"

Sylvia shook her head. "Your screwed up love life's not my business, Vittorio, but you know that black guys don't like white guys messing with their women."

This was the first time I'd heard someone refer to my love life as being screwed up. Exciting, over-the-top, sometimes indiscriminate, selfish, all of which was totally false, but never had I heard screwed up. Was this her view of me, or did other people have the same idea? I let the question hang for a moment, then I dismissed it. As for the black-white thing, she was probably right, but screw 'em if they can't take a joke.

"Sylvia told me about Winona's husband," Vincent said. "I understand wanting to get photographs of him for Carter, but why the hell didn't you get out of that jungle once the riot started?"

I ignored the reference to tropical climes and wild animals as unintentional. "You should have been there, Vincent. It wasn't that easy.

It was like everybody was trapped in their own anger. The cops had the entire area surrounded. By the way, Mario was there."

Sylvia said, "I thought I saw him after I brought you the camera. But I wasn't sure. He was with a gal who looked like she could play center for the Warriors."

"That was him, alright. Her name is Grace."

"Mario? Damn," Vincent said. "I think our brother lost some of his mind along with his hand in Vietnam, hanging out with all the crazies."

"Grace isn't crazy. And you're wrong Sylvia. Her group is called PeaceLinks. That was a peace sign on her beret."

"And bats in her belfry," Sylvia countered.

"Is that an original cliché?" I asked.

"All those people down there, they got screws lose," Sylvia replied.

Tired of the way this conversation was going, I said, "Forget the riot. Let me tell you what I did." I explained the letter I'd sent to Sweets via his lawyer.

"You did the right thing, Victor," Vincent said. "And, believe me, I appreciate you doing most of the heavy lifting."

The relief on Vincent's face was visible.

"Glad that's over," Sylvia said. "Now we can get back to making money."

"Nothing can make me happier," I said, wondering if that were true. These last days had done something to my mind. Maybe there were a few screws lose.

The rest of the morning, Vincent and I went over our inventory. Carlton Motors, which had been so badly damaged by fire, called and offered us a couple of cars. They were closing down their East 14th store and moving over the hill to Danville.

I got on the phone to Joe Carlton.

"Got to get away from these Black Panthers, and their radical friends. You know it's them stirring up all this trouble," he stated. I almost said something, but kept my mouth shut since the prices of the cars were too good to antagonize him. You got no balls, Brovelli, I thought to myself as I hung up. This wasn't the first time I'd listened to racial slurs and said squat. I told Vincent of my telephone call to Carlton, and that I felt badly. He told me I wasn't the only one without balls. According to him, when it came to confronting the blacks, half the Caucasian male population had lost their *coglioni*. This was not what I meant, but explaining would have led to an argument. The emotions of blacks, whites, and Chicanos, already hot, were on the verge of a melt-down. I suddenly began to see my twin and me on opposite sides of the political and social divide. As twins we'd always been in tandem, and the thought made me sad.

Sylvia dropped us off at Carlton Motors, and we drove back to the lot, Vincent at the wheel of a powder blue '66 Lincoln Continental with forty thousand miles on it and me looking sharp in a red '65 Camaro with custom rims. I knew of a guy who was looking for low mileage wheels for his teenage age son. The Camaro sported red with white stripes, a kid would think was cool. The Lincoln had an eight-track tape deck mounted between the center console and the dash that would give the asking price a boost.

Sylvia sat us down in the office and went over the state of our finances. She cautioned us that we shouldn't take the bank increasing our line of credit as a signal to go on a buying frenzy. Vincent and I agreed, but I could tell by the set of his jaw that Vincent was determined to keep going. When he's like this, you don't get in his way. But she did raise our spirits by pointing out an uptick in profits. Once again I was struck by the irony of our success while all the other businesses on the street had been suffering major hits. Vincent noted that if we could have a good rest of April and May, going into summer when sales historically increased, we might be able to buy a few more classic cars. Vincent and I both knew that the real money in the used car business was in well maintained, classic automobiles. Our ace in the hole was Jitters, whose mechanical genius would allow us to offer three-year warrantees on all moving parts, an unheard-of guarantee in the used car biz. But first we needed to accumulate a substantial inventory and about two years of rainy-day cash. I placed my legs up on my desk and leaned back in my chair. Maybe now was the time to taste Pappy Van Winkle's fine bourbon. I stood up, then changed my mind and sat down again. I was jumping the gun. The time to celebrate would be after summer, within sight of our goal.

I spent a couple of hours at my desk, making cold calls and doing paperwork. At noon, I declined Vincent's offer of Flynn's chili. I needed to pick up the photographs and deliver them to Carter. I got there just in time before he left the office for lunch. He was delighted with the news, explaining that the appearance of Jordan Fournier gave him an additional "wrinkle" to present to the jury. He spread the photographs on his desk and examined them one by one. Most were of the riot.

As he was looking through them, I said, "Let me see that one."

He handed me a photograph of a man in a hood throwing what looked like a Zucchini or a skinny eggplant. The hood concealed much of the miscreant's face, but I recognized it. I placed it in my pocket.

"What're you doing?" Carter asked.

"I know the guy in the photo. I got to check it out for sure." The negatives were in the glovebox of my car.

"Anything to do with Sweets?"

"No. Something else entirely." The face in the photograph was of Captain Halpern of the Station Defense Team. Jay would have a heart attack.

"You know, Victor, it's not Winona's murder I'm worried about," Carter said. "It's Arabella's that's the problem. Sweet's fingerprints in her apartment, I can deal with, but the old gal across the hall puts Sweets at the scene at the time of the murder."

"Have you spoken to her?" I asked.

"I haven't and I'm too far behind with other cases I'm supposed to be working on. My father warns me not to let your father down, then he sends me work he needs yesterday, and screams at me if it's not done."

He looked up at me, with a gleam in his eyes. "Uh, oh," I thought.

"Could you interview the woman for me, Victor, it would be a huge favor."

"Can't do it, Carter. You read my letter to Sweets, my days as a detective are over. *Fatto, finito.* Pop has a saying, the best armor is to keep out of range. My brother and I are staying as clear of Sweets from now on as possible."

"Come on, Victor. Do me a favor. My dad has me in the frigging law library for the next three days. One of our investigators is vacationing in Mexico, and his partner is working on another case that is a money-maker. Your old man is giving my old man a headache about Sweets, so my old man is doing the same to me. Look, you see that vein in my forehead throbbing? Migraine coming on."

I began inching backwards. "Sorry, no can do. Take an aspirin. I've got work too, you know. Cars to sell, promises to keep. Bankers to see. No way. Sweets is your responsibility now, Carter. Send the bill to Brovelli senior." By the last word I'd reached the door and had my hand on the knob poised to make my exit.

"I'll fix you up with Veronica," Carter said.

I took my hand off the door knob. "Your cousin, the stewardess?"

"Yeah, that Veronica. She flew in last night. Got a two-day layover, and would love nothing better than to go out on the town, say a nice dinner at the top of the Mark, a little nightclubbing after, etc, etc. if you get my meaning."

"By all means," I said. That damn Carter was not playing fair. His etc, etc, was turning into a candle lit bedroom and Veronica in a see-through negligee. "Tell me, has Veronica changed since the last time I saw her?" I asked. "She hasn't gained a bunch of weight, got in an accident and ruined that gorgeous face, anything like that?" I was imagining that face: eyes too big, nose to slender, mouth too wide - but the sum of the parts forming an unlikely but stunning visage. Not to mention the stunning body.

"Nope, still runner up for 1964 Miss Illinois."

"You're a very persuasive guy, you know, Carter. I got to give this some real thought."

"Here, let me show you a recent photograph. It might help you make up your mind."

Carter opened his desk and removed an envelope, fingered through the contents and pulled a couple out. "Here's some family snapshots from a get together in Bermuda. You'll appreciate this one on the beach in her bikini."

I was now back standing in front of Carter's desk, feeling like I was the biggest hypocrite in the world. I took the photograph.

"You'll be doing me a big favor, Vincent. Gael alums have to stick together. Interview the old bag and save me from fornicating with my first cousin, which is a sin in the eyes of the church."

"What are friends for," I said. "I don't have her phone number. Give it to me and I'll give her a call."

"No way," Carter said. "I'll set it up and call you after I get your interview on paper."

"You think I'd go back on my word?"

"I'm not taking any chances, Victor. Remember, I grew up with you dagos."

"Not very P.C., Carter. I might have to call the ACLU.

"Fuck those assholes. When shall I tell her you'll pick her up tonight?"

Oh, Christ, I had plans. "It's got to be tomorrow night."

"You got some frigging love life going, Victor," Carter said.

He just assumed I had a date. I didn't have a date, but I had a plan.

"Veronica's staying with a friend. The set up will be that she'll meet you in the lobby of the Mark at eight o'clock tomorrow night. Unless you renege on your word, that is."

A Brovelli's word is always good, I told him. A matter of *onore*. As I walked out of the office, I said, "Victor, my boy, you have the will power of a nit," Carter's secretary looked up from her desk. "I know what you mean," she said, fluttering her fake eyelashes. I hadn't realized I'd spoken aloud.

Let's get the interview over with, I said to myself. Earn my date with Veronica, and put the last obligation to Sweets behind me. For good. *Yeah, you heard me, for good.*

Thinking of the tall, willowy Veronica, I recalled that our last date had not turned out exactly the way I wanted it to, that is, the two of us between the sheets. I wondered if I should rent a room at the hotel, you know, like have a great meal at the Top of the Mark, overlooking *Baghdad by the Bay*, then entwine in said sheets.

I felt guilty, planning the seduction of Veronica, while I had a tentative seduction plan for Dila Agbo. Not to mention that I had an ongoing thing with Renee. But I couldn't really feel guilty about Renee, could I, since we had an understanding that had to do primarily with satisfying sexual urgency. It's like when you get hungry, you head to the refrigerator, right? When it came to Veronica, the metaphor was more like going to your favorite 4-star restaurant, something that's expensive and you don't do very often. As for Dila Agbo, thinking along the same lines, metaphorically speaking. . . Nothing came to mind. It would take a lot more of Dila to see how she would fit into my life. Or, for that matter, how I would fit into hers.

• • •

I hadn't been fed for a while, so I stopped for a quick lamb curry at a little mom and pop Indian joint called the Taj, close to Arabella's apartment. They baked their own nan and their curries were fabulous as long as you didn't order spicy hot. I ate to the sound of Indian music, which always reminds me of belly dancers.

After my meal, I left my car parked in front of the Taj and walked the rest of the way to the apartment. The elderly woman I had to interview was named Rachel Winslow, a very dignified name I thought. I rang her doorbell and heard a voice like sandpaper asking me who I was. I introduced myself first, then explained what I wanted. Reminding me there was building security available to all residents with a push of a button, she buzzed me in. When I arrived at her door, it was opened a crack but secured by a chain. Half a wrinkled face was peering out behind half a pair of spectacles. The one eye behind the spectacles looked like a kind of marble I played with as a child called allys for alabaster.

"You got any identification?" she asked.

I showed her my business card and Carter Innis's card. One eye examined them.

"Used car salesman," she said, in that tone, I've come to despise, meaning a guy who was willing to tell any lie in order to make a sale, like the jerks over at Dynamite Auto Sales in Hayward who never passed up the opportunity to turn back an odometer. They were also known for grooving bald tires so they looked like they had tread left. Once, they'd tried to pass off a few of their disguised beauties to us, but Jitters, our mechanic crawled under the cars and come out shaking his head. Assholes give us honest car salesmen a bad name.

"I'm helping Innis Attorneys at Law," I said.

"Doing a little moonlighting, eh? Sales must be down."

"The Brovelli Brothers are doing fine, Mrs. Winslow. If you ever need a dependable vehicle, you come see me. I will personally see to it you drive away happy. Now, may I come in?"

"Can't drive," she crackled. "Eyesight. Bastards took away my drivers' license."

I felt a little heart-rush. If she couldn't see well that meant her identification of Sweets as the guy knocking on Arabella's door was unreliable. Good news for the Sweet-tooth-man.

I felt I needed to be sure. "Would it be possible I could come in and chat. I promise I won't take up much of your time."

"You get that scar in a barroom brawl or some kind of prison fight?"

"You don't have to worry. I've never been in a barroom brawl and never been in jail. I've never even gotten a parking ticket." Not the truth, since there were two in my desk drawer waiting to be paid. I explained about my youthful baseball injury. When I mentioned baseball, she unhooked the chain, explaining America's principal pastime was her principal pastime, seeing she was old and widowed and had once dated Ty Cobb.

"Made love like he ran the bases," she said, as she escorted me down the hall into her living room decorated with Oakland A's and Milwaukee Brewers posters and pennants. "Fast is good in baseball but not much use to a woman, if you know what I mean."

She batted fake eyelashes that looked like she'd murdered a couple of moths and stuck them on her lids. I assured her I understood completely. She directed me to an overstuffed easy chair, and I mean overstuffed, with lumps the size of cantaloupes. She sat down opposite me on an antique settee. Her hair was a blueish white. If you ignored the wrinkles and the stupid eyelashes, you could tell she'd once been very cute. The coffee table between us was covered with baseball magazines and racing forms. A corner of it was reserved for a black and white television set. A game was on. She turned off the sound and leaned back.

"You like baseball?" she asked

"Not especially," I answered. "In college I played rugby."

"Don't pay much attention to foreign sports. What college did you attend, young man?"

"Saint Mary's College, in Moraga."

"Catholic, right? Got no use for Catholics, although I once dated a real nice dago by the name of Ping Bodie. His real name was Francesco Pezzolo. Caught him on the downside playing in the Pacific Coast League in 1922, or thereabouts. His game wasn't the only thing on the downside," she cackled.

I wasn't interested in why she didn't like Catholics or why an Italian changed his name to Bodie, which seemed dumb. Time to do the interview and get out of this aging ball park. I pulled out a small notebook and pen from the inside of my blue Brovelli Brothers blazer and spoke in my best detective voice. "Would you mind, Mrs. Winslow, describing the person you saw knocking on Arabella's door the day she was murdered."

"I told the police officers. Guess they don't like to share information. Perry Mason always gets real upset with that silly district attorney, Hamilton Burger, for withholding crucial evidence. I met Raymond Burr one time at a Dodgers' game. Nice fellow. I think he was coming on to me, but he wasn't my type, and I was a little too old for him anyway by that time."

Not a subject I wanted to pursue. I nodded as if to acknowledge that she was way too good for the likes of Raymond Burr. "You're right about not sharing information. The defense attorney has been kept completely in the dark." This was not true, but not exactly a lie. "So, could you describe the man?"

"Fellow's back was turned to me, so I didn't see the face. He was wearing one of those tan trench coats that spies wear. You know the kind that belts in the middle and has straps on the shoulders. The big thing was the yellow hair, part of it standing up on top of his head like a rooster, rest of it hanging down. Didn't look all that clean either."

A trench coat without a hat? The two seemed to go together, but that might be only in the movies. I continued. "You said you lost your driver's license because of poor eyesight. Are you sure that's exactly what you saw. Couldn't have been a yellow hat, say?"

"My left eye is in bad shape, but my right eye is 20/20."

I recalled that same good eye peering out at me suspiciously through the crack of the door just a few minutes ago. I looked carefully at the left eye, its retina covered by a cataract. Twenty- twenty or no twenty-twenty, the old girl was half blind. Carter could use this.

"Was there anything else you remembered about the man?"

"He wasn't real tall."

"How tall would you guess?"

"About your size."

"So he wasn't a real tall man?"

"No, but you're no shorty."

If the guy had been over six feet, that would have put Sweets out of the picture, I thought. "You didn't hear anything?"

"Not a sound, and I have perfect hearing."

I remembered seeing a door chain. "So, did Arabella open the door and let him in? Or did she kind of peek out like you just did?"

The old gal hesitated. "Well, she must have. The hall got empty real quick."

It was an odd way to put it.

"So, did you or didn't you see him enter?"

"Well, hell, dearie, he was there, then he wasn't. Where else would he be?"

"Did you see him leave, by any chance?"

"Eighth inning, tied with two men on."

Made sense, I thought. Eighth inning, two men out, a crazy baseball fan like her. Why would she even bother? Perhaps Carter could get the jury thinking about this. It *was* only her word. She could be lying, but I couldn't imagine why.

I couldn't think of anything else. I'd done what Carter asked me to do. As I stood up to leave, she'd already turned on the sound and was concentrating on the game, poised on the edge of the settee, leaning forward toward the set like a catcher crouching behind home plate. I thanked her. She waved me away.

"See yourself out, kiddo."

Outside, on my way to my car, I said aloud, "Adio Sweets. Ciao, Veronica."

A woman walking toward me moved closer to the building as I passed her.

• • •

When I returned to the lot, Sylvia told me I had a call from Carter Innis. I dialed. Carter's secretary put me through. I listened without commenting and slammed the phone down.

"You don't look as if you got any good news," Sylvia said.

"Winona's husband, Fournier," I said, glumly.

"What about him?"

"The cops found him in his motel room last night, shot to death."

"Since you're no longer helping Sweets, what does it matter?"

"*Minchia*," I swore.

"Well, at least, they can't blame Sweets for this murder," She said.

Right, but an important part of Sweets defense was gone. Three shooting deaths, the first two connected by the same kind of weapon. Not the third one, according to Carter. He explained that Fournier was shot with a larger caliber pistol. The news was depressing.

Sylvia stood up from her desk and gave me a hug, her big breasts crushing into me. "Don't look so down, Vittorio. You said you were finished with the whole thing, didn't you?"

I had and I intended to stick to my decision. Why the hell couldn't Innis use the other dude did it defense anyway? Vincent was out on the lot. I joined him and filled him in. His reaction was much the same as Sylvia's.

I waited for the phone to ring and Pop's voice admonishing me for letting Sweets down. I was sure that by now the Raging Cajun, ancestor of

Jean Laffite, had called and whined and begged and resorted to reminders of the favor he did for the Brovelli family, evoking the sacred importance of *onore,* or as Vincent calls it, the frigging *onore.* But no call came, and by five o'clock, I sent Sylvia home and told Vincent I'd close up. Vincent was all too happy to get home. He said he'd drop off Sunny Badger's roses to the Church because he had to pick up some stuff Mom had for his wife. I spent the next hour making cold calls to prospective customers. It was a theory that I'd come up with: Call telephone numbers at random and tell the person who answers that they've won the chance to buy a used automobile at the unheard discount of 30%. Thirty percent, I reasoned, sounded like a lot, but depended entirely on what we took the car in for. In the case of certain cars, if we discounted half, we'd still earn a fifteen percent profit. Cold calls were time-consuming and tedious, and for every twenty calls we made, we might only get one person to take our offer seriously and come down. It was a little like standing at the bus stop waiting for a good-looking woman to get off and asking her if she wanted to go to bed with you. Odds on, 99% of the women would slap your face, but that 1% that said yes might be worth the pain. Vincent had assured me that this was one of my stupider theories. Today, the odds increased. One man and one woman said they were looking to buy and gave me their names, promising they'd be down by noon tomorrow.

After I wrote down the names of our prospective buyers, I went to the storage unit in the back room, slipped on overalls and spent the next hour washing and polishing cars. While I was polishing a pink and white 1958 two-door Impala, the thought crossed my mind that I hadn't asked Carter a couple of things that were still bugging me. I put down my buffer rag and went to make the call, hoping he was still in the office. I reached for the phone, then stopped. What was I doing? I was no longer a part of this. I'd promised myself and I'd promised my brother.

I went back to cleaning cars. Ten minutes later I was on the phone to Carter. I'd caught him just as he was leaving. He sounded down. I told him what was on my mind. No, he replied, there was no rental car issued to Fournier. No automobile of any kind registered to him abandoned. No car registered to him at all, even in New Orleans.

A guy without wheels, no fucking way. It wasn't American.

Innis continued with the bad news. The cops had checked trains and buses. They had no idea how Fournier had traveled here and when he'd arrived. I thought this was too weird. I asked Carter if he could still use the alternative suspect theory. He could try was his answer, but now that the man was dead, it would be more difficult. If only Fournier had been shot with a .22, Carter groused.

I hung up. Outside, I began pacing. I stopped at a 1964 Ford Galaxy. Well, hell, I thought, some buddy of Fournier drove him here. Fournier shot Winona and Arabella, and whoever the guy was who drove Fournier shot him. It was possible. I went back to polishing. My thoughts turned from Fournier to a pleasanter subject, Dila Agbo. At six-thirty and little chance of a sale before closing time, I took our key box, and locked the office. I drove my car on to the street, parked, and placed the chain over the driveway. I'd grab a quick beer.

Flynn's was about half filled when I entered. Swanee was standing by the jukebox, cigarette dangling from his lips, shoving dimes in. Simon and Garfunkel were singing "Mrs. Robinson". Stuart was behind the bar, but Body was sitting on a stool, a bowl of pretzels and a mug of beer in front of him. He waved me over.

I steeled myself.

"Brovelli, me boyo, tell me, why is Italy shaped like a boot?"

"He's going to tell, me, right Stuart," I said to the grinning Tamberg.

"That I am, that I am, lad. But mull it over in that tiny Dago brain of yours for a minute; it's so obvious."

Stuart placed a frosty mug of Anchor Steam on the bar, and I drank. It went down smooth. "I give up," I said.

"Do you think, they could fit that crap in a tennis shoe?"

"Obscure," I said.

"Vince stopped in for a cold one before heading home," Body said. "He told me you guys are out of the detective business, that true?"

"You bet your Irish ass," I said. "Sweets is now in the capable hands of Innis and Innis Attorneys at Law."

"Which Innis?" Body asked.

"Carter."

Body chuckled. "Guess the ancestor of Jean Lafitte will be taking the needle won't he, Stuart?"

The bartender nodded his head. "Better than the electric chair."

"Nothing fried can be good for you," Body said.

"You're a sick man," I said.

Body might be right, I thought. Stay tough, Victor, stay tough, I thought to myself. Don't go looking for a way to break your promise, but the part of me that liked Sweets kept nagging, *have you really done enough?* Obviously, Winona's ghost didn't think so. She was standing by the pool table pointing to her Mickey Mouse watch and tapping one of her feet like Sister Marie Rose did when I walked into her fifth-grade class late.

No way, I thought. I blinked, hoping Winona would disappear. She didn't. Screw it, I'd ignore her. The bar talk had turned to boxing. I tuned out. Let the boxing aficionados argue I nursed my beer and allowed my mind to drift to Dila Agbo. It drifted from idea to idea until I came up with The Idea.

I left without goodbyes and hurried to my Mustang. There was just enough time to go home and change before the eight o'clock performance of *Othello*. The plan that I'd come up with seemed reasonable in its simplicity: I'd attend tonight's performance of *Othello*, and after the performance, surprise Dila with my appearance. I'd wow her with my knowledge of Shakespeare, and convince her to have a late-night dinner with me.

CHAPTER 29
OTHELLO

I do perceive here a divided duty.
Desdemona

As there wasn't much of a crowd, I bought a ticket for a seat in the fifth-row center stage. In college I'd seen the movie version of *Othello* staring Lawrence Olivier playing Othello in blackface. At the end of the film, the business majors, except yours truly, had to be awakened by the humanities majors, all prissy, complaining the snoring interfered with their hearing the actors. I recalled being fascinated by the evil Iago. I'd experienced the same curiosity in college over Lucifer in John Milton's *Paradise Lost*, sent plummeting out of the heavens with his cohort angels into the depths for challenging the Almighty. When I expressed this interest in evil to Vincent, who was in the same college class and hated every second of it, he told me I was too weird to be his twin. That might have been the day I stopped talking to Vincent about my interest in literature.

In tonight's production, the Moor was being played by a Black. I did not say Negro. *Did you hear that, Dila?* Desdemona was white, and Emilia was Adila Agbo. Iago could have been Mexican, and were it not for the dark hair looked somewhat like Sweets' – with the same facial structure, same cunning eyes. That wasn't fair. Sweets eyes weren't really cunning, but in the process of helping him, he'd become somewhat more sinister to me, no longer my pop's savior, and local Robin Hood.

When Emilia entered the stage, in Act II, I clapped, which the people sitting around me didn't appreciate. But I think I got Dila's attention, and that's all that mattered. I vowed to restrain myself for the rest of the play. But that didn't last because when Iago, talking to Cassio, said of his wife:

"Sir, would she give you so much of her lips

As of her tongue she oft bestows on me

You'd have enough,"

I joined in laughing with the rest of the audience but didn't stop when they did, which earned me a lot of shushing noises.

In the final scene when Emilia told Othello how she found the handkerchief and gave it to Iago was a stellar piece of acting by Dila, I thought, but then I was prejudiced, a strange way of thinking about it given the circumstances.

Emilia slumps to the floor murdered by Iago. Othello kills himself and Iago is condemned to be executed. Good riddance, I thought. These days, liberals were proposing doing away with the death penalty, citing there was no evidence that it deterred killers. Maybe so, but I believed that there were people like Iago and worse out amongst us who had, by their violent acts, lost the privilege of life. My brother Mario and I had gotten into a discussion about the death penalty shortly after his return from Vietnam. He was against it. I'd argued that his position didn't make sense since he'd just come back from killing a whole bunch of people, many of whom were probably no guiltier of a crime than he was. That had shut him up, but I could tell I'd hurt his feelings. After the curtain fell, and the applause ended, I followed the audience into the lobby. Coffee and drinks were still being served, so I ordered a glass of red wine and waited. I had no idea how long it would be before Dila and the other actors arrived. I nursed my drink. Time ticked by. The lobby cleared out except for people I figured, like me, were waiting for the actors – friends and family most likely. I'd finished my wine by the time Dila emerged, arm in arm with one of the actors, a real flamer-looking guy. She didn't see me as she walked past, but I heard her complaining about some idiot in the audience clapping inappropriately. She released him with a kiss on the cheek and walked to an older couple, both wearing long African gowns similar in style and color to the one Dila was wearing at the vigil, except the man had an embroidered white cloak slung over his shoulder. Both wore their hair in Afros, and the older women was Dila thirty years from now. They were smiling. So was Dila.

Ah, shit, the parents. Now, what was I going to do? I hadn't come down here for an amateur performance of *Othello.* I moved slowly to my right into Dila's line of vision, hoping she would see me. What she'd do once she did was anybody's guess. I waited, edging this way, then that way, trying to look cool, but unobtrusive, until she spotted me.

Which she did. Her eyes widened in surprise, and her lips formed the word, *Victor*. I bowed, and began walking slowly towards her, casual-like. As I did, she shook her head and those beautiful, lush lips formed the word, *no*. I've never been very good at accepting that word, so I continued walking. When I arrived, I turned on my biggest used car-dealer-smile.

"Miss Agbo, I thought your performance tonight was brilliant." Before she could come up with a response, I turned to the man and woman I assumed were her parents. "Didn't you think so? Truly wonderful. A performance worthy of Stratford on Avon." *My obsequiousness was sort of making me sick.*

"You mean Upon Avon, don't you?" the woman said, and I knew I'd made some kind of mistake. Not knowing what it was, I said, "You must be Dila's mother. The resemblance is uncanny. And you, sir, her father. My goodness, you've got to be real proud. My name is Victor Brovelli." I stuck out my hand.

The man looked at me like I was a lower form of life, which was okay, since that's what lots of people feel used car salesmen are anyway. By contrast, the mother's original frown turned into a thin smile.

"Yes, we are Dila's parents," she said, in the same lilting voice as her daughter. "And we are definitely proud of our daughter. Shake the man's hand Kahil."

Papa Kahil towered over me. I guessed around 6'7" or 6'8". His face was wide with high prominent cheekbones. His skin color was the color of mahogany. He had long eyelashes over dark piercing eyes. Dila got the green of her eyes from her mother. Papa Kahil stuck out his hand, but he didn't look real happy doing it. It was a firm grip, which seemed to me he held too firmly and too long and meant to be slightly painful. I tried not to act like my bones were breaking. All the while Dila was looking back and forth from her parents to me. I couldn't tell from her expression whether she was angry or amused.

When Kahil let go of his death grip, I stepped back and said. "I'm sorry to interrupt. I just wanted to tell Dila how much I enjoyed her performance before I headed home, well not exactly home. I'm going up the street to Ettore's and have a drink and a bite to eat. Say, you folks wouldn't care to join me. Still early. Best calamari in the East Bay."

I was out there on the end of the branch, over the abyss and hoping I wasn't sawing myself off. "You'd be my guests."

"Mother and father, Mr. Brovelli is the automobile dealer that sold our organization a van recently."

"We're pleased to meet you, Mr. Brovelli," the mother said.

"Yes, ma'am. A very reliable van, I'm sure the . . ."

Before I could finish, Dila interrupted. "You know, mother, how the PeaceLinks have needed a good vehicle to move our workers around the city. Mr. Brovelli gave us an excellent discount."

Okay, I got the picture. "The PeaceLinks are a worthy organization," I said, placing an emphasis on the name. My brother's girlfriend works for PeaceLinks. She recommended The Brovelli Brothers' Used Cars. That's where I met your daughter."

"Well, It's been nice meeting you young man," Dila's mother said. It was a dismissal.

I stood my ground.

"Yes," the father said, which could have meant anything but not happy to meet me was the tone I got.

Dila was making small gestures with her chin that were signals, like get lost Brovelli. Failed plan, I thought, but it had been worth a try. After telling Dila again how much I enjoyed her performance, I said my goodbyes. Dila's father looked relieved. Dila's mother's smile was long gone. I walked out of the theater feeling like a failure.

• • •

I was not lying when I told Dila and her parents that Ettore's served the best calamari in the East Bay. I had just been taken my first bite. I took a sip of a very nice Chianti, wondering what in the hell had I been thinking. Dila's parents looked like African royalty. I wasn't sure what African royalty looked like. The last movie about Africa I'd seen was a few years back called *Zulu* about a squadron of British Soldiers surrounded by thousands of Zulu Warriors in South Africa. All the Zulu chiefs wore leopard skins and carried long shields and short spears. I'd also seen *African Queen* with Humphrey Bogart, but the natives in that movie were pretty primitive. What did I know about Africa? What did I care about it, for that matter? Until Dila came into my life - and that had been totally by chance - my relationship to African-Americans had only been as customers. The only friend of color I ever had was in high school, and he was Mexican. I forked a piece of calamari and concentrated on eating. A moment later a shadow fell across my table. I looked up and saw Dila Agbo smiling down at me.

"Do I get my own plate?" she asked.

I leaped up, dropped my fork, damn near knocked over the table, regaining my balance, all the while grinning like an idiot. I pulled out a chair. She sat down. I waved at the waiter and ordered more calamari - and her own plate. She took a sip of my wine and said she'd have the same. This was Berkeley, so we weren't drawing any attention except from a group of older white guys who looked like they might be football coaches. They were frowning. *Si fottano tutti*, fuck them all, I thought.

"So what did you *really* think of the performance?" Dila asked.

I answered in the native tongue, "Favoloso, profonda, e straziante." *Okay, I was showing off.*

"Got the first two. What's the last word mean?"

"Heart-wrenching."

"What did I tell you about my bullshit meter, Victor."

"Look," I said, "You were splendid. I mean it. Too many of the actors, I don't know, seemed a little stiff. I don't know much about acting. I do know from my business if you're not sincere and relaxed, customers pick up on it." I thought maybe Dila would be offended, comparing actors to car salesmen, but she nodded in agreement. For a moment we sat in silence, then I asked, "Your parents don't know you work for the Black Panthers, do they?"

"My parents would freak if they knew. It's not that they are anti Black Panthers, they're only worried about the guns and stuff."

"Guns and stuff is an understatement. I saw some pretty powerful looking weapons. One in particular, was in the back seat of your car."

"I know what I'm doing. I knew from the start that the Black Panthers advocated self-defense. I'm licensed to carry firearms."

"It's more than that," I said. "The Panthers really will pull the trigger. They think we're the enemy."

"Who are you talking about?"

"White people."

Dila gave me a quizzical look. "So, Victor, who tipped you off during the riots? How come your business wasn't trashed?"

Dila made her point, and I was happy to concede. "I promise never to tell your parents." I said, sealing my lips with a twist of my fingers. Dila's calamari arrived and her wine. Explaining to me that she was famished, she tucked in, and we remained quiet for a while. Goddamn, she was beautiful, I thought. Those eyes were hypnotizing. Maybe I was in a trance. I recalled reading a poem in college about a woman who took her men captive to an elfin grot. She closed their eyes with four kisses is all I could remember. I'd settle for one kiss from Dila.

For an entree, I ordered lasagna. I would have ordered linguine con vongole, my favorite, but the clam sauces is rich in garlic, and I was hoping. . . Hope, springs eternal, right? Dila ordered Veal Parmigiana.

I poured more wine.

"There are some guys over in the corner staring at us," She said. "You want me to go over and straighten them out?"

"They're pretty damn big. You might need that carbine you're totting in your car."

Dila laughed. *Oh how that fountain bubbled over with laughter.* I started laughing. Soon we were holding our napkins over our mouths, both of us laughing for different reasons. Damned if I wasn't smitten. Smitten, yeah, smitten. *Whoever says smitten these days?*

When we calmed down, Dila turned around and stuck her tongue out at the football coaches, and we burst out laughing again. She was a hell raiser, and I suspected she would never stop being a hell raiser. When we'd run out of laughter, I asked Dila about her and her family and she told me her story.

She'd graduated from Cal Berkeley last spring with a theater arts and communications degrees and was taking a year off to be more active politically. She played the piano well and until last year sung in her church's choir. About the Black Panthers, she explained that despite their rep for violent confrontation, it seemed to her that they best represented today's black youth. Pointing to herself, she said, "I'm part of that youth." The other two activist organizations, as far as she was concerned, were Elijah Muhammad's *Nation of Islam*, and the *OAU* that stood for *Organization of African Unity*, founded by Malcolm X.

She went on to tell me about how her father and mother had raised their children to be Pan-African, meaning that they should be aware of and proud of their West African heritage. Before she was born, her father had sponsored a tour to West Africa of a group of prominent black businessmen, writers, and political leaders, where he had learned that his roots began in the country of Benin. Although he'd returned energized about his African background, he refused to join the radical movements, claiming that in the United States the only power that mattered was who controlled wealth, a concept, which made a lot of sense to me. I almost interrupted to say, *Right on, dad* but luckily I didn't. From the way she went on about her father, I could tell she had mixed feelings about him. Perhaps it had something to do with the scarring.

"But he changed your name."

"Yes, to what he believed was our traditional African name, Agbo. My parents gave me a traditional female Benin first name "And," she hesitated, "when I reached puberty, Father had me scarred."

I said, "I don't see any scars."

"They're not on my face."

"Where are they, if it's not too personal?"

"Just below my stomach. It means I'm strong enough to be a mother. You know, if you can take the pain of the scarring, you're ready for the pain of child birth. My mom went along with it but she wasn't happy."

From the tone of her voice, I couldn't tell if she was angry at her father or not. I was horrified, but tried not to show it. In the next sentence she answered the question I wouldn't ask.

"I'm not mad at him. It was all about finding an identity and a culture to go along with it that wasn't all about slavery. It didn't really hurt very much. He might have gone a little extreme, but a lot of older Blacks his age were as conflicted as he was. He still is, probably. You saw the African robes. When he's in his African mood, he actually wears them to his office."

I nodded my head. I knew a little about culture, my pop being a good example of a man who prided himself on being Italian, and more specifically a Napolitano.

She told me a little about her mom, a graduate of Howard University, who went on to get her law degree from the UCLA.

"Okay, Victor," she said. "That's enough about me. Tell me about your family."

I had a ton of questions for Dila I would have liked to ask, but didn't. I began the Brovelli family story with Big Sal and my mom meeting at a wedding. She'd been the maid of honor. I named my older siblings and their children. I spent some time on Mario, Vietnam and his girlfriend and *PeaceLinks*. Dila said she approved of PeaceLink's work. Considering she worked there I told her, to which she replied with a smiling, "Touché."

I explained how Vincent and I took over the car business. Dila was a good listener, nodding her head, smiling, encouraging me to delve. I delved. Into my pop's obsession with family and *onore*, my concern that Vincent was becoming a little too politically conservative. I did not delve into Winona's murder and aftermath. I wasn't ready to admit to my part in the crime.

When I finished, she asked, "How's it feel being a twin? I'm an only child."

Being a twin is so natural that I'm surprised when people are curious.

I began with the first thought to cross my mind, "Being a twin is always having each other's' back. One time when we were kids, we were punching each other. . . "

She interrupted. "Why were you punching each other?"

"Doesn't matter; that's what male twins do." I continued. "Another kid stepped in and hit me, believing he was helping my brother. Vincent was all over the kid in a hurry, and I jumped in to finish the job. Word got around that if we were fighting, it didn't pay to take sides.

"Let me tell you a story that says everything about my twin. We were repossessing a 1965 Chrysler Imperial. The car was in a garage with chains on the doors. My twin figures he had about ten minutes max to get in and out. As he snapped through the chain with cutting shears, the chain snapped back and sliced off his forefinger at the knuckle."

"My God," Dila whispered.

I continued, "A wise man would have stopped and found help. Not Vincent. He wrapped the piece of his finger in a handkerchief, stuck the bloody hanky in his pocket, then turned his belt into a tourniquet. Keeping the belt tight, he rushed into the garage and repossessed our car, backing it out of the garage and driving with one hand to the nearest hospital where they sewed his finger back on."

"You're making this up."

"As God is my judge," I said. "You can always count on Vincent."

"I'll remember that if I ever lose a body part."

"There's no braver guy in the world than my brother."

"You know you were pretty brave yourself when you stood up to the cops."

I shrugged.

Dila lifted her wine glass. "Here's to two brave Brovelli's."

She took a sip, the light of the chandelier directly above us momentarily causing her green eyes to glisten, the one more emerald than the other, like it had emerged from a richer vein of the earth.

Dessert menus appeared, saving me from the ancestral search. I ordered a raspberry gelato and she ordered a crème Brule. Both of us had coffee flavored with crème de mint.

I asked her if she thought there was some symbolism about tonight, considering *Othello* was about an inter-racial relationship. She said that was a little too, you know, coincidental for her. I told her I believed in coincidences. I didn't tell her I also believed in miracles, the Holy Sacraments, the Trinity, and the ghost of Winona Davis.

The waiter brought me the check.

I asked Dila if we could do this again sometime.

She hesitated, then replied, "Why not? But let's do it from now on in San Francisco. The East Bay is too close to home. My family would have a fit if they knew I was seeing a white man, particularly my father."

"What was it that Desdemona said to her father?" I asked.

"I do perceive here a divided duty," Dila answered. "But let's not get ahead of ourselves. This isn't even Act I. I got to admit I like you Victor Brovelli but I'm not willing to go to war with my parents over you."

I appreciated her honesty. I wondered what my mom and pop's reaction would be to Dila and me. Not bad if they thought Dila was just another of my girlfriends. If it became more serious, there'd be trouble.

"You're looking kind of startled, Brovelli. You don't think whites have an exclusive on prejudice, do you?"

"Nah," I said, lying. "You think I'm naïve? My brother and I've been doing business on East 14th for six years. We interact with blacks all the time. A few of my best friends are black."

Out came that lovely bubbling laughter followed by, "Oh, Victor, Victor, listen to what you just said. If that's not the most over-used cliché, it's surely in the top ten. I can only count one white female friend and not a single white male."

"Who's your white friend?"

"A girl I met years ago at a summer music and theatre arts camp in Travis City, Michigan. We're both grad assistants at the camp now."

"A long distant friendship. Doesn't count."

"No, Renee's finishing her senior year at Mills College."

If I hadn't gotten the napkin over my mouth, I'd have spit my coffee all over the table.

"What?" Dila asked. "Did I say something funny?"

I shook my head.

"We used to get together for coffee or drinks regularly," Dila continued," but with the political work I've been doing and her senior thesis, we're down to once every couple of months. I miss Renee a lot."

"*Oddio*, I thought.

I regained my composure, and we spoke a while longer about friendship. "Are we going to be friends?" I asked her. She didn't answer, but her smile did for her.

By this time the restaurant had thinned out until we were the last people seated. I examined the bill. I dropped four twenties on the table, and Renee's best friend and I left.

In the romance novels my sister used to read, couples would step out of a fancy restaurant after a romantic meal into a balmy moonlit night with a street musician strumming a love song on his guitar. But this was Berkeley, April, 1968 and what we encountered as we walked out of the door was fog, a couple of stoned hippies, and two police cars, sirens whooping full blast, hurdling down the street. And, from somewhere, too far away to understand, the sound of angry voices.

I walked Dila to her car. *Small talk. Both of us nervous.* I think we wanted to say more, about the night, about us, but didn't. She leaned into me, and we hugged. No elfin grot, no kisses four, not even one, but Tennyson's Knight couldn't have been more in thrall than Victor Brovelli. Before getting in the car, she gave me her telephone number.

Dila said, "I told you, Victor, you'd be dangerous for my health."

As she drove off, I thought, Victor, if you're not careful, you're about to leave your heart in San Francisco.

CHAPTER 30
JITTERS

*The world is full of obvious things, which nobody by any chance
ever observes.*
Sherlock Holmes

Being it was Ash Wednesday, I briefly considered dropping in to
Saint Joe's on my way to work and having some ashes smudged on my
forehead. I nixed the idea because I was feeling too happy for such a
religious downer. I stopped at the gas station to fill up and was greeted by
Jitters. He topped off the Mustang and cleaned the windows all around.
I groused about gas prices going up to 34 cents a gallon. Somebody was
making big bucks. Not us, we agreed. After last night's dinner, I was in a
great mood. A gorgeous woman in my future, and I was free of Sweets. I
wished the weather was sunny to match the way I felt. I was paying Jitters
when he picked up the Tribune laying on the counter.

"You know that f'fellow, got himself murdered over in San Leandro.
See here. . ." He pointed.

"I seen this g'guy around."

It looked like a passport photograph of Jordan Fournier, side by side
with the grainy photograph in yesterday's newspaper of a body sprawled
face down on a motel bed.

"Around here?" I asked.

"Yep. Couple of d'days ago. Drove in to gas up."

Jitters practices what I call selective stuttering. He'll stutter one letter,
then pronounce that same letter perfectly the next time. "You sure it was
the same guy?" I asked. Sometimes Jitters, who'd lived through a North
Korean prison camp, suffered lapses of memory.

"Maybe it was a little longer ago, but I'm sure of the guy and the car."

"Could you have seen him before Winona got killed?" I asked, getting my hopes up.

"Nope, not that long ago. Just a c'couple of days. Three at the most."

"What kind of car?"

"A Mercedes. You know, like the one Sylvia got from her p'pappy."

"You saying it was the same car?"

"N'no, not saying that, just like it though, same year, same make, model, colors and all."

"Did you talk to the guy?"

"You know m'me, Victor. friendly is my middle name. But this fellow didn't say much. Asked if I could direct him to the Oasis. He thanked me p'polite like, you know, real southern gentleman talk, sounds like they got m'mush in their m'mouths."

Damn. If Jitters could put Fournier in the area before Winona's murder, Carter would have more fuel for the Other-Dude-Did-It defense. Hell, even if Fournier was around before Arabella's murder that would work too. I paid Jitters and drove up the block to our lot. After I parked, I sat staring through the windshield. Fournier going to the Oasis could not be a coincidence. Jitters said he didn't think it was Sylvia's Mercedes, but what if it was? How many exact same models, same year and color Mercedes were there around in our part of town? Not many. Could Sylvia's customer have been Fournier? Nah, if that had been the case, she'd have recognized him at Romano's when she brought me the camera. But she'd been surprised.

I left the Mustang and walked around to the front of the building. Vincent was leaning inside a Corvette, doing something and didn't see me. I waved at his backside, hollered, "Yo!" and entered the office. Sylvia looked up from her desk and said, "*Ciao*,"

I ciao'd in return and went to my desk. For a while, I sat trying to remember exactly what Sylvia had said when she saw Fournier in Romano's. Did it matter? Probably not. I stood up and went to the coffee pot. I poured a mug and returned to my desk. I swiveled in my chair, "Hey, Sylvia, you know that Mercedes you sold. Who'd you sell it to?"

"Why you want to know?"

"No reason. Just curious."

"A priest friend of my father's. Actually, he's got a parish in Sacramento. I forgot the name of the church. You want me to look it up?"

"No, no reason to."

Just then, Vincent came through the door, and I left to take my ups. I took a walk through the aisles, inspecting the cars, not that any of them needed inspecting. Knowing Vincent, he'd already checked them out this morning. They were all spotless. I looked up at the sky. The sheets of cloud-cover on the eastern horizon were backlit by a sun trying hard to break through, creating a fuzzy light. To the south, in the direction of San Jose, I could see swatches of blue sky, like patches on a gray blanket. The weather was mild. Extreme weather is foreign to the Bay Area. The rest of the morning my mind raced back and forth between two subjects, Dila Agbo and Sweets. As much as I was resolved to forget about the *ciuccio*, I was having trouble managing my resolve. This did not make me happy. On the other hand, the subject of Dila gave me a warm feeling. I tried to concentrate on Dila, but Pop's voice kept popping into my head, *onore, onore, onore* like popcorn, pop, pop, pop. Sweets was like the needle on a compass pointing in my direction. Maybe I should talk to my twin. Could I confide in him that I was considering continuing to help Sweets, which I wasn't, *hell no, absolutely not, not for one second. You hear that Winona.* I looked around to see if the murdered woman's ghost was within hearing distance. I shook my head. The whole thing from the start had stupid written all over it. I was too damn young to be a private eye. Private eyes were mature men with experience, according to the book, ex-cops, ex-military police; they carried *gats* in shoulder holsters, and talked like Robert Mitchum. What was I? A twenty-six-year-old car salesmen only five years out of college with a degree in business administration and a secret love of literature.

In my mind, I heard Vincent: *It's high time we asserted ourselves, Victor. We're our own men, adults. No more Pop. Just you and me, the Brovelli Brothers.*

But my resolve, which seemed rock solid yesterday, was cracking. Like I couldn't help myself. I was a total weenie. There was, I had to admit, something loveable about Sweets not that I ever found anybody who'd been able to tell me exactly what it was. He took advantage of Pop's friendship, disrespected women, broke into people's homes, lied, cheated at cards, dressed like a clown, and left his frigging candy wrappers for other people to clean up. The only specific good I could name was the rumor of Sweets' donations to poor single moms. Maybe that's what endeared him to me. He *did* keep the cars we provided him with in immaculate condition. Like me, he was a lover of cars. If you did well by your automobile, how bad could you be? It's what my mom once told me about one of her friends from her women's church group who said she'd married her husband because he was kind to animals. In all other ways, she admitted, he was a complete ass.

An hour went by without customers. Vincent relieved me, and an hour later I relieved him. By noon I was ready for chili at Flynn's. I told Vincent I was taking an hour, then I'd handle the afternoon so he could spend the rest of the day with his wife. Vincent was stressing out over Gloria, who was in the last month of her pregnancy. Winona's murder and Sweets' arrest had compounded the stress. No way could I tell him I was having second thoughts.

Larry Hughes' wide ass was taking up two stools. There was an empty on his left. I sat down. A pair of cabdrivers, known as Abbot and Costello, sat next to Larry. There were a couple of Pacific Gas and Electric workers two stools down seated to my left. Stuart was behind the bar. He explained Body was at the dentist and asked me for my order. He returned with a steaming bowl of Irish stew. It came with a thick slice of crusty French bread and my usual frosty mug of Anchor Steam. Hughes was eating his stew and watching the TV that was showing the public memorial for Doctor Martin Luther King Jr being held at Morehouse College, King's alma mater. I figured if Body had been tending bar the funeral would have been quickly replaced with a sporting event. As I ate, I played over in my mind everything I remembered about Jordan Fournier, from the first time I saw him standing in front of Romano's. In my last memory of him, he was talking to one of the Brown Berets before I lost him in the crowd. What the *hell* was Fournier doing talking to the Mexicans anyway? As far as I knew he wasn't Mexican, nor was he a political radical. The way Sweets had described him, he was a small-time gopher for the principal New Orleans' mafia family.

I was mulling this over, when a hand clapped my shoulder, and I heard the familiar voice of Body Flynn. I steeled myself for what was coming.

"Victor, if Tarzan and Jane were Eye-talian, what would Cheeta be?"

"An Irishman because they all look like gorillas," I answered, turning in my seat to face the grinning Flynn.

"Wrong," Body said. "The answer is the *fooking* monkey would be the least hairy of the three." He erupted into laughter that turned into a knee slapping Irish jig. He was wearing a vest covered with green shamrocks. Sometimes Body was a parody of himself. That is until he got with his Irish buddies on Saturday nights, then he was all IRA business and a little scary.

"Knock yourself out, Body," I said. "I've got too much on my mind to listen to your dumb jokes."

"What's the problem, me boyo?" Body asked. "Don't tell me you're still trying to help that jerk off, Sweets."

"No," I said. "Well, maybe, just a little. But you can't say a word to Vincent." Body crossed his heart. "It's just there's some things that seem odd." I explained about Winona's husband as well as I could. I didn't mention the Mercedes.

"So, he might have been around the neighborhood earlier than you knew."

"If Fournier was here earlier, like before Winona was murdered, doesn't it stand to reason he'd try and get in touch with her?" I asked.

"Or he might *not* have wanted to get in touch," Body said. "Divorced guys don't usually carry on a relationship with their ex's. What the hell difference does all this make anyway? The guy is in the morgue."

"They weren't divorced," I said.

"Doesn't matter, estranged, whatever. The man might have had business in the Bay Area."

"Okay, can you give me a reason why Fournier was yakking it up with one of those Brown Berets at the Little Bobby Hutton vigil?"

Body said. "Probably has something to do with the Oasis. If Fournier works for the Mafia in New Orleans, like you said, he might be having dealings with some of our local gangsters. The Amigos handle most of the dope in the East Bay. Except for weed, which is the domain of our very own neighborhood Satans.

Duh, I thought. "So you think Fournier was into dope?"

"Absolutely, Victor. Look, if Carter wants a defense, he needs to focus on the beaners."

"Don't let Jitters hear you talking about *beaners*," Stuart said as he put down a mug of beer in front of Body. "He'll get his Mexican cousin Raul, the weightlifter, after you."

"Jitters is only a little bit Mex," Body said. "Besides, if he gives me any shit, I'll make him pay his tab. It's approaching *the fooking* national debt."

Body looked like he had more to say about Jitters, but stopped. "Jesus, Mary and Joseph, Stuart," Body exclaimed, looking up. "What the *fook* you have on TV. Get that morose shit off and find some sports. There's got to be a baseball game."

"That's Doctor King's memorial," Larry Hughes said.

"Ah shist, Larry, me boyo, I didn't see your black ass there. Sorry."

"Pretty hard to miss my black ass. It's taking up two of your skinny-white ass stools."

Body hollered, "Keep it where it is, Stuart, what the *fook* were you *tinking* trying to change channels. That's important *stoof* there."

All the while this exchange was going on, I was thinking how appalled Dila would be with Body's racism. Until now, as often as I heard Body and some of the other guys in the tavern talk about people's race and religion, it has been like background noise, like traffic on the street.

Body said, "Larry, me boyo, you know I admired Doctor King. I'm all for fighting the fooking oppressors."

"If you didn't make the best chili and stew in the city, I'd stop coming here, you Irish prick."

I changed the subject. "I think I have to go back to the Oasis and talk to the Amigos."

"And you'd be crazy if you do." Body said, raising his voice. "Did you hear what our esteemed Italian friend is proposing, Stuart?"

"I hope you have your life insurance paid up," Stuart said. "You're definitely persona non grata there."

"On second thought," I said. "Maybe I'll send Vincent. He's more likely to survive than me."

The cabbie called Abbot said, "Like the time he stuck a gun to the head of that pimp and saved your ass, Victor."

Larry Hughes leaned into the conversation. "And the time the robber put a gun to your brother's head and your bro bluffed him out of killing him." He chuckled.

Thanks for the memories. "That happened just after we took over the lot from our pop."

"What was that all about?" Stuart asked. "I wasn't around then."

Stories about my brother were becoming mythic in the neighborhood. I have to admit I love telling them, and occasionally embellishing. This particular tale was a classic. I began, "So, you see, this guy calls and tells Vincent he he's got a 1966 Thunderbird convertible for sale and how much would he give him. Vincent tells him, $2,000.00 dollars if it's in good shape. Great the guy says, he'll be right down. He drives up in the Thunderbird, points a gun at Vincent's head and says to fork over the money. Vincent pulls out his check book. No, no, the scumbag says. He wants cash."

"Jesus Christ," Stuart said. "What did Vince do?"

"Yeah, what *did* happen?" the PG&E guy two seats down from me asked.

For a moment I thought, if only Renee were here, I'd get laid, and instantly felt guilty talking that way about Dila's only white friend. I continued. "Vincent says, he doesn't have cash. The robber says he'll shoot my brother's muthafucking head off. Vincent says go ahead and fuck you, and you'll be doing him a favor, since his business was going down the tubes and his wife took their children, cleaned out their bank account, ran away with the green grocer, and his dog just got run over by a truck. The dude gets a frightened look on his face, tells Vincent he's one crazy sonavabitch, runs out the door and jumps into a '67 Lincoln Continental like he's going to drive away. Of course the key is not in the ignition."

"What did the looney do then?" The question came from a guy sitting at the end of the bar.

"He jumps out and sprints back to the Thunderbird and roars away. By then Vincent has been on the phone, and the cops catch the guy before he gets to the Bay Bridge."

"He had a Thunderbird, why'd the dummy try to steal the Lincoln?" Body asked.

"The cops asked him the same question. He told them the Lincoln was a better made automobile than the Bird."

"I agree," Stuart said. "You know granddaddy Ford was a Nazi lover?"

"The Fuhrer couldn't have been all that bad," Body said. "Bombed the hell out of the *fooking* English, didn't he?"

Body started laughing as if what he said was funny. "I'd be joking you pissants. It's a joke.

I love the *fooking* English."

That started me laughing and the rest of the bar joined in.

"Must have missed a good one," Jay Ness said, closing the door behind him.

"It's our favorite member of the constabulary," Body announced. "Welcome Detective Sergeant, you've arrived just in time to keep me boyo here from winding up in your morgue."

"Victor," Ness said. "Are you still playing detective? I heard from Sweets' lawyer, that you'd resigned."

"I did, Jay. I swear. But there's a few things that are bothering me, you know like when there's a rattle in your car and you can't figure out where it's coming from. You take it to the mechanic, but he can't find anything. It drives you crazy, right?"

"How many beers has my good friend Victor Brovelli had, Stuart?"

"Victor believes he has to interrogate the Amigos," Body said. "Because, the fool thinks there's a connection between those assholes and the dead guy from New Orleans."

"Sweet Jesus, Victor. What's this all about? If you know something, you need to tell me."

I told him.

"Well, now, that *is* interesting. Maybe you have a future as a gumshoe. We knew about his record in Louisiana, small potatoes. We didn't connect him in any way to those Mexican hoods."

"Could be drugs," I said. "You know he worked for the mafia?"

"Yeah, we knew that too."

"Sweets knew him when he lived there."

"Interesting. Sweets didn't say a word to us. "

Why wouldn't he, I wondered.

"If there is anything to this, it's a good bet it *is* about drugs. In that context, Fournier's murder makes sense. The way things have been going, we haven't had any let up to deal with ordinary crimes like murder and robbery, not with all this political and racial unrest. I haven't had four hours of uninterrupted sleep since Doctor King was assassinated."

With dark, saggy patches under his bloodshot eyes, Jay looked as if he hadn't slept for a month. He'd definitely lost weight. Jay was a good guy and a good cop in a profession that often, unfortunately, attracted arrogant pricks. I know that isn't a common belief, but all the guys from my high school class that went into law enforcement were bullies and complete assholes.

I felt bad for my friend Ness. Maybe this information about Fournier would provide him with some brownie points with his superiors.

Ness sat down next to me and ordered a shot and beer, dumping the shot into the glass.

"Now, what's all this about going to interview the Amigos?"

Ness had heard about how the Amigos had intimidated my father and how Sweets had saved the day.

"It seems that Fournier could still have murdered Winona and Arabella if this whole thing is about drugs. Or he could have been up here because of some shady business with the Amigos, seen Winona and shot her. They weren't even divorced. She ran away from him."

"If it bothered Fournier that much, why has it taken him this long for paybacks?" Ness asked.

"Who knows? He had other work to do. And he probably didn't know where she was."

Stuart said. "Don't forget Winona temped part time tending bar at the Oasis."

"There you go," I said. "That's how he found out about her. Her ex-pimp works as a bartender there, along with his sister."

Jay said. "That foxy little blonde is dangerous."

"Yeah, Fredericka," I said. "A real cutie."

"Cute, all right," said Jay. "But those long pins in her hair are deadly weapons."

I wasn't sure if Jay knew about my little altercation with the cutie and her brother.

If he didn't he was about to as Body began sharing my adventure with Jay and the rest of the tavern, all of whom were intently listening to our conversation as though it were the featured lunchtime entertainment. When Body finished his tale that ended with Vincent saving my ass, the bar erupted in applause.

I sighed. "Thanks, Body," I said.

"A tale worth telling, me boyo. That twin of yours has got some bollocks."

"Victor, I should arrest you for being a dumb shmuck." Jay said.

"Don't arrest me, Jay, you're the police, go with me."

"Where? What are you talking about?"

"Let's you and me go to the Oasis. We'll question Fredericka, her brother if he's working and some of the Amigos."

"I'm not going in there half-cocked. If the Amigos shot Fournier, I'll need evidence. I'm not going to tip my hand. I need to talk to my snitches, probe a little. See what surfaces. If there're new drug deals going down, the word will be out on the street."

He was right, of course. But I was disappointed. In *How to Be a Private Investigator* I'd read that good P.I.'s know instinctively when they're close to solving the crime. Well, that took care of that. I wasn't a hundred miles close. Anyway, I was donating the book to the library.

"Excuse me," Jay said, getting up. "Got to use the phone."

"Give him the bar phone," Body said to Stuart.

"I'll use the payphone in the back. I don't want half of East 14th Street listening."

My stew had grown cold, and I asked Stuart to heat it up. I tried not to listen to the bar talk, which centered mostly on different episodes in my twin's life. The more I listened, the more Vincent began to sound like James Bond. He was daring enough and certainly was handsome, but I couldn't imagine him with a martini in his hand sweet-talking lovely Pussy Galore. Like Pop, he was a one-woman guy.

Jay returned and slapped me on the back. "Thanks for the information, Victor. I got the ball rolling. I'll put you in for a police commendation if this drug connection turns out. Perhaps the mayor will give you the key to the city."

"*Va fangul,*" I said.

Jay slapped my back again. "I could arrest you for telling an officer of the law to go fuck himself, you know." Picking up his change from the bar, he ignored my second "*Va fangul!*" and hurried out the door, laughing.

Body took Jay's seat next to me. "Hey Victor, do you know what an Italian nativity scene consists of?"

Give me strength, I thought, shaking my head.

"Jesus, Mary and three wise guys."

Screw the stew, I threw a couple of bucks on the bar and left, the sound of Body laughing trailing me out on to the street. One of these days, I thought, I was going to knock him on his ass. I walked back to the lot and told Vincent he was good to go. Sylvia looked at me longingly. I gave her the rest of the day off too.

In the office, I tried to do paperwork, but I couldn't keep my mind focused. I went outside and ran a rag over a few cars that didn't need dusting, and straightened out a couple of price tags. Not a customer in sight. As usual, there was a lot of traffic coming and going along East 14th. If I closed my eyes, after a while the sound was comforting, like wind in trees or ocean waves were to a nature lover. A foursome of Satans roared by on their hogs, Sunny Badger riding the lead hog, the trio spread out behind him, taking up both lanes of traffic. The drivers in the cars behind the Satans were smart enough not to blow their horns. I thought of waving, but they were long gone.

Back in the office, I spotted another of Sweet's candy wrappers under Sylvia's desk. Sylvia was a meticulous bookkeeper but a lousy janitor. I grabbed a broom from the back, swept them up and dumped the irritating reminders of Mr. Sweet Tooth into the trash can. When the hell was the last time Sweets was in this office, I wondered. I put the broom and dust pan away and returned to my desk. It was two o'clock. The phone rang; Carter Innis on the line reminding me I had a date with his cousin tonight. I assured him I hadn't forgotten Veronica - which I had forgotten - completely. I hung up without mentioning that Jordan Fournier was once again a possible alternative suspect. Until I heard from Ness, I didn't want to get Sweets' hopes up. Or Innis' hopes up of becoming the next F. Lee Bailey.

Veronica, a 10 out of 10 on the stewardess scale, Top of the Mark for dinner. How in the world did I forget? I tried to imagine her naked on a bed, but instead I was looking at the face of Dila Agbo across the table from me at Ettores. I opened my wallet and withdrew Dila's telephone number, trying to figure out if asking her for a date less than twenty-four hours after last night's dinner would seem as if I was too anxious. Unlike women I'd dated before, Dila worried me. She possessed a combination of traits that I'd not found in my other. . . what was the P.C. term the hippies were using to describe lovers? Significant others, right? Not that Renee, one of my others, was by any means insignificant. But, I'd long ago figured out our relationship. Dila would not be so easy to pigeon-hole. Nor did I really want to. I simply enjoyed being with her. For the first time in my life, when I thought of a woman, I did not immediately think of sex. If I shared this thought with any of my local buddies at Flynn's the derision would be universal: *Next step is the altar, Victor. Guess we won't see you at the poker games anymore. Pussy whipped, eh? Victor, my friend, say it isn't so? Tell me, me boyo, what do you call an Italian who doesn't immediately think of sex when he sees a good-looking woman?* Not to mention, Dila was African-American, what an uproar that would create in the tavern. The thought occurred to me that, perhaps, the first indication that you were falling in love was when you didn't think of the woman in question in terms of sex. Don't be stupid, Brovelli, I said to myself. That contradicts the entire history of male behavior.

I dialed Veronica's number. The phone rang. "You are about to do something really dumb," I whispered as I listened for her to pick up. On the fourth ring, she answered in the same sultry voice I remembered hearing for the first time on a flight to Chicago when she'd stopped at my seat and asked me for my luncheon preference. When I told Veronica important business had come up, and I couldn't get away, her sultry voice turned petulant. As she was scheduled to fly out tomorrow, I promised next time she was in town we'd get together. By her response, I didn't believe that would happen. I should have felt like a dumb fuck passing on Veronica of the scrumptious body. Instead, as I hung up the receiver, I felt pretty damn good, like when you go to confession and you don't leave any sins out.

The next couple of hours dragged, until two old ladies with blue gray hair marched onto the lot – and I mean marched, not a cane or a limp between them. We'd been recommended by their colleague, Mr. Stokes, they explained. It took me a moment to realize they were talking about Jitters. Unless they were drag-racers or mechanics, I wondered what they meant by colleagues. They explained they wanted to purchase an automobile with a little giddy-up. I showed them a number of cars I thought they'd like. After test driving a few sports cars, including a sharp 1966 Corvette, the two senior citizens selected a gunmetal gray 1955 Chevy 3100 series pickup. It definitely had giddy-up-and-go. Under its hood was a rebuilt 347 cu in Ford engine with 350 horses. It was too much car for them, but they offered cash, so who was I to dissuade them? I wrote them up, followed them out to the lot, and watched them drive off, their arms out the windows waving at me. When they hit the street, the pickup peeled rubber and was gone.

Back in the office I tossed the paper work in Sylvia's in-tray, which caused another of Sweets' candy wrappers to pop into the air. It fluttered to the floor like a miniature bird. Cursing, I picked the wrapper off the floor and held it between my fingers. It smelled faintly of orange. The thought came to me that instead of the wrappers in Arabella's apartment being proof Sweets was the murderer, didn't it prove the opposite? Why would the killer leave behind such obvious evidence of his presence at the murder scene? Sweets was not a genius, but he was no dummy. On the other hand, it would have been smart of the real murderer to place Sweets' candy wrappers at the scene. The candy wrappers wouldn't have been hard to come by since wherever he went, he left a trail of them behind him like Hansel and Gretel left breadcrumbs. Only in Sweets case, it would have turned out better for him had the script stayed true to the fairy tale and a flock of birds had eaten the trail. I'd pass on this thought to Carter, in the event he hadn't already thought of it

The phone rang. I picked up and listened to Renee inviting me to an Academy Award Party at a friend's house. Because of Doctor Martin Luther King's memorial service, Gregory Peck, the President of the Academy, had postponed the ceremony that was scheduled for the 8th to the 10th. According to some of the guys at Flynn's the Awards had been high jacked by the liberals with two movies about race relations: *In the Heat of the Night* that I thought was boss, and *Guess Who's Coming to Dinner*, that I hadn't seen. Both movies starred a black actor named Sidney Poitier. I told Renee, maybe, but not to count on me. One thing about Renee, she didn't waste her time being disappointed. I'd never doubted that my quasi-girlfriend had alternative males in her address book. She made kiss-kiss sounds, said "later" and hung up.

Closing time was still a couple of hours away. So far, we'd had a slow day. One sale did not fire my engines, albeit a cash deal. Screw hanging around. I began closing up. First, I checked the cars to make sure they were all locked. I sorted through the paperwork on Vincent and my desks to be sure there wasn't anything that Sylvia needed to do in the morning. Accounts receivable was always welcome; accounts payable, not so much so. I found a post-dated check on Vincent desk. I wasn't sure what transaction it belonged to. I left it for Sylvia with a note. I took the key box and locked the office. In the distance, I could hear the grinding sound of rush hour traffic on the freeway and the occasionally whine of semis as they geared down. East 14th had cleared out some. The sun had broken through and was low on the horizon, turning the Oakland Tribune clock tower the color of burnt orange. I watched the sunset for a moment, then walked behind the office and got in my Mustang. I turned on the ignition, then turned it off. I slapped the steering wheel. Ever since Jitters told me about Fournier, this whole pain-in-the-ass business was making those irritating noises in my head. Sweets' conviction hinged on the evidence in Arabella's apartment and the testimony of the old lady across the hall from Arabella that put the bird-man at the scene of the crime. But did it place him inside?

Not necessarily. However, the candy wrappers and his fingerprints on the glass did. Was there any way Fournier fit into this? Could he have killed the two women, then wound up getting shot because of some drug deal gone bad? Of course, but where was the proof? Jitters saw Fournier at his gas station, driving a Mercedes. All that proved was he was there *after* the murders, but not *before* the murders.

My gut told me there was evidence that would clear Sweets, if only I could figure out what it was. Then I heard myself say, "But you're too dumb to figure it out." If that's the case, I thought, it wouldn't hurt to talk to someone, would it? Just talk. I wouldn't be going back on my word to Vincent. I was always able to bounce ideas of Renee. Only she'd think this was really exciting and dangerous, which would get her thinking sex. Besides, she was heading to an Academy Award party. No, the person I really wanted to talk to was my Black Angel. I got out of the car and returned to the office. I took her telephone out of my wallet. Three rings and she answered.

"I had a fabulous time last night," I said.

"Victor?"

"The only Italian white guy you know."

"I can't talk. I have another performance tonight, and I'm late."

"Are you free afterwards?"

"What do you have in mind?"

"How about an assignation in San Francisco?"

Dila laughed. "Give me an assignation designation quickly, and I'll meet you."

"Ten-thirty at Vesuvio's on Columbus."

"Is that the place across the alley from City Lights Books?"

"Right."

"I know it," she said. "See you there. Sorry, got to run."

The phone went dead, but I felt very much alive.

CHAPTER 31
NORTH BEACH

Poetry is the shadow cast by our streetlight imagination.
Lawrence Ferlinghetti

When I was in my sophomore year of college, the year most students discover they're intellectuals, the freshman year being too scary and the junior and senior years too consumed with studying, Frank Shirley, the school's chug-a-lug champ, and I used to drive to the North Beach in San Francisco on weekends. Our destination was a tavern called Vesuvio's, where we knew there'd be a plethora of hippie chicks waiting for two handsome college studs. It was Frank's idea that we take some poems with us to impress the maidens with our literary skills. Being business majors, those were skills neither of us possessed. No problem, Frank said. All we needed to do was hit the library, find some archaic Greek or Roman poems in translation, write them on the back of an envelope and present them as our own. Plagiarism was not a consideration, hippie chicks were.

The memory of those nights of mellow fruitfulness followed me into Vesuvio's. I'd arrived early. I sat down at the bar and ordered an Anchor Steam. The television above the bar was tuned to the concluding portion of the Academy Awards, the announcement for Best Motion Picture of the Year. A cheer went up when it was announced that *In the Heat of the Night* was the winner. The camera panned into the audience to the smiling faces of Sidney Poitier and Rod Steiger. A guy next to me, told me, Steiger won for Best Actor in a leading role. Poitier had already won an Oscar for Best Actor in 1964 for his role in *Lilies of the Field*, a movie my twin said couldn't possibly be good with a wussy name like that. I saw it anyway, but didn't tell him. Didn't blow me away. I was on my second beer when the door opened and Dila walked in, hip in a purple waistcoat with fringes draped over a white silk blouse tucked into black flared trousers from which emerged the tips of two high heeled black boots. *Madonna, protect your good Catholic boy.* I wasn't being altogether insincere.

I was trying to decide whether to give her a hug, or perhaps a peck on the cheek, some sign of how happy I was to see her, when she surprised me by kissing *my* cheek.

"The electrical system failed in the fourth act," she said. "I hitched a ride with the director who lives in the Marina. I'll ride back with you so you won't be lonely."

The hell with Sweets, I wasn't going to ruin what appeared to be the start of a propitious evening with talk of drug dealers and murders. The guy sitting next to me moved over, and she sat down and ordered a white wine. She looked up at the TV and asked who'd won for best picture. "Right on," she said when I told her *Heat of the Night*. We talked about the movie. She said the scene in which Mr. Tibbs slaps the white plantation owner was one hell of a brave move by Hollywood. She brought up *Guess Who's Coming to Dinner* as another brave Hollywood flick. I agreed, thinking to myself what the reaction my folks would have if I brought Dila home for pasta. If Dila brought me home, her father would probably shoot my honky ass. We talked a little about *Othello* and some more about Shakespeare. She reminded me that the Bard always included scary stuff like witches, clowns, somnambulists, and ghosts in his plays to appeal to the common folks. I kind of knew that. I didn't mention that the ghost of dearly departed Winona was following me around.

After Vesuvio's, we crossed Columbus Avenue to the Anxious Asp to hear a singer named Mose Allison, who Dila assured me was fabulous for a blues singer. "You'd think he was black," She said. "If you didn't see his face." The club was located in a basement where I imagined Beats like Allen Ginsberg, Jack Kerouac, writers like that hung out. I remembered our English professor lauding the Beat writers and only the English majors giving a shit. I had a copy of Ginsberg's *Howl* on my bookshelf. Read it once, thought it stunk. The club was dark and crowded, cigarette smoke covering the ceiling like cirrus clouds. The sweet scent of weed permeated the air. Through the gloom, I spotted a couple leaving their table, and we got there before a trio of hipsters. We had a good view of the small stage. A couple seated to our left were huddled over a chess board oblivious to the piano and the singer and the people circling around them. We ordered drinks, white wine for

Dila, Anchor Steam for me. Mose started singing with an accent much like
Sweets', which was not surprising since, according to Dila, Mose Alison grew
up in Louisiana. The song was called "Seventh Son". I liked it.

During a break, Dila leaned across the table and asked me what
was wrong.

"Nothing," I said.

"Nothing will come of nothing," she said. "Speak again."

Couldn't fool me, that was Shakespeare, but I didn't remember the
play. If I spoke again, I'd have to lay out the whole, from start to finish,
including Vincent and my part in the cover-up. How would Dila take
having a relationship with an accessory to murder? On the other hand,
since Winona was African-American, wouldn't Dila be more motivated
to help find her killer, than if she was some white girl from the burbs? So,
I took a deep breath and explained everything, ending with my present
frustration.

"Ohwee," Dila said. "You snuck that poor girl's body into the Satans'
clubhouse and left her alone."

"We were real respectful," I said, thinking being alone wouldn't have
mattered to Winona. I hadn't counted on her ghost. But I was not going to
tell Dila with my ghostly encounters.

"That was cold, Victor."

"I know, I know. If I could take it back, I would, believe me. I feel really
shitty about it."

"Trying to save your ass."

"And Sweets' ass," I added. "And our car dealership. Not to mention
our family honor was at stake."

That drew a chuckle. "Good lord, whites talk about black families
being fucked up."

"Honor makes a man strong as a mountain," I said quoting my father.
It was a belief I held on to, but recently my grip on the paternal ledge was
slipping. *Sorry, Pop.*

"That's beyond strange," Dila said. "So, what do you want from me?"

My black angel didn't sound happy, and I didn't blame her. "Another
view point. I've run out of ideas. And suspects."

Dila shook her head. "Look, this is messed up, to say the least. I'll try,
but no guarantees. Why don't you start over again, from the beginning,
and don't leave any details out.

She was right. My detection manual made the point that it's all in the details.

Our conversation was interrupted by Mose returning to the piano. He started singing "Parchman Farm" that Dila explained was his signature song about a convict picking cotton. I thought of Sweets describing the penitentiaries in Louisiana, not that the liar had ever actually been inside. Dila explained that "Parchman Farm" or "Parchman Farm Blues" was first recorded by a black guy named Bukka White in 1940 about his experiences in the Mississippi State Prison, notorious for its harsh conditions. I told her about Sweet's trying to get my sympathy by lying to me that there was an outstanding warrant for him from Louisiana.

"I don't know Sweets," she said, "but I heard a few things from the brothers."

"Like what?"

"Like he's got some kind of weird mojo."

"The Panthers," I said.

"No, not the Panthers, but some of the older brothers helped him a while back."

My pop never knew what Sweets actually did to get the Amigos off his back. Perhaps those older brothers had helped.

"I'm ready to hear the next episode of the Brovelli boys," Dila said. "You can tell me the rest on our ride home."

Second Street led to the Bay Bridge onramp. At this time in the morning, traffic was light. I stayed in the slow lane so we could talk better. I shook my head. "You know, Dila, I don't think Sweets did it, but I don't think Fournier did it either. Something in my gut tells me I should be able to figure out who did?" I told her my analogy about the unexplained car noise. "So, you see, you're my expert mechanic. I need you to bring all your objective prowess into play."

"Damn, Victor. I'm pretty good at figuring out government tactics or interpreting lines in plays, but a Girl Friday I'm not. Isn't your job to get Sweets off, not find out who the real killer is?"

"I guess," I said. "The reality has very little to do with Winona, who I hardly knew. But I liked Arabella."

"Aha," she said. "This is the very ecstasy of love."

"I like this line better. 'Who ever loved, that loved not at first sight?' "

"You loved her at first sight?"

"I'm talking about you."

"You can't tell, but I'm blushing."

No way was I going to step on that P.C. landmine. "It's the truth, Dila, from the moment I woke up in the Panthers' office and saw your face looking down at me."

"We better get back to talking about the murders."

Forget the murders. I wanted to talk about her and me, but I felt pushing it would not help my cause. "Okay. Lets." I said. "You have any flashes of insight?"

"Nothing specific, but I remember a problem-solving strategy one of my professors taught us. It's called webbing. You start out with a blank sheet of paper in the center of which you place your subject. In your case it would be Winona or Arabella or both. Then you start writing down words or phrases that you associate with the subject and place them around the subject, drawing arrows from the center to the satellites. The key is to write every little thing you associate with the subject, no matter how trivial. It's kind of a free flowing thought process. Let your mind go. Soon you'll have a page filled with circles all interconnected. You see what I mean?"

"Not exactly."

"The sheet of paper will look like a galaxy."

"Like a bunch of gaskets."

"I don't know what those are."

"Just car talk. All right, I get it."

"You're weird, Mr. Brovelli."

"Once I've run out of things to put in the holes, then what do I do?"

"You fixate. Ask yourself why you wrote them down? For each of your little satellite subjects you have to be able to answer that question. My prof used to tell us that there are unexplored places in everyone's mind where one's best ideas are hidden."

"It sounds a little hippie-dippy to me."

"There's nothing hippy about it. You don't have to drop any acid, all you need is a blank sheet of paper, a pencil and your mind."

"I'll try it tomorrow first thing. Thanks."

"You can go a little faster, Victor. You can't keep a girl out to all hours when she has to go to work early in the morning. I'm not just a volunteer, I get a paycheck."

I accelerated. Dila turned on an R & B station, Gladys Knight and the Pips she told me when the voices started singing, "Do You Love Me Just a Little Honey?" Followed by another of their hits, "Every Beat of My Heart". We reached the turnoff to Berkeley, from there she directed me to her house. I parked in front of an attractive two-story shingled home with a wrap-around porch on a tree lined street close to the University of California. There was no ghetto in this woman's life. She turned to face me.

"My daddy owns a successful business. A very successful business."

Anticipating my question, she said, "I wouldn't want the Panthers to know."

"All your secrets are safe with me." I said, thinking the Panthers probably knew anyway.

"You're a good man, Victor." She leaned forward and placed her hand on my cheek.

I reached for her, but she was too quick. I started to speak, but she shushed me with her finger on my lips.

"Remember, we're only in Act One."

With that she opened the door, stepped out of the car and ran to her front door.

"*Madonna*," I whispered, as I pulled away from the curb. I was thinking about Act Two.

CHAPTER 32
BRAINSTORMING

The brain is a world consisting of a number of unexplored
continents and great stretches of unknown territory.
Santiago Ramon y Cajal

The morning sun was shining through the window, sending dust motes sliding down long streams of light to my bedroom carpet. For a moment I watched their descent through a hazy, romantic vision of happiness with Dila Agbo, then tossed off the blankets and headed for the bathroom. I showered and shaved. I congratulated the person looking back at me from the bathroom mirror on a successful evening. In the past, success would have been measured by the presence of a warm female body lying next to me. But this morning I redefined my definition of success. It was a work in progress, I knew, but you had to put the car into drive before you could go anywhere. I started with the word friendship. Returning to my bedroom, I dressed, went to the kitchen, turned on Mr. Coffee, and retrieved my newspaper. While I drank, I scanned the front-page headlines:

Berserk Youth Slays Mother;
Reserves Get 24,500 Call-Up;
Johnson to Sign Rights Bill Today.

President Lyndon Baines Johnson was going to sign a civil rights bill that prohibited discrimination in housing sales. Dila would be thrilled. I felt like calling her, but she'd already be at work unless, like me, she'd slept in. I dialed her home number. No one answered. Calling her at work didn't seem like a good idea.

Hi, can I speak to Dila Agbo?

Who's calling?

Victor Brovelli.

Why you want to talk to one of our sisters, whitey?

That I imagined would be the dulcet voice of James the Ferocious. I had no desire to antagonize him. This whitey would wait to talk to her face to face in the evening after the make-up performance of *Othello*. No doubt Dila was current on all the latest political news anyway.

Time for work. I knotted the blue tie with red Gael insignias on it, slipped on my blue blazer and headed for the door. The Mustang was waiting for me at the starting line of a new day. According to the radio, the new day was partly cloudy with a chance of rain. On the way, I reviewed Dila's suggestion to create a web of details based on Winona's and Arabella's murder. It was a good idea. Last night, I'd decided I was going to break my promise to Vincent and continue to help Sweets. Breaking a promise to my twin was *not* a good idea. On the other hand, we hadn't had one of our knockdown, drag-out fights in a long time. I thought back to our last fight and couldn't remember what it had been about and how long it lasted. In the Twin Ring, our fights always turned out to be draws. I did remember that our battles cleared the air between us, the way storms do after they blows through, leaving the skies blue and the air fresh. *Yeah, and sometimes they leave a black eye or two and a couple of loose teeth.*

Why was I breaking my promise to Vincent? The only answer I could come up with was that I've have always be stupidly stubborn, an opinion of myself that has been substantially and repeatedly proven in the past.

I got to work and parked. Vincent was standing in the middle of the lot surrounded by cars, gazing at them as if they were prize cattle he'd raised on his ranch. Sylvia was sitting at her desk. Vincent waved to me over. He was wearing his red tie with blue Gael insignias.

"We've lucked out for a couple of more cars," he said. "Jitters got the word O'Keefe and Sons have also decided to move their dealership."

"Like rats from a sinking ship," I said.

"Whatever," Vincent said. "The point is we have first dibs on their cars. You want to go or should I?"

"You got the ball rolling, bro, you go. I'll take the lot."

"The early bird, right? See you around noon." He started walking, then stopped and turned around. "Oh, Sylvia says her Daddy's got another car for her. Wants to know if she can take a couple of days off to go get it. You decide."

"Not a problem."

He took off, happy as an Italian who'd fallen into a barrel of Chianti. I'd completely forgotten to ask him how his wife was doing. But he was already behind the building out of sight. I heard his engine turn over and watched him drive off the lot.

In the office, Sylvia looked up from her desk and asked, "Interesting looking woman you were seen with last night, Vittorio?"

"You got someone following me, Sylvia, or what?"

"Or what," she said. "Got a cousin tends bar at Vesuvio's. He called me and said there was a guy who looked a lot like you having a drink *with una donna nera.*"

"I'm surprised your cousin didn't say the N word."

"Come on, Victor, when did you become so sensitive? I'm just asking. It's strange times we're living in. The coloreds are getting pretty damn restless."

"Like the Injuns on the reservation, huh?"

"There you go again. You're sounding awful liberal these days. You got to admit there are a lot of stirred up people."

"Like our brother Mario and all his friends, is that what you mean?" I asked. Life in the Sixties was getting to me, getting to the entire country. It was like the country was suffering from a migraine.

"All right, point taken," Sylvia said. "Let's drop it okay. I don't give a crap who you date. But aren't you seeing some college sweetheart pretty steady?"

"Renee and I have an agreement," I said. "And since you're being such a Pinocchio, that *was* me having a drink with a black woman. And the night before, after her performance in *Othello,* we had dinner together at Ettore's. You want to know what we ordered. I had. . ."

"*Basta.* No, I don't want to know. Sorry I mentioned it. Hey, go have a drink, calm down, you *ciuccio*"

"Too early in the morning." I was angry and tempted to tell Sylvia she'd have to wait to go to San Diego and pick up her damned car, but that would have only antagonized her more, and she seemed plenty on edge this morning. I took a deep breath. "Okay, I'm calm, all right?" She gave me a tight smile. "Vincent says you'd like to go down to your daddy's. How long will you be gone?"

"Yeah, Victor. Papa called and said there was a real nice Volkswagen Custom Van he'd let me have. It's Easter weekend. I'd like to go to mass on Sunday with the folks. Be back on Monday. Is that okay?

"Go ahead," I said. "Once Vincent comes back, you take off. We can handle the intake. Motor vehicles doesn't open 'till Monday anyway. Go, have a good time. Enjoy, all right?"

"Thanks, boss. Sorry I called you a *ciuccio* I'm sure your Negro woman is a lovely person."

"The term is Black, not Negro. Negroid is a race. You don't say I have a lot of Caucasian friends, do you? "What's going on with you, Victor?""

"Nothing," I said, wondering what in hell I *was* talking about. "Would you mind taking the lot for a while, while I'll do some paperwork?

Once Sylvia left, I went to my desk. I began looking through my messages. There was a call from Carter Innis and a call from Pop. Sylvia had written urgent at the bottom of both messages. I had no desire to talk to Pop, but I needed to talk to Innis. I sat back in my chair and closed my eyes, trying to think. There was something bugging me, but I couldn't figure out what it could be. Something odd that had to do with Sweets. I opened my eyes and stood up. I looked around the office hoping to trigger my memory. Nothing doing.

Through the door I saw Sylvia talking to Nick Parsegian next to a two-tone red and white 1961 Nash Metropolitan. The last time I'd talked to the Armenian, he was in the market for a small car for his daughter. I got into my salesman mode and went to greet him.

They were chatting about Winona, not the car. Parsegian nodded to me as I approached.

"We were just discussing that dear girl Winona." Parsegian said. "How sad such a thing could happen. I was saying it was made more dreadful that she was changing her life, enrolled in Laney College."

Sylvia was nodding in agreement. "She did good work for us."

I could do without the subject, particularly since her ghost was standing only a few feet from us, an ethereal smile on her ghostly face. It was not cold, but I shuddered. I shook my head and Winona disappeared. I waited for a second, then changed the subject.

"Are you by any chance here to buy that car for your daughter?" I asked, pointing to the Nash. "You won't find a safer car for her than this baby. I took it in on a '66 Pontiac GTO. I don't think the guy knew how good a shape the engine was in. You ask Jitters what he thinks. He tuned it." Evoking the name of Jitters was a sure-fire selling point with all who knew the skills our mechanic possessed. In Parsegian's case, it was definitely a plus. "It doesn't have a lot of power, but you don't want your daughter drag racing, right?" Parsegian looked horrified at the mention of drag racing. I'd made another sales hit, *a palpable hit.* I smiled, thinking that ever since I'd met Dila I was definitely into the Bard.

Sylvia left, leaving me alone to close the deal.

I gave Parsegian my rock-bottom price. He withdrew a notebook from his pocket and wrote the number down, with a promise to think about it.

Rather than have him walk off the lot, I lowered the price two hundred. The discount made an impression on him. Discounts are at the heart of his business. I went to the office and returned with the keys. He took the Nash for a spin, which I was sure would wind up at Jitter's gas station for a Q & A. Sylvia poked her head out of the office door and asked was it a sale. I told her I figured it was. My instincts proved correct. After Parsegian drove back onto the lot, he asked for another hundred off. I stood my ground, but told him I'd pay the tax. He took out his checkbook. "My little princess will very much like this automobile," he said. She was his princess all right. Her name was Marian and as far as I could tell, having only met her a few times, spoiled rotten. I sent Parsigian into the office to finish the paperwork and provide him with the opportunity to ogle Sylvia's large jugs. A half hour later, a big smile on his face, he drove off the lot and across the street in the Nash, believing he'd managed to get a good deal out of this Brovelli Boy. Based on the Blue Book price for a Nash for this year and model, he had. But what he didn't know was how much we bought the car for. It's odd how salesmen are knowledgeable about their particular business, but are often ignorant of general sales principals when it comes to other businesses.

Sylvia stood at the office door, "Four big ones," she said.

Vincent would be happy with the profit. I started walking around the lot in order to check our stock, but wound up considering Dila's brainstorming suggestion. I decided it wouldn't hurt to try it out. I went to the office and left the door open, telling Sylvia to keep an eye out for customers. I placed a sheet of typing paper on my desk. Moving my chair to my left, so Sylvia couldn't see what I was doing, I began, as Dila had instructed, by drawing a circle in the middle of the paper with the name Arabella in its center. Why Arabella and not Winona? I felt the most damaging evidence against Sweets had to do with Arabella's murder. I stared at the name and the circle and the white empty space around it and concentrated. Details and names began to appear in their own gaskets extending out from the center. Let your mind go, Dila had instructed. *Don' think, just feel and write.* By the time I was through, I had over twenty interconnected circles that actually looked more like a galaxies of planets than automobile gaskets.

"What you got there?"

I looked up at Sylvia standing behind me staring down.

"Nothing."

"Looks like something to do with those murders to me."

"Loose ends. Just trying to get everything straight."

"I thought it *was* straight. *Finito*," Sylvia said, her voice hardening. "Vincent will be furious if you change your mind."

"Not to worry, cuz. I'm done with it." To make my point I crumpled the paper into a ball and sunk a nice little hook shot into the wastebasket.

"Why should I worry? I'm not the one who messed up," She asked, "I'm going for lunch, okay?"

"Yeah, go for it," I said.

After Sylvia left, I reached into the wastebasket, removed my ball and flattened it out on the desk. I read what I'd written a couple of times, trying to do the free association thing, but came up with no new ideas, nor was I able to put a name to that irritating noise in my head. In fact, the more I looked at all of the details in their little planets, the more I knew there should be one more just beyond my understanding. If only I had some kind of interplanetary brain telescope. Damn, I balled the paper again and shot - air-ball. Screw it. I forced myself to think of last night with Dila. That did not take a great effort.

The phone rang. It was Vincent. O'Keefe had three more cars he was willing to get rid of, all primo automobiles, of which one was a 1956 DeSoto.

"And guess what, it has a Highway Hi-Fi unit in it."

I could only imagine my brother's excitement. In that year, Chrysler Motors had come out in some of their models with a record player mounted into the dash. It was not practical because you could only play seven-inch records made for Columbia Record Company. This car, Vincent explained came with a bunch of Broadway show tunes. Collectors would jump all over this car whatever its condition. The other two would earn us a decent profit even after factoring in Jitter's bill. There was a risk in absorbing too much inventory. He agreed, but argued we'd never have such a chance again. If we couldn't sell some of these cars fast, I warned him, we'd be up shit creek. I finally relented, when he reminded me that we were the

Brovelli Boys, and standing back-to-back nobody could take us down. I'm a sucker for that kind of fraternal machismo. I said that I'd get a hold of the bank and for him to go for it. I hung up the phone.

The Brovelli Boys were on a roll. We were taking a financial plunge, pedal to the metal. We'd either crash or come blazing across the finish line, the checkered flag waving.

There is no accounting for how my twin and I were acting, suddenly willing to take risks with our business when we had only three weeks ago been terrified we would wind up bankrupt. It occurred to me that perhaps it was the craziness of the times that was emboldening us. I was suddenly feeling pretty dam confident that Brovelli Brothers' Used Cars was on the highway to success. When Vincent got back we'd celebrate to our future.

Pappy Van Winkle here we come. The bottle stood proudly on the shelf behind Sylvia's desk flanked by two glasses, one for me, one for Vincent. Sylvia didn't drink whiskey. I took down the bottle, brought it to my desk and set it down, light from the window illuminating it. "*Che cazzo,*" I said, examining the bottle. The level of booze had dropped below our last marker. Eyeballing it, I couldn't be sure, so I took a pencil off my desk and lowered it down then back slowly a number of times until the tip came up wet. Yep, definitely, somebody'd been doing some drinking. Since I knew I hadn't been taking a nip, it had to be Vincent. Maybe his wife's pregnancy was driving him to drink. I left the bottle on my desk for Vincent's return. I stood in the open door looking out on the lot and imagining where we'd place the new cars. But my mind took me to Arabella's murder. Ten minutes went by. I went back inside the office and retrieved my brainstorming out of the wastebasket. That paper so wrinkled now that I had trouble reading it. I worried over it for a while, but came up with zero. Dunked it back in the basket. "*Mavaffanculo*" I said.

"You know it's against the law to swear in a foreign language." Jay Ness said, stepping into the office.

"Gee, Jay, between you and Body, I'm surrounded by comedians. You here to see me or to check out Sylvia's tits?"

"Take your mind out of the gutter, Victor. That woman doesn't know how much I admire her mind. I'm considering proposing."

"You better get in line. It's common knowledge that Sunny Badger is about to pop the question."

"That's got to be a lie."

"A fact, but I'm sure Sylvia would rather be the third Mrs. Jay Ness, than the first Mrs. Satan."

"That hurts, Brovelli. No I'm not here to see Sylvia, although it crossed my mind. I'm here to thank you. The Fournier tip paid off big time. There sure was a drug connection."

"They admitted to killing him?"

"Of course not. But we've got witnesses who saw Fournier arguing with a couple of Amigos. And one of our snitches confirmed it was about cocaine. So thank you, and my lieutenant thanks you. We might be able to solve a real homicide instead of spending all our days hauling in and booking hippies and black nationalists and commies and other dirt-bags for misdemeanor assault and batteries and other small-time criminalities."

"You're welcome," I said, wondering if this helped Sweets or not. Was there any way to tie the gangster to Arabella's murder, I wondered. I asked Jay.

"No connection between Arabella and Fournier that we can ascertain. Sweets' counselor will certainly tie Fournier to Winona's death, now that it's proven he was in the area when it happened. And no doubt he'll try to make the same case as it pertains to Arabella."

"Any luck finding Winona's diary?"

"Nothing, but if she'd written that many, she'd have to have stored them somewhere."

At that moment Vincent walked in the door.

"What's up, Jay?" he asked.

Jay said, "I was filling your brother in on the murder cases he's been pretending to solve.

"No longer trying to solve, right, bro?"

Vincent was smiling, but the smile had a question mark at the end of it.

"Absolutely," I said. "Wasn't I just telling you, Jay that I'm out of the P.I. game? My exact words, right? Not my concern anymore." Good old Jay, quick on the up-take nodded.

"That's what he said to me, Vincent. He's no longer in the P.I. business, much to the relief of the Oakland Police Department."

"Why don't I believe you?" Vincent asked.

"On my honor, Vincent," I said. My twin made a face at me like yeah, yeah, yeah.

"So what the hell were you talking about?" he asked.

Jay explained.

"Great. So, this gets Pop off our backs. We helped Sweets by helping the police. Now the police department is taking over. All's well. We move on with our lives, right, Victor?"

"Yes siree. We're moving on," I said.

"Well, I'll be moving on myself," Jay said. "Anyone want to join me next door for chili and a brewsky?"

"Later," I said. "We got some car business to discuss."

As Jay left, Vincent placed his hand on my shoulder. "You weren't lying were you, Victor. You're no longer a P.I.?"

"*Sul mio onore.*"

"I don't want to hear on your honor. In fact, I don't want to hear the word honor for a long time, if ever again. You understand, Victor? There's enough crap in the world and my life. Gloria is totally stressed over the baby. If she keeps eating everything in sight, she'll turn into a Sumo Wrestler."

"You never told me," I said.

"Not your problem, but remember the last time we were in Italy and mom's aunt who looked like a beach ball. And pasta, pasta, pasta, every meal was some kind of pasta. That's what my dear wife is going to look like if the baby doesn't show up soon."

I remembered mom's aunt and nodded. Vincent sighed.

"You should see O'Keefe's place," he said, changing the subject. "The fire bomb gutted their showroom. Five of their cars were trashed. But we wound up with some great deals. We suddenly have a chance to come out of all this *merda* smelling like a rose. You can't screw it up."

"I'm not going to be a P.I. ever again, Vincent. That's a promise." I raised my hand like I was taking an oath.

"*Meno male*" Vincent said.

"Yeah," I repeated, "Thank goodness." I gave him a big smile and a double thumbs up.

"Now that's straight," Vincent said, "here are the invoices for the cars I bought at O'Keefe's. He gave us a fleet deal and a little discount on top of it. You think we should call the bank?"

"What for? They've already raised our credit limit. We're good to go."

"*Bene,* Victor, *bene.* It's time. We'll toast to the Brovelli Boy's Used Cars and toast to being our own men, not a slave to Pop's screwed up notion of honor."

"And toast to being free of Sweets," I said, although I had my doubts.

"You can say that again," Vincent said, stepping behind Sylvia's desk and removing the bottle of whiskey from the shelf.

"Get the glasses," he said, twisting the cap off the bottle.

I returned with two glasses. "Been doing some nipping on the sly, eh." I said.

Victor look startled. "Not me. I know how much that bottle cost. I wasn't about to drink without you."

"Well, somebody had more than a nip. You think Sylvia's is a secret tippler?"

"Nah," Vincent said. "Vino only."

"Could be a covering up an alcohol problem." It was wrong the minute I said it.

"Who else has been in the office, lately, beside the three of us?"

"You mean someone who'd have the *coglioni* to drink our booze without asking us?"

We both said the name at the same time. "Sweets."

"I'm going to kill the fucker," I said.

"You may not have to. The state could do it for you."

It wasn't funny, but I started laughing. And is the case with twins, Vincent started laughing too.

"Well you two are in a good mood," Sylvia said, walking into the office. She hung up her coat and purse. "What are we celebrating?"

Vincent explained. She gave a whoop.

I held up the bottle. "You know that fairytale about Little Red Ridinghood tasting the bear's porridge, well we have our own little taster. Someone's been tasting our whiskey, and we know who it is."

"Don't look at me, Victor."

"I wasn't talking about you, cuz. It's that frigging Sweets."

"You mean Sweets just came in the office and drank the Pappy Van Winkle your father gave you? When was that?"

"I don't have any idea."

"I don't let him near me, and I'm usually in the office."

"Hell, Sylvia," Vincent said. "You could have been running errands. I never pay much attention to Sweets the way you do. When he comes by I treat him like background noise."

"It couldn't have been recently," I said. "He's been in jail most of the time. Wait a minute. I sent him over here to get my car. Could he have snuck a taste then?"

"Let me think. Well, yeah, possibly," Sylvia said. "He did hang out some, kept slurping on those candies and complaining you wouldn't do the old freebee auto deal anymore."

Vincent groaned. "You didn't leave him alone in the office, did you?"

Sylvia's head dropped a little. She looked up sheepishly. "I might have left him alone, maybe to go to the bathroom."

"Anyway, it's done," I said. "I'll take care of Sweets. Let's have our toast and forget Birdman for one Goddamn minute of our lives.

Sylvia said, "I'll join you." She reached to the shelf and brought down a bottle of Chianti we kept for our lunches and another glass.

I poured Vincent and me a shot of whisky. Sylvia poured her wine. Before drinking, Vincent described the best cars out of the bunch he bought, all 1966 models: an olive-green Ford Fairlane; a Ford Galaxie; a maroon Pontiac Bonneville convertible and his piece de resistance, a Cadillac 75 limo that he got for two grand and would make us a fine profit. Not that there was a big market for limos, but at that price we couldn't miss. Vincent had every right to be proud of himself. They were all fabulous buys and the prices were close to rock bottom, a testament to how badly O'Keefe wanted out of the neighborhood.

Not the Brovelli Boys, loyal to the neighborhood. Our glasses clinked in the air.

"To us," Silvia said.

"To the Brovelli Boys," Vincent and I said simultaneously.

"And to our future partnership," Sylvia added with a grin.

"Stai sognando, cugino," Vincent and I said together, which translates into you're dreaming, cousin.

CHAPTER 33
WHERE'S THAT NOISE COMING FROM?

Instinct is a marvelous thing. It can neither be explained nor ignored.
Agatha Christie

After we toasted, Sylvia started on the Parsegian's paperwork, but she was pouting. Vincent helped her, and I worked the lot. It was a good thing too, because I was getting that I can't-identify-the-irritating-noise-in-my-car-feeling again. I walked to the end of the lot and back a couple of times, stopping occasionally to wipe a windshield or buff a spot on a grill or bumper. What could it hurt if I tried to figure out what was bothering me? It didn't mean that I was going back on my word to Vincent. Right? It was just a matter of satisfying my curiosity. I'd thought of something that I needed to ask Jay. My twin would understand. Right?

Right. I'd try calling him at the police station, but not from our office.

I went back to the office and poked my head in. "You guys mind if I take a quick break?" Both were too busy to object. I hurried out before Vincent realized I was leaving the lot unattended.

The door to Flynn's opened, and Jay almost knocked me down. "Just the detective sergeant I was looking for," I said.

"The chili was fantastic." He held up a bag. "I'm taking some to my partner in criminology."

"I need to ask you a question about Arabella's murder."

"Victor, boy. I thought you'd sworn on a Bible to lay off."

"There's swearing and there's swearing an oath. And I don't remember a Bible anywhere near my hand. Listen, you found Sweets' fingerprints on a glass, right."

"Yep."

"Was there a lab test done on the contents?"

245

"Of course."

"What were the results?"

"Vodka."

Was I relieved or annoyed, I couldn't tell. *If it had been Pappy Van Winkle. . .still. . .Madonna.*

Jay interrupted my thinking. "But forensics also picked up traces of whiskey.

I closed my eyes. I heard myself ask, "What kind of whiskey?"

"I don't know. I'm not sure forensic can isolate brands. Ask Carter Innis. He has all the forensic results."

"Yeah, I guess I will."

He looked at me and cocked his head. "All right, Victor. Pony up. What do you think you know?"

What could I say? I didn't know in what direction this was going, but I suddenly felt like I was driving toward the edge of a cliff, and couldn't put on the brakes. I needed to go to Carter's law office. I needed to see a photograph of the glass, find out what brand of whiskey. "Sorry, Jay. Got to run. Don't worry. Everything's cool." I took off running back to the lot. I sprinted past the office to the back and jumped into my Mustang, fired up the engine and sped out of the lot, burning rubber as I turned onto East 14th. I imagined Vincent and Sylvia standing next to each other at the open door to the office wondering what I was up to. Vincent probably figuring it out quick enough, and cursing me for a liar.

As I drove, my thoughts were pin-balling around in my brain, lighting up corners of memory.

Parsegian telling me that Winona was a snoop; Winona always short of money; Winona with an accounting degree. There were only two possibilities. The first would either stick Sweets in the gas chamber or set him free. The second possibility I didn't want to think of.

My off-ramp appeared suddenly on my right. I veered across two lanes of traffic, ignored the horns and screeching tires, and dropped into the city. I made it to Carter's office without wreaking my car. His secretary said he was on the phone. I brushed past her. Carter looked up from his desk, and said something into the phone and put it down.

"You got some balls, Victor. You tell me you're going to interview that old neighbor. I don't hear from you, then you call my cousin and cancel your date, and she calls me absolutely furious. Now you come rushing in like a crazy person. Shit, you look like you're on drugs."

"Carter, calm down," I said.

"You telling *me* to calm down. Why don't you calm down yourself. This is my office that you just barged into."

"I need to look at evidence from Arabella's apartment. Jay said all the evidence along with the lab tests were sent to you. I need to look at photographs of the glass that had Sweet's fingerprints on it."

"You mean Detective Sergeant Jay Ness?"

"Yeah, that Jay. I just talked to him. He told me the DA is required by law to hand over all the evidence they got on Sweets to his defense attorney. That's you, right?"

"You're correct there, Victor. I'm an attorney for that dumb-ass friend of yours, but not because I want to be, but because my old man dumped it into my lap to drive his son crazy."

His sad tale struck a familiar cord. *Familiar, as in family, as in Pop, as in Onore.* "I understand completely, Carter. Believe me my pop has been on our backs ever since Sweets was arrested. But, seriously, I think I'm on to something that can get your client off. Could you just let me look at the physical evidence? Please."

Carter scrunched his little eyes, wrinkled his brow like he was thinking. I didn't say anything else, but I placed both hands on his desk and leaned forward.

"You have your hands on the evidence," he said. I looked down and saw I was leaning on two portfolios with the seal of Alameda County on them. "Sorry," I said.

"Pull over a chair, Victor. Take a look. I'll get us some coffee. He rang his secretary and ordered. I was already reading when she arrived with two cups on a tray with sugar and cream. I wouldn't have noticed if she smiled at me the way she usually does. I was too busy looking at a photograph of a glass, marked Exhibit #4. Exhibit #3 had been a set of fingerprints that were removed from the glass. The fingerprints belonged to Sweets. The glass looked exactly like the kind we bought at the Five and Dime for our office. But those were cheapo glasses found in any Woolworths, so that meant nothing. I turned back to Exhibit #2, candy wrappers. I counted ten, photographed as they were found on the floor of Arabella's apartment. Exhibit #1 were fingerprints retrieved from the wrappers, most were partials, but two were identical to Sweets' fingerprints found on the glass. But there were no fingerprints on any of the furniture or any other object in the apartment. Carter was standing behind me, looking over my shoulder.

"What is it, Victor? Why are you so worked up?"

"I'm not worked up, at least not yet. Where is the laboratory report on the contents of the glass?"

Carter leafed through the portfolio and withdrew a page. I began to read. The Vodka was Smirnoff and consistent with the bottle found in Arabella's kitchen. The whisky traces were of straight bourbon. Not Scotch or rye. A specific whiskey could not be isolated, but a notation read that it was detectably of a high quality followed by a list of possible brands, one of which was Pappy Van Winkle. No bottle of whiskey of any kind had been found in Arabella's apartment. My head slumped onto the open portfolio where I let it rest. "Fuck, fuck, fuck," I whispered.

"What, what, what, Victor, talk to me. I'm a lawyer. Attorney client privilege. I'm as good as your priest."

"I'm not your client, you *ciuccio*, Sweets is."

"You're my detective," he said.

"Yeah, yeah." It didn't matter. I couldn't tell Carter what I was thinking. If I was right, there was a whole lot I still didn't understand. "Jesus, Mary and Joseph," I said under my breath.

"Victor," Carter said.

"Carter, you'll have to trust me. I wouldn't let a fellow Gael down. It's just right at the moment, I'm totally fucked up. Engines can't operate without carburetors. I'm missing the Goddamn carburetor and a few sparkplugs and I'm not sure what else."

"Are you insane? What's with the carburetor and sparkplugs?"

"I'll be in touch." I stood up and headed to the door.

"You can't leave me hanging like this Victor. My father will want to know."

"For Christ's sake, don't tell your father anything. I promise I'll be back to you very soon.

Very soon," I repeated as I opened the door and closed it behind me. Mouthing thank you to Carter' secretary, I hurried out of the office and got on the elevator.

Outside I found my car with a parking ticket on the windshield. I stuck it in the glove box and started the engine. I needed to think. My thinking Porsche was too far away. My Mustang would have to pick up the cognitive slack. I drove to Berkeley and Grizzly Creek Road, I passed the turnout and drove down the other side. At the tunnel road I turned around and curved my way back up, this time pulling off onto the turnout. Going through the gears relaxed me. I sat, looking out through the windshield toward Treasure Island. In the distance the sun was hovering above Coit Tower. If only I could run this by my twin. All our lives we'd been able to confide in each other, but if I'd made a promise to him there'd be no more detecting.

I did not start out my life believing in a spiritual world that coexisted with our physical one.

But as this began to unravel and the ghost of Winona Davis continued to appear like she was now, in the backseat of my car, what else could I believe? I was not hallucinating. You might argue that ghosts are a form of hallucination, but I knew what my mother's crippled cousin had meant when she had said *fantasmi*. So, I did not bother to ask Winona's ghost why she was there and what she wanted. I knew. I didn't need ears.

Twenty minutes later I was parked in front of the Black Panther's headquarters with a bunch of really scary black guys in leather jackets hanging out in front giving me the evil eye.

CHAPTER 34
THE TRUTH BE TOLD

*The affairs of the world are no more than so much trickery, and a
man who toils for money or honor or whatever else in deference
to the wishes of others, rather than because of his own desire,
or needs lead him to do so, will always be a fool.*
Johann Wolfgang von Goethe

Any African-American walking down the street who saw a white man
sitting in a car in front of the headquarters of the Black Panthers, in the
heart of West Oakland with both hands on the steering wheel, talking
to himself, would no doubt become the target of suspicion. So, I wasn't
surprised when the door to my car was jerked open, and I was pulled
roughly out onto the sidewalk and heard a voice like thunder.

"You got some business, here, Wonder Bread? Or you just like to hang
around a black neighborhood drawing attention to your white ass."

It was Behemoth James. My head came up to his shoulders. My health
was in jeopardy, but I wasn't in the mood to be intimidated. "I'm here to
see Ms. Adila Agbo. If you'll take your hands off me, I'll go inside to see if
she's available."

"Available for what?"

I didn't like the tone of the question. It called for a what-the-fuck's-it-
to-you response, but I kept my cool. "That's not your business, is it?"

Wrong answer. His hand tightened on my shoulder like a vice. "Damn,
that hurts, man." I said, wrenching free. I started walking to the door of the
building, but half way there I felt myself being lifted by my collar and belt
into the air and driven forward until my face was pressed to the door, my
nose bearing the brunt of the pressure. I banged on the door and yelled,
help, as loud as I could. The door opened, sending me and my assailant

stumbling forward into the office. Terrance Bowles stepped back to avoid being knocked over. He recovered in time to catch me as Big James let go of my clothes, and I fell into Bowles arms.

"Victor Brovelli. How nice of you drop in. You here to sell us our other vans?"

"Jesus," I said, pulling my briefs out of my butt- crack and straightening my clothes. I tested the cartilage of my nose. "I only have one of these sniffers and your body guard here, almost broke it."

"I could've broke lots more, honky, you keep smart-mouthing me."

"What's with the honkey and white-bread crap, Mr. Bowles. Don't you teach your men anything about political correctness? It *is* the Sixties, you know." I sounded like a hippie dork.

"Accept my apologies, Mr. Brovelli. James, I think you're needed in the back. A shipment has come in we need your help unloading."

The look on James' face clearly said he didn't like being talked down to, but he lumbered off, grumbling, probably about some awful things he'd like to do to me. I turned to Bowles.

"I was wondering if Dila Agbo was around. I really need to speak to her."

"It's been noticed that you and our sister have been seeing each other socially. Is that true?"

I could have said it wasn't his business, but thought better of it. He didn't seem angry. "That's true. We had dinner two nights ago and last night we had drinks and went to a hear music in the North Beach. Both were pleasant evenings."

"The Black Panthers do not have a policy regarding racial fraternization, but we don't encourage it. White men with black women in particular has a negative history among our brethren, if you get my meaning. I know that sounds hypocritical since some of our brothers consort with white women. But I'm a purist. That said, I'll see if Sister Agbo is available." Bowles turned and left the room.

Being a purist, probably meant he objected to my seeing Dila. But I was already too far gone to worry about it. Five minutes later the door opened, and Dila appeared, wearing another of those long African dresses of many colors that fall straight to the ankles, leather sandal on her feet. She was not wearing a turban and her afro encircled her face. *Oh, those green eyes, the one shining touch of amber.*

"You are either very dumb or very brave, Brovelli. The only whites that come around this office are armed cops and lawyers. I don't see any badge, and I know you're not an attorney, so you're lucky you made it this far without James actually breaking your nose. You might want to avoid meeting the big fellow alone on the street. He was muttering all the way back to the storeroom about what he'd like to do to you."

"How are you, Dila. Nice to see you, Dila. You're looking fine as wine. If you haven't noticed outside the sun is out, birds are singing, and I need to talk to you. Can we take a walk?" I took a deep breath. There were only a few sparrows hopping around and they do not sing. The sun was out. Inside me, however, the weather was overcast.

"In this neighborhood?"

"Why the hell not?"

"It's my rep you're talking about."

"*Madonna*," I said, looking up at the ceiling. "Okay, we'll drive."

"I was only kidding, Victor. Let me get my shawl."

Dila took my arm and guided me up the street to a small park a block away. As we entered, an old woman guarding her grandchildren playing in the sandbox, looked up from her knitting and frowned. I pointed to an empty bench out of her hearing. What grass there was badly needed watering. The jungle gyms and swings needed repair and paint. The gray walls of the two small restrooms were covered with graffiti. On the opposite end of the park, was a basketball court, wooden backboards and chain nets on the hoops, barely visible boundary lines. A shirtless, skinny black teenager was shooting jumpers and draining them, looking like he might be rewarded with a college scholarship one day if he kept at it.

"So, what's so important that you risked your life to see me?" Dila asked.

"Things are totally screwed," I said.

"You're telling me," she said. "The flying gestapo have been harassing us again."

Shocking, but it didn't surprise me. "The same guys?"

"The very same."

"Those cops give cops a bad name." I said, thinking of Jay Ness, one of the good guys.

"Terrance is writing an article accusing Whites of committing genocide against blacks."

The photographs I took at the recent riot at city hall were in the backseat of my car.

"I think I've got something he might be able to use in his article." I told her about photographing Halpern.

Dila clapped her hands joyfully. "He's going to give you a big sloppy kiss for this, baby."

"I'll settle for a kiss from a certain black angel I know. Cheeks don't count."

"Hrumph," she said. "We'll see. Now tell me what's bothering you."

"Remember last night when I explained about the irritating unidentifiable automobile noise theory of mine? Well, I might have identified the noise."

"And what was it?"

I related what happened to me since arriving at the lot this morning, ending with going to Carter Innis' law office and checking out the state's evidence against Sweets.

"My goodness," she said. "So let me get this straight. The whiskey is this famous type that you guys have in the office. And, the way it looks, Sweets sneaked a drink. Then, you are supposing that the glass he drank out of turned up at Arabella's apartment with Sweets fingerprints on it."

"That's about it."

"Correct me if I'm wrong. You're thinking Sweets would have been totally crazy to have taken that glass with his fingerprints on it to Arabella's and left it there so the cops could find it."

"Right again."

"Which means?"

"You tell me."

"Well, it wasn't your brother."

"Absolutely not."

"That leaves your bookkeeper, your first cousin? That's really heavy. Are you sure?"

I shook my head. 'No, I'm not sure, that's the point. But I don't see how it could be anyone else."

"Why? Because, the brand of whiskey in the glass found in Arabella's apartment is the same as the one in your office? Couldn't other people have the same kind of booze?"

"It's pretty damn rare and very expensive. I don't see Arabella having that kind of money. Plus, the cops only found vodka in her apartment. I don't even think there are big time night clubs that carry Pappy Van Winkle."

"And you found candy wrappers in your office, proving what? That Sweets is pretty messy."

I explained that Sweets' fingerprints were definitely on the candy wrappers, which is a problem. As for other prints, "Sweets admitted he'd been inside Arabella's apartment when he was dating Winona, so that can be explained."

"Okay, moving on. Didn't you tell me that your cousin owns a pistol?"

"Yeah, but that doesn't amount to much. It's an old Second World War Beretta, not a .22 that was used on Winona and Arabella."

"No reason she couldn't own two guns," Dila said. "What else?"

"Jitters said he saw Fournier, Winona's ex, in a Mercedes just like the one Sylvia's daddy gave her to sell."

"So?"

"She told me she sold it to a priest in Sacramento."

"But that could be a lie."

"I suppose so. But Sylvia is a real good Catholic."

"What in the world does that have to do with it?"

Dila was right; it didn't. "How about the old lady across the hall who saw Sweets, or someone who looks like Sweets knocking on Arabella's door just before she was killed?"

"That's pretty damming. But, makeup, costume. I've been in lots of wardrobe rooms and seem some pretty convincing transformations."

"Okay, then, that's possible," I said.

"Ask yourself, Victor, is your cousin the kind of person who'd murder people? More importantly why would she murder them? What would her motive be?"

"Blackmail," I said. "When Winona was temping for us, she must have found out something bad about Sylvia."

"I'll tell you what you need to do?"

"What's that?"

"Find out if that priest really did buy the car from your cousin. See if you can catch her in a lie."

"Got it. I'll get right on that."

"Fournier was some kind of gangster, wasn't he?"

I nodded. I knew she was thinking of a connection. "The family story is that Sylvia's daddy is mobbed up."

"Is there any truth in it?"

"My pop says it's all jealousy because the old man is so successful. Mom thinks it's true, but he's married to her sister and according to Mom, her sister is in a loveless relationship. Mom's all about *amore,* Pop's is all about *onore.*"

There was movement next to us. We looked up into the smiling face of the old black woman we'd passed as we entered the park.

"You young people mind keeping an eye on the children while I go to the restroom?"

"Be our pleasure, grandma," Dila said.

The old woman moved slowly away, leaning on a cane to keep her balance. From the back, dressed all in black and black scarf covering her head, she reminded me of Nonna Rosa, my mom's mother, who'd lived in our house while we were growing up and died five years ago at the age of ninety-six.

Dila said, "Grandmothers are black parents' day care system."

"Grandmas love taking care of their grandchildren," I said, thinking of my mom, who'd drop anything she was working on to babysit her grandchildren.

"Yeah, but it's not the same. That old woman probably has no choice in the matter."

"Why's that?"

"May not be true, but there's a good chance that those kids' daddy's disappeared and the mommy's strung out," Dila said, her eyes darkening with anger.

It occurred to me that if whites and blacks wanted to have a conversation about the normal, daily struggles in their lives, they'd need translators; my understanding of grandmothers' roles in a family being markedly different from Dila's.

Grandma returned, thanked us, and went back to her knitting.

I resumed talking about Sylvia. Dila stopped me with a touch.

"Victor, I think you definitely are on to something, but I've got to get back to the office. I'm helping edit Brother Bolwes' article. Can you get me those photographs?"

"Copies are in my car. You can have them. I need to keep the negatives. Just in case."

"Copies will work." Dila said. "I'll be finished in a couple of hours. Give me a call, and I'll wait for you outside the office. I'll help you with your investigation."

"You can be my girl Friday."

"You mean like Robinson Crusoe? I'm the darkie native and you're the smart white guy?"

See what I mean about a translator?

"No, no," I stammered. "Like in detective novels."

"You're sure?"

"Come on, Dila. What do I have to do?"

"All you have to do, is do, Victor. Saying never cuts it. That's what whites forget. The reason Terrance respects you is that when push came to shove, you did the right doing. And now, giving us these photographs. You see?"

"Well, I appreciate that, especially with guys like James around." I stood up and held out my hand. She took it, and I tugged her to her feet, pulling her into my arms. For a moment I held on to her, and surprisingly she held on to me. Then I tilted her chin up and kissed her, slowly, carefully, softly. She kissed back, pressing her body against mine. It was a soft, full body. It felt like comfort.

From behind us, came a crackling voice. "White man kissing a black woman in broad day light in West Oakland. You two childrens know how foolish you being?"

We turned to see grandma smiling at us. The two little kids in the sandbox were puckering their lips and making kissy sounds. *Too young to care about race and the grandma too old for it to matter.* Over Dila's shoulder I saw the teenage basketball player, ball tucked under one arm, staring. He was definitely not smiling.

"*Amore,*" I said. I caught the kids' kisses and blew them back to them. They giggled.

Dila took my hand. "Amore sounds like onore," she said.

"Your first Italian lesson," I said.

"Okay, then I'll have to teach you Ebonics."

I had no idea what that was, maybe a tribal language.

The kids went back to their sand castles, and we walked back to the Black Panther's office. I tried to hold her hand. She told me we shouldn't push our luck. I left Dila at the door, holding the envelope with photographs of Captain Halpern and his fellow defense team inciting a riot. I wanted to kiss her goodbye, but thought about James. When it came to Dila, I was okay with being "foolish. But not insane.

On the way back to East 14th, I segued to downtown to visit Sweets. After I harassed his ass for a while, he finally admitted to drinking our Pappy Van Winkle, explaining that it was not in its usual place on top of the file cabinet, but sitting on my desk. His words were, "As if Pappy was calling my name, man."

I did not believe him for a second. That bottle never left its hallowed place, but I let the lie slide for the time being.

I left him wondering what this was all about. I couldn't tell him yet. I gunned the Mustang on to the street and headed for East 14th. I reconsidered my earlier thought to keep Vincent out of it. There was an upside and a downside to that, both of which, it seemed to me, would result in the two of us rolling around on the ground trying to beat the shit out of each other. So, I decided if either way we were going to have a fight, I'd postpone the event until I had irrefutable evidence. I swung into the lot and parked.

Sylvia was not at her desk. "Where's Sylvia?" I asked Vincent, hoping she wasn't in the bathroom. My concern was that I wouldn't be able to keep my suspicions about her from showing. We Italians have very expressive faces.

"She said you gave her the go-ahead to fly to LA. There was a flight leaving at five."

"Right," I said, relieved, looking at my watch. It read two-thirty-three. Hopefully by the time she got back from LA, I'd have the proof I needed to take to the police. No, I'd take it to Jay first. I wondered how he'd feel having to put the cuffs on a woman he had romantic feelings for.

"Did she tell you when she'd be back?"

"Through the weekend."

Plenty of time, I thought.

"Where you been?" Vincent asked.

I wasn't about to tell him where I'd been and with whom, not that I thought my twin was prejudiced, but the way he'd been talking recently I was no longer certain. Besides, I couldn't take the chance that he'd say something to our parents.

I said, "Visiting Renee.

"I sure could use a little bit of what you got these days," He said. "I'm feeling like a monk."

"Not to worry, bro. Once the baby comes, you'll be so tired you won't even want any sex."

"You're real encouraging, Victor."

"Think of it as a lesson in patience."

"I used to know a girlfriend named Patience," he said wistfully.

"And you were the doctor, and she was the patient," I said.

"Funny man, funny man."

It was distressing for me to banter with my brother as if we were back to our normal give and take; that this entire incident with Winona and Sweets was behind us; that we were back to being The Brovelli Boys salesmen of classy pre-owned automobiles.

The phone rang. It was O'Keefe and Sons with more cars for sale. This time a couple of vans and a pickup. It was as if our luck was getting better and better. I remembered Minister Bowles saying the Black Panthers could use more delivery vans. Since Vincent made the contact, I told my bro to be my guest. I was happy to see him drive away, so I could have the office to myself. We kept a number of city telephone directories in the lower drawer of our file cabinet. I withdrew a Sacramento Metro directory and wrote down the numbers for all the Catholic Churches in the area from as far west as Placerville and Auburn in the foothills through the valley and west to the city of Davis. I began calling, pretending that I worked for an advertising firm representing Mercedes International. I explained that I was looking for priests who drove Mercedes Benz automobiles for an ad campaign, that it would be splendid to include a men of the cloth, yada, yada, etc, etc. I talked fast and hopefully convincingly. Two hours later, I'd placed my last call. No priest, no monsignor, bishop or archbishop in the entire Sacramento Valley as far down as Stockton and as far north as Chico had purchased a Mercedes Benz, new or used. I stood up and stretched. I paced around the office, stopping occasionally to smack my forehead or to release an expletive, most of which were in Italian, but with a few good old American, *fucks* mixed in. I can't speak for other languages, but it's my theory that swearing in Italian is much more effective than swearing in English because the language is more dramatic, the result of which the swearer feels a greater reduction in tension. The reduction in tension may also have something to do with English speakers relying entirely on their voices while Italians use their bodies as well as their voices. I continued in this state, reducing tension, until I looked at my watch.

"*Madonna*," I said, remembering that I'd told my Girl Friday that I'd pick her up. Vincent was late coming back. What to do? I couldn't close the lot. I'd have to call the Black Panther's office.

I dialed. I recognized Minister Bowles deep voice.

"She's just getting ready to depart," he announced. "I'll stop her."

I heard him call her name.

Back on the phone, he said, "Brovelli, I thought we were even, but I guess the Panthers owe you another favor."

"If your organization is still looking for more vans, Brovelli Used Cars will have one available this weekend."

Bowles laughed. "Once a salesman, always one. We'll take it. And we can use one more."

"Right," I said. There was a moment of silence, then Dila's voice came on, "Girl Friday speaking."

I explained about Sylvia's bogus car sale.

"It sure does look like your cousin lied to you."

"Damn straight. I don't know where to go from here. "I want to meet, but I'm stuck in the office waiting for my bro to get back. Can we meet somewhere later?"

"There's a poetry reading going on at the Student Union at Merritt College. When your brother shows up, meet me there. You'll recognize me by the color of my skin."

I ignored the comment. "I'll recognize you because you'll be the most beautiful woman there."

"Flattery will get you somewhere, sir," She said and hung up.

Actually, I did know where I should go from here, straight to the homicide division of the Oakland Police Department and Detective Sergeant Jay Ness. I thought about that. I'd have to explain that my cousin, a woman whom I'd known since we were kids, with whom I'd once played spin-the-bottle and had been a part of The Brovelli Boys' Used Cars for the last five years, was a murderer. A member of my family - a murderer? My mother's niece? All of the evidence pointed in that direction, but I still couldn't wrap my mind around it. Why? I asked myself, why? What could Winona have had on Sylvia that she'd go to such lengths to protect? I remembered a philosophy professor pompously lecturing our class: *Young scholars, I suggest to you that there are no whys in the world.* And upon leaving that lecture, hearing my twin grumble, "*What the fuck did that mean?"* And the student next to him saying, *"I hate philosophy."* Until I could figure the motive out, I was reluctant to go to Jay.

A few singleton customers walked onto the lot, inspected cars and strolled off, ignoring my offers to provide them the deal of a lifetime. Jitters came by on his way to Flynn's. I waved to him. He waved back, made a drinking sign with his right hand. I shook my head. From west on East 14th, I heard a siren approaching. An ambulance turned the corner and skidded to a stop in front of Discount Furniture and two medics, holding valises in their hands, rushed inside. I walked down to the sidewalk. Soon, one of the medics emerged, running to the back of the ambulance. He opened the back, withdrew a stretcher and hauled it inside. Customers from Flynn's, the Donut Hole and other shops close by joined me on the sidewalk to see what the ruckus was about. After another couple of minutes the medics came out rolling the stretcher upon which, covered by a blanket, was a body followed by Nick Parsegian. By the anguished look on Parsegian's face, I assumed that the body was Ron Sharifi, his partner. It was. Parsegian saw me and, pounding his hands on his chest, yelled, "Heart attack. Hospital." When the ambulance moved away, its siren blasting, Parsegian threw his clasped hands above his head in a gesture of despair and hurried back inside his store.

For the next hour, seated in my chair, my legs up on the desk, I put all of my faculties to work trying to understand Sylvia's motive for killing Winona and Arabella. I didn't attribute Fournier's' death to her, but I didn't exclude it either. I was drawing blanks. I'd already searched her desk for any clues, but found nothing that connected Sylvia to any of the murder victims. I stood up, and went through each of her desk drawers again, this time item by item. I even pulled the drawers all the way out, having read in *How to be a Private Investigator* that sometimes people taped things in the spaces behind drawers. All I found was dust and one torn candy wrapper.

I had just finished replacing the drawers when Vincent returned. His cocky smile told me he'd made some more good buys.

"So what did you get?" I asked.

His smile widened. "Man-oh-man, you won't believe it. There were three vans. All three in good condition. Need tune-ups. The pickup was junk. I passed. But, listen to this, I bought two cherry 1957 Olds Starfire Nighty-eights."

I whistled.

"And get this." He puffed his chest out. "A 1957 Olds F-88 convertible Showcar. You know, the kind with the front grill that looks like a shark's mouth."

"*Che fortuna,*" I said, hoping I sounded excited enough. Normally I would have been jumping up and down, but my mind was filled with images of our cousin with a smoking pistol in her hand.

Vincent didn't notice my lack of enthusiasm. "I don't know what's going on with O'Keefe," he said. "but he's giving his cars away. It's like he's having a nervous breakdown."

"Lots of violence," I said.

"No kidding," Vincent shrugged. "I'm sorry for the O'Keefe's, but the cars are ours. I tell you what I want to do with the Starfires."

I half listened to Vincent's plans to repaint the Oldsmobiles in bright colors to attract the growing population of young Mexicans in the neighborhood who were into creating low-riders.

"Where's Sylvia," Vincent asked. "She's got to get on the phone to the bank. I wrote a check, and we need to get it covered."

"You said she left for San Diego, remember."

"Damn it, forgot completely. I'll do it." He went to his desk, put the paperwork down, and reached for the phone.

Before he could dial, I placed a hand on his shoulder. "Hold on a second, bro. If you can handle this on your own, I'm late for an appointment."

"Business or pleasure?"

"Business," I said.

"Yeah, right." He winked. "Go ahead. I got you covered."

As I headed out the door, he was already talking on the phone, a dreamy look of fame and fortune on his face. Not that the F-88's had not given me the chills, but his uttering Sylvia's name brought on a different kind of chill.

CHAPTER 35
POETRY READING

. . . Luminous triangle! Whoever has not known you is without sense.
Comte de Lautreamont

Sunlight had disappeared and flat gray clouds were replacing the white cirrus, possibly bringing rain, which meant work in the morning wiping down all our spotted cars. My pop's biggest complaint about living the Bay Area was its lack of enough sunlight. He'd grouse. "No sun, no vegatables." Since he turned over the store to us, life for Pop has been all about his vegetable garden. As I drove, I thought of Pop and how this had all begun because Sweets had saved his life. Sweets, who had been set up by our cousin. If I was right, and I believed I was, my parents would be devastated. My mother's sister would be, I don't know what, suicidal. Sylvia's father? His little girl? But would he be? Perhaps like father, like daughter? So much roiling in my head, I almost missed the entrance to Merritt College.

Trying to find parking proved difficult. By the time I got inside, the reading was just about over. I found Dila sitting in the last row in the packed Student Union auditorium. I stood behind her and rested my hands on her shoulders. I started to whisper my apologies, and she shushed me. I stepped back out of the aisle and moved to the back wall, waited and thought.

The poet declaiming was a frail little stick, with a voice like a club. I couldn't figure out much of what she was saying, but I did get the impression her subject matter was about being a lesbian. I looked down on Dila's afro, hoping that her choice of a poetry reading didn't have anything to do with her sexual preference. Modern poetry really throws me. I used to worry that I wasn't smart enough, but I finally decided poetry belonged to the same category as modern painting or dissonance in music, subjects that could not be understood with the rational mind. That left the irrational mind. Since I'd been accused of been irrational, I figured I should give poetry a chance before I gave up on it. To this case, I decided I'd wait for another poet to give poetry a chance and tuned out the poet on stage. I felt a nudge at my elbow. I turned and almost bumped heads with Renee.

"Watch it buster. This is my only nose," she said, taking my arm and kissing my cheek. "You thinking of joining the East Bay Alliance of Gays and Lesbians, a good Italian hetero like you."

"*Madonna, mia,*" I thought. Panicking, I grabbed Renee by the arm and hustled her out of the exit behind me.

"Hey, hey!" she said, tugging to get away from my grip. "I was listening to the poem."

"No you weren't, you were talking to me."

"You haven't called back, Victor. Weren't those Academy Awards great? I missed you."

"I'm sorry Renee, honest to God, there's been so much crap going on, I simply could *not* get away." I looked at the door, then back to Renee, then back to the door.

"Aha, I get it. There is someone in there you'd rather be with than me. Is that it? That's why you dragged me out of there in such a hurry."

"No. Yes, I mean she's a friend, okay?"

"She? Victor, sweetee, you don't have any women friends. You may have trysts, relationship, even mutually agreeable liaisons, but friendships, I don't *think* so."

Why is it that women can find the exact word in the sentence to elevate while, voila, I'm feeling guilty? I swear to God, if boys are taught machismo by their fathers, then girls are taught the various ways to inflict guilt on males by their mothers.

"Liaison," I said. "Is that all our relationship has meant to you. I thought you and I were friends. It's not all sex, you know. I appreciate your mind, your musical talent."

"Ohmygoodness," Renee said, drawing out each syllable, cocking her head like a bird who's just spotted a tasty worm. "Do I detect some male sensitivity emerging out of that delectable chauvinistic body? I want to meet this woman, who's got you thinking of friendship with females."

As she spoke, the double doors opened and people began pouring out, Dila Agbo leading the way. She waved to me.

Ah, shit.

I waved back, and she headed my way – our way. "Victor, where did you disappear to?" Dila asked as she approached. When she saw Renee, a look of delight spread across her face. She skipped forward, embracing my mutually agreeable liaison.

Totally screwed, I thought.

"Girl, I haven't seen you for ages," Dila whooped. "Where have you been keeping yourself? No don't answer that, you been making that awful clanging music."

"Dila, you're such a traditionalist."

They hugged some more, then separated. Holding Renee's hand, Dila asked, "You know this Eye-talian, here?"

"Victor Brovelli, you mean? Do we know each other Victor?"

"You want to answer the woman, Brovelli," Dila said.

There was that tone again. I was one dead goombah. This reminded me of one afternoon during my short-lived high school baseball career when I tried to steal home and got trapped between the third baseman and the catcher, scampering back and forth between them. They kept flipping the ball to each other, toying with me until one of them finally ran me down. Either way I ran I was going to be out. My obvious consternation caused both of them to break out laughing.

"Victor, you don't even need to explain," Renee said. "If Dila Agbo is raising your consciousness, I gladly pass you on to her."

"And what should I graciously do with this person?" Dila asked.

The baseball scene disappeared replaced by one from track. I was now the baton being passed from one sprinter to the next. My ego was taking some serious hits, and I needed to get back my masculine control.

"Hey, you two can stop talking about me like I'm not here. You can't pass me on to anyone if I don't want to be passed on," I said, looking at Dila. "We Italians have our pride, you know." I knew this sounded defensive, but by raising my voice, I hoped it didn't sound lame. .

That started the two laughing even harder.

"Oh, don't be so sensitive, Victor," Renee said, wiping the tears out of her eyes. "I'll always be willing to listen to those terribly dangerous dilemmas you twins get yourselves into." She winked. "Has this man ever regaled you with stories about his brother, Vincent? They're really hot."

There was more toying going on, but now it was directed towards Dila, who, thankfully, wasn't picking up on the significance. How could she, unaware of Renee's sexual inclination.

I was glad when Dila changed the subject.

"Renee, Victor and I are off to work on a project. Why don't I call you tomorrow, and we'll get together and talk. We have a lot of catching up to do. You can tell me all about this guy."

"Oh, I'd be thrilled to fill you in," Renee said, leaning toward Dila and brushing her cheek with a kiss. Good luck on your *project?*"

She started to walk away, but skipped back and threw her arms around my neck and gave me a wet kiss. Had I opened my mouth, I would have drowned. As Renee strode away, I saw Dila grinning at me. I could feel myself blushing. Luckily blushing, as is the case with Blacks, is not so easily visible through the dark skins of southern Italians.

"You're blushing, Brovelli," Dila said, proving me wrong.

"I feel like a jerk," I said.

"Why? Because you date a friend of mine. Or do you have such a big ego that you think I'm madly in love with you after only two dates and one kiss. You're acting like you've been caught in some kind of love triangle. What's the Sixties all about if we're not open about our love life?"

"That's a good question," I said.

"And one that you don't have to answer," Dila said, "until you have come to grips with the decade we're living in, dig? So let's get on with the problem at hand."

Dila took my arm and led me down the steps of the student union.

"I bused this morning," Dila said. "So it's your car."

We reached my Mustang that had a parking ticket on the windshield. *Minchia.* Two tickets in two days. Jay's poker debt to me might not be high enough to cover both tickets. I opened the door, and Dila slid in. We sat in the car, and I explained everything.

CHAPTER 36
SYLVIA VITALE

The common woman is as common as a rattle snake.
Judy Grahn

We parked at Grizzly Peak turnout. Dila and I moved out of the car and went to sit on a rock at the edge of the ravine. I could hear the occasional tick of the Mustang's cooling engine, the occasional crackling of crows, the rustling of the Eucalyptus leaves, the distant hum of freeway traffic. Soon it would be that early evening horizon glow, fog moving in, darkness rising behind it, but for now the vista from here was clear, both bridges like arms spread wide from its white high-rise body. Romantic. I placed my arm over Dila's shoulder, and she allowed her head to rest there like a cushion. For a moment I thought of the old woman in the park calling us foolish. I also imagined the young teen basketball player's angry face, staring at us. I forced to get back to the subject at hand, solving the murders.

Motive, motive, you just don't kill without a reason, unless you're a psycho, and Sylvia was definitely no psycho. I said. "I'm still at a loss for a motive."

She raised her head. "If you're right about Winona finding something bad about Sylvia, it must have been something that threatened her so badly her only recourse was to silence her permanently. Do you have any idea what that could be?"

"Money is the only thing I can think of," I said. "Sylvia loves money. No, I take it back, Sylvia adores money. But I don't have a clue in what way money could be part of it. We couldn't afford to pay our cousin much, but we let Sylvia sell cars her daddy gave her at his costs off our lot. I think Sylvia made out pretty well. She's never without customers. Even when our business was down, she found people to buy her cars. Winona temped

266

for us for five days. I guess Winona had the opportunity during that time to discover something, but I looked through our books for evidence of financial wrong-doing and couldn't find anything."

"She'd have her own books, or no books at all."

Back and forth we went, trying out different motives and drawing no conclusions, until we looked at each other and shrugged. Twilight was turning to night. A foghorn sounded in the distance. It was getting chilly. We returned to the car and I turned on the heat. The warmth swept over us like a blanket, and we gave up thinking about murder. I leaned across the console and cupped Dila's face in my hands and kissed her. She returned my kiss, softly at first then with more passion. Our mouths opened. My hand cupped her breast. She placed her arms around me, hand on my neck, fingers in my hair. The next thing I knew she was over the console and in my lap, straddling me.

Finally, exhausted from the effort, Dila whispered, "Let's go to your place."

It didn't enter my mind that I'd never brought a woman to my apartment before. I drove like I was on automatic pilot. Dila leaned her head against the window and closed her eyes, the radio on her favorite rhythm and blues station, Smoky Robinson filling the car with his falsetto: "I Second That Emotion". I third it and fourth it, I said to myself. I tried to imagine what she was thinking. It seemed to me it would have to be about us, but hopefully not about race. I'm not a deep thinker and don't pretend to be, but it seemed to me that our love - because this is what I realized it had become - made the subject of skin color not only superfluous, but stupid.

We reached the Fruitvale Bridge and crossed into Alameda with Smokey Robinson singing, "The Tracks of my Tears". In my apartment, our clothes came off fast. We fell on the bed giggling like two teenagers. Considering that we were both only half a dozen years removed from being teens, why not giggle? *Why the hell not?* And then, our giggling stopped and our bodies turned serious.

• • •

When I awoke the next morning, my first thought was that the sun's *got to be* shining and birds have *got to be* singing. I turned to the window. No such luck. A drizzling rain was washing the window. A water-logged crow perched on a telephone wire was staring at me, his head cocked to the side, trying to figure out what he was observing. He squawked and flew off. So much for post coital romantic sunlit mornings. On the other hand, the object of romance was still curled asleep, half covered by the comforter, breathing softly.

I pulled the comforter over her shoulders. I moved out of the bed quietly and into the bathroom where I showered, shaved and donned a bathrobe. In the kitchen, I got Mr. Coffee going. Soon it was bubbling, and I heard Dila calling.

"Is that coffee I'm smelling?"

"Come and get it," I said.

She did, naked. "*Madonna mia*," I exclaimed. "The coffee can wait."

Smiling, she pushed by me. "No fool, nothing stands between me and my morning coffee."

So we sat on the couch next to each other, drinking mugs of dark brew, me in my bathrobe and her au natural, totally at ease with her own nakedness. When we'd finished, she led me back to the bedroom, explaining that she was now fully awake and ready to devote her attention to my physical needs.

After we'd spent ourselves, we lay back breathing heavily and smiling at each other like two crazy idiots, which is what I'm sure Vincent would have called us, or maybe worse. After a while I found myself tracing the Betamaribe tribal scars on her stomach with my finger. Three columns of tiny, raised beads began at her belly button and ended at the hair line of her pubis. Two smaller horizontal rows of four beads extended at right angles on either side of the mid-point of the column, curving slightly downward so they looked more like the wings of a bird than a cross. I marveled at how brave it must have been for Dila, at such a young age, just beginning puberty, to have gone through such a painful scarification. I asked her if it had hurt. She shrugged. I thought her father was some kind of sadist, but didn't tell her. What I *did* tell her was that the pattern looked like the bird of happiness. Dila said I was a weird Eye-talian, but she could live with it. For a moment, the thought occurred to me that I could live with her. I mean really *live* with her. The thought frightened me. I chastised myself for being such a coward.

The next time we woke up it was close to noon. It was still raining. I called work and told Vincent I'd be in later. Dila and I showered together. No sex, just slowly, dreamily rubbing soap over each other's bodies. We drank our second cup of coffee fully clothed watching television. There was a show on about the Academy Awards. My black angel was still stoked about *Heat of the Night* winning.

I was thinking how much I admired that 1966 Alfa Romeo Spider 1600 Dustin Hoffman was driving in *The Graduate*. The show ended, and I turned off the TV. I checked my watch. "You're late for work," I said.

"I took Friday off."

"I told my brother that I'd be in later, but I'll call him back and tell him I won't be in until tomorrow."

"Don't do that, Victor I've got graduate school stuff I need to get in the mail, and you got a murderer to find."

"Grad school?"

"Yeah. I was accepted into a couple of Masters in Theater Arts programs."

As if reading my thoughts, she continued, "I've played better roles than the one you saw me in. But what I really want to do is write plays."

What else could I say except terrific and good luck? She gave me a thank you-smile and a very tender kiss.

"Before I go," she said. "Let's consider this murder investigation of yours. All the movies I've seen, the detectives say follow the money. Maybe Sylvia's money will lead back to Winona."

When I'd searched Sylvia's desk, I hadn't found any of her personal bank records. All Brovelli Boys' records had seemed to be in order. I explained this to Dila.

"Yeah, but you told me where she lives, and those places are pretty darn pricy."

I reminded Dila of the deal Sylvia had with her father.

"So, she makes all this extra bread. And you say her papa is tied in to the mafia, right?"

I knew where she was going with this thinking. "Not really. But it's like I told you, it's just that Vincent and I like to kid her about her dad."

"So, you don't think there could be any truth to it?"

I hesitated because I wasn't certain. I thought about my mom's dislike of her sister's husband. It wasn't like Sylvia's father was ugly, or brutish, or a bad provider. Perhaps there was a seed of truth from which the jokes sprouted. It was worth asking my mom, but I'd have to be careful. Getting into family affairs was always tricky and in Italian families could be dangerous. Her sister's husband might be an asshole in her mind, but he was still part of *La Famiglia*.

We talked some more about Arabella, trying to figure out how her murder related to Winona. I told Dila about the telephone message she'd left with Sylvia.

"So, it has to be about the diary. Arabella read the diary and there was stuff in there about your cousin."

"That's got to be it," I said, thinking back. Between the time Arabella left the message about finding Winona's diary and the time I found the message, twenty-four hours had elapsed, plenty of time for Sylvia to go to Arabella's apartment and kill her. God, I thought, that message wouldn't have meant a thing to Sylvia except that I had already told her it was bound to have a clue about Winona's murderer in it. Had I kept my mouth shut, Arabella might still be alive. I told this to Dila.

"You couldn't have known."

"How about the old woman across the hall," I asked. "Only Sweets has that kind of screwed up blonde hair."

"A blond wig. And all you need to do is tease it and apply enough hair spray to make it stick up like Sweets' doo."

The more Dila talked, the more convinced I was that Sylvia Vitale had murdered Winona and Arabella. "The way Sylvia loves money, it had to be something about her car deals," I said.

"Isn't that where you said she was going, down to her father's dealership to pick up another car to sell?"

"Can you get into her apartment?" Dila asked.

"Maybe. But I don't have a key."

"Brothers at the office said Sweets is supposed to be this legendary burglar?"

Why not, I thought. Sweets could give me another lesson in breaking and entering. Hopefully this one would provide better results. "You're right. I'm going to pay Sweets a visit."

Dila looked at her watch and stood up. "I can send off the graduate forms tomorrow. I'm going with you."

"Not a chance. One burglar might not attract attention. Two will. Go do what you have to do and I'll call you."

"Didn't you say I was going to be your Girl Friday? Today is Friday."

"Please," I said. "I'll be nervous with you along. I'll call you before I start out."

"Give me the address and I'll meet you later close by. In front of store or at a bus stop Okay?"

I agreed. We kissed. After she left, I remained standing at the closed door, inhaling the scent of soap and the faint, musky, delicious fragrance of sex.

• • •

It was too early for visiting hours at the county jail, so I drove to Saint Joseph's. It was Good Friday. I'd pass on confession, but a prayer wouldn't hurt. The morning drizzle had turned into a steady rain. Why, I wondered, was Good Friday called good? It always made me feel bad. Jesus being crucified and the consequent suffering of his apostles was a spiritual downer. Afterwards, with ashes decorating my forehead, I drove to the lot. I explained to Vincent I was going to visit Sweets and would be back by noon. He made me promise I wasn't going to pretend I was a private eye again. I lied to him that this was a purely humanitarian visit. I hated to lie to my twin, but he definitely would not have understood what was about to happen. I drove off, the windshield wipers slapping back and forth. I hit the freeway. Ahead of me, downtown Oakland was barely visible through the downpour.

Rains this heavy are unusual in the Bay Area. I hoped it wasn't a sign of future trouble.

• • •

At the county jail, the guard brought out the jailbird. Sweets was looking more haggard than the last time I saw him.

"Victor, dude, I read your letter. How could you, man?"

"I bet you immediately called Big Sal and started guilt-tripping him."

"Not guilt-tripping, just reminding."

"Well, it didn't work. I'm not here because my pop put the screws to me, I'm here on my own. I think I know who the killer is."

"Dude, really? I knew you wouldn't abandon me. Who is it? It's that horny old bastard Sharif, isn't it?"

I told Sweets about Sharif having a heart attack.

"Couldn't happen to a better person. Got to be Parsegian, right?"

"I'm not telling you, Sweets. I've got to get more evidence. I need your burglar skills. I have to get inside an apartment."

"Not a problem. You know where my tool kit is, right?"

I nodded.

"In it you'll find a set of lock picks. You got some paper. I'll explain, you take notes. It's not hard."

For the next fifteen minutes Professor Sweets gave me a crash course in lock picking. As I was leaving I heard the guard yelling: "Sweets, you pick up those fucking candy wrappers off the floor. You born in a God damn pigsty?"

The guard was not too far wrong. I left. I found a pay phone at a gas station and called Dila. I told her my plan with instructions to talk to Detective Sergeant Jay Ness, should anything go wrong. My response to her question was, you never know. My D.I manual stated to be always prepared for the worst. There was a tavern at the corner down the street from Sylvia's apartment. I gave her Sylvia's address. My Girl Friday promised she'd be there waiting.

• • •

An hour later I was standing in the middle of Sylvia's living room. Hell, if this was all it took to be a burglar, maybe I was in the wrong business. If I'd had any question that Sylvia was involved in some kind of illegal, financial enterprise, the furnishings eliminated all doubt. I don't know much about oriental rugs, but I figured I was standing on something ancient and very expensive. All of the paintings looked like originals, and though I didn't recognize any of the artist's names, the impressions of San Diego landscapes no doubt cost big bucks. The sound system was state of the art, and Julia Childs would have committed murder - pardon the pun - for the kitchen. Sylvia's closets were filled with I. Magnin labels. I'd never seen so many shoes. Such a lifestyle was impossible on the salary we paid her, and improbable on the profits she got from her Daddy's cars, no matter how high she marked them up.

Once I'd made a cursory look-through, I started searching in earnest, delving deep into closets, under the mattress, into drawers, checking for secret cubbies. I wasn't sure exactly what I was looking for. Some significant evidence to go along with what I already had. I needed to convince Jay

Ness that the love of his life was a murderer. In an MJB coffee can I found a roll of twenties wrapped in a rubber band hidden beneath the coffee grounds. I counted them. Two thousand dollars. Come-on Sylvia, I thought, first place any good P.I. would look, as per instructions from *How to Be a Private Investigator*. I carefully placed the envelope into a plastic bag. I could hear Jay now: *So, she's got a bunch of cash, so what? Her daddy's as rich as Midas*. I needed more. Remembering the person standing at Arabella's door, I rummaged through the bedroom closet looking for a raincoat and a blond wig. None that I could see. There was a wall safe hidden behind the clothes. I wished Sweets were here, he'd be able to get in to the safe. I heard him say once, "I put my fingertips on a combination, and it starts talking to me." On the shelf were hatboxes. I opened them. No wigs. I was about to move to the hall closet when I spotted the bottom of a tan garment sticking out under a full-length mink coat. I removed the mink coat and there it was: a tan raincoat that buckled at the waist like the kind the old woman described. My heart started beating faster. As I was placing the coat on a separate hanger, I noticed a couple of blond hairs caught in the right shoulder epaulets. *Gotcha*, I thought. The hairs went into a separate plastic bag for forensics to identify as part of a wig. I'd saved Sylvia's address book for last. I took my evidence and sat on the couch leafing through pages. Nothing until the page marked Z, where I found one number with an unrecognizable area code. There was a telephone on the end table. I reached over for it and dialed the operator. It was a code for a district just outside of New Orleans. Sylvia Vitale and Jordan Fournier, I thought. This proved Sylvia knew him. Jitters was probably right; it was Sylvia's Mercedes Fournier was driving, but without the car I couldn't prove it. I dialed the number. It rang five times then went to a voice announcing, "Jordan Fournier is unavailable, leave a message." I put the phone down and closed the address book. I stared at the book. Safe combinations talked to Sweets, this address book was trying to tell me something. When I realized what it was, I leaped up, grabbed my evidence and headed for the door. Half way there, I heard the key in the lock. I reversed direction, but managed only a couple of steps.

"Is that you Victor Brovelli? What are you doing in my apartment?"

Slowly, I turned around to face Sylvia, standing with her hands on her hips, a scowl on her face, her large bosoms heaving as if she was out of breath.

What could I say? I smiled. I coughed, I thought. And I thought some more. She tapped her foot, looking like an angry school teacher waiting for a bad student to come up with the predictable lie. The silence between us reaching a crescendo. *What did I have to lose?* "This is very embarrassing, Cousin." I said. "The truth is. Well, the truth is. . . "

"Spit it out, Victor."

My brain cells spun one direction, then another, synapses firing on all cylinders. This had to sound exactly right.

"I've always loved you, Sylvia," I blurted out. "You may not have been aware of my feelings for you. But, you know, you're my first cousin and the church frowns on those kinds of relationship." I stopped talking to see if she was buying it. I couldn't tell, so I blurted on. "I just wanted to be close to you, without. . .you know. . . being close to you. Like I wanted to *feel* your aura, inhale the perfume, see how you lived your life. Love makes a man do strange things."

"You're so full of *merda*, Victor. Why are you holding my raincoat, and is that my address book you have in your hand? I forgot it when I left for the airport. Luckily I wasn't that far, so I came back for it."

Lucky for her, unlucky for me. "How come you're not in San Diego?"

"If you really need to know. There was a pile up on the Bay Bridge and I missed my flight. The next flight wouldn't have been until ten o'clock at night. So I decided to take a flight today. Now that I've told you, you need to answer my question."

"Well, I sure as hell not trying to steal your frigging raincoat." *Act indignant.*

"You've also been searching through my apartment. I can tell."

Sylvia was between me and my escape. I could charge and knock her down. But maybe I couldn't and what if she had a gun in that huge purse she was carrying. It was time to try the romance ploy again.

"Sylvia, why don't we sit down on the couch, put our heads together, if you know what I mean."

"I won't let you toy with my emotions, Victor," she said, reaching into her purse and withdrawing a pistol.

It was larger than a 22. I said. "Is that real? Should I be worried?"

"Cousin, you should be damn worried."

"You're pointing that gun in my direction. You're aware of that."

"I'm completely aware of that. Now, I want you to move back into the living room and sit on the couch, but I won't be joining you. A long time ago we could have put a lot more than our heads together, you *ciuccio*, but you were off nailing all your glamourous college sluts."

"Sylvia, Sylvia, this isn't what it looks like."

"You keep your mouth shut. And I mean shut. I gotta think."

If Sylvia's hand had been shaking even slightly, I would've made a grab for the gun, but her hand was steady as a surgeon about to perform brain surgery. Without the pistol, Sylvia looked as harmless as a big-bosomed songbird; with the gun, she looked like a raptor about to swoop down on a rat. That rat would be me, one fucked Italian goombah.

"Sylvia," I said.

"*Sta 'zitto*. You and your father's God damn *onore*. Why the hell couldn't you have done the smart thing, the legal thing when you found Winona's body, and called the cops? Nothing can be the same anymore."

Her jaw was set, but her eyes were glassy with anger.

"Tell me what's going on?" I asked, trying for the voice of innocence. "We're Italians. We stick together."

"Liar," she said. "Italians never stick together. Every goddamn town is a separate country. My father would screw your father in a heartbeat if he could profit from it. Italians are bandits. We were all suckled by wolves."

Ah, geez, I thought. Sylvia philosophizing was not a good sign.

"I don't know what I'm going to do with you, Victor. Put my things on the coffee table and sit on the couch and, *per favore*, don't move a muscle."

Keeping her eye on me, she reached for the phone and dialed. She spoke in a whisper. She hung the phone down. "We'll wait," she said.

"For what?" I asked.

No answer, only a ferocious silence filled with images of a bullet blasting a large hole in my chest.

Fifteen minutes later the phone rang. She picked up, whispering again before hanging up.

"We wait some more," she said.

"Why did you have to kill Arabella?" I asked. She ignored me. I asked again. She sighed like I was a silly child.

"I couldn't take a chance that she didn't read Winona's diary. There was too much in there. The Bitch would have taken me for all my hard-earned money."

Follow the money, I heard Dila say.

"What about Fournier?"

"Tying up loose ends. Besides, he abused Winona. She told me all about him when she worked for us. We women had to stick together I felt sorry for her."

"Not sorry enough for her," I said, thinking what crazy convoluted mental shit was that? It occurred to me that Sylvia had a crew loose. Why hadn't I noticed? Why hadn't my twin? All this time we had a nut-case working for us.

Sylvia's frown grew deeper and her eyes began to take on the hooded aspect of a reptile. We waited. Any time I started to say something, she waved her gun. An hour later, the waiting came to an end when the doorbell rang.

CHAPTER 36
AMIGOS

If you have a lot of what people want and can't get, then you
supply the demand and shovel in the dough.
Al Capone

You can guess what my expletive was when the two walked in, and I saw JR, Winona's ex-pimp and the big sonavabitch Vincent thumped on the head in The Oasis. The big Mexican, sporting Amigos' colors, rumbled over and gave me a vicious gold-toothed smile. Then he Duct-taped my ankles and my arms behind my back. He slapped tape over my mouth, after which the three moved to the other side of the room and began whispering, no doubt trying to decide how best to kill me. This is all your fault, Sweets, I thought. And yours, Pop. Your son will soon be dead for trying to uphold your frigging Italian idea of honor. *How does that make you feel? I know you'll sniffle into that long white handkerchief of yours that you keep stuffed in your back pocket. Mom will weep. Vincent will be shattered to lose his other half. My other siblings will stand around the grave solemn in their black funeral attire. Mario will blame my death on the Republicans. He blames everything on the Republicans. All the guys from Flynn's would be at the funeral, and lots of toasts and Italian jokes remembered. There might possibly be an article in the Oakland Tribune. Surely there'll be something in the Northern California Used Automobile Monthly Newsletter concerning the murder of an up-and-coming used car salesman. I've never given any thought to what should be inscribed on my tombstone. What's that Sinatra tune? "My Way"? Here Lies Victor Brovelli, He Lived Life His Way. Nah, too corny. Here Lies Victor Brovelli, Victim of a Bad Decision. That's more like it. Or, perhaps this, Here lies Victor Brovelli who died pretending to be a PI.* I thought of Dila waiting for me at the tavern down the street, looking at her watch, worrying. I thought of us together last night. Some sound like a moan escaped my mouth. Sylvia turned and frowned, then returned back to the two Amigos. No, I thought, I hadn't given Dila the address. I was relieved that she was safe. Dila would come to the funeral also. So would Renee. Dila and Renee would stand together. My parents would wonder who the beautiful black woman was. Would Sylvia be there? No. Sylvia would be on the lam. Dila would have followed my instructions and told Jay.

From the other side of the room came the sound of arguing, Sylvia's voice rising above the others. The arguing died down. Time passed. With my hands tied behind me, I couldn't see my watch. There was no clock on the wall. At last the three came out of their huddle and approached me. The smiles the Amigo and JT bore and the solemn expression on Sylvia's face did not bode well for me. She stripped the tape from my mouth. It hurt, but I didn't yell.

That's when I saw Winona framed by the hall entry staring at me, disappointment in her eyes like I had let her down. Well, hell, I thought, it's your own fault trying to blackmail a Catholic woman with homicidal tendencies. Winona just shook her head.

"Victor, these boys are going to remove the duct tape. I've explained that you and your brother are pretty damn headstrong, so they'll be on their guard in the event you decide to do anything crazy. I have a pistol. You might mistakenly feel I wouldn't shoot you. Well, sorry to inform you, cousin, but I'd blow your good-looking head off. I'd rather let JR work his magic on you with his stiletto. Less noise the better. Capisci?"

I nodded.

Big Amigo tore the duct tape from my mouth, not gently. Then my wrists and feet. I rubbed my wrist, and felt blood returning to my fingers.

"Is that the pistol you used to shoot Fournier?" I asked. She didn't reply, but she didn't need to. I saw it in her face.

"We're heading to your car," Victor. "The boys will be on either side of you, and I'll be right behind you with my pistol under the raincoat. We'll walk out talking and joking around like we're lifelong friends."

"We *are* lifelong friends. We're cousins. You dated Mario, remember? We're family."

"Stop groveling, Victor. And I *never* dated Mario."

"Well, he always wanted to. He told me. It's not too late. He and his girlfriend are breaking up. I'll arrange everything. How about that?"

"*Basta,* Vittorio. Move to the door. Let's get this over with. It's Easter Sunday coming up."

I wasn't sure what that had to do with my perilous position. "The Church doesn't condone murder, Sylvia, you know."

"You got to know the right priest," she said.

At which point Amigo Gigantus stepped close to me and nudged me forward. What the hell else could I do? If I'd been Vincent, maybe I'd have done something creative and unexpected, saved the day, saved my ass, been a hero, got a medal from the governor. I never backed down from a fight, but there was no fight in me. Perhaps some notion of flight, but I couldn't run faster than a bullet. Would she dare to shoot in the street? I opened the apartment door and stepped into the hall. Sylvia locked the door behind us. Prolong things, I thought, be patient until my natural intelligence kicked in. At the moment, it seemed to be on vacation.

In the lobby, Sylvia went into the street first. She waved to us, and out we went into the gray light. The rain had stopped and the sun had broken through the clouds.

"You guys wouldn't have a pair of sunglasses, would you?" I asked.

"Be a smart ass," Brovelli," JR said. "I'm going to enjoy slicing your throat. You messed with my sister's affections."

Jesus, when the hell did I do that? We began walking down the street to my car. The big Amigo had a wrestler's grip on my forearm" J.R., your sister is a lovely woman. I'd be honored to be her husband. I'd never. . ."

"Shut the fuck up," he said, piercing my skin with the point of the stiletto.

"That hurts," I said.

"Shut the fuck up, you two," Sylvia hissed.

"Not a problem," I said, thinking here I was at death's door and still wising off. I must be some kind of *ciuccio.*

"Give me your keys, Victor." Sylvia said.

"Can't Mr. Amigo has my arm locked down."

Amigo relaxed his grip, and I pulled the keys out of my pocket and handed them to Sylvia.

"When we reach your car," she said, grabbing the keys from my hand,

"You will get in the backseat with JR and his knife. Hector will drive, and I will follow you in my car.

"Where are you taking me?"

"You're going to have an accident cousin. Everybody knows how much you like to drive fast. So no one will be surprised when your Mustang is found in the canyon below Grizzly Peak Road. Isn't that where you go to make out with your little hoity-toity college sweetheart? You'll probably die from the impact, but if not the fire will finish the job."

I could tell Sylvia was warming to the topic. The closer we came to my car, the less chance I had of escaping. There were people on the other side of the street, but they were not paying attention to us. If I yelled, would they come to my aid? Probably not. People in cities are programed not to get involved. With each step, my Mustang drew closer. At the end of the block, across the street, was a tavern, called The Embers, and to the left of the tavern was a telephone booth. Standing in front of it was a woman with a wild looking afro. She was waving her arms over her head and yelling.

"Keep walking, Victor, don't pay attention to the drunk."

The woman started stumbling drunkenly in our direction. As she stumbled closer I saw it was Dila. *Madonna.* She'd scuffed up her afro and torn her blouse. Half way across the street, jaywalking, unconcerned about the traffic, she stopped and began screaming.

"There you are, muthaaafuckaaaaa, lying bastard. I sees you. You gots all your gambling friends wit you. Who are these, muthaafuckaaaas? How much money you be owing them. What bout us? Whadabout the baby? You ever think of anybody but yoself?" She was swinging her arms and crying, beseeching anyone within hearing distance to consider the plight of a mother whose husband gambled away the grocery money. Jesus H Christ, I thought. Cars were screeching to a halt rather than run her over, blowing their horns, one driver leaning out the window yelling to get the fuck out of the way. People on the sidewalk across the street were staring, looking at each other and shaking their heads. Surely the two white guys weren't this crazy woman's husband. Must be the Mexican. Despite the predicament I was in, I was impressed. This was an Oscar-winning performance.

"Jesus, Mary and Joseph," Sylvia said. "Keep walking. Don't look around."

Sylvia invoking the names of the Holy Family with murder on her mind seemed a little irreligious. I told Sylvia. Her reply was a death stare.

By now Dila had wobbled drunkenly closer to our side of the street, her purple brassiere showing through a tear in her blouse. "You see, you see what happens to a good black girl marry a white man? You see that man over there," she yelled, pointing in my direction. "My chilluns are going hungry and the muthafuckerrr," she screamed.

I kept getting punched in the back to keep moving, but I was frozen, fascinated by the performance and scared to death for Dila's safety. I tripped and fell. Or, perhaps, I tripped myself on purpose. The two gangsters lifted me to my feet, but I dug in my heels. A cab slid to a halt in front of Dila. She slammed both hands on the hood and stared the driver down. Then, she pivoted to the gathering crowd on the opposite sidewalk. "My chilluns are going hungry and the muthafuckerrr is out here consorting with gamblers." She began to sob, tears streaming down her cheeks. In the meantime, my assailants had lifted me under the shoulders and kept heaving me forward.

We were just about to reach my Mustang, JR holding me up by my belt and the big Amigo holding me under my arm. The barrel of Sylvia's pistol was pressing into my side.

Someone from the other side of the street yelled, "The woman's got a gun."

Then, in succession, coming from different directions:

"Where's a gun? I don't see no gun."

"You see a gun?"

"She's got a knife."

"No knife. I don't see no knife."

"Shit, she could kill him with her teeth."

"Where the hell are the cops?"

As if in response to the question, or in response to my fervent prayers, a siren sounded in the distance.

Sylvia pushed her pistol harder into my back. If I got into my Mustang, I was a dead goombah. No way. I dropped to my knees, feeling the pain in my crotch until JT let go of my belt. Dila's performance had given me an idea. It was my turn to please the Bard.

"Oh baby," I yelled at the top of my lungs. "I'm so sorry. It won't happen again. Don't shoot. Please don't shoot." Now the attention of the crowd turned to me, which is what I was hoping would happen. If Dila was Act I, I was going to be Act II. I started sobbing and wailing for forgiveness. My forehead dropped to the sidewalk. The big Amigo tried to lift me, but I let my body go slack, slumping forward, continuing the dramatics. I shut my eyes tight and whispered a quick prayer to the Virgin Mary: *Madonna, if only you get me out of this , I'll start going to mass every Sunday.* I felt hands under my arms trying to lift me, but an inert body is twice its normal weight. Grunting, followed by cursing. Sylvia's high-pitched screaming followed by Dila's equally high-pitched screeching. It was a cacophony of madness. In the screaming match Dila was winning. I kept my eyes shut and continued wailing at the top of my voice. Sirens sounding closer. I felt a sharp pain in my back and a terrible burning sensation. Then more yelling. More sirens and the screeching of tires. "*Oddio,*" I sighed and passed out.

• • •

I woke up in a hospital bed. Around the bed stood my twin, Detective Sergeant Jay Ness, Mario, and my parents.

Jay spoke first and not very kindly, "You are one stupid piasan, Victor. I told you to stop playing detective, but would you listen. Uh, uh. You got to do it your way."

Vincent placed a hand on Jay's arm. "Give it a rest, Sarge. Victor just had a knife stuck in him."

"I'll live," I croaked. "What happened to Sylvia?"

Jay answered, "As far as we know when JR stuck you, she vamoosed in your Mustang. Left the other two hoodlums there. They took off running but we got 'em."

I groaned.

"The Mercedes she sold Fournier was in her garage along with twenty kilos of cocaine. JR talked. Sylvia was selling drugs right under your noses."

I was pretty woozy, but I sensed that Jay was giving me the old needle. I didn't need anything else stuck in me.

"How were we to know, Jay?" my twin asked. Why would we even be suspicious? She's family."

"Well, anyway, Victor, I'm not really mad at you. You solved the murder, and we got most of the bad guys. You should be proud of yourself. I must say you're one stubborn son of a gun."

I guess my stubbornness paid off. And, Jay was right, I *did* feel proud.

"I always knew the Vitales were crooks," My mom said. She moved around to the other side of the bed and took my hand and began patting it.

Leaning down close to my ear, she whispered, "Vittorio, chi e donna nera in piedi alla finestra?"

I looked to the window and saw no one. "What black woman?" I asked.

"She was there just a second ago. She was very beautiful."

Dila, my black Angel, I thought. This was definitely not the time to explain our relationship. "I'm tired, Mom," I whispered. "My side is burning and my head is dizzy. I need drugs."

"I'll call the nurse," my mom said.

"Sylvia couldn't have gotten far. We'll find her," Jay said.

Pop said, "Your mama and me are proud of you, Vittorio. The family honor, you and your brother keep it strong." He made a fist and shook it.

I looked at Vincent. He rolled his eyes. My eyes closed, and I fell asleep.

• • •

My eyes opened. My mouth felt like I'd just finished eating chalk. . I grunted for water. A nurse about the size of a defensive lineman was standing by my bed holding a tray with my breakfast on it along with the morning Tribune. She put the tray down and handed me a water bottle. I sipped gratefully.

"A Negro woman left this for you," she said, removing a folded piece of paper from her apron pocket. I could tell it had been unfolded then refolded and probably read. The note said, **I love you Victor Brovelli**. By the unpleasant smirk on the nurse's face I figured she was the snoop, *like really, a Negro?* Did she have any idea times were changing? Probably not. I read it again, happy for the words and the image of Dila, it conjured. Nurse snoop raised the bed into a sitting position. I ignored the food that looked like it was prepared yesterday. The coffee was bitter, even with lots of sugar and cream. I opened the paper to the front page. The headlines read from top to bottom:

FBI Checks Clues in King Slaying;
Hanoi Accuses U.S. of Stalling Talks,
Worlds Christians to Celebrate Easter.

It was Easter Sunday. I'd slept through Saturday. Pope Paul VI would have already celebrated mass in Saint Paul's Basilica. Easter was Mom and Pop's favorite feast day. They'd be dressed in their best attire, heading into church, flanked by the Brovelli sibs, spouses, and grandchildren, minus

Mario and me, Mario because he'd announced he was an atheist, and me because the nurse told me the hospital would not release me until tomorrow.

In the lower left of the front page was a small article about the Alameda County Police Department breaking up a heroin ring masterminded by a Mexican gang called the Amigos with connections to certain members of the Mafia in New Orleans. Nowhere in the article was Sylvia's name mentioned. What the hell had become of our cousin, I wondered.

A couple of minutes later, Sweets, descendant of Jean Lafitte, sucking on a hard candy, bounced into the room with a smile on his face. How he managed both smiling and sucking and bouncing, and talking, I couldn't tell you. He was a man one could imagine being on puppet strings and being manipulated from above by someone with a crazy sense of humor.

"Yo, Victor. You're the man. I knew you wouldn't let me down."

Sweets was wearing a jacket of many colors, envy of the Old Testament's Joseph. The jailbird pallor was gone, and he looked rested. "I was praying they wouldn't release you," I said.

"Funny man, Victor. The stuff you found in Sylvia's apartment was enough to spring me. I'm not entirely off the hook, but they let Carter post bail."

"On Pop's dime," I assume.

"You eating that sausage?" Sweets asked, picking it off my tray and popping a wrinkled piece of meat into his mouth where it joined the hard candy to form something akin to sweet and sour goop.

Better him with indigestion than me. "There're two more, go for it," I said.

"How come you have to stay in the hospital once they sewed you up, man?"

"The blade didn't hit any of my vitals, but I lost a bunch of blood. I got kicked in the head. They're worried about a concussion. The doctor said I could probably get out the day after tomorrow."

"You heard about Sylvia? JR sang like a tweety-bird all about your cousin being in cahoots with the Amigos. She's on the run."

"In my Mustang," I said. The image of Sylvia at the wheel of my Mustang, cop cars chasing her until the shoot-out, Sylvia and my Mustang riddled with bullet holes. "Ah, man," I groaned.

"Bet you money she'd heading back to San Diego and daddy."

"Have they connected her to her father?"

"Stands to reason. Who supplied her with all those cars? Jay told Vincent that she had heroin stashed inside the back seat of the Mercedes she brought up from San Diego. The Amigos deny any involvement. They've got lawyers. Not sure how long JR will be singing before some guy in the county jail sticks a shiv in his voice box."

"Sylvia, a drug dealer, who'd have thought it" I said.

"I never liked her," Sweets said. "Shifty eyes. Those tits were too big."

Funny, I thought, coming from the man with the shiftiest eyes I'd ever seen. "So, Winona must have found out about her heroin business."

"Probably Winona confided in Arabella and Sylvia got wind of it."

"I'll be happy to get back to selling cars again," I said.

"Speaking of cars," Sweets said. "Now that I'm back in circulation, I needs some new wheels."

"Sweets, your arrangement with the Brovelli Boys is terminated. As Pop said, honor has been upheld, which means you no longer can hold us up."

"I resent that, Victor. I truly resent that. I'm not a stick-up-artist, I'm a burglar."

"Fine, I'll gladly sell the burglar a car, cash or with a substantial down payment."

"You're such a kidder, Victor," Sweets said. "You want a candy?"

The nurse walked in just as I was about leap out of bed, damn the stiches, and ring Sweets' scrawny neck.

CHAPTER 37

WOMAN WITH A ROSARY

Holy Mary, Mother of God, pray for us sinners...

Christians around the world had finished celebrating the ascension as the doctor released me in the evening on Sunday, earlier than he'd previously stated into the waiting arms of Dila Agbo, He warned me not to do any physical exertion for a while to allow the stiches to heal. Dila drove us to my apartment. I didn't interpret physical exertion to include making love, an act we both decided could be accomplished without breaking my stiches or suffering further brain damage. It was taken for granted by both of us by then that Acts I, II, and III were over and we were into Act IV. Thus, after proving sex could be gentle and even peaceful, we sat next to each other in bed, propped up on pillows. I continued my futile effort to finish *War and Peace*. Dila read a script for a play written by someone named Amiri Baraka in which she was to play the female lead.

I leaned over and kissed Dila's shoulder. "My mother thinks you're beautiful."

"That's strange. She's never seen me."

"At the hospital. Mom said you were standing by the window."

Dila shook her head. "I was only in the hospital once when I came by and gave a very grumpy nurse a note. The only person in your family I've met is Mario."

"Oh, well," I said, trying to sound natural. "You are certainly beautiful."

"Could have been another nurse," Dila said.

"Doesn't matter. Mom's getting a little old." Not that old, I thought. I could ask my mom if the woman she saw by the window was wearing a Mickey Mouse watch. Nah, I thought, what would be the point?

286

Dila and I napped; we made love again – gentler, *peacefuler*. The rest of the day, the phone remained disconnected. When Dila finally left to go home, Lazarus could not have been more thankful for life than Victor Brovelli.

The evening church bells of Saint Joseph's rang out. I had heard those same bells ringing *Christ had risen. Christ had risen*, as long as I could remember all the Easters of my life.

I decided to make seven o'clock mass and take communion, even though I hadn't gone to confession. I figured the Good Lord knew I'd been in a hospital. As for the sex, I've got a theory that an All-Loving Deity knows the difference between love and lust. Lust, you head straight for the confessional. Love, well, that's what God's supposed to be, right? Okay, so the Pope wouldn't go for that idea. It's all about what truly in your heart anyway.

• • •

For the next three days I stayed home. Dila visited often, once when Vincent was there. According to Dila, he was polite, but not embracing. On Thursday, I woke up ready to get back to work. I didn't think I could break my stitches talking to customers. My Mustang had disappeared with Sylvia, and Sylvia, according to Detective Sergeant Jay Ness, was still in the wind. As far as I was concerned, she could stay that way riding her broomstick. I called Vincent to pick me up. As usual, morning traffic was heavy. We arrived at the lot. I got out and unlocked the chain. Vincent drove in and parked in the back. As he walked around to the office. I told him I was going for coffee and donuts. He placed his order for two maple squares.

The front window of the DoNut Hole had finally been replaced. The minute I stepped in, I knew it was a mistake. Half the neighborhood was there in line waiting for their morning cheer. They all turned to look at me expectantly.

"Well, if it isn't the hero of East 14th," Body Flynn said. "I always thought you Dagos were lovers, not fighters."

"I always thought you Irishmen were assholes, not politically incorrect assholes," I replied.

"Gotcha, there Brother Flynn," Larry Hughes said from behind the counter.

Parsegian patted me on the back and congratulated me. Stuart and Jitters slapped me on the back. Swanee pulled me aside and whispered that he'd known something was wrong from the start, "You know, when you brought the Impala in to have it detailed and there was no rug in the trunk. I poked around and found a few specks of blood."

"For Christ's sake, man." I said. "Not a word about that, okay. The cops don't know she was in the trunk." He looked alarmed and promised not a breath.

Jitters added he always knew there was something weird about Sylvia. A couple of other car salesmen from down the street offered to buy my donuts. I felt sort of foolish since I didn't think of myself as a hero. I *was* thinking that perhaps I hadn't been such a bad detective after all when a hand fell heavily on my shoulder. I turned around and faced Sunny Badger. *Minchia*, what the fuck was Badger doing here, I wondered. The Satans wouldn't be caught dead buying donuts from Hughes because he was black.

"Congrats, soldier," he said and stuck out his hand.

His voice didn't sound congratulatory, but I couldn't ignore his outstretched hand. He gripped and squeezed, hard, pulling me close.

"I know who put the black whore in our club," he whispered into my ear and released my hand.

Before I could say anything, he walked to the door where he stopped and turned around. "Hoowah," he yelled and left.

"What was that all about?" Body asked.

"Nothing," I said, but I knew better, and it sent a shiver down my spine. It occurred to me that maybe the stiches needed a couple of years to heal. Perhaps in Tahiti.

"Coffee and donuts on me," Hughes yelled.

My stomach was in a knot. I told Hughes I'd be back and hurried away to inform my brother that we were not long for this life.

As I was leaving, I heard Body Flynn holler, "Yo, Victor, why do Italian men have mustaches?"

I opened the door quickly, hoping to escape before the answer. I didn't make it.

"So they can look like their mothers," he yelled.

Body's laughter followed me back to the lot. Vincent should have been putting price tags on the cars by now. The door to the office was closed. I opened the door and stepped in.

He was sitting at his desk staring straight ahead.

"You taking a day off?" I asked.

My twin raised his chin in the direction of the filing cabinet. Standing next to it was our cousin, holding the same revolver that she'd recently threatened to blow my head off with. She waved it in the direction of my desk.

"Close the door and take a seat, Victor, over there by your brother, facing me. We need to settle some things."

Sunny Badger and now our killer cousin. "I was so worried about you Sylvia," I said, trying to look worried. "You here to return my Mustang? Great, but you can keep it if you want. It's a present. Me to my favorite cousin."

"Don't start with the con job, Victor. It didn't work in my place, and it ain't going to work now. I'm in deep *merda* and you and your brother are the cause of it. I'm here for some well-deserved *vendetta*."

"Vincent didn't have anything to do with this, Sylvia. He told me to leave it alone, and I didn't. So you can blame me, okay. He's going to be a daddy. You can't kill a new daddy."

"You can't grovel for me," Vincent said. "I'll handle my own groveling."

"Oh, yeah, I'm a hell of a better groveler than you."

"Oh, yeah." Vincent, yelled, jumping up with his fists balled.

"Shut the fuck up, both of you," Sylvia yelled. "You Brovellis are pathetic. I could've made millions if it wasn't for you. Sit, sit."

Her eyes were getting smaller, her bosoms growing larger, the gun waving at us. We sat. She walked to the door and flipped the sign to *Gone Golfing* and released the Venetian blinds. Keeping her gun trained on us, she moved to her desk, sat on top and crossed her legs. Her arm with the gun at the end looking like some kind of prehistoric bird.

"Why, oh, why did you two have to be so stupid? I was working on some things with my daddy. He could have supplied us with lots of great automobiles. A little more time and I'd have convince you two knuckleheads to let me buy in. We could have cornered the used car market in the East Bay. But, oh nooo, I was just your little accountant. You never paid any attention to any of my ideas. I had lots of profitable ideas. I'm not stupid, you know."

Right, I thought. Ideas about how to smuggle more heroin into the country.

With her left hand, Sylvia reached into her purse and extracted her rosary.

"Oh, oh," Vincent whispered.

"No kidding," I whispered back. You better think of something quick."

"*Stai zitto*," she hissed between clenched teeth.

There is no more terrifying sight than a woman with a gun in one hand and rosary beads in the other telling you to shut the fuck up.

"Sylvia," Vincent asked, "would you mind pointing that weapon away just a little bit?"

"What, you don't want those good looks splattered all over the wall?"

"No, I just don't want you to get nervous and pull the trigger before thinking this over completely."

"Yeah," I chimed in, "shooting us doesn't make sense. Give yourself a little time and you'll realize that. Hell, you could tie us up. By the time anyone checked, you'd be in Mexico. Your daddy's connections will help you I'm sure."

"There you go again about my daddy. Can't I get it through your thick skulls, he's not a member of the Mafia. He's a car man. Never been closer to the Mafia than the movies."

She paused, her eyes going squinty again, the rosary chattering between her fingers.

"But his daughter is. It's me with connections. No one else. From the start, this was all my idea. You were born to be used car salesmen, I was born to be in the Cosa Nostra. And do you know what side of the family I get it from? Do you?"

Vincent and I shook our heads.

"Not from my daddy's side and not from your daddy, but from the bitch who's always putting down the Vitales, your dear mama, her Rizzo side of the family. The Ferraros are either a bunch of witches or Cosa Nostra. You ask her if I'm lying."

"Hell, yes, I'll ask her. As soon as we leave, we'll get right over to our house, and we'll give her all sorts of hell. You know what, if my mom is mafia, that makes you and me sort of mafia too, right. We're blood kin."

Vincent was looking at me like I was stupid.

"Do something, Vincent," I said. "I just fell in love. I can't die now."

Sylvia sneered, "Victor, you continue to amaze me with your ridiculous crap about romance and love and sex. You're a walking hard-on. I'll be doing women a favor killing you. In fact I'll start by shooting off your *coglioni*. How about that?"

Instinctively, I placed my hands over my crotch. Sylvia saw me and started laughing hysterically, like she was going totally berserk. But her laughing stopped abruptly and she looked toward the door. I heard it too, the sound of motorcycles.

The sound grew louder and louder until it stopped in front of the office. Engines gunning.

"What are the Satans doing here?" Sylvia asked.

"Maybe Badger wants to ask you out."

"Fuck him," she said.

Before I could say what was one my mind about them deserving each other, Badger's voice roared from the other side of the door. "Hey, in there, Victor Brovelli, no use pretending you're closed. That's your Mustang in the back. Come out and take the ass kicking you deserve."

Vincent and I looked at each other. Sylvia looked confused.

Vincent said. "Get on out there, Victor."

"If you don't come out," Badger yelled, "We're coming in. You fucked with the wrong guys. You weren't even in the army, you little shit, and the Goddamn car you sold me is a lemon."

I'd like to believe I did what I did next because I'm one smart piasan, but it's more likely because Badger insulted my vehicle.

"We've never sold a lemon in our lives, you bozo," I yelled. "You so goddamn tough, you try to get in here. We got guns."

"Will you shut the fuck up," Sylvia said.

"I don't think so, not you weenies," Badger yelled.

There was a second of silence then the door crashed inward. Sylvia leaped back. As Badger thundered into the office revolver in hand, she shot him in the chest. Blood burst like a spider web across the front of his leather jacket. His eyes widened in surprise. As he dropped to his knees, he whispered, "Sylvia," and fired. The force of the bullet drove Sylvia backward. She landed seated on the couch, beneath our pop's photograph of his beloved Naples, groping at the blood oozing from the cleavage between her enormous breasts.

Vincent was yelling in Italian. From outside, I heard lots of cursing and yelling. A guy jumped in, brandishing a shotgun, saw Sunny dead on the floor and jumped back outside. Then there was the sound of boots running and motorcycles firing and screeching of tires. Followed by silence. Such silence I experienced for the first time in my life in which, for a moment, time ceased to exist and motion seemed impossible.

And then, reality

Scrambling to my feet, I rushed to Sylvia. Her eyes were glazing over. She was coughing blood. The hole was huge. I had no idea what to do. Stop the bleeding with pressure was all I remembered from a first aid class I took years ago. I pulled off my sport coat, folded it, and pressed it over the gaping wound.

As if from a long distance, I heard Vincent calling emergency on the phone.

With the pressure, her eyes focused. Her mouth moved. I leaned down next to her face. Her breasts heaved, then she whispered hoarsely, "You Brovelli Boys, what am I ever going to do with you."

Those were our first cousin, Sylvia Vitale's last words.

• • •

A few days after Sylvia had almost killed the Brovelli Boys, we sold the '61 Impala convertible in which we'd found the dead body of Winona Davis. As I'd suspected all along, there was a lot of profit in that car. The woman who bought it will never know what the trunk of her automobile had once contained. I prayed that there would be no residual ghostly effects to haunt her and wished her safe driving and long-time ownership. Given the circumstances, this was one car I would not consider as a future trade-in. As for Winona's ghost, she was gone with the sale. How did I know? As the Impala drove off the lot, the driver's side passenger seat window opened and an arm appeared. On its wrist was a white Mickey Mouse watch, the hand waving goodbye. I waved back. In the future, if another ghost entered my life, I would not be surprised, but for the time being I was happy to see Winona's ghost departing my life.

Having watched the Impala drive off the lot, I'd told my brother Vincent that I was taking the rest of the day off. I drove away to pick up Dila, leaving him arguing with Sweets who'd arrived on foot, whining about how it wasn't fair that the Brovelli Boys had severed their automobile sales arrangement with him. Wasn't the fact that he was the descendant of Jean Lafitte worth some consideration? He was relying on the Lafitte strategy because Pop had also severed ties with the burglar. Perhaps Pop no longer believed that crooked logs make straight fires.

CHAPTER 38

AMORE

L'Amore domina senza regole.
Love rules without rules.

If Victor Brovelli would have been the same man as the one who helped cover up a murder and almost screwed up a police investigation, and almost got himself killed, while solving three murders in the process, instead of the man with a raised consciousness he is today, guess what he'd have done? Let me tell you. He'd have jumped in his Mustang and run all the red lights driving to Mills College, hustled Renee out of her dorm, sat her in the back seat of his Mustang, and imparted the story of his dangerous encounter with death. Can you imagine the sexual creativity this tale that included the Black Panthers, pistols, switchblades, mafia bag-men, a crazed rosary-toting female killer, and shoot-outs with the notorious biker gang, the Satans would have inspired in Renee. It gives me goosebumps.

But I was *not* that same man. The events of the last month that later came to be known as The Sweets Fuck-Up, had changed me. It wasn't the closeness I'd come to dying, or the dangers of thoughtless decisions, or the turbulent political times, or even coming to grips with family pressure. It was the sudden and inexplicable love and admiration I felt for Dila Agbo.

So there we were, Dila and I, the top down on my Porsche, the sun chasing the fog back to the Pacific horizon, taking the curves down Coastal Highway 1 on our way to Santa Cruz for some theater, poetry, fun in the sun, and a whole lot of *amore*. That afternoon when I'd picked Dila up, her father, dressed in his usual long African gown, came to the door, looking none too pleased. Neither had my pop been pleased when I told him my heart's desire was a black woman. It was their problem, not mine. It's my theory that the rulebook of love contains only two rules: 1) Follow your heart. 2) Anything that stands in the way of the first rule must be ignored.

The End
Coming Fall 2023

A Brovelli Brothers' Mystery
THE CASE OF THE '66 FORD MUSTANG

EXCERPT FROM CHAPTER ONE

The voice of sanity is getting hoarse.
Seamus Heaney

Vecchi peccati hanno le ombre lunghe.
Old sins have long shadows.
Italian proverb

CHAPTER 1
GRIZZLY PEAK ROAD

In the end, one needs more courage to live than to kill oneself.
Albert Camus

"Brovelli?"

"Yeah," I replied.

"Which Brovelli am I talking to? I never can tell your voices apart."

I recognized the voice of my friend, Detective Sergeant Jay Ness of the Oakland Police Department. "The Brovelli who took you for fifty bucks last Thursday with a pair of nines."

"Yeah, yeah, Victor. Look man,"

Jay coughed like he was trying to clear his throat. Jay can't tell our voices apart because we are twins. Vincent is my older brother by 32 minutes, and me, Victor Brovelli. We are known in the neighborhood of East 14th Street where we have our used car dealership as The Brovelli Boys, the sons of Big Sal Brovelli, an Italian-American icon, whose dealership he turned over to us when he retired.

Jay coughed again.

"I've got bad news," Jay said.

I had a bad feeling, but I made light of it. "What? You're going to stop playing poker and deprive me of my livelihood."

"Victor, this is serious. Get serious."

Serious dropped Ness' already deep voice a couple of octaves below bass, and in it I detected sadness. "Sorry, Jay," I said. "I'm listening." I knew that when Jay got serious it had to do with being a detective sergeant and his job with the homicide bureau.

"It's your brother, Mario. Look, there's no easy way to say this."

A knot called death tightened in my stomach. "Go ahead."

"He and his girlfriend were found at the lookout off Grizzly Peak road. It looks like ah. . . Christ. . . damn this is hard. It looks as if your brother shot his girlfriend then turned the gun on himself."

I was in our office standing at my desk, looking out onto our used car lot facing East 14th Street. Mid-morning sun trying to break through cloud-cover. The window was open. Traffic was heavy. An ambulance sounded, then a truck blew its air horn. In the distance, an airplane from the nearby Oakland Airport rose into the sky like some kind of prehistoric bird. Normally the sound of urban rock-and-roll comforted me. Not today. First the air was sucked out of the room, then out of my chest I collapsed into my chair. I shut my eyes - *impossible to breathe* - in that dark space between the eyelids and the universe an image of Mario and his girlfriend Grace appeared waiting on the sidewalk in front of San Francisco International Airport. They had been in Washington D.C. at one of the protest rallies representing PeaceLinks, a political organization Grace had co-founded a little over two years ago with another woman named Carol Hosty. Mario and Grace were full of stories about the protest, happy and energized by the expanding anti-Vietnam War movement and relived to finally be home in time for Christmas. I heard myself whisper, "Jay, I don't believe it." What I really meant to say is that I don't want to believe it, that any talk of death of a loved one would always be unbearably unbelievable. Just yesterday, I'd talked to Mario on the phone, and he'd sounded perfectly fine.

"I'm really sorry, Victor," Jay said. "You or your brother need to come to the Alameda County coroner's office to officially I. D. the body. Cops in Berkeley are trying to contact the girl's family. One of the homicide detectives at the scene recognized your brother's name and knew I was a friend of yours. I figured it was better to call you guys than your father."

"You did right," I said. *Madonna*, Mom and Pop would be devastated. How could I break this to them? It was Monday, the 8th of December, 18 days before Christmas. Mondays would never be the same again, and there would be no joy this Christmas. The New Year would end the 1960s. Our office was decorated inside and out with bulbs and tinsel and wreaths. *Have a Jolly Christmas* was playing on our loudspeaker.

I lifted the Kelly's Blue Book off my desk and hurled it with all my might at the small Christmas tree on top of the file cabinet next to the couch. The tree toppled to the floor, red, blue and white ornaments shattering in all directions.

I heard Jay yelling into the phone. "Come down, Victor. Hurry up," I brought the speaker back to my ear.

"The last thing you want is for your parents to hear about this over TV or radio," he said. "There was media all over the place."

Jay gave me the address on Fourth Street and Washington. I hung up and let my head fall between my legs, still gulping for air, tears blurring my vision. Mario was the third of the Brovelli siblings. Carlo was the first born followed by Costanza and four years later by Mario. It took four more years before Vincent and I arrived. I straightened up, thankful that I was the only one in the office. Vincent was on the lot talking to a middle-aged couple about a 1967 Ford Fairlane, and Theresa Bacigalupi, our new accountant and secretary, was at the bank making a deposit.

I stood up and walked to the open door. Vincent was turning on the charm. I could tell from here that the woman was letting herself be charmed. It's easy to charm when you have my twin's thick black curly hair, swarthy complexion that is a backdrop for gray blue eyes and a sturdy jaw in addition to an athletic body. Since we're identical twins, you'd think this description fits me too. It does, except that my face is marred by a half moon scar under my left eye that runs from the bridge of my nose almost to my ear like a hammock, the result of trying to steal second and getting tagged by a line drive that left me unconscious between bases and no longer handsome.

About the Author

TOM MESCHERY is the author of the memoir *Caught in the Pivot* and four books of poetry: *Over the Rim, Nothing We Lose Can Be Replaced, Some Men, Sweat: New and Selected Poems About Sports,* and *Time Out.* Meschery was born Tomislav Nikolaevich Mescheriakov in Harbin, Manchuria. He and his mother and sister spent four years during WWII in a Japanese internment camp in Tokyo. Following the war, the trio were reunited with father and husband in San Francisco where Tom Meschery attended Lowell High School, played on the basketball team and was named an All American Player. He attended Saint Mary's College on a basketball scholarship and earned College All American honors in 1961. He was drafted by the Philadelphia Warriors (now Golden State Warriors). He played NBA basketball for the Golden State Warriors and the Seattle Sonics from 1961-1971. After retiring from the NBA, he earned an MFA in creative writing from the University of Iowa. He believes he inherited my love of writing from ancestors on his maternal side, The Tolstoy's: Leo, the Novelist, and Alexie, the poet. Meschery was inducted into the State of Nevada's Writers Hall of Fame in 2002. Meschery has traveled extensively through West Africa, coaching basketball and lecturing about American Literature. In retirement, he continues to write poetry and fiction. He lives in Sacramento, California with his wife, artist Melanie Marchant Meschery.

CPSIA information can be obtained
at www.ICGtesting.com
Printed in the USA
LVHW092026131222
735113LV00005B/606